I0658332

IMMORTALITY

THE EVOLVED SERIES

VOLUME 2

IMMORTALITY

THE EVOLVED SERIES

VOLUME 2

STEVE WOODS

ISBN-10: 0-9966883-8-2

ISBN-13: 978-0-9966883-8-3

Freeze Time Media

Cover Illustration by Tom Meyer, FX Design

Dedication

This book is dedicated in the memory of my little brother, Michael Lane Woods, July 19, 1970 to the summer of 2002. You will always be my hero.

Acknowledgments

A special thanks to those that spent endless hours bringing Immortality to the world: Di Freeze, Freeze Time Media, a talented and patient editor and publisher; Caroline Winders, creative director and publisher for Oregon Valley Verve; Michelle R. Woods, my beloved wife, who spent endless nights reading with me as I wrote and rewrote the book; Tommy Meyers, FX Designs, an outstanding artist and friend who created the cover; and finally, my amazing friends and readers who inspired me to keep writing. Thank you all.

Contents

Chapter 1

Immortality

When I first opened my eyes, it was nearly pitch-black in the back of the SUV. I was lying next to Ben in the cargo area, and we were both pretty messed up. My mind seemed to be playing tricks on me, and it seemed as if the whole day had been a dream. Hell, the last couple of weeks could've been a dream and I wouldn't have minded one bit.

The nanites Cornelius had injected into me had stopped the bleeding, but I was still fighting for my life. When this day began, I had no cares one way or the other whether I lived or died. Yet, ever since Katherine had read me the message from Ray, I had a renewed will to live. My beloved wife, Michelle, was alive. I still wasn't sure how I could face her after all that had happened, but nonetheless, the love I felt for her was enough to give me the strength to live another day. Even if she couldn't forgive me for becoming the man this war forced me to be, I'd still spend the rest of my days making her life as close to paradise as possible.

Since the day we met, she'd inspired me to face life head-on. It was her passion for living that even now filled me with hope and joy. Yet something was amiss. I'd been fortunate the gunshot had missed my vital organs and I felt very little pain or discomfort. What bothered me was rooted much deeper than any wound could ever be. The problem came from deep in my psyche.

Visions of my childhood haunted me. It wasn't like a normal memory coming back from a long forgotten time. No, it was more like my mind was having a hard time separating my past from my present. One second I was lying there in the SUV and the next I was literally ten years old again with no thoughts of my current life.

I'd spent my whole childhood as a dreamer, never quite accepting life at face value. In fact, my little brother and I both enjoyed our childhoods this way. As young boys growing up in California, we often found ourselves passing the time by sharing stories with one another. They weren't separate stories but ongoing magical journeys we would create together. This was more than just a way to pass the time; it also helped to pass the many miles we walked together.

During the spring and summer months, we routinely made the trek from Redding to Anderson every weekend to watch the stock car races. It didn't take too many of these trips before we perfected the art of what-if scenarios. Coming from a large family with meager finances, our imaginations were our favorite form of cheap entertainment. The stories we found most exciting always stemmed from the desire to be superheroes. We'd endlessly save some poor soul from certain doom, and in return we'd be richly rewarded. The reward was just a bonus part of the fantasy we'd throw in for good measure.

The stories always started the same. He and I would be walking along minding our own business when something terrible would unfold right before us. We would discuss in great detail the life-threatening situation and how it all came to be. Then, as if we were each a miniature Sherlock Holmes working on an important case, we'd share different approaches to the situation. We tried to be as realistic as possible for our adventures. We never encountered a mystical beast or alien from another world. Even the way we went about saving a life or fighting a villain had to be plausible. We couldn't rely on brute strength. At eight and ten respectively, strength wasn't yet in our arsenal of weapons.

Over time our stories developed many different and creative ways of using items around us as either weapons or tools depending on the threat. It didn't matter if we were pulling a family from a burning vehicle, or saving a young mother-to-be from a deranged purse snatcher. We'd figured out a solution for any situation. Our stories never did reach the part of receiving our great reward.

Our eight-mile journey was never quite long enough to go over that part of the adventure. That never bothered us though; it was the chance to battle evil and be victorious that was the real thrill. After all, being a superhero is what little boys truly dream of.

I know it seems odd that I'd compare these memories to a fate worse than being shot. It wasn't the memories as much as the reality that followed. I lost my brother to the Biscuit Fire years ago in Oregon. The memories I had weren't dreams but a physical state of mind.

I relived it over and over, each time ending in the same spot: the death of my little brother. That pain tore me apart the first time. To relieve it time and time again was like being in my own personal hell.

I'd just snapped back from my latest bout with the past when Josh suddenly pulled the SUV to the side of the road. My eyes had adjusted to the dark and I was able to watch his reflection from my position in the back glass. He quietly exited the vehicle and stepped to the side, facing Katherine's door as she and Robert slept in the backseat. Then, as if it were a totally normal thing to do, he calmly reached into his jacket and removed his handgun from its holster. He never even flinched as he fired round after round into his unsuspecting companions. Without the slightest sign of remorse for what he'd just done, he peacefully reloaded his gun and put the barrel to his own head. A bright flash from the muzzle followed by the ear-piercing report conveyed to me my friend was gone.

I lay there in stunned silence, unsure of where to turn. Ben was lying next to me broken and bleeding; the sounds of the gun going off repeatedly never disturbed him in the least. My last hope would lie in Cornelius. As my mind raced, the rear hatch suddenly flew open. With the aid of the moonlight, I was able to make out the figure standing before me. It was Cornelius, the person I'd trusted and in whose hands I'd unwittingly put my life. He stood there eyeing Ben and me without saying a word. I could feel the hairs on the back of my neck standing stiffly on end. It was as if somebody had put ice water into my veins. I could feel the cold rush through my body as he finally made a noise. It was a cold and sinister laugh, the type that makes your skin crawl.

I had the feeling things were about to go from bad to worse, and they did. Cornelius walked over to Josh's body and retrieved the handgun. A second later, another bright flash and loud report left Ben's body lying lifeless next to me. I wanted to fight back, or at the very least get up and run, but it was to no avail. My body was frozen with fear. With Cornelius now standing over me, I drew in a deep breath and waited for the inevitable. He stared coldly at me, until he finally raised the gun and pointed it at my head. He paused for what seemed to be an eternity. Then he turned the barrel back to Ben and fired a second shot.

My mind raced. What was going on? Why in the hell was Cornelius doing this, and how had he gotten Josh to help? I could feel a warm tear running over the edge of my cheek and into my ear. Cornelius laughed again, and as a final point, spoke.

"You're so naïve and predictable," he said. "It was people like you that not only made all of this extremely easy, but also necessary. None of you had what it takes to survive in the new world. You were always so busy trying to help others, even when it meant putting yourselves at risk. That made you weak, and there's no place left for the weak."

He leisurely raised the gun once again, pointing the barrel directly at my forehead. This time, however, I no longer felt the cold through my veins like I had before. I could feel my blood start to boil as the rage quickly built inside me. No longer were my muscles frozen with fear. Adrenaline pumped through every vein in my body, and I was ready to fight. I wasn't willing to just lie there waiting for him to make the first move. I drew my leg back in one rapid, deliberate motion and extended it full force into his jaw. I felt the impact as his head flew back, absorbing the full force of the blow. I pulled my leg back and again drove it forward with all the strength I could muster. It met its target with little resistance and continued forward until my leg was fully extended.

"What the hell are you doing?" I froze at the sound of Katherine's voice. "What the hell is your problem?"

Shaking violently, I opened my eyes to see Katherine hovering above me, her hands pressing firmly against my chest, holding me to the floor. Ben flailed around violently next to me, screaming in agony. Confused, my mind raced wildly while my eyes quickly shot to my foot. My leg was fully extended, but Cornelius wasn't the apparent recipient of my rage. Instead, my foot and a good portion of my leg were now sticking through the glass of the rear hatch. I turned my attention to Ben as Robert climbed over the seat and took him into his arms.

"What am I supposed to do?" he yelled out, not really caring who answered.

About that time I slid forward, hitting my head on the seatback in front of me. I could hear the tires skidding on the dry pavement. I was now more confused than ever. Was I still dreaming, or was all this a hallucination? I could hear two of the doors open and what I deduced at the time could only be Josh and Cornelius. After some discussion outside, someone grabbed my foot and shoved it back through the broken window. At the same time, the rear hatch opened and I stared directly at Cornelius. Without wasting another breath, I used all my might and shoved Katherine off me. Forgetting all else that was going on around me, I grabbed hold of anything I could and slid my body out of the vehicle, instantly diving on top of Cornelius.

"Whoa! Not so fast, cowboy," Josh yelled out, pulling me off of the scared young man.

Cornelius jumped back to his feet and entered the back of the SUV. His hand visibly shaking, he inserted a needle into Ben's neck and then fell to the floor. With his heart pounding rapidly, he turned to face his patient. Ben was no longer screaming; his body relaxed as the medicine rapidly took effect. I, on the other hand, wasn't so fortunate. Robert had slid back into his seat and out the door. In what seemed to be a single step, he was around back and assisting Josh. The two of them grabbed me and forced me to the ground.

My eyes darted back and forth, swiftly going from one person to the next as I tried to piece things together. I finally got my answer after Cornelius finished with Ben, slid out of the back, and knelt over me.

"I'm so sorry, my friend. What's happening to Ben and yourself is just a side effect from the nanites."

Without another word, he reached down and stuck me in the side of my neck. Within moments, I was once again unconscious. A crisp, aromatic breeze woke me early the next morning and I found myself back in the rear of the SUV. I found this to be a much more pleasant way to be awoken than the night before. The scents were all so strong it was as if I smelled them for the very first time. They weren't new to me, just extremely fragrant. I lay there with my eyes closed, taking in all I could through my nose. One by one, I tried to identify the source of each sweet smell: the cool water from a nearby brook; the overwhelming smell of lilac growing on its banks; and even the faint, pungent smell from a far-off skunk.

What I didn't notice were the smells I'd been getting all to used to this week, that of my friends. My eyes now wide open, I exited the vehicle through the open rear hatch when I realized I was alone — even Ben was missing. I became very uncomfortable and darn near terrified. I'd been alone before since all this took place, but I'd always known why. This was a scary new world, and the idea that everyone could just disappear didn't seem too far-fetched.

I was able to relax as the breeze changed direction. From the north I caught the unmistakable scent of my un-bathed band of rebels. It was a faint scent, so I knew they were still a ways off. It comforted me knowing I wasn't alone. While I waited, I took the opportunity to get a look around. I found the creek with the lilac growing near it and filled a canteen I'd gotten out of the SUV. I was walking back, enjoying a cool drink when I finally had time to analyze all the bullet holes in our ride. It must have been hit twenty to thirty times. Three of the shots had come right through the front windshield.

It made me think of my own wound. I slowly removed my shirt and ran my hand across my chest until I reached the site the bullet had entered. I had to do a double take. I was expecting a bloody bandage or at least some type of patch. There was nothing, no bandage, and no hole to speak of. All I found was a slight indentation and a soft spot not unlike the one on a newborn baby's head. Off in the distance I could hear the distinct sound of Katherine's laughter. I was so caught up in playing with the spot where the hole should've been that I didn't notice them coming down a path next to me.

"Dude! Quit touching your bare chest that way; your weirding me out!" Robert hollered out, causing everyone to laugh. "We really need to get you back to your wife so you can satisfy your urges."

"Ha ha. Very funny, asshole," I shot back to him. "I can't figure out why I don't have a hole in my chest. Also, what the hell is Ben doing walking around with you guys? Shouldn't he be lying in the back half dead? His body was all broken up and mine had a hole through it. What's going on?"

The others turned to Cornelius, waiting for him to fill in the blanks. The last memory I had from the night before was when Cornelius stuck us both with a syringe. He'd mentioned something about some sort of side effects from the nanites. Then he apologized and out went the lights. Once again my mind was trying to make sense of it all. Could my heightened senses be a side effect also? What more could I expect?

Anxious to hear more about the nanites and what they were doing to us, I turned my attention toward Cornelius. He didn't face me at first. His attention was more on Ben's dog. He was lying on a blanket a few yards from us in the shade. I hadn't noticed him earlier. He too had been severely hurt when the bus crashed through the fence. The only difference was he was still broken, while Ben and I were more than just healed; we were thriving.

Finally, he turned toward me and squished his brow like he was concentrating extremely hard. He hadn't done so because he didn't know what to say; it had more to do with the magnitude of what he was about to tell us and how he thought we might perceive it.

"It's going to seem a bit implausible, but please hear me out," he stated. "After you got shot, I injected nanites into you and Ben. That's why you're both still alive. They work in somewhat the same way the nanites that killed everyone worked. With one simple difference: these nanites attack damaged cells and flawed DNA chains. The others attack plasma platelets."

"How can killing bad cells make you better?" Josh interrupted. "Wouldn't it just leave a void?"

"It would if that is all that happens. If you used a knife to cut out a section of flesh, new cells would form to close the wound. When the nanites destroy the damaged cells, the body goes into overdrive to replace those cells. Since they no longer have the damaged or flawed cells to replicate themselves after, they use the blueprint from your original DNA. The old cells were damaged, so they took longer to replicate and thus slowed down the total reproduction of cells. Without the flaws, the new cells tend to reproduce at an alarming rate. What would normally take months, or years can now be done in days, hours, or even minutes. Besides, they do a little more than just kill cells."

He grinned slyly at us. "The best is yet to come. The first twelve to twenty-four hours can be excruciating, sometimes even deadly. Now you will start to see your body get younger and stronger. Not you, Ben. You will gain muscle mass and possibly even become a bit more mature looking."

Now he had my attention. "What do you mean younger? Are they like some sort of diet pill or wrinkle remover? How exactly will I look younger?"

I didn't care much about the strength part because I still felt strong. It was my looks that I wanted to repair. Like I mentioned before, the reason I colored my hair was to make myself look younger. If all I needed was a nanite shot to do that, I was all for it.

Cornelius continued on. "This is the most amazing part. Your DNA naturally wants to be at its most mature, unadulterated state. That's usually somewhere between the ages of twenty-two and twenty-nine. Each person is different, so the age varies."

Katherine's eyes lit up as she stepped forward. "Does it work for women as well as men?"

"It does," Cornelius told her. "Unfortunately, the side effects for women are more severe."

"Are you saying it's more painful than it was for Ben, or does it mess with your mind even more than it did Steve's?" she asked.

"It has to do with the reproductive system. Men become more fruitful, but women become barren. The male can create sperm cells clear into his eighties, and in a few cases, even longer. The female, however, has most of her eggs when she's born. An unsubstantiated amount is produced in her ovaries until menopause. For some reason when the nanites take out the damaged cells in a female, the body thinks it's in menopause, thus destroying the remaining eggs."

We were all expecting Katherine to get upset by this bit of information, but in true style, she smiled and shared her wisdom with us. "That shouldn't be a problem. A woman doesn't start showing her age until after she has children. I'd never even consider taking them until after I had my family."

"What would be the point in having them injected into you anyhow?" Robert asked. "I don't see going through any amount of pain just to lose a few wrinkles."

"It allows the body to stay young a lot longer," Cornelius told him.

"How much longer?" I asked.

"According to our research, you would never age another day in your life as long as you kept taking the nanite injections."

"Screw that noise!" Ben shouted out. "There is no way in hell I'd ever want to go through that much pain every couple of months, or even years, for that matter."

"You wouldn't have to," Cornelius said. "The first shot is the only one that effects a body that way; you would hardly even notice subsequence shots. Your first dose lasts about five years due to all the work the nanites have to do. After that, our research shows you should only need to do it about every one hundred to one hundred fifty years."

"Holy shit!" Robert exclaimed, shaking his head. "I can't even imagine what that would be like. Are you really saying we could live to be one hundred and fifty?"

Cornelius corrected him. "You're not quite getting it. What I'm saying is you would never die, at least not from old age."

"Oh my God," I blurted out. "You've figured out how to make man immortal!"

"Yes and no," Cornelius said. "To be truly immortal, you'd have to be impervious to death. You can still die. You'll just never die of old age."

"I'm still a bit confused," Ben admitted. "Steve and I would be dead right now if it wasn't for the nanites. That has nothing to do with old age; it's more like being invincible."

"That's true, Ben," Cornelius nodded his head in agreement. "It can bring you back from the brink of death. It can also stop you from ever contracting a cold or any other type of disease or cancer. It just can't bring you back after your brain is dead, and it can't stop you from getting your head shot off."

"Holy shit!" I hollered and then laughed out loud. "If getting my fool head shot off is the only way to die, I'd say that makes me about as immortal as any man could ever be."

The excitement in the group was electric. We discussed what it would be like never having to fear death, not to mention the advantage we now had over our adversaries. Then something hit me like a ton of bricks.

"Cornelius?" I asked softly, almost hoping nobody else would hear. "Does that mean the people we are fighting have the same technology?"

"No, I don't believe they do. Other than a few choice scientists the only individuals permitted to have this technology in their possession or to even have knowledge of these certain nanites were at the base in Coos Bay. Since we were able to kill everyone there, I feel secure they never got out."

Robert seemed to be in disbelief. "That's crazy," he said. "We had this amazing gift to live forever and nobody ever got to use it?"

"That's not one hundred percent accurate," Cornelius stated.

"Go on," I said, sounding a bit pissed off. "What the hell are you leaving out?"

"It's nothing that could harm any of us," he said. "Back in the early twenty-first century, we injected a select group of one hundred men and women with these exact same nanites. For the sake of the continuity for all those left behind, nobody else was ever injected."

"Left behind?" I asked quizzically.

"It's like this," Cornelius said. "Everyone who had received the nanite injection was quarantined to Antarctica for the next two years. There they were trained for space travel and taught a variety of different trades. In 2004, they started being deployed to a space station on the dark side of the moon. They spent the next ten years there building a massive spaceship capable of traveling to other galaxies. Their sole mission was to locate a new planet to call home. Scientists believed that was the only hope for mankind to continue on. This planet has less than two hundred years before the population's growth rate exceeds the planet's capabilities to sustain life."

"Why only take a hundred people?" Robert asked. "There are billions of people on this planet. Do they plan on coming back for the rest of us?"

"The planet that was chosen is nearly a thousand light years away," Cornelius said. "By the time they settled it and made their way back to us, our planet would be barren."

"That still doesn't make any sense!" Katherine interjected. "Everyone would be stuck at the same age and could never have any more children. What kind of a society could they establish with a population at a constant one hundred?"

"We took all that and more into consideration," Cornelius said. "Everyone on the ship was chosen for certain skills they possessed. Not to mention each of them passed a psychological exam showing them to be abnormally passive. Their cargo consisted of spores and DNA from every species of plants and animals on earth we wanted to replicate. That included a half billion human eggs."

For the rest of the trip little more was said on the subject. Cornelius may not have seemed bothered by sharing that knowledge with us, but we were caught totally off guard. Even if the drone attack had never happened, man's days on earth were numbered. Mankind wasn't only starting a new life far off on a distant planet, but we were never even allowed in on the decision. For some strange reason, it felt that only the crème de la crème had their gene pool carrying on. The rest of us were to die out on this planet just as so many outdated species had before us. It was Ben that finally brought us all back to reality.

"Why didn't you give my dog a shot?" he asked, glaring at Cornelius. "He did just as much as the rest of us to secure our victory."

Cornelius put his hand on Ben's shoulder. "Do you remember those other dogs we encountered? You know the ones with distemper?

"Yes, I remember," Ben said.

"Well, those dogs all ingested the altered nanites. Now, I'm not totally sure if these nanites would have the same effect, but I didn't feel it was my place to take that risk. It's your decision, Ben, but remember, if for any reason Artemis develops distemper, we have to put him down."

Chapter 2

FOLLOWED

The decision to inject his dog with nanites was tough on Ben. The answer finally came as Artemis looked into his eyes and his breath became labored. If he did nothing, his dog would be dead in minutes. At least the nanites gave him a chance.

We all stood back as Cornelius gave him the injection. Almost as if we were waiting for a miracle, everyone stood over Artemis.

"Well, when will we know if it worked?" Ben asked.

"That's hard to say," Cornelius answered. "It could be anywhere from an hour to a full day. The focus of our research was humans. What happened to the dogs was just a side effect."

"So did you ever do any testing on animals?" I asked.

"We did some," Cornelius said. "It just seemed any of the research that was done on them tended to be highly exaggerated."

"What are we supposed to do to help him then?" Ben asked, hoping for a clearer answer."

"The main thing, above all else, is somebody needs to stay with him at all times. When he wakes up, he'll be in pain. You'll have a limited amount of time to give him the second shot. Just remember that if he turns, well, you know what you need to do."

"Why can't I just give him a shot now while he's asleep?" Ben asked.

"It's a very delicate balance in the first stages. The nanites still don't have a clear picture as to what's good and what's bad. The second shot needs to be given to keep the first ones from eating away the tissue from the inside."

"Tell you what," Ben said, "the rest of you can round up some grub. I'll stay here with Artemis."

"Sounds good to me," I said. "Robert and I will gather the food, if the rest of you can get some wood and build a fire. Then as soon as we eat, we can get loaded up and head home. It seems like a lifetime since I've seen Michelle. I have no idea how she'll react, but I'm going crazy wanting to see her."

Robert put his hand on my shoulder while Katherine wrapped her arms around me. No words were said, but their actions spoke volumes. Afterwards, Robert grabbed the rifle from the SUV and handed me a pair of binoculars and a buck knife.

"This should be all we need," he said as he counted the shells in his rifle.

Then taking a quick look around, he told me to follow him. We took off to the north, walking into the breeze. After about a quarter mile, we turned slightly left and headed uphill onto a game trail.

"This is going to be a bit tricky," he said.

"Why is that?" I asked.

Robert started telling me something, but I really didn't pay much attention to him. I was more focused on an object off in the distance.

"Hey! Are you even paying attention to me? I said it's hard to shoot animals when they walk right up to you."

"Sorry, buddy. I thought I saw something moving off in the distance."

Robert turned to face the direction I was looking. Several seconds passed as he stood there quiet and motionless. I wasn't sure what he was up to so I also remained still. Then, without a word, he reached over and took the binoculars out of my hands. Putting them to his eyes, he turned and looked in the opposite direction. Scanning the horizon, he turned a full three hundred sixty degrees. Afterwards, he slowly lowered his hands to his sides.

"Do me a favor, Steve," he said. "Don't look back to where you were looking earlier; just make your way into the clearing off to your left. I want you to hang out there for two minutes. Then, head back to the others and quietly load up."

I trusted Robert with my life and very seldom questioned him. Doing as he said, I took off into the clearing while he headed into a large group of trees. For the next two minutes time seemed to stand still. I could tell by the tone of his voice that he had seen something, even though he didn't say what it was.

My mind raced wildly. Was it an animal, or maybe even a drone? If it was a drone, why hadn't he said so? Was he using me as bait? We'd started taking the gadolinium a week earlier, so there was no way the drones could see me. At least not the drones we were used to.

Two minutes had passed, and I still had no idea where Robert had gone. I decided it was probably best to do as he requested and head back down the hill to load up. Ben was sitting quietly with his dog's head in his lap, while Katherine and Cornelius were seated on a log next to a small fire. Josh was in the bushes off to my left taking care of his morning ritual.

"Hey, where's Rob?" Katherine asked, sounding a bit concerned that we weren't together.

"I'm not exactly sure, but he requested we all quietly load up in the SUV."

I could tell everyone had questions, yet nobody said a word. We'd known each other a little less than a month, yet we all felt total trust for one another. We knew sometimes it was best not to question it when someone said we needed to do something. I'm not sure how to explain it; we all just knew this was one of those times.

I helped Ben load his dog into the back, and then he hopped in with him. Josh went over to put the fire out, as Katherine and Cornelius got into the backseat of the SUV. It was then that we heard Robert coming down the trail whistling to himself. Nothing seemed wrong except for the robotic way he was doing it. It sounded more forced than just a natural tune.

I felt the hair on the back of my neck stand up as Robert quietly told us we needed to go. Josh didn't waste any more time on the fire. He turned and made his way to the SUV and joined Katherine and Cornelius in the backseat. Robert took a seat up front, leaving me to drive.

With everyone inside, I fired up the motor and started to pull away. Robert's head was down, and he slowly shook it back and forth.

"What was it, Rob?" I asked, trying not to sound overly nervous.

"Instead of being the hunters, we were the hunted," he said quietly and then turned towards Cornelius. "Do you know if the drones all use the same technology?"

"I'm not sure what you mean?" Cornelius questioned, a little thrown off by Robert's demeanor. "The drones all share some of the same characteristics, but for the most part, each design has a specific function."

"We have several drones following us," Robert said, doing his best to stay calm. "They don't seem to be interested in attacking us yet, but they're definitely following our every move."

"It's hard to say without seeing them. The drones we were using mainly used DNA to track. We did have some that used more conventional methods, such as thermal imaging, and regular cameras that relied on GPS. Those were pretty basic, though. We didn't have a lot of access to most of the military's drones. If we had, a whole new can of worms may have been opened."

"Are you telling me none of those drones that killed everyone belonged to the military?" Robert asked.

"At one time they did, but by the time we got them they were considered discards. If we're being followed, I don't believe they're military. At least none that I can recall."

"What makes you say that?" I asked. "How can you be so certain they're not using the same weapons our military used?"

"It's because we're still here. Trust me, if they had access to everything the government had we wouldn't stand a chance. They could basically track every human left just by using our satellites and thermal imaging."

Robert turned towards me and then back around to face the others. Slowly looking over the four of them in the back, he started to laugh.

"That's some funny shit!" he said with a fake laugh.

"What's funny?" I shot back at him, a bit bewildered.

"Us!" he said, laughing again. "We were so busy pretending to be warriors that I never really saw how ridiculous we all looked. Cornelius is right; if we were actually fighting our own government's drones, they would've kicked our asses by now. We're just normal people; it makes no sense that we're doing as well as we are."

"I have to admit, Robert has a point," I said. "Let's have it, Cornelius. You're a genius and all; what do you make of all of this?"

"I have a good idea of what's going on, but I need all of you to trust me."

"I believe everyone here trusts you," I said.

Cornelius looked around at the others. One by one, they all nodded to show their support.

"First off, we can't go home right now. If the drones are following us, there's a reason for it. They may not be military drones, but one thing is for sure; somebody is on to us. I don't believe they want to kill us, at least not yet. They more than likely want to see if there are more of us out there. That means they don't know about the others, and if we play our cards right, they never will."

"Are you saying I can't go home and see Michelle? I don't care about this damn fight anymore! I just want to be with her."

"If we go there now, they'll follow us," Cornelius said.

"Then you guys divert them. You'd do that for me, wouldn't you?" I asked. "I can get out here and hike home while you guys continue driving."

"I'm sorry, Steve, but you know they'll still be following you also," Robert said, putting his hand on my shoulder. "Come on, man. Remember, think with your head and not your heart."

In a fit of anger, I punched the dashboard, breaking out the radio.

"Fucking drones!" I yelled.

Katherine reached up from the backseat and put a hand on my other shoulder, joining Robert in trying to console me.

"I'm so sorry, Steve. We all know you miss her, and we share your pain. Just be grateful that Ray found her and is taking her home. I promise, nothing will stop us from eventually getting you two back together some day. Today is just not that day."

I knew they were right. It just hurt so damn bad.

"Well, can I at least call her on the CB or send her a message?" I asked.

"I'm sorry, Steve, but I don't think that would be a good idea," Cornelius responded. "In fact, we need to destroy all the devices we've been using to communicate. If someone tries to contact us, their signal could be used to locate them."

I stopped the vehicle and turned towards Cornelius.

"You're joking, right?" I really thought he was kidding around with me. The idea that I couldn't even speak with Michelle seemed ludicrous.

"Sorry, Steve," Josh said. "Cornelius is right. It's not worth the risk, and I'm sure deep inside you know it too."

I wasn't real keen on the idea, but regardless, I exited the SUV with the others. One by one, Josh handed us all the cell phones that had been converted to send and receive Morse code. Then, using a large rock we found on the side of the road, we thoroughly smashed each one.

"How about the other phones?" Ben asked. "You know, the ones we used as weapons."

"Those should be fine," Cornelius said. "Now let's hurry up and get out of here."

"Everyone returned to their seats, and we were off again.

"OK, Cornelius, where to now?" I asked."

"San Francisco," he said without hesitation. "If we can get there without getting killed, I may be able to help get us the edge we need."

"What do you mean?" I asked.

"It's a long story," he said, "but now that all of you have accepted me as one of your own, I want you to know how this all went down. It was a week to the day before the attack. My grandfather and I were working on an artificial protein we used in 3-D printers to create food.

"You make food in a printer?" Josh interrupted.

"Please, Josh, I don't want to seem rude, but if you could, hold your questions until the end," Cornelius said.

"Anyhow, my grandfather and I were mainly just doing busy work. We'd already perfected the process and decided to have a little fun while making lunch at the same time. It was about noon when we caught an image in one of the monitors. Several all-black SUVs pulled in through the gate at our research facility. We weren't the ones in charge, so it really didn't bother us much. Things were done there on a need-to-know basis, and apparently I didn't need to know a lot of things. As the lot of them entered the building, they gathered in the cafeteria. A few minutes later, we were summoned to join them.

"Once there, we were each given a bottle of gadolinium and directions on when to take it and how much. My grandfather balked at the idea at first but was quickly informed it was not a choice. They also informed us that it wasn't their job to tell us why we needed to take it. It was their job just to make sure we did. Grandpa and I were still extremely confused as we went back down to our lab. We'd just started discussing what might be going on when our boss walked in, followed by the other men.

"Now remember, we may have worked for the military, but we were still civilians. None of us at that lab had any proper military training. These men, however, all looked as if they might've been CIA or SEALs. You know, not your average grunt types. In fact, now that I'm looking back on it, I'm sure they were mercenaries.

"As they entered our lab, my grandfather asked them what they wanted and said that he would be glad to show them around. Without a word, one of the men pulled out a Taser and let us have it. When I came to, I was in the backseat of one of the SUVs. My boss was up front, and two of the men had their weapons pointed at me. I was told I had two choices: I could help them and someday be reunited with my grandfather, or I could refuse and we'd both die.

"Now, I've never been one for violence, and the only person I've ever loved was my grandfather, so the decision was quite simple. After I agreed to be their minion, they injected me with a sedative and I was out again. This time when I came to I was on a cot in the middle of a large network of computers. The two men that had held me at gunpoint earlier were standing guard at the front of the room. When they realized I was awake, one of them radioed a third man.

"It was obvious to me that he was the one in charge there. Certainly not of the whole operation, but definitely this part of it. Still, I had little to no faith in his promises. I knew enough to know that anyone not at the top was only given enough power and information to complete his task and nothing more.

"However, he made it very clear that he'd personally recruited me for the position. Apparently the former recruit, as he put it, had opted not to help and had to be eliminated. My job, he said, was a simple one. I was to use my skills in molecular biology to create a fuel additive that would pollute our air with an inert gas. Not just any gas, though. This gas would have to be able to dissolve a specific lining that they'd used to coat the nanites. Then, after the lining no longer encased the nanites, a unique radio wave would activate them.

"I was also informed that the last recruit was nearly finished when he got cold feet. If he hadn't, my services would never have been needed. That meant he would still be alive and my grandfather and I wouldn't be. I believe it was his way of letting me know that even if I backed out, someone else would eventually get it done."

Cornelius paused for a brief moment. I couldn't tell if he was doing so for effect or if the memory of that day was still eating at him.

"Believe me, I'm nobody's fool," he continued. "I was well aware of their intent to kill us. The only chance we had for survival was to make them believe I was on their side. I put on a good show of being totally committed to their cause and added input that would ensure them success. I must've been very convincing, because after only a few days they trusted me enough to leave me alone in the lab.

"The program they wanted me to write was so simple a child could've done it. It only took three days to finish, but I had them convinced I was still working on it a week later. What I was really doing was infiltrating their system and figuring out their complete game plan. I couldn't believe what I was unearthing; I felt there was no way this was really going to happen. The government had entrusted the scientists to all of their outdated weapons and technology in hopes they could create even greater tools to protect our allies and us. Over the years, they made some astounding breakthroughs in nanotechnology. Since they policed themselves, not all the weapons they produced made it into the hands of the government.

"I quickly discovered these men weren't alone. Hundreds, if not thousands, of scientists and computer programmers from all over the world were in on it. The one thing they all had in common was that each one worked for his country's government. I had no way of telling whom I could trust and just how deep this all went. I had to face the fact that I was alone and even though I couldn't stop it, I could limit the amount of firepower they had.

"When I first started hacking their systems, I noticed the only drones commissioned to them were a few thousand reconnaissance drones. The Apollo and Zeus drones were never meant to be in their control. It was one of our own government's programmers that moved them from weapons status to discard status; they also changed the files to show that they were never mass-produced. In fact, an inventory report showed less than ten thousand total for both types. It took only a few emails from them to convince the military brass that a cargo ship full of toasters was actually a shipment of newer drones — ones that used sonar waves and lasers to kill.

"We're fortunate that they did trust me. These men had full control of nearly all of the technological weapons created over the last couple of decades. They could gain access through a backdoor anytime they wanted. That was the first thing I changed. I put a worm in the system that would counter any launch command within milliseconds. It would then eat every line of code, making that weapon useless. This included all nuclear and satellite devices.

"There was no way for me to stop the initial attack from happening. The gas I'd created was only for the nanites; it had nothing to do with the drones. If I sent out a warning to anyone, everything would be set in motion automatically. If I tried to disarm their weapons, then the drones would be activated. The worm was the only thing I could do to save what I could. That would keep these guys from being able to launch every weapon this wonderful species had created. It had to be done in such a way nobody could detect my encryption until it was too late.

"I had no way of checking my work, so I didn't know if it had been effective until you took over the mill. If they had all the technology they planned on having, you could never have done that."

We all listened intently to every word Cornelius had to say. When he finished, I quietly pulled to the side of the road. Turning towards him, I was nearly speechless.

After several seconds, Katherine spoke up. "What is it, Steve? Why aren't you saying anything?"

"I'm fine. I'm just at a loss for words. This whole time I thought it was sheer luck that we were all still alive and fighting back as well as we were. In fact, I actually thought I was a large part of the reason we were all alive. It turns out we owe it all to Cornelius. If he hadn't done what he did, there would've been zero chance for rebellion against these monsters."

I watched the light as it came on in the eyes of everyone else as they put it all together. Suddenly, all at once, everyone was either hugging Cornelius or trying to shake his hand. He'd truly been the first rebel in this resistance. By closing the backdoor on the men controlling this massacre, he'd inadvertently opened one for us.

That gave me a really good feeling about our future. Before, we were just a group that had somehow beaten the odds. Knowing that it wasn't just luck that saved us, but rather, help from the inside, gave me hope. It wasn't only possible to have other pockets of resistance, but it was also highly plausible.

I started back down the highway, and while Cornelius chatted with the rest of the group, my mind began to wander. I tried to piece together places other survivors might hide. There were so many possibilities that I was beginning to get excited. That was about the time that Ben's dogs suddenly seemed to go ballistic.

Artemis jumped to his feet, growling and barking. Then he let out an ear-piercing noise that was somewhere between a scream and a howl. My first reaction was to get the hell out of there. We slid to a stop as I locked up the brakes. Everyone quickly jumped out of the vehicle. Everyone, that is, except Ben. Artemis had him cornered in the back, with no clear chance for escape.

Thinking the dog had gone rabid and fearing for my friend, I grabbed my handgun, raised the barrel, and aimed it directly at the dog's head. As I squeezed the trigger, Katherine grabbed my arm. The bullet tore through the glass panel next to Ben's head.

"Don't shoot, you damn fool!" she yelled. "Everyone, please just hold on a second."

Robert had already drawn his weapon and was about to fire as Katherine's words sank in. He still kept it aimed at Artemis but held off shooting.

While we were listening to Katherine, Josh quickly made his way to the rear of the SUV and opened the hatch for Ben. We all expected a wild dog to jump out at us, ready to defend his life. What actually did happen was a relief to us all.

Artemis forced himself between Ben and the open door, knocking him flat on the floor. Then, using all the strength he could muster, he forced his entire body under Ben's. As he lay there shaking and whining, Cornelius realized what was happening. He wasn't rabid, as we'd feared; he was healing. Much in the same way Ben had reacted, Artemis just wanted to get away from the pain.

Cornelius quickly shot back into the SUV and grabbed his bag next to Ben. He pulled the bag open to get to the syringe he'd loaded earlier. As he did, the entire contents dumped onto the ground. Cornelius froze for just a second, as each of the glass bottles dropped to the pavement, bounced, and then safely came to rest. With a distinct look of relief, he turned towards Artemis.

He looked both Ben and the dog up and down. He feared that any attempt he made to get to the dog would be met with razor-sharp teeth. A soft smile formed on his face as he handed the needle to Ben.

"Quickly!" Cornelius said. "You must stick him in the neck and inject all the serum."

Ben took the needle and rolled off Artemis. Wrapping

one arm around the big dog's neck and head, he stopped and stared for just a second.

"Hurry, Ben, you don't have time to waste!" Cornelius yelled.

Ben inserted the needle deep into Artemis's flesh and forced every drop into him. With a rush of relief, he fell to the floorboard, his dog lying next to him, unconscious but alive.

Josh's eyes went from Ben to his dog.

"What the fuck just happen?" he blurted out. Why did Ben's dog do that? Is he viral? Is he rabid?"

Cornelius laughed at Josh's choice of words. "No, he's not rabid, and he isn't viral either," he replied. "He's just reacting to the nanites."

"Does everything react that way?" I asked.

"Not exactly that way," Cornelius said. "Some reactions are mild and some are extremely dramatic. It all depends on the host and how much work the nanites might have to do."

With Artemis passed out next to him, Ben raised up slightly.

"What was the deal, having to get it done so quickly?" he asked. "Was it because he was in so much pain?"

"Yes and no," Cornelius responded. "The amount of pain helped to indicate we only had a few seconds to respond, but the shot wasn't just for that. There's a window of opportunity after someone or something reacts to the nanites. For some it's several minutes, and for a few it's a matter of seconds. The shot is more than just a painkiller. It neutralizes the nanites that are in the system and adds fresh ones. For some reason, the first batch goes rogue. They start the process to repair the damage but get confused. They repair your nervous system first, but then for some reason they start eating your insides. If you're not in a lot of pain, they're still eating you but at a much slower rate."

"That is so gross!" Katherine said as she walked away.

"So, what happens if you don't destroy them?" Robert asked. "Would you eventually just die?"

"That's the scary part," Cornelius told us. "The nanites would keep your entire nervous system in perfect condition basically forever. With all your nerve endings exposed, you'd be living in an inescapable hell for all eternity. You're not even considered a vegetable. Your bones, flesh, and organs all disintegrate until you're just a pile of mush — a pile of mush in agony, that is."

"Don't tell me you've actually seen this happen," I said, almost afraid of what he was going to say.

"More times than I care to remember," Cornelius replied. "For the most part the initial reaction tends to be more psychological instead of physical, like yours was. When that's the case, there's plenty of time to react. With Ben and Artemis, time was of the essence. A few seconds could mean the difference between living and dying in the most excruciating way possible. There's literally no worse fate."

"How would you know that?" Robert asked. "How can you judge someone else's pain?"

"We can't judge what they're feeling; we just know what it does. It would be like dipping every nerve ending you have in acid all at the same time. Except it wouldn't last just a few minutes; it would last forever."

Ben offered his input. "I know the pain I felt was the worst I've ever felt in my entire life."

"Believe it or not," Cornelius said, "they hadn't even gotten to the nerves yet. That's when it's the worst, and we can no longer stop them."

"How do you know that?" Ben asked.

"Because I've seen it," he said. "I've tried everything to stop it, but the way we're built, it's like lighting a fuse — a very fast fuse. From the time it attacks the first nerve cell until they're all inflamed is a matter of seconds."

"So couldn't you just set a timer and give them the shot a little early?" I asked.

"No. Unfortunately, it has somewhat of a narrow window for the second shot. If you do it too early, they instantly attack the nervous system; too late, and it's time for a bullet."

"What do you mean a bullet?" I asked. "What good could a bullet do?"

"That's the only way to stop them at that point. A bullet to the brain destroys your nervous system to the point the nanites can't bring it back. No more nervous system, no more pain."

"Damn!" Robert let out. "Immortality hardly seems worth the risk."

"Believe it or not," Cornelius said, "for anyone who has seen the dark side of it, few to none are willing to take that risk."

"Just promise that if that ever happens to me, you won't hesitate shooting me in the head!" Robert said.

"Shit, Rob," Katherine said with a grin, "I really doubt sometimes if either you or Steve even have a brain to shoot."

Robert took off after her and chased her around the vehicle until she fell to the ground. I thought how happy the two of them looked together as Robert flopped on the ground next to her.

Chapter 3

HEADING SOUTH

Cornelius gathered up all of his glass jars and took a seat in the SUV.

"You sure looked awfully nervous when those things hit the ground," I said.

"That's for a couple of reasons," Cornelius replied. "For now, these may be all the good nanites left on this planet. If we lose them and something happens, we'll have no second chance."

"Are you sure that's all of them?" I asked skeptically.

"Yes, we had total control of this type of nanite. The only lab ever set up to create them is the one in Coos Bay. When all this is over, I promise I'll make all we need."

"So, big deal," Robert said. "We've lived this long without them; breaking the vials wouldn't have been the end of the world."

"It might've been for us," Cornelius said.

Katherine raised an eyebrow. "I think you need to elaborate on that," she said, staring hard at him.

You see, when I give an injection I use very few nanites. The amount I have here is enough for more than one hundred shots. They don't just die if the glass breaks; they go rogue. With all of us being so close to them, they would've entered our bodies very quickly. With that many entering our system, we'd never have stood a chance."

"Then why the hell would you have put them in glass tubes in the first place?" Katherine asked, visibly annoyed.

"It's the only substance we know of that can contain them," he said sheepishly. "We were so caught up in creating them that we never gave much thought to how to store them."

"Wow, isn't that just like a scientist," she said. "You're always wanting to take that next step without ever considering the consequences."

Cornelius didn't respond.

When we'd first learned about how close to being immortal you became with the nanites, it sounded too good to be true. Now that we knew the risk, it hardly seemed worth it. We'd never seen anyone die that horrifically, but after hearing Cornelius describe it, we didn't want to either.

We'd gotten back into the SUV and continued heading south. Ben was lying down with Artemis, and everything was once again calm and peaceful. In no time at all, we were almost out of Oregon. Since most of the cleanup had been finished, the freeway was relatively easy to maneuver. All the vehicles were either moved to the sides of the road or far enough apart to leave a nice path.

We ran into a small snag around Medford, though. A large section of freeway had been built over the city instead of cutting through it. The viaduct was at least a half-mile long, which normally wouldn't have been an issue. We still had some road ahead of us when I first noticed an abnormality in the roadway.

"Hey, guys, look up ahead," I told them, "Something doesn't look right."

"Slow down," Robert said. "It may just be my eyes playing tricks on me, but it looks like the road is gone."

"I don't think it's your eyes, Rob," I answered, bringing the SUV to a crawl.

More than half of it was missing. We could see remnants of a fire on either side of the bridge. It looked as if there'd been some sort of explosion right in the center of town. It was still early enough in the day that the morning sun cast its glare against the windshield. With almost no cloud cover to help shield its rays, we were forced to squint. On occasion, the carnage left on the freeway would play tricks on our eyes. Many times, we had seen something moving between the cars and swore it was a person. Then, after we had come to a complete stop, we would lose them. It wasn't until the third or fourth incident that we realized it had only been shadows playing with our minds. This time, however, it was no shadow.

"Son of a bitch!" Katherine said, climbing over the seat as we got closer. "Steve, quick, stop the damn car."

I pulled to the shoulder and stopped our SUV. I didn't need to pull to the side, but it was still a force of habit. Katherine had not only slid over the front seat, but also right past Robert, and she was the first one out. The rest of us got out behind her, but nowhere near as quickly as she had.

For a moment no one said a word. We just stood there, mouths opened, and stared at what we could only assume used to be a shopping center.

"What do you think happened here?" Josh asked.

"My best guess would be that this is a plane crash," I answered him. "I just can't believe how much destruction there is, though."

We shook our heads in disbelief. We'd gotten used to the fact that practically every person on the planet was now dead. Yet, we'd assumed everyone died basically the same way. It was just so hard to fathom the terror of being in a plane as it went down.

Standing on what was left of the bridge, we were high enough to get a good view of the city. Straight ahead of us, where the freeway once stood, was a long section of bridgework that had been torn away. Below was a debris field of cars, trucks, and pieces of fuselage. It looked like something had not only torn through the roadway but also had taken several buildings with it. Remnants of the fire that followed made it almost impossible to distinguish between the initial destruction and what happened afterwards. We even saw what could've been melted drones over a large section of the landscape.

"You know, with nobody here to fight the fire, it may have burned for several days before it ran out of fuel," Ben commented. "I can still see a few hot spots over to the east."

"Look over there!" Katherine called out frantically. "Is that the tail of the plane?"

"We all turned to where she was pointing. It wasn't easy to make out at first, but our eyes slowly adjusted to the chaos. Soon, it was easier for us to make out the object she was referring to.

Sure enough, the whole tail section had remained intact and had avoided being burnt. The last row of seats was still connected to the hull. I couldn't tell if the partial remains still strapped to those chair were victims of the crash or the drones. No matter how they died, it was evident something had been feeding on them.

We 'd gotten all to used to the death around us, but this was different. It wasn't the same as seeing it on the news or in a movie. This seemed so much more violent and horrific than anything we'd ever witnessed. The immediate impact zone was anywhere from a quarter to a half mile long. The destruction from its aftermath was evident for as far as the eye could see. Off to our left, we could make out what was once a small mall with a theater. It appeared the plane had hit there first and then continued onward, leveling the raised section of the freeway as it was ripped to shreds.

I turned to face the group. "Sorry, guys. We're going to have to hoof it from here."

Katherine turned her head away from me so I wouldn't see her crying. I could tell the others were also pretty shaken, but they did their best to hold it in.

"How far?" Ben asked.

"It shouldn't be too far," I told him. "I really don't see any way of driving around it, and for now I'd just as soon we stay real close to the freeway. We'll just make a path through the center and grab a new rig on the other end."

I thought that made everyone feel a little better. There was something about the SUV that really seemed bleak. Once we made it through all this, we could find something that didn't remind us so much of losing Kenny.

Everyone gathered what he or she could easily carry and we headed off. It wasn't going to be an easy jaunt. With Artemis sticking close to Ben, we made our way down a broken section of bridge that took us to ground level. The first section we passed was mainly chunks of charred metal and large pieces of concrete. A little further on, we were able to make out the remains of burnt vehicles. Unfortunately, we could also make out the bodies that were still in them. Most were scarcely more than a burnt shadow of a figure, but a few were nearly complete.

The ones that resembled shadows weren't bad. They were nothing more than a reminder that a person used to fill that seat. We all cringed when we passed a spot where the fire hadn't been as hot and the charred remains were easily recognizable. One such encounter was a minivan that had been only slightly burnt. It had also been partially crushed by the falling bridge. Inside we saw what we thought to be a young family. After a closer look, we spotted one of those bloody drones. We saw no sign of anyone being ripped apart by it though. We figured it must have torn its way into the van just as the bridge came down on them.

Robert found a stick and poked at the charred remains. Suddenly, one of its rotors started to spin. Without a second's hesitation, Josh grabbed a cell phone and pressed send. As quickly as it started up, it shut down again.

"Good job, Josh," I said, glaring at Robert. "We're not safe by any means, people. Let's make sure we do our best not to attract attention."

"What about those drones that are following us?" Katherine asked.

"It would appear they have a different agenda than these other ones," I told her. "I'm sure when they realize we're not leading them to our home base, they too will attack us. For now, though, the real threat comes from the unknown. Just be ready for anything."

"Copy that," Cornelius said, sliding in between Robert and me.

He really wasn't the fighting type, and I guess he figured Robert and I could protect him if something attacked us. Either that or maybe he just figured if he was between us, we'd get it first.

We didn't say much during our walk, so everything was quiet, for the most part. Occasionally, though, a piece of falling debris or some animal climbing over the ruins in search of food broke the silence. We could all feel the tension growing around us; it wasn't a matter of if, but when someone would snap. And just who would it be?

We were about three-quarters of the way through the rubble when Josh finally lost it. He was climbing over the burnt-out shell of a car when the vehicle shifted. As it did, the partial remains of a highly decomposed body fell from where the door had been. It landed at Josh's feet, catching him off guard. In a panic, he fell backwards, coming to rest in a pile of dried flesh-covered bones. As he scrambled to get his footing, it was clear to the rest of us that Josh had gone off the deep end. He was now running from one vehicle to the next, yelling incoherently at the remains inside each one.

After a few seconds we realized he wasn't just screaming, but he was also yelling for his wife and son, running to each vehicle in search of them. As he made his way through the labyrinth of decay, he tripped over a downed drone. With a crazy look in his eyes, he raised his rifle and opened fire. He fired shot after shot into the bloodstained demon until he finally collapsed to the ground in a fetal position.

Not wanting to get killed, we waited until he'd not only spent his ammunition, but also his energy. Once he was no longer a threat, we all rushed to him. Katherine was the first to reach him. She pulled him into her arms and he began crying uncontrollably.

"I can't do this anymore," he said between sobs. "I don't want to go on without my family."

So many times in my life I'd told somebody how sorry I felt for them, yet I never truly understood their pain. This, however, wasn't the case. We were all running from the pain we felt. We'd all lost loved ones. I myself still had my wife but I did all I could to close my mind to the fact that my children were gone. I had to. Every time I even thought about them no longer being with me brought me one step closer to insanity. Yes, I felt Josh's pain; each one of us did. We were all just a hair's breadth away from losing it just as he had.

Sadly, it was also the one thing that kept us going. Our own lives had lost their value and we were willing to do anything to change that. The only thing we could think of that might help was revenge.

We stayed there in a tight group until Josh regained his composure. All of us understood his meltdown and quickly forgave him. Unfortunately, his outburst had gained some unwanted attention.

We got Josh back to his feet only to find ourselves surrounded by a pack of dogs. Most of the dogs we'd run into over the last week or so had been rabid or close to it. These dogs had a different look to them. We could tell they'd been eating well, because none of them looked too malnourished. However, they did look surprised to see us.

I don't think they were expecting to see humans. They'd come running at the noise, expecting their next meal. Judging from what we'd seen in this city so far, no cleanup efforts had taken place. For that reason, we may have been the first living people they encountered since this all began.

Artemis stayed close to Ben's legs. He too seemed unsure of what to expect from these visitors. They'd gotten to us swiftly and quietly. They even made sure to stay downwind from us until they were ready to attack. Then in one swift move, they surrounded us before making their presence known.

"You're the hunter, Rob," I said. "What's our next move?"

"Well, Steve, if we shoot, they'll attack us for sure. There's far too many of them."

"And if we don't shoot?" I asked, a little unsure of their intent.

"Your guess is as good as mine," he said.

I was scared as hell; we all were. None of us had a clue how to get out of this.

Suddenly, Ben's dog did the unthinkable. He leapt out from beside Ben's legs and faced the intruders. The other dogs took a step forward, showing their teeth and growling. Slowly we raised our weapons, waiting for what seemed to be the inevitable. What happened next taught us all a lesson in humility. Ben's dog rolled over onto his back, exposing his belly and making himself defenseless to the pack. He whined softly and waited for their response.

The dogs instantly changed their demeanors. It was as if we'd walked into a pet store and every one of them was looking for a new family. They started whining and wagging their tails as they made their way towards our group.

"Oh my God, Steve!" Katherine cried out. "What will we do with all of them?"

By that time, she was on her knees, hugging and petting all those lovesick canines. I'd never seen such a sight before. Eleven dogs of all shapes and sizes bid for our attention. They weren't rabid; they were confused and alone. Just like us, they'd banded together for strength and companionship.

Artemis had made his way back to Ben and took a seat at his feet. As he sat down, he turned his head to face him. His tail was wagging a hundred miles an hour and his tongue was hanging out. If I hadn't known any better, I would've sworn he was grinning at him. It was as if he somehow knew what a good thing he'd done. Not to mention he was probably pretty stoked to have a few of his own kind around.

I'd heard in the past how pets are supposed to be good therapy. I got to witness it that day. To see the change in everyone, including myself, as the dogs showed their affection was almost surreal.

Josh sat on the car that had just set him off and played with a border collie. Robert and Katherine played with a group of five dogs, all about three months old. It looked as if they might've been from the same litter. Cornelius kept to the smaller dogs. One was a black and tan Chihuahua. I didn't recognize the breed of the other, but it was about the same size. Ben stood next to me as the rest of the dogs came over to greet us.

They may have all been a bunch of mutts, but the smiles and laughter they brought made them worth more than any old purebred. It was one of those moments we all really needed. For a short time our minds were no longer focused on the death around us. We literally got lost in the moment and just enjoyed all the affection those dogs had to offer.

Robert and Katherine had a great time playing catch with the puppies. They'd wait for Robert to throw a stick that he found and then they'd take off barking and yelping. For some strange reason I didn't fear the noise they made. We were invisible to most drones and the dogs gave us a sense of security.

Katherine looked over at me with a big smile. "So, Steve, how are we going to take care of all these dogs?"

"I'm not sure." I laughed as an overly excited dog nuzzled my hand, looking for attention. "I guess we'll just have to make do."

To this day, I'm still not sure exactly what happened. The big dog I was focused on suddenly stopped playing, took two steps away, and then barked once. All the other dogs instantly stopped what they were doing and came over to him. Then, giving us one last look and a wag from their tails, they were gone.

"You're considered a genius," I said, turning to Cornelius. "What do you make of them just leaving like that?"

"I don't really know," he said, scratching his head. "It was like they were glad to see us but for some reason had no intentions of staying."

"Maybe they like the freedom they have now," Katherine said, shrugging her shoulders.

Robert gave us all a quirky look. "I'm just glad we didn't have to shoot them."

"Isn't that the truth!" I exclaimed. "Well, it's nearly one p.m. What do you say we get the hell out of here?"

With everyone in agreement, we continued on our way. We had a little more spring to our step and didn't focus so much on the travesty around us. Ben seemed relieved Artemis hadn't left with the others. Even though the other dogs appeared to be enjoying their freedom, Artemis was content just being with him.

As we reached the end of the burnt-out section, Katherine spotted a small garden. It was growing right behind an old Chinese restaurant on the south end of town. A broken water line a few feet from it supplied just enough water to keep everything green and flourishing. It was still too early in the season to harvest the vegetables, but a small planter of potatoes proved to be an amazing find.

After we ate a few of them raw, we stuffed several in our pockets for later. With very little food and an overabundance of exercise, I noticed my old body was becoming much firmer and my energy level was through the roof.

"Wouldn't it be great if Michelle could see me now?" I thought.

I was already past my prime when we met, yet with her, I felt young. Even with my graying hair and sagging midsection, Michelle doted on me like I was her first love. She claimed the years had treated me well, but many times I found her staring at pictures of me in my younger days. She'd smile and refer to them as her eye candy.

So many times I've looked back on my life, wishing I'd chosen different paths. When I was young, I'd often hear my mom wishing she could have a do over. It wasn't until I myself had a laundry list of poor decisions in the wake I left behind that I understood what she meant. It isn't that we don't make it through without some good memories; we all have some great ones. The problem is life has a funny way of making us pay for our poor decisions as we get older.

On this day, however, I felt as if I were getting my do over. I felt young and full of life. My joints and muscles didn't hurt and even my hair seemed to be a bit thicker. I had the feeling that if Michelle could see me at that very moment, she'd have a new picture for her eye candy.

The day had started rather rough, but the further we got into it, the better it seemed to get. It had less to do with the things around us as it did our own peace of mind. The dogs showing up may have been just what we needed to remind us we were still alive.

What we were going through was the darkest times our world had ever known, yet I'd made some amazing new friends. Together we'd created some of the happiest memories I'd ever known.

My mind was adrift, wondering if Michelle had made it back safely. I often wondered if she missed me as much as I did her. Deep down, I knew she did, but time has a way of messing with us. It becomes easy to think someone you love has stopped thinking about you when you go so long without him or her.

"Oh yeah, baby! It's Christmas time," Josh called out, pushing those thoughts from my mind.

We all looked up to see what had caught his attention. There on the edge of the fire line was a row of brand-new motor coaches. These were not your run-of-the-mill motor homes. No, these were the high-end models rock stars drove around in.

Josh was right; it did feel like Christmas. We took off towards them in damn near a full run. Ben was the first to reach the lot, with Artemis right beside him. Approaching the first motor coach, he stopped and peered in a window. Katherine, however, had no intention of just window-shopping. Bypassing Ben, she went straight for the door.

"Yes!" she exclaimed as she pulled it opened.

The dealership must've been open when the attacks broke out. The RVs were unlocked and next to the office was a pegboard with all the keys. It hadn't been a very busy day for them. We only spotted one body, lying on the office floor. For the most part, he still looked normal, other than his clothes being nearly torn off him; he appeared to just be napping.

"What's up with this?" I asked Cornelius, pointing to the dead man's body. "Don't they ever decompose? And why would something rip his clothes like that and not eat him?"

"In time, they'll shrivel up some, but they're basically mummified. They could last thousands of years unless the elements get to them. As far as the clothes go, the only thing I can figure was an animal. It must have smelled something on his clothes and tried to eat them."

"Then why didn't they eat the body?" Josh asked.

"For pretty much the same reason you don't eat your plate," Cornelius said, almost dumbfounded by such a silly question. "To the animals, these bodies aren't food; they're just some object. There's no smell and no taste."

"Is everyone the drones killed mummified?" Ben asked, still sounding a bit confused.

"Not everyone," Cornelius told him. "Those that were chopped up by the bloody drones just decomposed like anything else that dies. The others the drones killed fell victim to a solution of nanites on the arrows. That was what vaporized their blood. It would appear many of the people around here were killed in the same way as this man was: by the nanites."

"Then aren't nanites bad?" Ben asked.

"Actually, most nanites are good. They were all created to do good things. Most of them were being designed for the consumption of waste. It was going to be the future for waste management in a few years, not just for household waste, but also biohazardous and nuclear waste."

Josh gave Cornelius a strange look. "With so many good uses for the nanites, why did they get used for evil instead?"

"Unfortunately, that's just how life works. It's not just with man; it's with everything in the universe. For every positive there's a negative; every good has its bad. There's literally nothing I could ever create for good that some yahoo wouldn't figure out something terrible to do with it."

"Hey, guys. Get over here and check this out!" Katherine yelled. She'd gone through nearly all of the coaches before finding the one she wanted. The rest of us hurried over to join her inside the coach.

It was amazing. It didn't have any slide outs like some of the other models, but it was luxury all the way. It was the widest of the models on the lot at eight feet wide and forty-five feet long. The living room had plush furniture and a gas fireplace. The kitchen had a nice marble countertop, a large double-door refrigerator, and a full-size oven. The rear of the coach had a fully furnished bedroom with a queen-size bed. There were plenty of pillows and a thick comforter. It also didn't have one of those little bathrooms; it had a nice tub and a separate walk-in shower.

None of us could've cared less about the fancy kitchen. That was almost useless to us, since we currently didn't have anything but a few potatoes to cook. Our eyes were all on the large shower and soft bed.

Robert was already sitting in the front of the coach reading the owner's manual. "This thing holds enough fuel to go between fifteen hundred and twenty-five hundred miles, depending on the driving conditions. It also holds more than three hundred gallons of water," he said excitedly.

"Tell you what, Rob," I said after grabbing the keys off the board. "I noticed this dealership has a gravity-fed fuel station. Why don't you fuel it up and check the water tanks? There's a clothing store across the street. The rest of us will run over there real quick and grab us all something fresh to wear. We'll meet back here in twenty minutes. You good with that?"

"Yeah, I'm good with that."

"Could you pick me up something sharp, please?" he asked, looking at Katherine. "I want to get all spiffed up for you tonight."

Katherine shot him a warm smile and nodded.

There were several bodies outside the store, but we really didn't pay any heed to them. I was more worried about how it would be inside the store. The front glass was broken out and a dozen or so bodies were heaped together towards the rear of the store. These people appeared to have all been killed by the bloody drones. They'd been decomposing for a while now and the smell was anything but pleasant. Katherine and Josh didn't seem bothered by it much, but as for Ben, Cornelius, and myself, it was almost overwhelming.

Ben grabbed a cart from one of the aisles and we made our way through the store together. Using our flashlight to help guide us, we quickly loaded the cart with tons of clothes and returned outside. We also made sure to grab some soap, shampoo, and plenty of other items we'd been without lately. Once outside, we sorted through the mess of items to find what would fit us.

None of us wanted to spend any extra time inside looking for the perfect outfit. It wasn't just the smell; it had more to do with the visual effects. The store was dark and dreary inside, and the light our flashlights gave off was inadequate for the conditions. It seemed more like a house of horror than a department store.

Dark pools of dried blood covered the floors. The bodies were contained mostly near the back of the store. Pieces of bodies were another story. We passed arms, legs, and even some parts we couldn't identify throughout the store. Being killed by the bloody drones allowed for plenty of scents to attract different types of hungry animals. From what we could tell, there must've been plenty of them. Most didn't want to sit in the store and eat; they wanted their food to go.

After sorting through our mess, we quickly pushed the cart back across the street to join Robert. When we got there, he was still filling the RV with fuel, and he'd already finished topping off the water.

As the rest of us loaded the items we'd just gotten into the coach, Ben went into the sales office. He'd spotted a few vending machines earlier and decided we needed some snacks for our trip. When he returned, we had plenty of warm sodas and enough candy to satisfy even the worst sweet tooth.

"Let's go!" Robert called out as he removed the nozzle from the RV. "This world isn't going to save itself."

We all laughed as we entered the vehicle. Ben took his rightful spot behind the wheel and fired it up. That thing was so well insulated that we could hardly even hear the large diesel motor. Ben did a magnificent job making his way through the mess of vehicles in route to the freeway. Every now and then he would slow the bus, and then using the bumper, he would carefully push a vehicle or two out of our path. Once back on the freeway, driving was a lot easier. Except for that city, the other roads and towns we passed were all cleared of bodies and obstructions.

With the RV at a steady speed, Katherine made her way back to the shower. Robert went to join her, only to be shot down.

"Hold it right there, cowboy," she said. "I'm not exactly feeling very attractive right now. Not to mention you smell about as appealing as a locker room. Let's get cleaned up a bit and maybe I'll let you take a nap with me."

Robert stood there dumbfounded as Katherine winked at him and shut the door.

"Sorry, Rob, ole buddy," I said. "She's right; you don't smell very pleasant. Not to mention, with your dirty clothes and unshaven mug you look a little less than appealing."

"You don't look that great yourself, asshole!" he shot back. "None of you jackasses do."

We all laughed at his remark as we kicked back on the sofa. Robert sank into a La-Z-Boy chair directly across from us. In a matter of minutes they were all asleep. The gentle rocking of the RV just seemed to take the fight right out of them. Not wanting to be alone, I made my way to the front and took a seat near Ben. It was nice and peaceful chatting together as we made our trek south.

Roughly a half hour later, Katherine appeared in the hallway near the back. Seeing the others sleeping peacefully, she figured it was her duty to do something about it. In her usual sweet way, she woke them all back up.

"Rise and shine, you losers!" she yelled out. "You guys need to crack a window in here and go get cleaned up."

She had a rough, unrefined way about her, but regardless, when she entered a room Robert totally lit up.

One by one the rest of us showered and cleaned up. Even Ben traded off driving with Josh so he too could smell a little less manly. The odd part was it took the five of us combined less time to shower and change than Katherine took.

While the rest of us had gotten cleaned up, Katherine found a frying pan in the cupboard and cooked up our potatoes. She may have been lacking a bit when it came to tact, but that girl could sure cook. Even though she had no spices to speak of, she still managed to make an amazing meal for us. After she'd finished cooking, Ben pulled the bus into a nice shaded area next to the freeway. We all sat together near the kitchen and enjoyed our meal together. Artemis bypassed the plate he was given and focused on eating off Ben's.

After we ate, we relaxed a bit while Robert did an impromptu comedy routine. He was telling jokes and acting out different characters he'd seen at a Jeff Dunham concert when the hum of a drone caught our attention. It wasn't just one drone but several of them. The surveillance drones that had been following us were no longer in hiding. They'd come down to eye level and were now buzzing around the RV.

"What do you want us to do, Steve?" Ben asked.

"Well, it appears the little bastards have figured out we aren't going back to any base camp," I said. "Personally, I don't think it will make much of a difference if we just blow their little asses out of the sky. What do you guys think?"

"Hell yeah!" Robert yelled as he grabbed a rifle.

Everyone else was on the same page and followed suit. Exiting the RV, we made note of the drones flying around us. None of them had any weapons, but we could tell from the lights on the front of them that they definitely had cameras.

"How do you want to do this?" Robert called over to me. "Do we have to take them out one at a time, or can we do a free-for-all with everyone shooting?"

"Hell, I say we all have a good time and do a free-for-all," I yelled back.

Chapter 4

CAVE DWELLERS

We'd all been a little surprised when the drones first started buzzing around the RV — surprised, but also a bit relieved. These things had been following us for a while and we were growing tired of it. Leaving the cover of the RV, we didn't care what they were up to — we just wanted to shoot them.

We didn't know if shooting them would have any real impact on them. The bloody drones had seemed nearly invincible when it came to being struck by a bullet — at least not with the guns we had. We didn't have access to any large caliber weapons in the beginning — just your standard hunting rifles and shotguns. I'm sure a fifty-caliber would've done some damage though.

Robert decided to take a test shot to give us some idea what to expect. Taking aim at a drone not more than twenty feet from us, he squeezed off a single round. It was a perfect shot. The bullet entered what we deemed to be the front of the drone, directly through a small, red eye. The results were better than we could've imagined.

The bullet penetrated the material, leaving just a small hole where it entered. It was the damage it did exiting that we found so entertaining. It didn't just make a nice, little hole; it ripped nearly the whole back section completely off the drone.

We saw a bright flash of light as the bullet tore through it, followed by an explosion that emitted a beautiful array of colorful sparks and flames. It was almost like watching a miniature fireworks display.

This wasn't one of the fancy drones with all of the independently moving rotors. These things looked more like the drones you'd buy at a hobby shop. They had four rotors affixed directly to the body. It had what appeared to be a built-in camera on its underbelly. We couldn't figure out what the red eye was on the front. It might've been put there as a bull's-eye for us to shoot — which was what we did.

The stricken drone instantly came crashing through the windshield of a nearby pickup truck. The fire from the drone soon had the cab of the truck fully engulfed in flames.

"Holy shit!" Josh exclaimed. "That was awesome."

With that, everyone raised their weapons towards the other drones and opened fire. Soon dozens of bullets were flying through the air. Many of them had missed their intended targets, but for those that didn't, it meant instant doom for the drones.

When the drones first started crashing to the ground, everyone laughed and cheered on their destruction. One after another, they burst into flames and crashed to the ground. Most of them did little more than hit the ground and slowly burnt out. In an ironic twist of fate, one of the drones crashed through the side window of our coach.

We didn't think a whole lot about it at first. It seemed more whimsical than anything else. A few seconds later, as flames raced up the curtains, we thought better of it.

"I've got it!" Robert yelled, dropping his rifle and rushing back inside. With the last of the drones eliminated, the rest of us were hot on his tail. Most of the fire was contained to the recliner and the curtains above it. Fortunately, Robert had been playing with the fire extinguisher earlier and knew right where to find it. In a matter of seconds he had the last of the flames put out and tossed the chair out the door.

Cornelius was the last one in and the chair nearly knocked him over as Robert tossed it.

"Hey, watch it, Rob!" he hollered at him.

"Sorry, buddy, no time!" Robert yelled back, jumping out the door right behind the chair he'd just tossed. "I've got to get my rifle."

Robert quickly retrieved it and stormed back into the RV. Soot covered his face and arms. Katherine pointed to the damage the fire had done. She was just about to speak when Robert cut her off.

"No time to cry about the damage, hon," he said, slamming the door behind him. "I have a funny feeling we need to be getting the heck out of Dodge."

"Copy that," Ben said, jumping back behind the wheel.

"Everyone had better reload," Robert said as he opened a window and threw what was left of the curtains out of it. "I'm sure whoever was spying on us wasn't just doing it for prosperity. We should know what their true intentions are here shortly."

"Where to?" Ben yelled back to us.

"Just keep going south," I replied. "If we can make it to Redding before whatever is going to happen happens, we should be able to find someplace to hide out."

"Should I pick up the pace?" he asked, sounding way too hopeful.

"You can pick it up some," I said nervously. "Just please don't get us killed or maimed in some stupid car accident."

Ben didn't reply; he just grinned and stuck the pedal to the floor.

"If it's all right with you, I can take over the driving for a bit when we get to Redding," Josh said. "I know the area quite well, and I'm sure I can get us around a lot safer than Ben can."

"You've got it, Josh," I said, grabbing something to hold onto. "For now, I'm just praying we can even make it that far."

Ben had the RV pushing close to seventy-five mph. Vehicles and debris were still on the roadway to make it precarious even at that speed. I'm sure it had nothing to do with a lack of power; we could've gone much quicker if the road were wide open.

He was doing a great job threading the bus through the labyrinth that lay before us. Sections of the freeway that had little to no congestion made it possible to take the RV at even greater speeds. I didn't bother to look at the speedometer during those stretches. If I had, I would've replaced him as the driver long before Redding.

The miles seemed to fly by as we put as much distance as possible between the drones we'd destroyed and us. After about thirty minutes, the initial surge of adrenaline began wearing off; we started feeling less threatened by our stalkers. Our biggest fear now was that Ben might crash. I was just about to have him slow down when I heard an explosion.

"Too late!" I thought to myself as I felt the RV drop hard to the left.

The driver's side steer tire had exploded into a million pieces, instantly sending us out of control. Ben's first instinct was to step on the brakes. He did so only for a second, but that was enough for the rear of the RV to slide wildly to the right. Fortunately for all of us, we'd just entered a long, sweeping, left-hand turn at the time the tire let loose.

"Gas it, damn it!" I screamed at him from my new position on the floor.

Ben did as I told him, and I could feel the RV begin to straighten out. It was too little, too late. We were all thrown forward as the left side struck the concrete divider. Ben did his best to hold onto it, but we shot across the freeway and into the back of a second motor home parked on the shoulder.

It wasn't a solid coach on a bus frame like we were in. It was a Chinook that Toyota used to make. The Toyota came apart in more pieces than our tire had. The impact was spectacular but did very little to slow us down.

We finally slid to a stop about a hundred feet further after colliding with the hillside on the right side of the roadway. I could hear the moans from everyone in the RV, but before I could ask if everyone was all right, Robert spoiled the mood.

"Damn it, Ben, you asshole!" he moaned. "I'm pretty sure I need another shower, thanks to you. I think I may have shit myself."

I was relieved to hear the familiar laughter from each person on board. We knew he hadn't actually soiled himself. He was scared for all of us, and that was just his way of dealing with fear at times.

I made my way to the front to thank Ben for getting us stopped safely. For being as young as he was, he did a good job handling a difficult situation. It wasn't until I reached him that I discovered he hadn't faired well through the ordeal. It hadn't been laughter we'd heard from him but gurgling.

The front of the RV was crushed clear past his seat, and he was hanging out of a large tear in the driver's side caused by the divider. The steering wheel had crushed his rib cage and torn the flesh away. His internal organs were partially outside of his body, sitting on his lap. I nearly threw up as Ben turned toward me and gave me a weak smile.

"Cornelius! Get your ass up here!" I screamed.

Cornelius rushed to the front as quickly as possible. Katherine was nearly right on top of him.

"Not so fast," I said as I grabbed her. "There's nothing up there you need to see."

"Don't tell me what I can and can't see," she said, pushing past me. "He's my friend too and just maybe I can help."

A second later she let out a bloodcurdling scream and fell backwards into my arms.

"Here, take her, Rob," I said, handing her off to him. "I think I'm going to be sick."

"Calm down, you two," Cornelius ordered. "He's going to be OK. He already has the nanites in his system. It's just going to take a little bit for them to repair his body. For now, I need you and Rob to help me get him out of his seat so we can lay him down."

Katherine was still freaked out by the sight of him so messed up and made her way to the bedroom in the back. Robert and I did as we were told and helped pull him back to the living room. Josh did his best to help us, but soon he took off to join Katherine.

"Are you sure about this?" Robert asked in disbelief.

"Yes, you just have to trust me," Cornelius reassured him.

Artemis lay next to Ben, whining and trying to lick his wounds. I wasn't sure if Cornelius was right about this or if he were just trying to comfort us by saying everything would be OK. It was Ben who finally made the difference.

"I don't understand the fuss," he said calmly. "I really don't feel all that uncomfortable; in fact, I feel pretty darn good." He scruffed his dog with his right hand and spoke softly to him. "It's OK, boy. I'll be up and around in no time."

Cornelius had me get him a wet washcloth so he could clean up some of the blood that was beginning to dry on Ben's skin. Then he told Robert and me to find him some clean clothes. He didn't have to tell us twice; we were both more than willing to leave the room while Cornelius tended to his wounds.

We headed back to the bedroom, not only to find him a shirt and pair of pants, but also to check on Josh and Katherine.

"Is he going to be all right?" Katherine asked as we entered the bedroom.

"Oh yeah. It really isn't as bad as it looks," Robert said, hoping to put her fears to rest. "You know how a little blood really makes something appear a lot worse than it really is? Do you remember that cut on Steve's head back at the coast? It's pretty much the same deal."

I didn't know if she believed him or not, but it did seem to calm her down. We gathered up the items we needed and headed back out to the living room. It only took us a few minutes, yet when we came out, Ben was already sitting upright.

"What the hell are you doing, Ben?" I asked. "You need to be lying flat so Cornelius can stop the bleeding."

"What bleeding?" he asked as he raised his bloodstained shirt.

Robert took one look and dropped to his knees.

"What the fuck is going on?" he stammered. "I saw your guts hanging outside of your stomach, and now there isn't even a hole."

"I told you," Cornelius said. "There's nothing to worry about."

"We get that," I said, staring at Ben's stomach. "What I don't get is how quickly it healed."

"Over time, the two of you will start to heal faster and faster. In fact, some day you'll heal almost instantly."

"Hell!" Robert said. "I think that was pretty damn close to instant as it was."

"I know you may think so, but if this had happened a month from now, Ben would've been completely healed before Steve had even gotten to the front of the RV."

About that time Josh and Katherine appeared from the bedroom.

"Is there anything we can do to help?" Katherine asked. "I think I can handle it now."

"There's nothing to help with," Cornelius said. "Unless you want to undress him and put the clean clothes on him."

"What are you talking about? Have you gotten him stitched up already?"

Ben stood up and turned to face her. As he did, he raised his shirt.

"What the fuck!" Katherine exclaimed. "I saw your guts hanging out. How can this be possible?"

"Wow, you're sounding more like Robert all the time," Ben laughed. "I think what you saw was the blood on my shirt, and you panicked."

"I know what I saw, Ben. I'm not so old that I can't remember that far back. What I don't know is why you aren't dead. Hell, you don't even have a scratch on you, yet your clothes are covered in blood."

Josh didn't say a word. We could all see the wheels turning as he tried to make sense of the whole thing, yet nothing seemed to add up for him.

"If you all don't mind," he finally said, "I'm going to step out for a bit. Rob, would you mind if I had one of your cigarettes?"

"Not at all," Robert answered. "In fact, I think I'll join you."

As the two of them left the RV, Katherine and I took a seat and watched as Cornelius helped Ben change his shirt and pants. His boxers were still covered in blood, but we didn't have a replacement pair.

STEVE WOODS

"Looks like I'm going commando," Ben said as he dropped his shorts.

"Not so fast there!" Katherine hollered. "At least give me time to turn my head."

She'd already seen more than she cared to and was nearly as red as Ben's shirt as she turned to face the back of the RV.

"Smooth move," Cornelius said as Ben pulled up his pants.

"I'm sorry, Katherine. I guess my mind was elsewhere."

"No problem. Just don't let Robert find out or those nanites may not be able to bring you back."

"Hell, I thought it was pretty damn funny myself," Robert said, peeking in the open door. "I can tell the nanites can't fix everything."

"Screw you, Rob!" Ben said, retrieving his shirt from the floor and throwing it at him. "It's cold in here."

"I'm just giving you shit," Robert said, still laughing. "Besides, it's at least ninety in here."

"Well, that's my story, and I'm sticking to it," Ben laughed, not truly bothered by Robert's comment.

After he finished getting dressed, we all went outside. It was easy to see that Katherine was still shaken up by the whole ordeal. She kept trying to touch Ben's arm as he looked at the damage to the RV. She even tried to raise his shirt.

"Really, woman!" Robert yelled from just outside the doorway. "You already saw the man's junk, and now you're going in for a second look."

"Very funny, asshole. I just can't understand it. I know how badly he was hurt, and nothing you guys can say will change that."

"Do me a favor," Ben softly said to her. "This is hard on me too. I know I was messed up and I don't fully understand it myself. Regardless, I just want to forget what we all saw and go on like nothing happened. I'm going to have a hard enough time dealing with this as it is."

"I'm sorry, Ben," Katherine replied. "I can't even imagine how you must feel. Just let me look one last time, and I promise I'll never bring it up again."

"How about the rest of you?" Ben asked. "If I let you all take one last look, can we all just put it behind us?"

We all agreed and Ben raised his shirt. I stood back and watched. Even though the nanites could heal the body, the mind continued to hold onto all of it. I already had enough to deal with after my own experience; I didn't need to focus on Ben's as well.

Cornelius stood back with me as the other three ran their hands over Ben's arm and stomach. They were nearly speechless until Robert ran his hand along the spot where the steering wheel had pushed through.

"Tell me, Rob," Ben nonchalantly said, "is it turning you on to touch me like that?" Then he kissed the top of Robert's head.

"Why, you little son of a bitch!" Robert yelled, tackling Ben to the ground. "I ought to kick your ass."

It would've seemed that Robert really was pissed at him if they both weren't laughing so hard. The two of them rolled around while Artemis barked and nipped at Robert's feet.

"Come on, you two," I said, ruining their fun. "I don't think we should waste any more time around here. There's still a good chance that whoever was in control of those drones may want a little revenge. Let's find us a new ride and get the hell out of here."

We all did our best to keep our promise to Ben. Even though we often thought about it, we never spoke of that incident with him again — well, almost never.

"Do we need to make it all the way to Redding today?" Josh asked.

"Not necessarily," I said. "What did you have in mind?"

"Well, according to that road sign up ahead we're only ten miles from O'Brien. We could use the caverns at Shasta Lake to hide out in for the night. The rock walls and ceiling should keep us hidden from whatever may be looking for us."

"What do you think Cornelius?" I asked. "Is it possible the caves could keep us hidden from any more of those drones?"

"It all depends on how thick and how dense the rock surrounding us will be. It would have to be at least a good four to five feet thick. We also need to be pretty deep so they can't detect us through the opening."

"If that's all it takes, we'll be plenty safe," Josh said happily. "It's not like a lot of caves that are cold and cramped either. It's deep in the side of the mountain and the caverns are large enough to hold more than a hundred people."

"Let's get there quickly," I said. "I don't feel safe right out here in the open."

"Maybe we can use that pickup truck over there on the other side of the freeway?" Robert suggested.

"I'm not sure if that's a good idea," Ben carelessly said. "We'd need to go back the other direction at least five to ten miles before we could get back to the southbound lanes."

Everyone stared at him for a moment and then broke out into laughter.

"I know I promised not to say anything about your little accident, but it seems that you may have done some brain damage to yourself, young man. I doubt that we'll get into a whole lot of trouble if we use the northbound lanes to drive south."

Ben thought about what he'd said for a second and then blushed.

"Yeah, I guess maybe I did," he smiled.

I turned to Josh. "If you want to make sure the truck runs, the rest of us can grab our gear from the RV and meet you over there."

"You've got it, Steve," he said, jumping the divider.

Josh seemed excited that he was going to drive and not Ben. Actually, I think that made everyone feel a little better.

It took us only a few minutes before we had the truck loaded and were back on our way. I admit it wasn't the posh ride we had before, but it wasn't your run-of-the-mill pickup either. It was a large Ford F-350 crew cab with plenty of room for us upfront as well as ample storage in the bed. Even though we'd enjoyed the room and comfort of the RV, this made more sense.

A short time later, Josh pulled off the freeway and started heading down a narrow tree-lined road. I wasn't feeling overly excited about not having multiple escape routes, but Josh seemed confident about the choice.

"Can we drive right to the caverns, or do we need to hike a bit?" I asked him.

"We might have to hike a little way," Josh said. "That all depends on how low the lake is and how close to the opening we can get the boat."

"Boat! What boat?" Robert asked excitedly. "You never said anything about no damn boat. All you said was that it was a hole deep in some mountain."

"Don't worry," Josh said. "We won't be in one for long. We just need to take it from the dock to below the entrance to the caverns. That makes it even safer for us, though. It'll be harder to locate us when there are no roads to follow."

"I sure hope you know what you're doing," I said skeptically. "In case you haven't been paying attention, we brought a truck with us and not a boat."

Robert leaned forward from the backseat where he and Katherine were sitting with Cornelius. Without touching Josh, he put his lips up next to his ear and quietly whispered.

"Did you not see the truck you passed a few minutes ago pulling the boat behind it? Don't you think that might've been the time to tell us we needed one?"

"It's OK, guys. You just have to have faith. There are always some tied up at the dock once we reach the water."

Josh was right; we needed to trust him more. Every one of us had something to offer our group, and we needed to have faith in each other.

A few seconds later, I heard Josh mumbling to himself as we approached a crowd of cars at the end of the road. We could all see the dock from where he stopped the truck, but what we couldn't see were any boats.

"What's that you're saying, Josh? We can't seem to hear you," I said to him.

He lowered his head and repeated himself just loud enough where we could hear him. "I said I didn't plan on there being this many vehicles down here. I think they might've taken all the boats."

We were still a hundred yards from the water, but the road leading to it looked like a used car lot. We saw everything from small cars to motor homes crammed in so tightly that we couldn't see the whole dock.

"Tell you what," I said optimistically. "Let's grab everything we can carry and make our way down to the water. Maybe there's still something there and we just can't see it from where we're at."

Gathering what we could, we wove our way between the vehicles and made it down to the dock. Taking a slow look around, it became apparent Josh had been wrong in his assumption.

"What the hell do we do now?" Robert asked, throwing an armful of blankets to the ground.

"Wait here," Ben said excitedly as he took off back towards the truck. A second later he called out to us, "Hey guys, I need a couple of you to come give me a hand."

"Why don't you take Boy Wonder with you and see what Ben needs?" Robert asked, sulking. "I'm going to sit here and pretend to load the boat dumbass told us about."

I was laughing to myself as we made our way to Ben. Normally I would've given Robert a good ribbing just for being so pissy. This time, however, I opted to let it go. He was already having a bad day as it was, not to mention the fact he still had a gun.

Artemis danced around wagging his tail at the back of the motor home as we passed, but we couldn't see Ben anywhere. Stopping for a second, Josh knelt next to Artemis and took a look around. He was just beginning to look up when we heard Ben call out again.

"Look out below!" he yelled, pushing a small aluminum skiff off the top of the motor home.

Josh grabbed Artemis as we both dove out of the way. The fact that he'd found us something to get across the water kept me from chewing his ass for almost crushing us. It wasn't a very big boat; in fact, there was barely enough room for all of us without our gear.

"What do you think?" Ben asked, jumping down from his perch above us.

"It ain't much," I replied, "but it's a heap more than we had before. Good job."

Ben and I each grabbed an end and hoisted it into the air above our heads. Josh and Artemis walked quietly behind us. I could tell he was worried about the way Robert might react. He didn't have long to wait. Robert spied the boat before we even made it to them.

"What the hell!" he called out. "That thing is freaking awesome. I love it. It almost reminds me of the one I had as a kid. You know, the type your mom gives you when you take a fucking bath!"

"Oh come on, Rob," I said, no longer able to contain my laughter. "You know this boat isn't that big."

"You're an asshole. You know that, don't you, Steve?" he said, glaring at me.

"You know, Rob, you may be right," I said, still laughing. "But at least I can swim."

"How the hell did you know I couldn't swim?"

"Let's just say it was an educated guess. Now, come on; it won't be that bad."

Robert and I held back for a moment as the others put the boat in the water and hopped in. Artemis jumped in next to it and swam around. He'd already made the decision it was going to be a safer trip in the water than in the boat.

"I really don't have a very good feeling about this, Steve," Robert said, staring at that little metal shell floating on the water. "It's not that I can't swim. It's just that I kind of suck at it."

"Don't worry, my friend. I spotted this lying on the other side of the dock," I said as I handed him a kid's life jacket. A huge smile crossed his face. It was as if I'd just given him the greatest gift he'd ever received.

"Sorry about calling you an asshole," he said as he climbed into the boat. "You really are a good friend."

I climbed in after him and took my seat. The boat was now only sticking out of the water a couple of inches but at least it was still afloat.

"Hold on tight, everyone," I said, handing Josh an oar. "Whatever you do, don't try to stand up!"

Cornelius already had the other oar, and soon they were working together to get us moving.

"Don't worry," Josh joyfully exclaimed. "We'll be there in a moment. The entrance is just around the bend."

He was feeling good about being able to do something more than just following along. In the beginning he was always busy, either making weapons or working on communications. Lately, though, he hadn't felt like he was contributing much at all.

Personally, I was beginning to think we might've been worried about finding a place to hide for nothing. It had been close to two hours since our run-in with the surveillance drones and we hadn't seen or heard a thing.

It was about that time I heard a low humming off in the distance. I couldn't pinpoint exactly where the sound was coming from. The large surface area of water from the lake caused the sound to echo, giving the illusion it was coming from every direction.

"Shhh, quiet everyone," I said, putting a finger to my lips. "Can you guys hear that?"

Josh and Cornelius quickly pulled their oars from the water and listened. Ben carefully reached over the side of the boat and wrapped an arm around Artemis. The dog seemed to sense something was up and hung lifelessly in the water.

We glided slowly across the surface, not making a sound. Whatever I'd heard was now gone and an eerie calm overtook the lake. We sat there listening and waiting without so much as a bird chirping.

Suddenly, we heard a loud sonic boom as what appeared to be a fighter jet shot past us. It was going so fast that in less than a second it was again out of sight. The jet appeared to be following the freeway, trying to find us. Fortunately, we were now nearly a mile away, off to the east — far enough off its path that we hadn't been seen.

"Holy shit! What the hell was that?" Robert asked, nearly stuttering.

"I'm not sure. I think it might've been a jet," I said, still staring in the direction it had disappeared.

"I didn't think the Army was still around — not to mention the fact that they're helping those wackos," Josh said, sounding a little surprised.

"That wasn't a normal jet," Cornelius informed us. "That was another type of drone. It's about half the size of a regular jet and is run by someone on the ground, or by using a computer program. Sometimes they use both. The computer will assist in finding the target, and then a real person takes over for the kill. It uses a screen like a video game, so it's very impersonal to the controller."

"One thing is for sure," I said. "We now have our confirmation that someone is following us and they don't appear to be friendly."

Josh and Cornelius were already back to paddling and had that boat humming across the water. We'd just started to clear the bend and were making our turn when we got another surprise. Boats swamped the shoreline below the cavern.

"Check it out," Josh triumphantly said. "Those are what I was telling you about. They should've been moored back at the dock."

We pulled up next to them and carefully made our way onto shore. Artemis was already out of the lake, vigorously shaking the water from his fur. We weren't overly concerned that he was giving us quite the bath because our focus was on getting under cover as quickly as possible.

The only things we'd taken with us on the boat were a couple of rifles and our handguns. Josh also had a small bag with the cell phones we'd set up to kill the drones. We figured once things had calmed down a bit, we'd go back for any other supplies we might need.

Since the water in the lake was close to the top, the entrance to the cavern was only a stone's throw away. We had barely reached it when Artemis stopped in his tracks and let out a low growl.

"What do you think is upsetting him?" Ben asked.

Before any of us could answer, the large, unmanned drone flew back over the freeway. We couldn't see it from our current location, but we could sure as hell hear it.

"At this point, it really doesn't matter," I answered him. "Just make sure you all have your guns ready."

We entered the cave as quickly as we could, yet still erred on the side of caution. The last thing I wanted was to have to fire our weapons and attract even more unwanted attention. I was hoping whatever was in there would either share the space with us or move out peacefully.

Surprising us with a flashlight, Josh took the lead. The small light easily lit up the entire room, which proved to be empty. There were several other chambers in which something could've been hiding, but that didn't concern us. This first section would allow us plenty of seclusion from wondering eyes.

Carefully, we followed the path down to the bottom of the cavern and gathered together. There were a few abandoned chairs for us to sit in, and Robert even found an old lantern and matches. The light from it allowed Josh to conserve his batteries for a later date.

It wasn't the most comfortable of places, and the occasional sound from the drone made us feel uneasy. It didn't take long before everyone in the group became restless. Robert and I opted to go deeper into the hillside to find a more suitable place to hide out. As we made our way towards a tunnel leading into the next section, Artemis decided to follow us.

"That damn dog won't give us away, will he?" Robert asked.

"I don't think so," I told him. "In fact, you may be glad he tagged along, if some wild animal jumps us."

Using Josh's flashlight to lead the way, we slowly made our way into another large cavern. I was using the light to admire how high the ceiling was when I heard a noise in front of us. As I lowered it, I saw something that caused me to lose my balance and fall backwards. Quickly jumping back to my feet, I found myself face-to-face with a young woman covered in dirt. Behind her, I could see the outlines of several others.

Robert and I were momentarily speechless. We'd seen the boats down at the water, but for some reason the thought of survivors never crossed our minds. If anything, we were expecting some wild dogs or maybe even a bear. They were the first people we'd seen in nearly two weeks.

Regaining my composure, I quickly spoke up.

"Don't be alarmed. We're just here to find sanctuary from the drones. My name is Steve, and this man here with me is Robert."

It was almost like talking to a brick wall. The whole group just stood there staring at us without making a sound. It was almost as if we were some strange creatures from another planet.

"Do any of you speak English?" Robert asked sarcastically.

Still not getting any reaction from the crowd at all, I turned towards Robert.

"Hell, the lights are on but nobody's home," I laughed.

"Look at them, Steve. I've never seen people look so scared that weren't about to die."

"It's the dog," came a man's voice from somewhere in the crowd. "Is that dog with you?"

I looked down at Artemis and then back to the others. Suddenly it hit me. These people weren't staring at Robert or myself. They all had their eyes glued on Artemis. They were following his every move.

"Yes, he's with us," I called out to him.

Not wanting to cause these people any more grief than they already had, I sent Artemis back to Ben. He didn't want to go at first. It wasn't until I used a firmer tone with him that he finally headed back.

Once he'd gone, the young man who'd spoken came forward. He slowly made his way out from the others and walked over to me.

"We came here for protection from the drone attacks," he said weakly. "We've been hiding in here since all of this first began."

"Are you the one in charge?" I asked.

"Nobody is in charge," he answered. "We don't even know each other."

"Then who takes care of your group and makes sure you all have food and water?" Robert asked, walking up to him.

"We had some food in the beginning, but that ran out after a couple of days. There was a small group that would sneak off at night and get more. They were almost all killed off by dogs, though. The last time a large group went out, only one of them made it back."

"Where is he?" I asked.

"I don't know," the man replied. "He just wandered off a while back and we haven't seen him since."

"Then what have you been doing for food and water since then?" I asked.

"There's a small pool of water right over there," he said, pointing to a small puddle in the middle of the room. "As far as food goes, we've just been doing without."

I put my hand against my forehead and slowly drew it down over my face before removing it. I normally only did this to keep myself from screaming over something stupid I'd heard.

"So, let's see if I have this correct. The lot of you were somehow able to flee from the drones. You managed to make your way up here to this cave, and now you're all just basically waiting to die? Good plan! Well, I guess I'll just leave you to it."

As I turned to go, Robert grabbed my arm.

"Dude! What's gotten into you?" he asked, caught off guard by my reaction.

"Sorry, Rob, but it's been a month since the attacks and you'd think that somebody would've stepped up by now."

"Maybe that person just did," Robert said, motioning to the man standing before us.

"What's your name?" I asked him.

"It's Gary, sir," he replied.

"Well, Gary, I'm putting you in charge of your group," I said calmly but firmly. "The first thing I want you to do is make a list of any illnesses or injuries anyone might have. Make sure you put their names by the information you get, so I know who needs the help. Do you understand?"

"Yes, sir," he said with some enthusiasm. "Do you have a pen and paper I can use?"

I reached into my pocket and pulled out the pen and notepad I had with me. Since day one, everyone in our group always carried certain items with them at all times. Besides a knife and water, a pen and paper were at the top of that list. We never knew when it would be necessary to write down specific events or details.

"Do me a favor," I said, handing the items to him. "Could you please just call me Steve?"

The young man almost seemed to beam with excitement. "Yes, sir, Steve," he said as he headed off into the crowd.

"Thanks, Rob," I said, turning towards him. "Sometimes I just get frustrated. Now, let's go tell the others what we've found."

Robert took the lead as we entered the room where our group waited. Ben came rushing up to us as we did.

"Hey, guys," he said anxiously. "When Artemis came back alone, I figured everything must have been OK."

"OK, my ass!" Robert shot back at him. "That damn dog of yours ran off like some damn chicken as soon as the bear appeared."

"I had a hard time containing my laughter as Robert screwed with Ben's head.

"He did what?" Ben stammered."

"You heard me, damn it! That dog of yours left us high and dry."

About that time, Artemis came strolling up to greet us. His tail wagged and he had a pleased look on his face.

"I'm just messing with you," Robert confessed. "You really have quite the dog there."

Ben breathed a sigh of relief. "Thanks a lot, Rob. You really had me going for a minute. So, what did you guys find over there?"

By then, the others were hanging on our every word, waiting to hear what was over there.

"We found a group of survivors," I informed them. "There must be at least twenty or so people just on the other side of that wall."

Katherine was instantly excited. "Oh my God!" she yelled out. "I can't wait to meet them."

"Hold on just a second, young lady," I said. "These people are in pretty rough shape. They're like a bunch of scared rabbits. I think it would be best if we approached them in a nice, calm fashion. The last thing they need right now is to be overstimulated."

Katherine looked concerned. "I think I understand, and I promise to tone it down a bit. It's just that I'm so darned excited!"

"Maybe my dog would be good therapy for them," Ben said. "It might get them to relax a little."

"Probably not," I said. "Apparently that's why everyone in there is so timid in the first place. It seems that dogs have already eaten many of them."

"Oh, gotcha," Ben responded sheepishly.

I led everyone over to the next chamber. Ben agreed to hang back with Artemis a while until we could convince the others they wouldn't be eaten.

We'd barely entered the room when Katherine caught a glimpse of a group of children. Even though she'd promised to stay calm, we could tell she was on cloud nine.

Gary made his way to the front of the group and greeted us as we entered.

"Here's the list you asked for," he said, almost shoving the paper into my face.

"Whoa, easy there, big guy," I said to him.

"Sorry about that, Steve. We've been in here so long with little to no light that my depth perception is a little off."

"No worries, Gary," I told him. "I can only imagine what you've all been through. Why don't you and I go over your list and you can fill me in on everything?"

Chapter 5

CALISTA

Since there was virtually no light in the cavern, I loaned Gary one of my cell phones to use as a flashlight. His eyes had grown so accustomed to the dark that he was able to see clearly with very little light. I, on the hand, was having a hard time trying to view the list of injuries he'd made for me.

After several attempts to make out the writing, I handed the note back to Gary and had him read it to me. None of the injuries appeared to be life threatening, but it gave the two of us time to talk.

"Why don't you tell me what you can remember about the day of the attacks," I told him. "I'd really like to know just how you and so many other people ended up here in this cave."

"Up until that day, I'd been working at a place called Turtle Bay," Gary said solemnly. "It's not an aquarium like it sounds; it's actually a twenty-two-acre park near the civic auditorium. I mean it was. They had gardens, animals, and even a museum with a large playground. In fact, the whole place was based mainly around kids and young adults."

He recalled that he'd spent the morning demonstrating the effect of erosion to a class of third graders.

"I was supposed to work until six but ended up getting off early," he said. "I had plans but changed them when I saw the car show was going on. I've always had a fascination for things like that and was hoping to see some of the old muscle cars from the sixties.

"The ironic part was that this car show ended up being about cars of the future. They were mainly concept cars from the major manufacturers like Ford, Chevy, and GM. It turned out that many of the vehicles there were actually designed clear back in the fifties and sixties. Back then they seemed way too futuristic for the general public, so they never made it to production."

We could tell how excited Gary was getting by the way his voice rose. "My favorite part of the show was one whole section that was dedicated solely to drones and their future place in transportation. I was amazed by the diverse uses for them. I'd always figured they were just toys, not unlike remote control helicopters. It wasn't until that day that I found out the truth. They were originally created for military use some one hundred years ago."

He lowered his head for a moment and cried.

"I should've never lied to my mom. She called me early that morning upset about a dream she had. She didn't tell me what it was about — only that she needed me to come sit with her. I'd agreed to do it and even got my boss to let me off early for it. Then when I got off work and saw the car show, I called her back and lied to her. I told her I hadn't been able to get off early and that when I did get off, I had a date."

He paused for a moment and lowered his head, tears softly rolling down his cheeks. I felt sorry for him as he shared with me that not only didn't he have a date, but he'd also never even had a girlfriend. He was always stuck taking care of his mom and could never find the time.

"Shortly after five o'clock, I started feeling guilty about lying to her and gave her a call," he said. "I couldn't get a signal and tried a few more times with the same results."

He remembered looking at his watch and noticing the time: 5:17.

"I figured I might as well head home and grab a bite to eat. I was getting hungry, and the food at those places costs way too much. I barely made it out of the building when the sky suddenly grew dark. Thinking it was a spring storm quickly rolling in, I waited, hoping for a major downpour. Then everyone around me started screaming and trying to push his or her way back inside. I'm not an overly aggressive person, and I soon found myself lying on the ground being trampled by everyone. I was really scared they were going to crush me — there were so many of them. The next thing I knew, everyone started dropping to the ground. One woman fell across my legs and another over my head and upper body. I tried to push them off me at first, but when I realized they were dead, I just sort of froze."

He looked at his audience and then down at the ground before continuing.

"The screaming seemed to go on forever, but slowly, one by one, they quit," he said. "After a few minutes, I could hear people calling out to their loved ones. I figured if they were willing to come back outside, then whatever it was that did this must be gone. I gently pushed the two women off me, expecting to be covered with their blood. There was none.

"Both women had these horrified looks on their faces and were covered in what appeared to be porcupine quills. Other than that, I couldn't find anything wrong with them. One of the women really tore at my heart. She had long blonde hair and appeared to be about my age. I tried frantically to wake her, not wanting to believe she could really be dead.

"One of the men who was working at the car show came running out of the building. He kept yelling that more of them were coming and that we needed to get the hell out of there. I jumped up and tried to run past him to get inside, but he grabbed me. I turned to look at him and he had this crazed look in his eyes. He warned me not to seek shelter but to run and keep running or they would get me. After he let go of me, I stood there and watched him for a moment. He took off running to the street and stopped a man in a pickup. Then he suddenly hopped into the open bed and they were gone."

Gary remembered thinking there had to be somewhere safe he could hide.

"Then I suddenly remembered these caverns," he said. "I talked about them every day; it was a part of my job. I also remembered one of the stories I'd shared with the kids about a group of settlers using them during a harsh storm in the eighteen hundreds. I knew I needed to get to them!"

His heart sank when he remembered his car was clear on the other side of the parking lot behind the museum.

"I took off running to get it; that's when I came across a car already running, with nobody in it. Up until that point, I'd never stolen anything in my entire life. For some reason, though, I didn't think twice about it as I jumped in and sped away."

Gary painted a graphic picture of roads filled with abandoned vehicles and dead bodies.

"Fortunately, many cars and trucks were still moving. I managed to get behind a fast-moving semi pulling a fifty-three-foot trailer that was plowing through anything that was blocking its path, including people. At first, the sight horrified me. Body after body was either thrown clear by his low front bumper or crushed under the massive weight of the tires."

Fear and adrenaline pushed him harder than before.

"I no longer felt horrified by the way the truck tore

through both steel and flesh," he recalled. "I actually felt grateful he was there to clear a path for me."

Gary headed north on I-5. He'd just cleared the Oasis Road exit when he watched the sky turn dark behind him. As he looked back, he noticed between twenty and thirty cars and trucks following the semi. He watched in disbelief as the dark cloud began to overtake them.

"One by one, the vehicles behind me crashed," he said. "A few seconds later, something ripped into the roof of my car. I realized they were drones. We'd increased our speeds to around eighty mph, and the drone was having a hard time maneuvering as its blade cut the roof away. It wasn't until its third attempt that it actually made it into the car. I tried to lower my head and pull away from it, when an airplane tore through the trees off to my right. In an instant, it went from being a plane to being a giant fireball."

Gary didn't realize that in the seconds before the plane crashed, he'd been so focused on the drone that several cars managed to squeeze between him and the semi.

"In a strange way, that drone saved my life," he said. "The ball of flame instantly engulfed the tractor-trailer and all of the cars that had gotten around me. I could feel the intense heat, but somehow I managed to escape the flames. The drone fell lifelessly next to me just as I struck something in the road ahead of me. The last thing I remembered was the car doing a barrel roll through the air."

It was nighttime when he woke up.

"I hadn't been wearing a seat belt and found myself stuck in some bushes that had been next to the freeway," he said. "I was bleeding, but nothing seemed to be broken. The heat from the fire suddenly reminded me what had taken place."

Gary remembered pulling himself free from the thorny bush and looking around. Even though he'd been on that section of roadway at least a thousand times before, nothing about it seemed familiar anymore.

He could make out what was once an apartment complex burning in the background, but nothing between that and him remained intact.

"There was only fire and debris," he said. "I told myself to get to the caverns as quickly as possible, and I took off running. After about two miles, I spotted an RV entering the freeway. I was able to flag it down. When it stopped, the two men inside came to my aid. They were scared and shaking. After I shared my story and told them where I was going, they opted to join me."

"Where are these two men now?" I asked.

"Dead," he replied. "They were two of the men eaten by the dogs."

"Did they get eaten out here by the caverns or did they get killed someplace else?" I asked him. I was also wondering how long it had been since the last attack. I knew everyone here was afraid of the dogs and that they'd killed a few people. I just wasn't sure if the dogs had made it out this far yet. Gary could see the wheels turning in my head.

"What are you thinking?" Gary asked without answering my question.

"The dogs!" I said bluntly. "We've had many run-ins with rabid dogs ourselves. Yet a short time ago, we ran into a pack that weren't rabid. I'm hoping the dogs you're talking about haven't made it out of town yet. If they have, maybe whatever caused them to attack is wearing off. There's a small chance that they will no longer be a threat."

"I can't say for sure where the attacks took place," he said. "It happened when they went out for supplies. The last attack was just over a week ago, and we haven't left the safety of the cavern since."

We talked for well over an hour. During that time, the rest of my group attended to the needs of those we'd just found who were left behind. Josh and Ben even went back to the boat dock to retrieve the blankets and any food we may have had.

We also learned that only about half of those people made it there after the attacks. The others, mainly the children, were there on a field trip. A lot more people were on the trip, but they all headed back to town over an hour before everything had happened.

This group was stranded after the van they came over in wouldn't start. A mobile mechanic had just showed up to fix the problem about twenty minutes before the first of the people running from the drones got there.

Robert and Cornelius approached me as we finished talking.

"You realize this puts a new twist on things," Robert informed me. "We can't go into battle toting a bunch of scared women and children with us."

"I know, Rob," I said thoughtfully. "I've been running all of the different scenarios through my mind. If we leave them to fend for themselves, there's a strong possibility they'll be dead within a week or two. If we take them with us, it puts the whole mission at risk, and more than likely we'd all end up dead."

"So, what did you come up with?" Cornelius asked.

"Looks to me like we'll just have to leave them here in this cave and let them all starve to death," I said calmly, waiting to see how they'd respond.

Suddenly, I felt a hand smack me on the back of my head, nearly knocking me to the ground. Without even turning around, I knew it was Katherine.

"What the hell did you say?" she asked sternly.

Apparently, something I said had offended her.

"Holy shit, woman!" I shouted. "Can't you take a joke? I was just messing with these two. If I were going to leave anyone behind, it wouldn't be them. I'd leave your crazy ass here!"

She smiled and gave me a quick little wink. "Sorry, Steve. Since Michelle isn't here to keep you in line, I just figured it was my duty."

"Crazy bitch," I said quietly under my breath.

I didn't really mean anything by it. I loved Katherine and the others in my group more than anything. In a strange way, the little antics she used to keep me in line really did remind me of Michelle. Besides, she never really hit me as hard as I made it seem. We just had a playful way between us that kept the others guessing.

"To be honest," I said, getting their attention away from her little show, "the only solution I can come up with is to separate our group."

"How do you figure?" Robert asked, sounding a little surprised.

"Well, Rob, if we take everyone with us, I know things will go really bad pretty quick. We have way too much heat on us right now. We all know that drone that flew by earlier is looking for us. Alone, we can outrun or outmaneuver most anything. A crowd this size will make getting away nearly impossible. Unfortunately, they've already proven that they can't be left alone. Without leadership, they'll just sit still and die. We just need a small group to lead them back to base camp, while the rest of us make our way to San Francisco. We'll move out first, thus taking the threat from the drone with us and leaving the others a safe passage. Once back at camp, Michelle and the others can make sure the children are safe and fed. We just need to figure out how to break up the group."

"Well, that's a no-brainer," Katherine said. "You need to be the one to lead them back. That way you can be home with Michelle."

"That's not a bad idea," I told her. "How about you take them there instead, and I'll go on with the others?"

"Are you out of your head?" she yelled. "I'm not sitting back while the rest of you go fight these things. This is my battle too."

I smiled at her for a moment, waiting, as the wheels turned. Suddenly her eyes softened and she gave me an understanding gaze.

"What about Michelle?" she asked softly. "Isn't she the whole reason you've been fighting?"

"Really, Kat?" I said, sounding surprised. "Is that what you truly believe?"

Katherine stood there for a moment with a sad look on her face. "You always tell us how much you love and miss her. I just assumed she was the reason you were so willing to risk your life the way you do."

"Yes, Kat. I do love her, more than anything. I'll admit in the beginning she was my whole focus. I figured she was all I had left — my children, my friends, and everyone I'd ever known were all gone. That's no longer the case though. This war we're in is about a lot more than just one person. It's about every man, woman, and child who's having to live in fear — either as a slave, or hidden someplace just waiting to die. You are all my family and I'd gladly give my life to save any one of you."

Katherine had tears in her eyes as she stepped forward and wrapped her arms around me.

"I love you," she said softly.

"I love you too, Kat."

Josh and Ben had walked up behind us in time to hear the whole conversation. Robert and Cornelius were also within earshot. The next thing I knew, our whole group was in a giant bear hug. For several minutes, the six of us stood there; nobody wanted to let go. Dying was no longer what we feared in life; it was saying good-bye that truly tore at us.

"You know," I said, gently pulling away from the others, "before we split up and head off in different directions, we need to get supplies. These people need some food and good, clean drinking water."

"How about some more blankets also," Katherine added. "It can't be easy for them to sleep on the hard ground, and I bet the nights get pretty cold in here."

"That's a great idea, Kat," I said as I turned towards the front of the cavern. "I figure we can head out after it starts getting dark. It'll give us most of the day to rest up and more time for the drone to move on."

"Who's going to take the others back to camp?" Ben asked.

All at once, we all turned to Ben and smiled.

"Well, buddy," I said somberly, "to be honest, you're probably the best man for the job."

He turned slowly, looking at each one of us as tears began to fill his eyes.

"I don't know if I can do it, Steve," he said reluctantly. "What if I do something wrong and end up getting everyone killed?"

"You won't fail," I said, placing a hand on his shoulder. "We all have total faith in you. Just remember, these people are still visible to the drones. You'll need to locate some old welding curtains or anything that contains lead to cover them."

"And one more thing," Robert added. "Please try your best not to crash. These poor people have already been through enough."

STEVE WOODS

Ben laughed at Robert. He knew he was only giving him a hard time to lighten the mood. A second later, Artemis let out a soft whine, so Ben went over to sit with him. It was time for Katherine and I to address everyone.

For most of these people, being found still seemed much like a dream. Many of them stared blankly at me as I spoke. It was almost as if I were speaking in some strange language.

It went much easier for Katherine. As she began to speak, the women and children in the crowd instantly lit up.

"Hi, everyone. I'm Katherine." She spoke as if she were addressing a kindergarten class. Her tone was sweet and cheerful, and she made sure to make plenty of eye contact with everyone. The light from the lantern was soft enough to see without hurting their weakened eyes.

"We're here to take you someplace safe. We understand your fears and will do our best to answer any questions you may have. If any of you have any special needs, please let us know so that we may assist you."

A little girl stepped forward. She appeared to be only about five or six years old.

"My mommy told me never to talk to strangers," she said softly.

"What's your name, young lady?" Katherine asked.

"It's Calista," she replied. She spoke so softly that we could barely make out what she was saying.

"Well, Calista," Katherine said, bending down to her level, "you're too young to be part of the field trip. Is your mommy or daddy here with you?"

"My mommy was here with me. She brought me here to hide from the bad stuff."

Katherine had a look of concern.

"Do you know where your mommy is, Calista?"

83

"She went to get me something to eat, but she hasn't come back yet."

Katherine took a look around the group.

"Do any of you know where this little girl's mom is?" After a long pause with no response, Katherine called out again. "Do any of you recall even seeing this woman leave?

A middle-aged man who looked worn and haggard stepped forward.

"I knew one of the men in the last group that went out, but I wasn't aware of anyone else leaving since then," he replied.

"Where are those people?" she asked sternly.

"Only one of them made it back," he answered. "He never seemed quite right after that and just walked away a few days later. We haven't seen or heard from him since."

"What about the others? What became of them?"

"All he ever told us was that the dogs ate them all."

"Did any women in the group go with him?" Katherine asked, almost afraid of what he might say.

"No, it was just a small group of younger men. There weren't any women in the group at all."

Katherine was confused.

"Calista, honey," she said. "When exactly did you mommy leave?"

"I think it was this morning," she said. "My mommy told me she was going to get me some milk and cereal."

Katherine turned toward Robert and me. Without her saying a word, we knew exactly what she wanted.

"Gary, I have a question for you," I said, making my way over to him. "When we arrived here earlier, there were no boats tied up at the dock. Wouldn't it make sense that she would've taken a boat with her?"

"Well, yes, but that doesn't mean she would've gone that way. It would make more sense for her to take the boat straight to Bridge Bay. It's not very far from here, and the whole trip should've only taken an hour or so."

I turned back towards Katherine, and it was apparent she'd heard every word.

"Steve," she said, her voice trembling, "her mom may still be alive out there."

"Hey, Josh," I said, getting his attention, "how long does it take to get to Bridge Bay from here by boat?"

"Somewhere between fifteen and twenty minutes, depending on how hard you're pushing it. Why? What are you thinking?"

"I'm thinking these people need food and fresh water. If we leave while it's still light out, we can look for the girl's mom as well."

"You do know that drone is still out there looking for us, don't you?" he asked.

"I know. It's not the ideal situation, but lately nothing has exactly been ideal."

"Robert is going with you, I assume."

'Yes, and I want to take Ben and Gary with me as well."

"Who's Gary?" he asked, giving me a strange look.

"He's that young man I was speaking to earlier. If Ben is going to lead these people back home safely, I want him to have an ally. You know, someone he can turn to out there if they run into trouble."

"I could always go with him."

"Thank you, Josh. I really think you're a major asset to our team. If you feel you'd be better suited to go, I wouldn't stop you."

"Thanks, Steve. I appreciate that. Just let me know how Gary does out there. If you believe he and Ben can handle it, I'd prefer to stay with you."

After we finished talking, I took Gary and the rest of my team into the first cavern. We bounced ideas off one another until we all felt comfortable with what we were about to do. The discussion wasn't just about getting supplies or finding Calista's mom. It also had to do with working out a good escape clause should we encounter the drone or wild dogs.

I informed Gary of his role in the situation and was quite pleased by his reaction. For nearly a month, he and the others had stayed hidden. They were not only unsure of what to do, but they were also scared of what each day might bring. Death was beginning to seem more of a blessing than a curse.

He'd been praying early on for the opportunity to fight back, but as time went on, it seemed their fate was sealed. It wasn't until we showed up that he once again felt the desire to fight for his own survival.

"Let's do this thing!" Robert called out to us, after saying his good-bye to Katherine. "I want to be back in time for supper."

"Smartass," Ben replied, throwing us all for a loop.

"Holy shit!" I called out. "It looks as if those nanites are causing Ben to grow a pair."

He shot me a quirky smile as the four of us and Artemis exited the caverns. I was surprised at how bright it seemed after such a short time in the dark. Gary had to shield his eyes from the light, and even then, he needed assistance down to the water. Robert was just happy knowing he wouldn't have to ride in that little boat again. This time we could choose from several different styles.

There were two large skiffs capable of holding anywhere from twenty to thirty people, a bass boat, an older ski boat, and the little aluminum boat we came in. We opted to take the bass boat. It allowed us enough room to sit comfortably, and the power to quickly get us to where we needed to go. Gary also pointed out that a sleek powerboat that had been there when he first arrived was no longer there.

I kept a sharp eye out for anything out of place as the others took their seats. After everyone was secure, I untied the line and joined them. Robert was concerned at leaving Josh behind. Since this was his hometown, he felt Josh would've been more valuable to us than Gary.

This was quickly put to rest as I fired up the motor and pulled out away from the shore. Gary started filling us in with information about how to stay hidden along the shoreline. He also had a vast knowledge of the Bridge Bay Resort and where they stored certain items. As it turned out, he'd spent many summers there filling in during the busy tourist season. It was the little things he knew that would make all the difference on how well we succeeded.

When we made it to the resort and tied up to the dock, my first instinct was to head for the building marked "convenience store." That's when Gary pointed out where the restaurant kept all of their dry goods and bottled water. From the outside, it looked like a private garage nestled in the hillside. Once inside, however, we discovered pallets of canned goods, water, and even cases of sheets and blankets.

"Why didn't you come here before?" I asked Gary suspiciously. "Couldn't you have led the others to this spot much sooner?"

Gary sheepishly admitted that the first group told him they didn't need his help. Then, after hearing what had happened to most of them, he hid while they assembled the next group.

At first I felt anger and frustration towards him. How could I trust someone that hadn't stepped forward to help when called upon? I was about to say something when Ben beat me to it.

"Why would you hide, knowing people's lives were at stake? Didn't that make you feel like a coward to hide while others put their own lives at risk?"

"It did," he said, trying not to make eye contact with any of us. "I'd never thought about death before the attacks. Then to suddenly see so much of it in such a short period of time just scared the hell out of me." He paused for a second and turned to face us. "I had plenty of time to think since the last group went out without me. When only one of them made it back, I felt hate and contempt for myself. Every night I prayed God would give me the courage to put others ahead of myself. Then all of you showed up. I'm no longer afraid to die — I'm afraid to die without at least trying."

His answer and the way he spoke really hit home with us. We hadn't chosen to live the way we were. It was just one circumstance after another that directed the course we were on.

Robert took off to find us something to transport the food and blankets to the boat. We'd moved nearly everything we needed to the front of the garage when he pulled up in an old, rusted-out blue Ford pickup.

"Nice ride," I said snidely, poking fun at his choice of vehicles.

"Actually, it's just like the one my dad used to drive," he said proudly. "I saw this and it made me miss him."

I felt like an ass as we loaded the truck. I never would've made fun of it if I'd known that earlier. I was just thankful it didn't hurt Roberts's feelings.

In a matter of minutes, we had the bed loaded down with a variety of items: bottled water, several cases of dehydrated fruits, vegetables, and even some beef jerky. Gary located a large bag of powdered milk as well as several boxes of cereal. We also made sure to get plenty of cups and bowls, along with some silverware.

After we'd loaded all the essential items, we went back for some blankets and a few pillows. I couldn't imagine any of them had slept very well on that cold, rocky ground.

My mind kept drifting back to Calista's mom. We hadn't seen any sign of her so far, and I was pretty sure we never would. She did have the right idea about using a boat to get supplies, though. It kept us away from the freeway, and thus off the path of the drone that was stalking us. We hadn't seen that drone for a couple of hours, but since it hadn't found us, I was sure it would keep looking.

I'd noticed a vast variety of boats when we pulled into the marina. If we drove down to the docks, we could transfer the food to a larger one.

I informed the others of my decision and we headed to the water to find our vessel. Seeing all those houseboats lined up along the rental dock gave me the urge to use one of them. It would've been a beautiful replacement for the motor coach Ben had wrecked earlier. I glanced around at the others, and it was easy to see they were also very tempted by the luxury of these floating vacation wonderlands.

"Probably out of the question, isn't it, Steve?" Robert asked.

No, Rob, I think that would be a marvelous idea," I replied to him.

"Really!" Ben squealed. "Can we get a houseboat?"

"Are you that big of a dumbass?" I asked, staring at him. "Why not just put a big flashing light on top saying, 'here we are.'"

Ben gave me a sad look. "You said that the drones wouldn't be looking for us on the water."

Shaking my head, I turned towards Robert.

"That's what you said, Steve," Robert replied in nearly the same sad voice.

I took a deep breath and sighed.

"Fine, but no whining when the drones kill us."

"Hell yeah!" Ben yelled. He jumped from the truck, with Artemis close on his heels. "I'll go start it up."

"Freeze right there, young man," I said sternly. "You can get a couple of carts to move the food. I'll fire up the boat."

Robert and Ben resembled a couple of kids racing up the dock to each grab a cart. Artemis was caught up in the excitement and barked joyfully as he chased them. Gary gave me a look of uncertainty.

"You know, Gary," I told him, "sometimes you just have to risk dying to live a little." With that, I took off walking towards the houseboat. Robert and Ben were racing each other back to the truck with their carts. They were just passing me when Gary cried out.

Artemis stiffened up instantly, and a deep growl forced its way through his clenched teeth.

We all turned towards Gary. He was pressed up against the truck, fear in his eyes. At first, we couldn't see what he was looking at. Then, from behind a row of porta potties, three large, fierce-looking dogs emerged. I couldn't distinguish their breeds, but it was easy to see that they were definitely rabid.

The three of us carried our handguns, but the proximity of the dogs to the truck put Gary directly in the line of fire. With a rifle, any of us would've taken the shot, but handguns were another story. Still, we all drew our weapons and started running at the dogs. Artemis shot past us almost instantly and cut between the dogs and Gary within seconds.

I could hear the panic in Ben's voice as he screamed to his dog. It was to no avail. As soon as Artemis positioned himself between Gary and the dogs, they attacked. Artemis locked his powerful jaws around the first dog's neck, as the other two sank their teeth deep into his flesh. With a twist of his body, Artemis sent all three dogs sailing through the air. Then, before the other dogs could react, he again sank his teeth into one of his aggressors. This time, as he bit down, we could hear the audible sound of bones breaking. Artemis had nearly severed the dog's neck with his steel-crushing jaws. The dog gave one last cry and then went limp.

The other dogs froze in their tracks, unsure of their next move. They were defenseless against the savageness of Artemis's amazing agility and razor-sharp teeth. He grabbed a second dog, this time by the leg, and the animal let out a shrill of pain as body and limb separated.

Robert, now close enough to get a clean shot, put one of the remaining dogs to rest and then the other. What started as another rabid dog attack had ended up as more of a mercy killing that saved our attackers from a merciless death.

With Artemis calmly sitting next to Ben's feet licking his wounds, we all stared in disbelief. Then, as if he had the answer to the question now on our minds, we all turned towards Cornelius.

"Don't look at me," he said, putting his hands up in front of him. "I don't know what came over that dog."

"Could it be the nanites?" Ben asked, reaching down to pet his dog.

"It has to be," Cornelius said. "I've never seen a response to nanites anywhere near that magnitude before. In all of our studies, it was to prolong life, not to increase strength and agility."

Gary leaned up against the pickup truck, visibly shaken. "I thought I was going to die. How I can ever thank you?"

"Don't worry about it," Ben said, scratching his dog's neck. "It's just how we do things."

Robert and I looked at each other and laughed.

"Let's see how quickly you can get the boat loaded," I told him. "You have the nanites in you too. Show us something to impress us there, stud."

He shot me a sly grin and we all went back to work.

Chapter 6

Saying Good-bye

As the others loaded the boat, I took a little time to get familiar with it. I did a quick walk around, looking for possible obstacles and snags. I didn't want a repeat of the school bus incident.

After I felt secure that nothing was going to catch me off guard, I fired up the motor. Even though it had an inboard, it was a little louder than I'd anticipated. I think that mainly had to do with how tranquil everything had become. Without the overabundance of man and machine, life just seemed to be quieter.

When everything first happened, it was difficult not hearing all the noises we'd gotten used to. Even when it wasn't people or cars, other man-made devices always pierced the silence. I can remember camping with Michelle once and thinking how quiet it seemed. Yet off in the distance we could still hear the sounds of man. There always seemed to be some plane or other vehicle nearby.

For the first time since I was born, the world was truly quiet. The big motor on the houseboat would've normally been drowned out. Now, however, it tore through the silence, putting fear into me that others might hear it as well.

Robert came bounding onto the boat and confirmed what I was thinking.

"It's a bit loud, isn't it?" he asked.

"You're right; I was just thinking the same thing myself. Maybe we'd better find a quieter alternative."

"Oh, hell no!" Robert said assuredly. "If the gunfire didn't get their attention, I doubt we need to worry. Besides, there's no way I'm missing out on this just because of some damn drone."

"Well then, I guess it's time to make some waves."

I made my way back to the helm as the others loaded the last couple of items and untied us from the dock. Now, I've driven boats before, and I wasn't half bad at it either. This, however, wasn't a boat, but more of a floating timeshare — nearly twenty feet wide and over seventy feet long. To top it off, it had three different levels. The idea of trying to squeeze this beauty out of her slip should've made me nervous as hell. It was funny, though; since we had nobody but ourselves to answer to if I wrecked it, all fear was gone.

I shoved the controls into reverse and felt the gentle movement of the boat. It was nothing like the fishing boat we'd used earlier, where we took off quickly and felt every ripple. It felt more like being in an elevator, but rather than going vertically, we were moving horizontally. We could hardly feel any sway at all as we cut through the gently lapping water. It was solid.

With the bow safely out of its slip, I turned the wheel and continued back a little further. Then, as the boat straightened out, I slid the controls back into neutral and let it drift for a second. With my hand still on the throttle, I took one last look at the others. They were all grinning from ear to ear, just waiting for me to open it up.

I didn't keep them waiting long. I pushed the handle slightly forward, and there was a soft hum from the motor as the beast began to move slowly.

"Don't be such a pussy!" Robert yelled out as the others cheered. "Open the bitch up!"

Not wanting to disappoint them, I shoved the throttle control as far as it would go. It was nothing like I expected. I grabbed ahold of the steering wheel to keep from falling over. The others didn't have that option and tumbled onto the deck, laughing hysterically as they did.

Jumping back to their feet, they raced to the railing to watch the other boats. We'd created such a large wake by our size and speed that anything still at the dock was tossed around like a bunch of tub toys. I'll admit I too was quite amused by the havoc we had caused.

In almost no time at all, we'd reached a rather quick cruising speed. Due to the massive size and weight of the houseboat, our perception was somewhat exaggerated. We may have only been going thirty-five to forty mph, but it felt more like seventy.

Ben came rushing up to me. "You have to let me drive this thing!" he said excitedly. "I swear I won't hit anything."

"I really don't care one way or the other if you wreck it," I told him matter-of-factly. "Just be sure we can still make it back to the others."

I moved out of the way and turned the controls over to him. I was just about to make my way down the stairs when I had a flashback of the motor coach incident. Deciding it wasn't a good idea to tell him it was OK to crash the boat, I turned back and gave him new instructions.

"Why don't you slow down just a bit and do your best to stay out in the middle of the lake. Then, as soon as we pass the bridge, I want you to hang to the left. I'll send Gary up to help guide you."

It wasn't that I didn't trust his abilities. It was just that it was Ben, after all, and he seemed to make a habit of destroying anything he drove.

After sending Gary up to assist him, Robert and I decided to take advantage of our downtime. Stripping down to our boxers, we raced to the third level to try out the water slide. Now, he and I might not have always done the smartest things, but sometimes I really did think before doing. When I realized the problem with our plan, it was nearly too late. Robert hadn't given much thought to it either and was just about to go down the slide when I grabbed him.

"What's up?" he yelled as I pulled him off the slide. He quickly looked around, trying to see the danger.

"How far off the water is the bottom of the slide?" I asked.

"Fifteen feet," he responded, giving me a quizzical look.

"At our current rate of speed, how long would you have to tread water before we got back to you? That's assuming you don't get shredded into fish food by the props first. Remember, you're not really that good of a swimmer. "

"Oh my God, I never thought of that!" he exclaimed.

It was at that point that I realized Robert was worse than I was when it came to doing things we really shouldn't do.

"What do you think? Should we just bypass the swimming and do something a little safer?" I asked.

"We can go fishing!" he yelled out joyfully as he raced downstairs to get his clothes and locate a fishing pole.

Shaking my head at the cluelessness to his response, I made my way to the helm.

"How do you two feel about shutting down for a bit and taking a swim or doing some fishing?"

It was like watching a couple of kids at Christmastime. Ben reached over and turned the engines off, before racing upstairs.

"I've wanted to try that slide since the second we stepped on board!" he yelled.

Before I could say a word, Ben was in his shorts and heading down the slide towards the water. Artemis never missed a beat; he took two steps towards the edge, and with all his might, jumped from the top deck into the lake. It didn't take long before the two of them realized the boat was still coasting.

I waited patiently until Ben was safely on board before I took my turn at the slide. When I did, Gary was hot on my tail.

The weather was in the mid-nineties, and for some strange reason I expected the water to be as well. I've never been one for the cold, so my first reaction after hitting the frigid water was to get back on the boat. I reached the surface of the water, expecting it to be right in front of me. Man, was I surprised to find that it still hadn't come to a complete stop. The distance between the warm deck and myself was steadily increasing. Almost in a panic, I started swimming as hard as I could, trying to reach the ladder on the back. I honestly thought I was swimming faster than I ever had before and began feeling a bit cocky about my abilities. It was then that Gary swam leisurely past me; reaching the boat ahead of me, he turned and asked if I needed a hand.

I could think of plenty of things to say to that little show-off. I looked him squarely in the eyes as I mustered up the manliest voice I could and said, "Yes, please." I'll admit that I sounded more like a whipped puppy, but in my mind it was very manly.

Gary reached out and grabbed hold of my arm, giving me a final pull to the ladder. Once I was back on the boat, I opted to fish with Robert while the other two played in the water with Artemis.

"What was all the commotion back there?" Robert asked as I sat down on the chair next to his.

"It was that Gary character. Apparently, he isn't all that great of a swimmer, and I needed to give him a hand."

"Oh, I see," Robert said, eyeing me suspiciously.

I could tell by his shit-eating grin that he knew the truth.

"So how goes the fishing?" I asked, reaching for an extra pole.

"No luck yet. I've just been sitting here studying all these boats floating freely on the water."

"I take it from the way you're staring at that one over there that something about it has your attention?"

His eyes were fixed on an older ski boat about a quarter mile from us. There didn't seem to be anything special about it. A lot of boats in this section of the lake floated aimlessly.

"The way I see it, everyone out here was killed during the first attack," he said. "I mean, since all these boats are pretty much open, there wouldn't have been a need for the bloody drones."

"Yes, go on," I said, staring at him and waiting for the punch line.

"Well, for some reason the birds have been all over that boat."

I took a closer look at the boat in question. "Do you think there might've been some food left on board?" I asked him.

"There's definitely food on board; I just don't believe it's been there a month. That's what's attracting the birds."

I took another long look at the boat. Robert was onto something. There were birds on most of the boats. The difference was the amount of birds and the way they acted. We both sat there for another minute just watching.

"I know we're both thinking the same thing," I said, still staring at the boat.

"I figured she was dead," Robert said sympathetically. "I just didn't figure we'd actually find her."

When we left the caverns for food, it was also to look for Calista's mom. There's just so much lake, I never dreamed she would cross our path. I really only offered to look for her to keep Katherine and the little girl happy. Telling them we couldn't find her mom would've been one thing. If this was her, and we had the feeling it would be, we'd have no choice but to bring her remains back with us.

"Sorry, boys," I called out. "It's about time we head back with the supplies. Besides, I do believe we found the ski boat Calista's mom is on."

Ben and Gary slowly turned to see what Robert and I were looking at. Our fun was over, and once again the reality of our new world was thrust back in our faces. No longer jubilant and childlike, they slowly exited the water and joined me on the deck.

Cornelius had been taking advantage of our downtime to read a book somebody had left behind. To him, that seemed much more relaxing than running around in his boxers. While the rest of us got dressed, Robert reeled in his pole and went to inform him of the situation.

A few minutes later, the whole group reconvened near the bow of the boat. For a good minute, we stood there wondering if we really needed to bring the body back with us. After all, with all the birds picking at her carcass, there was a good possibility there wouldn't be much left. Finally making the decision, I sent Ben and Gary to grab some sheets while I made my way to the helm.

I didn't run the boat full speed as I'd done earlier; I pretty much kept it at a snail's pace. None of us had been overly anxious to even get there at all. We'd seen death all over the lake, but this one seemed a little more personal. This was the only one we had to explain to a little girl.

99

We were still about one hundred feet away when Artemis stiffened and growled. I shut off the motor and scanned the horizon. As we drifted towards our target, our eyes focused on everything but the boat. Something had set Artemis off, and we really needed to see it before it saw us.

I was watching from my perch above the others when Robert disappeared from my view. The other three stood motionless at the bow, continually scanning the skies around us. Ben's left hand was on his dog's head. It was his way of telling Artemis that we understood what he was trying to tell us, while at the same time keeping him from making any unnecessary noise.

We could tell something was still bothering Artemis by his demeanor. He was restless and constantly turned his nose in different directions. Perhaps he was trying to read the story his senses were picking up. Suddenly, he turned towards Ben, whined once, and jumped into the water.

"What the hell is your dog doing?" Robert asked, returning with his rifle.

"I'm not sure," Ben said, visibly confused. "He just took off."

Swimming like his life depended on it, he set his course directly towards the ski boat. In a matter of seconds, he was at the back of it, quickly pulling himself inside.

Still unsure of what Artemis was up to, we continued scanning around us as we drifted closer. We were within about twenty feet when I got my first glimpse into the boat.

"She's alive!" I called out as I spied her hand move slightly when Artemis nuzzled her.

This woman wasn't dead, but she wasn't far from it. At that moment, blood still pumped through her veins.

I leapt from the top deck, landing next to the others. Then, all five of us jumped into the water and swam the final distance. Pulling ourselves into the boat, we circled around the woman and slid down on the floor next to her. Ben carefully cradled her bleeding head in his lap.

"What do we do, Steve?" he pleaded as tears welled up in his eyes.

"Just hold her for a second," I told him, my mind racing. "Gary! I need you to tie us to the houseboat. Robert, I need clean water and a blanket."

"You've got it, Steve!" Robert said. He jumped onto the houseboat as it reached us.

"Gary, as soon as we tie off, I need you to find a first aid kit," Cornelius instructed him. "Check the kitchen and the bathroom."

Within minutes, they had the items we needed and made their way back to us. Artemis was at the woman's feet, watching our every move. As Ben moved back, Robert carefully placed the blanket under her head and used the water to wet her lips.

Cornelius and I went to work cleaning up some open wounds the birds had made as they picked at her flesh. Scanning the first aid kit, Gary pulled out some smelling salts and handed it to Ben.

"Should I, Steve?" Ben asked.

"Yes, but just slowly wave it under her nose. Don't actually shove it up there."

Ben broke open the tube and leaned over her. His eyes were fixated on her face as he carefully moved his hand close to it.

She moaned softly and slowly opened her eyes. For a second, she just stared at him. Finally, a faint smile formed on her lips, and she once again closed her eyes.

"Should I give her more?" Ben asked, holding the smelling salts out to me.

"No, just let her rest," I said. "We'll move her over to our boat and get her back to her daughter."

Ever so gently, Ben lifted the young woman into his arms, gazing warmly at her the whole time. She looked so frail and weak, we could tell she hadn't eaten much over the last month. If I had to hazard a guess, I would put her at around eighty to ninety pounds. She probably didn't weigh much to begin with; at best, she couldn't have been more than five feet tall.

What was left of an old pair of blue jeans and a torn t-shirt hung loosely from her body. She wasn't wearing any shoes, and from the looks of her feet, she hadn't for quite some time. Her long blonde hair was matted up around her shoulders and filled with dirt and twigs. The birds had managed to tear several pieces of flesh from her arms and feet, but for the most part, her face was untouched.

My hat was off to her, though; she couldn't have been much older than twenty. I'd say twenty-three at the most, yet she was willing to give her life for her daughter. Seeing the young woman starving and fighting for her life, I felt guilty about taking time to play.

These people may have looked OK in the dimly lit cavern, but it was easy to see they were in a crisis. Even Gary looked extremely haggard. I could tell he must've been a bigger guy when this started. He was average height, but he wasn't nearly as thin as she was.

With the two boats tied securely together, Ben effortlessly carried her between them. Once on board, he took her straight to the main bedroom. Holding her using only his right arm, he pulled the blankets back with his left and slid her in.

This wasn't the Ben we'd all grown to know and love. The lost young man, who was unsure of himself and looked for affirmation in most everything he did, was gone. In an instant, he'd changed; he was now sure of not only his next move but also of the sole reason his life had been spared.

We made a straight shot for the cavern and pulled up to the shore in a matter of minutes. For now, the young woman would stay on the boat with Ben. She slept comfortably on the soft bed as he gently cleansed her face and arms. The rest of us each took an armload of food and water up to the cavern. Katherine met us at the entrance.

"What happened out there? I could've sworn I heard gunshots earlier," she said to Robert as she lightened his load.

"Just a little run-in with a few dogs. It wasn't a big deal," he told her.

As we carried the food and water inside, Josh and Cornelius began passing it out. We were just about ready to leave the cave for another load when I heard a little girl call out. It was Calista. When I turned, I could see her eyes in the dim light; they had a look of urgency in them. Katherine tried to intervene, but I stopped her.

"It's OK, Kat. I do believe someone out there would love to see her."

Katherine's expression lightened up. "You mean…"

She tried to talk, but she was so choked up she couldn't say another word. Suddenly overcome with joy, she began to cry.

Good news had been in short supply. Finding the girl's mom alive was about the most wonderful thing any of us could've imagined.

Calista raced up to me and jumped into my arms. Instantly, my stomach was in knots. This little girl was scarcely more than a miniature skeleton. She'd lost so much weight that her little shoes wouldn't stay on her feet. I held her close to me as I told her the good news. Grabbing me tightly, she wrapped her arms around my neck.

"I knew you'd find her," Calista said as we made our way to the boat. "I talked to God before you came here.

He told me you would find us and bring me my mommy back."

I was choked up and couldn't say another word. I carefully carried her down the hill and onto the boat. Then, as we walked into the bedroom, her mom opened her eyes. I set Calista on the edge of the bed and watched as the two held each other. I motioned to Ben and we stepped into the next room.

"What's up, Steve?" he asked.

"Are you sure you're OK taking everyone back alone?" I asked him, half-hoping he would say no.

He glanced back through the doorway at the young mother and daughter.

"Something deep inside me tells me this is my destiny," he responded. "I swear to you, I will die before I let anything happen to them."

I wrapped my arms around his neck and pulled him close to me.

"I know you would," I told him as he hugged me back. I felt so blessed to have him in my life, just as if he were one of my own children. Suddenly, the sound of the drone off in the distance tore the silence apart. It was no longer flying over the freeway; it was now systematically flying a grid over the hillside. I let go of Ben and stuck my head out the window.

"We don't have much time before it locates us," I said to Ben as we reentered the bedroom. "I'll carry Calista if you'll take her mom."

"It's Amy," he said.

"What's that?" I asked.

"The woman — her name is Amy," he said happily.

I shot him a smile as I picked up Calista and headed out the door.

A buzz was coming from inside the cavern. As we got closer, it became clearer. The same people who only a few hours ago appeared to be lifeless were now talking and at times even laughing. Little by little, that spark they'd been missing for so long was coming back. All it took was a little food and water to lift their spirits and give them hope.

I lowered Calista to the ground as we got inside. For a moment, I just stood there and watched everyone's reactions as Robert spread out several of the blankets. It had been a month since any of them had a soft spot to sit or lie down on, and at first, they were a little unsure. It didn't take long, however, before both the children and the adults were laughing and running their hands all over them.

I figured we still had time before the drone located us, so I kept that information to myself instead of spoiling the mood. I don't think it would've made a difference though. Everyone was so overjoyed by that little bit of normalcy that hardly anything could've ruined it.

For nearly twenty minutes, I sat back and watched. For the first time since it started, all of them had the chance to relax and open up. They were soon sharing what they could recall with each other, hoping to find some reason for it all.

I was amazed as I listened to them. It turned out that the majority of them were already here when the attacks first happened. They had very little knowledge of what had really transpired. They just knew the world had changed and it wasn't safe to come out of hiding. One thing still bothered me, so I interrupted them to try to get an answer.

"I have a question," I said to get their attention, "for those of you who weren't already here before the attacks. How did you know to leave town and come clear out here?

"It was on the radio," one woman answered. "It was a little after five, and I'd just finished shopping in town and was getting on the freeway. Some guy interrupted the song

I was listening to. He told us an attack was about to take place and that we needed to find cover."

"So, did he tell you to come here?" I asked.

Another woman spoke up. "I heard the same guy. He didn't tell us where to go; he just told us to get under ground as deep as possible. He was so calm that at first I thought he was pulling our legs."

"Then why did you listen to him?" I asked.

"I don't know about everyone else," the first woman spoke again, "but there was just something about the way he said it that scared me. This was the only place I could think of. I still wasn't sure if it was a joke or not until I was almost out of town. I'd just gotten past Oasis Road when the sky turned dark. Most of the cars on the freeway stopped, and everyone was looking. I was scared and just kept going. The next thing I knew, people were running and falling down all over the place. I couldn't tell what was happening, so I drove like hell until I got here."

"How long did you plan on staying down here?" I asked.

Her head lowered as she continued. "To be honest, I don't think any of us ever planned on leaving. I'd personally come to terms that I was just going to die in this cavern."

For the most part, those that weren't already here had the same story. Gary seemed to be the only one that had witnessed the second attack.

"Did you all really just plan on giving up?" I asked.

Everyone stared at me. I could tell I'd already ruined the mood, so I decided to share the news I had.

"I'll be leaving in a few minutes and taking most of my group with me."

I could see the surprised look on everyone's face — everyone's except Ben's, that is.

"I thought we were staying another day or so?" Katherine interrupted.

"That was the plan, but the drone that's been chasing us is starting to close in. If it tracks us here, nobody will be safe."

They all nearly froze when I informed them we were leaving. It was as if I'd drained the life right back out of them.

"What about us?" asked one of the boys who'd been on the field trip. "Are you going to leave us here?

"No, definitely not. You'll all be going someplace safe to live. Benjamin is going to stay with you and take you all on a little trip into Oregon. He's a good man; he'll keep you all very safe. I'll be leaving with the others in a few minutes and will make that drone follow us. That is, if they want to go," I said hesitantly. "The rest of you will leave tomorrow."

"What do you mean if we want to?" Robert asked as my group approached me.

"Well, Rob, the way I see it, this is pretty much a suicide mission. The only way to ensure the safety of everyone here is to get the drone to chase us. That means we'll need to be in its direct line of sight before we run. I figure we'll try to start the chase on the other side of the bridge, where we got the food."

I could feel the tension as everyone quietly pondered his or her next move.

"I'm going with you," Katherine said. "You've brought us this far. If this is where it's all going to end, then so be it. I can't think of a better reason to sacrifice our lives than for all of these kids."

"You can count me in too, buddy," Robert said. "I really don't have any fear of dying."

"Same here," Josh chimed in. "I can't think of a more noble reason than this to follow you."

The three of them turned towards Cornelius.

"I don't know why you're looking at me," he said disapprovingly. "If you think for a second you could do this without me, then you're crazier than I thought."

Ben's head was down and he didn't say a word.

"What's up with you?" Katherine asked, trying to sound strong.

Ben looked up with a tear in his eye. "I'm not sure what to say," he said softly. "You're all so willing to lay down your lives for all of us. I just feel so guilty for not going with you."

"Hey, no guilt, dammit!" Katherine said sternly as she started to cry. "This is not about anything but our original promise to one another. No matter what it takes, we will make the people who did this pay. You're not out of this, by any means."

"She's right, Ben," I said, shaking his hand. "You're just securing the next generation of rebels to fight back. Just promise me you'll tell them about us and teach them to never give up."

"One last thing. Make sure you tell Michelle I love her."

"I promise," he said proudly.

We all moved in for a final hug before turning to go. No words were said; none were needed.

Chapter 7

FOLLOW US

Once outside, the mood lightened quickly. Katherine took her first real look at the houseboat and lit into us. "I can't seem to trust you guys to do anything without you throwing your own twist into it."

Robert and I both knew what she met, but it was always so much fun to push her buttons. I think it had something to do with her having such a strong personality. We knew we could always get a reaction.

"What do you mean?" Robert asked. "We needed something with plenty of room to bring back the supplies."

"I understand that, but this is massive," she said, trying to take it all in. "Didn't you ever once take the time to think it would be safer with a smaller boat?"

"Actually, we did think," he said. "Then we added in how much fun this one would be, and the risk to reward just made sense."

"That's what I'm talking about," she said, beginning to sound a little pissed off. "When the two of you are together, it doesn't matter how stupid something may be; if you think it sounds like fun, you're all for it. I swear, I truly don't see how the two of you ever stayed alive before the attacks, yet alone afterwards."

"That's easy," I spoke up. "We didn't even know each other before the attacks."

"What about after the attacks, smartass?" she asked, glaring at me.

Before saying another word, I walked right up to her until our faces were only inches apart.

"That's why we have you," I said and then leaned over and kissed her on the cheek.

Katherine froze for a second. Robert was laughing so hard he damn near fell off the boat. Finally, Katherine clenched her fist and screamed. Then she turned to Robert and yelled at him.

"You're supposed to be my boyfriend! When another man kisses me, you need to get mad — not laugh."

Everyone stopped and stared, including Robert.

"I'm your boyfriend?" he stammered.

Well, of course," she said, sounding calmer. "What did you think we were?"

"I was scared to asked," he said, staring hard into her eyes. "Things were so good between us; I didn't want to say something that might mess it up."

"But the others have called me your girlfriend all along. Didn't you ever catch on to the fact that I never corrected them?"

"Are you kidding?" Robert asked, sounding surprised. "I don't believe half the shit these guys say. I truly think they're all crazy."

Katherine stepped onto the boat and took Robert into her arms.

"They are all crazy," she said. "That's why we all get along so well." Leaning back a little, she looked softly into his eyes. "I love you, Robert!"

Then she gave him a soft but passionate kiss. The rest of us gave Robert a pat on the back as we joined them on the boat. We'd felt since day one that these two should be a couple. Now that they were, our spirits lifted again.

"You know this doesn't have to be a death sentence," I said, breaking the silence.

"What are you saying?" Katherine asked suspiciously.

"I'm not talking about you two," I said, giving her a wink. "I'm talking about this drone thing. We've dealt with drones before and survived. We still have the upper hand, so let's create a game plan and keep control of this."

"This is an actual military drone though," Robert said, as if I didn't already know. "Our weapons work great on the other drones, but this one would take serious firepower to destroy."

"That's correct. The other drones were weaker in that aspect compared to this one. On the other hand, nobody said we'd need to destroy it."

"What are you getting at?" Robert asked.

"If we can somehow convince it that we're dead, maybe it would just leave. We just need to know how it determines its target has been eliminated."

"I see what you're getting at," Cornelius said excitedly. "All we need to do is convince the drone we're dead, and it will leave under the impression it's finished its mission."

"This is where we need your expertise, Cornelius," I said. "How can we convince this thing it has finished its job?

"It's quite simple," he said. "The smaller drones could read our DNA and know everything about us. We couldn't trick them; we could only hide. This drone is much older and relies on antiquated technology. All we need to do is drop our body temperature and pulse rate quickly to make the drone think it's killed us. Then it will send a signal back to the operator that we're dead. The operator may be able to see us as well, so we need to do our best to look dead."

"That sounds easy enough," I said, laughing.

"There's a catch, though."

"What's that?" Katherine asked.

"It has to have a lock on us at the time we make the change. If not, it'll just think it's lost us."

"So, can we get the drone to fire at us, or something, and then just jump in the lake?" Josh asked. "The water should make it seem like our temperatures have gone down."

"The lake is way too warm for that," Cornelius said. "I like the idea, but we'd need the water to be colder than fifty degrees."

Josh's eyes lit up. "I bet the river is cold enough."

"That's highly doubtful," Cornelius stated. "It's nearly summer and most rivers are already between sixty and seventy degrees. That's just too warm."

"Most rivers, yes," Josh said. "But this isn't most rivers; this is the Sacramento. They pull the water from the bottom of the lake to keep it cold for spawning. If we can get in just below the dam, the water may be only forty to fifty degrees."

Everyone turned towards Cornelius and waited for his response. He thought quietly for a moment, crunching the numbers in his head. Finally, a huge smile came over his face.

"This might just work!" he said enthusiastically. "We still have one other small issue, though."

"What's that?" Katherine asked, her voice showing the excitement she felt knowing we had a shot.

"Hypothermia! If we drop our core temperatures too much, it can actually stop our hearts. There's also a strong chance we could cramp up and drown."

"Hell, those are just little things," I said happily. "We can figure out how to deal with that along the way. For now, we need to hurry up and divert the drones away from those kids."

The mood was almost electrifying as we took up positions on the boat. Robert and Katherine untied the ropes while the rest of us headed upstairs to the helm. I could feel my pulse quicken as I fired up the motor and carefully idled away from the shore. As soon as I felt it was safe, I pushed the throttle control all the way forward and started on our new adventure.

The five of us bounced ideas off one another, trying to figure out the best way to get the drones to follow us. It was going to be tricky. If we docked the boat at Bridge Bay, we'd be close enough to the freeway to easily attract the drone. However, we'd need to cover so many miles with the drone in pursuit that it would surely overtake us. We could take the boat almost all the way to the river, but then there was only a small chance the drones would locate us before discovering the others.

It seemed the more we went over it, the worse our odds were. Feeling a little discouraged, Robert and Katherine went to spend some time alone together. I'll admit things were once again looking rather glum and our enthusiasm was beginning to diminish. Over and over, I ran each scenario through my head.

As I looked out the windshield, I spotted them standing at the bow of the boat. He had his arms wrapped around her waist, while she stood facing the water. She was leaning out as far as she could with her arms outstretched. It reminded me of the scene in "Titanic," and I caught myself mesmerized by these two. They were so in love that even with so much at stake, the only thing that mattered was the moment. Watching them really got me to missing Michelle.

He didn't let go of her until I slowed the boat to pull into the docks. As I did, Robert grabbed the rope and secured our vessel. Josh and Cornelius had already joined them on shore by the time I got off the boat.

"I need everyone to follow me!" I yelled, running past them.

With everyone close behind, we ran past the pickup we'd used earlier and headed to the hotel. Katherine slowed for a second when she noticed the dogs lying next to the pickup.

"I thought you said you had a minor run-in with some dogs," she said, glaring at Robert as she caught up with him.

"I didn't want you to worry. Besides, Ben's dog whooped their asses pretty good."

She was still glaring at him as we reached the front of the hotel and made our way through the front doors. All the bodies were removed shortly after the attacks, but the place was still a total mess. Nearly every window in the lobby had been broken and blood stained the carpets and walls. Doing my best to block the view from my mind, I went straight for the printer. Once there, I pulled open the paper drawer and grabbed several blank sheets and some pens lying next to it. I quickly handed them out to everyone.

"What the hell are these for?" Robert asked.

"I want each of you to write something personal on your paper. You can write to someone in particular or just a note telling the world who you are. When I was watching you and Kat on the boat, I realized this is our moment. I don't want to take the chance of dying nameless like the billions who already have in the last month. I want us to be remembered."

"With so few people left, who do you think would really care?" Josh asked.

I shot him a smile. "Those alive in the future will care. The history books we read in school were full of normal people who somehow had their story shared. I don't care to be one of the nameless, like the billions of others who died in the midst of all of this. If we accomplish what we're setting out to do, we'll be remembered. This is our moment.

Let them know who we were, and remember, it never hurts to embellish a bit."

I could see the lights going on in everyone's eyes. Robert was already halfway through his page and writing like a madman.

"I don't know about the rest of you, but I'm telling everyone that I was six foot six and built like a brick shithouse."

"Oh come on, Rob," I said, giving him a shove. "This isn't a chat room; at least be a little realistic. Tell them you're five foot six and smell like a brick shithouse."

"Very funny," he said, enjoying the mood. "Then I'm telling everyone we followed a nearsighted truck driver to our doom."

I raised my head and thought for a moment. "Holy shit, Rob! That's pretty much exactly what you're doing."

Everyone was having a good time getting very engrossed in the project when Cornelius pointed out the obvious.

"You do realize, Steve, that the chances of somebody actually finding these papers are slim to none."

"I thought about that also," I said, putting my pen down. "We're not all going. In fact, only two of us need to go — Cornelius and myself. If by some stroke of luck we make it, I'll need him to help me get into San Francisco. Once there, we can disrupt the signal sent to the drones. That will give the rest of you ample opportunity to build armies using the manpower Ray and Shelley put together."

"That's bullshit, Steve, and you know it," Robert said. "Nothing personal, but you and Cornelius couldn't shoot your way out of a paper bag. Even if you get past the drones, there are still wild dogs out there. Besides that, we're all just as much a part of this as you are."

"I know you are, Rob, but you and Katherine deserve the chance to have a family."

"We do have a family," Katherine interrupted, "and I have every intention of following my family to hell, if need be. Screw the world, if our letters aren't found."

Rob reached over and put his hand on Katherine. "Steve," he said solemnly, "who did you write your letter to?"

"Michelle," I said quietly.

At that moment, I could tell they all understood. Michelle and I had crossed paths many times without being reunited. She'd always found a way to tell me she loved me, even when everything told her I'd never see it. I left my ring at the memorial Justin had made, but I never took the time to write her and tell her how much I loved her.

Josh stepped away from the counter and looked out the window.

"My family and I lived just a few miles from here. I can't stand the idea of never knowing their fate. Do me a favor and let me stay. After you get the drones to follow, I can sneak out and look for them. When I have what I'm looking for, I'll hook up with Ben and lead the others back to camp. Then Michelle can get your letters, and none of you will be forgotten."

"Are you sure that's what you want?" I asked.

"More than anything. I hope you guys don't think less of me, but this is something I need to do."

"How are you for firepower?" Robert asked him.

"I'm good. I have enough ammo for a few dog attacks, and to be honest, I doubt I'll need the phones anymore."

"How many phones do you have?" I asked.

"Six," he responded.

"Hold onto those, just in case," I said. "We still have enough to last us."

"Do you at least have some sort of plan to make it to the river?" Katherine asked.

"I have a great plan." I paused for a second and thought about it. "OK, I may not have a great plan, but I do have a plan that will be a shitload of fun. Give us a fifteen-minute head start. Then blow the piss out of this place. We'll set vehicles on fire every so often along the way. If the explosion can get the drone's attention, I'm hoping the heat and flames from the fires will lead them to us. Then when the drone does spot us, we'll be almost to the river."

Katherine closed her eyes and softly shook her head. "So, what you're saying is you plan on blowing stuff up, setting fires, and getting killed."

"Hell yeah!" Robert exclaimed. "That does sound like fun. Count me in."

"Just how am I going to blow this place up?" Josh asked, looking confused.

"We can just fill this place with gas," I said, pointing to the propane tanks. "That end of the building near the kitchen still has all of its windows. We can open the lines in there and give it time to fill up. Then you can put a lit flare by a closed window and get to a safe hiding place. After we have a fifteen-minute head start, shoot the window out. When the gas hits the flame, this place should go up like a Roman candle."

"Damn, that's a pretty trick way to set it off," Josh said.

"Thanks. You just need to make sure the window has a good seal; you wouldn't want the gas hitting the flare prematurely."

"Have you given any thought to how you want to set the cars on fire?" Robert asked.

"I figured we could douse them in gas," I told him.

"Instead of that, we should make a few Molotov cocktails," Robert suggested. "It would be easier and a hell of a lot more fun."

Katherine lowered her head and sighed. "I don't care what it is, you two always try to figure out a way to make a game of it."

"You only live once," Robert said, taking off to the lounge to get some bottles. "You get the gas going. I'll take care of the cocktails."

"Isn't it too soon?" Josh asked.

"No, I want this place full so it makes a really big boom," I told him. "We just need to make sure no pilot lights are on or it'll go off early."

Josh followed me into the kitchen while Katherine and Cornelius went to catch up with Robert. In less than fifteen minutes, we had everything in place. Josh would give us a ten-minute head start before lighting the flare, and then another five before shooting out the glass. Even if gas was leaking around the window, ten minutes should be enough of a head start.

We said our good-byes a little after seven p.m. and loaded into a newer club cab pickup we found in the parking lot. I could hardly believe the events of the day. When the day had started, the only thing I planned on was going home to Michelle. Since then, we'd been chased by drones, wrecked a beautiful RV, found a large group of survivors, and even saved a life. In the past, this much excitement would've worn me out. Today, however, I felt different. I could almost feel my muscles changing shape and the blood pulsing through my veins. I felt young and alive.

I was in the driver's seat with Cornelius riding shotgun. Robert was directly behind him and Katherine was to his left. Between them sat the two boxes of Molotov cocktails they'd made. As we started out of the parking lot, Robert lit his first cocktail and threw it at one of the cars. He did four more in the first mile and two the second. After that, he did another one to two all the way to town.

Robert was having too much fun. Katherine would light the rag that was stuffed partially into the bottle and then hand it to him. He'd moved from his seat and was now sitting on his door in the open window, the top half of his body outside the truck. He held the oh shit handle with his right hand and threw with his left.

He's naturally right-handed, so throwing this way looked awkward. Katherine was laughing her ass off making fun of him and telling him he threw like a little girl. Somehow, even with his throws as bad as they were, he still managed to hit his target. At least we think he did. Most of the time the vehicle was almost out of sight before the fire really got going.

We were lucky enough to get a good show from one of them at least. It was an old station wagon, one of those big ones from the seventies. Robert had his eyes set on it for nearly half a mile. Something about it had aroused his attention, and he made sure we all knew what his intended target was.

As we closed in on the vehicle, I noticed several red plastic fuel cans in the back. Hindsight being what it is, I probably should've stopped him. At that time, though, all that was going through my mind was "Oh yeah, this should be good."

Robert's aim was right on the money, and his flaming bottle hit the center of the rear glass. I don't know about most of the newer cars, but back then that rear glass was damn near bulletproof, and a good thing too. The bottle shattered when it hit, sending a nice ball of flame around the whole back of the car but only cracking the glass.

As near as I can figure, those gas cans must not have been sealed properly. After a month in the hot California sun, most of the liquid had evaporated. With the doors closed and the windows up, the car must've been full of gas fumes. We hadn't gone more than one hundred fifty feet when the flames and fumes finally made contact.

I watched the whole thing in my side mirror. The explosion looked more like the car was filled with dynamite instead of gasoline. The doors flew off and the roof ripped from the body, shooting straight into the air. Through the ball of flame that was now chasing us, I could make out the hood and possibly a fender coming towards us. They were going a little faster than we were and collided with the back of the truck. I've never seen Robert move so fast. He was nearly all the way back in the cab as the ball of flame passed over us. Something shattered our back window, spraying us with glass.

I locked up the brakes, bringing the truck to a sliding stop, and jumped out of the cab. Cornelius apparently had the same idea and exited the cab before the truck fully stopped. As he picked himself up off the pavement, we both turned to see if Katherine was going to shoot us. That girl has a hair trigger, and now I was really regretting giving her a gun.

Looking into the cab, I could see Katherine was facedown on the floorboard in the fetal position between the front and rear seats. Robert was sitting upright, with little shards of glass covering most of his body, and a great deal of hair missing from the top of his head. Nearly frozen in place, he still held the handle with one hand while the other gripped the back of my seat. His eyes locked on Katherine, and he was unsure of his next move. He desperately wanted to pull her into his arms and make sure she was OK. On the other hand, he still wanted to live.

She slowly rose up off the floorboard, her hair covered in glass. As she looked back, her eyes made contact with Robert's.

"Holy shit, that was awesome!" she blurted out. She was laughing so hard it made her eyes water. Not to mention she had the biggest smile on her face I'd ever seen.

"I get it now!" she said, throwing her arms around Robert. "I finally understand why you and Steve do the things you do. Oh my God, we have to do that again. I don't think I've ever felt such a rush of excitement."

Robert slowly loosened his grip and put his arms around his obviously delusional girlfriend.

"That was fun, wasn't it?" he asked cautiously as he turned toward me. Quietly, he mouthed, "What do I do?" almost pleading for me to help him.

I too was unsure just what she was up to; it didn't feel normal. Cautiously, Cornelius and I reentered the vehicle and continued. We still had close to a mile to go until our exit, and it was nearly time for Josh to blow up the resort.

I was beginning to feel a little concerned for his safety. After seeing the size of the explosion the last car made, I was afraid filling the whole building with natural gas might've been a bit extreme. He planned to take the shot from more than one hundred yards away; I just prayed he'd do it from behind cover as well.

We pulled up to our exit with only about a minute to go. After coming to a stop, I hopped out and opened Robert's door. I figured this gave him the opportunity to run, if need be.

"So, shouldn't we get going?" Katherine asked, still sounding a bit giddy.

"We will," I assured her. "We have a little prep work to do first. While you two were busy making your toys at Bridge Bay, I located a few items we'd need. The first are these inflatable life vests. If you start to cramp from the cold water, this will keep you afloat. I also got four watertight drawstring bags. We need to strip down to our skivvies and put our clothes and anything else we want to keep from getting wet in them. Once we get out of the water, we'll want to dry off and put warm clothes on as quickly as possible. If not, hypothermia could still get us."

Reaching into the bed of the truck, I grabbed a box I'd put in there earlier. Inside were four thin bath towels.

"These aren't much, but they'll get you dry, and one last thing," I said, pulling out a large thermos. "I boiled some soup before filling the place with gas. It will still be hot when this is over, and we'll need it to help raise our body temperatures."

I was already stripping off my clothes and putting them into my bag while the others exited the truck.

"Do we have to do this now?" Katherine asked.

"Yes. Once the drone is chasing us, I don't believe it'll take a time-out while you undress." I was being sarcastic, hoping to get a rise out of her.

Suddenly, a huge fireball filled the sky. It was the blast from Bridge Bay. Everyone froze for a second as we stared at the flames and smoke filling the sky.

Katherine's eyes shot back to me. "What now?" she asked. I could hear the panic in her voice.

"We need to finish getting undressed. I don't know how long it'll take for the drone to get here. One thing is for sure; if that didn't get its attention, nothing will."

Robert quickly took off his clothes and put them in his bag, but Katherine just stood there, her eyes pleading with me, as if she was deathly afraid of something

"Are you OK?" I asked, half expecting her to pronounce her fear of the drone.

"I can't get undressed," she said sheepishly.

"I never figured you for the shy type," I said. "It's just underwear; it's no different than a bathing suit."

Her face slowly turned a warm shade of pink as she confessed her reason for being embarrassed. She'd made the decision to give herself to Robert that night. It was going to be a surprise, so when we got clothes that morning, she'd picked out the skimpiest bra and panties she could find.

Robert's eyes quickly went back and forth between Katherine and me. I could tell what he was thinking. She was his girlfriend, and having us see her in next to nothing would embarrass them both.

"Darn party poopers," I said jokingly. "I had a feeling you might be a little modest."

As I spoke, I reached into the box and pulled out one last item. It was a very modest one-piece bikini. Katherine looked at me, almost overjoyed.

"How did you know?" she asked, grabbing it from my hands and racing for a hiding spot to change.

"I figured if Michelle were here, she wouldn't want to undress around others. Even though you act like one of the guys, you're still a lady."

She quickly changed and rejoined the rest of us.

"Thank you, Steve. I really appreciate this," she said, still trying to hide behind Robert.

"OK, everyone, grab your bags and hop in. I don't want to be caught with our pants down when that thing shows up," I ordered.

"Do you know how to get to the river from here?" Cornelius asked, his voice cracking. When Katherine was telling us about her undergarments, he pretty much went into hiding. I honestly felt that if Katherine had undressed down to her underwear, Cornelius would've died of embarrassment before she did.

I tried not to laugh at his voice as I spoke. "Josh told me to take the first exit at Shasta Lake City and just stay on that road. It'll lead us through town and to a stop sign, with the

123

school on our right. Then we're to continue straight ahead and climb the hill. He said we'd be able to see the lake and dam once we're on top; the river is just below them. He also told me there'd be a beautiful view of Mount Shasta."

After I finished sharing the directions with the others, I had Robert set another car on fire before starting the truck and pulling to the top of the off-ramp. Then, we sat and waited for the chase to begin.

From the top of the ramp, I could see the destruction Gary spoke of off in the distance. It closely resembled the same destruction we witnessed in Medford. The only difference was that this was a far less populated spot. It took out a lot of trees and a flat section of the freeway but no large buildings that we could see. The plane that went down in Medford tore right through the center of town. The force was so great that some buildings had been leveled to their foundations.

We sat there in disbelief, pondering how many plane crashes we'd passed without even knowing it. We had a good view of the ones on the freeway, but what about all the others? There were probably thousands of them. I was deep in thought when Roberts's voice brought me back.

"I think we have company!" he yelled.

Turning around in my seat, I could see what appeared to be a small plane off in the distance. It was flying about fifty feet above the ground, directly over the freeway. I took a deep breath and readied myself. I'd just reached forward to put the truck in gear when the drone flew past us.

"What the fuck was that?" Robert asked, visibly shaken. "That wasn't what I was expecting at all."

Not wanting to wait for the second pass, I slammed the truck into drive and sped off, spinning the tires as I did. The speed of the drone caught us all by surprise. At first, I let fear take over and drove somewhat erratically. I glanced over at Cornelius, expecting him to be white as a ghost. I turned back towards the road ahead of me, and then did a double take at him. He had a big grin on his face as he looked at me.

"Did I miss something?" I yelled. "Why are you scared of women, and this drone seems to excite you?"

"It's an obsolete series of drones," he said cheerfully. "It's even older than I'd originally thought it to be. That style was scrapped clear back in the eighties due to its guidance system. At the time, they were the fastest unmanned drones ever produced, but they had one major flaw."

"What's that? I asked.

"Well, for lack of a better description, they couldn't hit the broad side of a barn. They maneuvered more like a missile than an airplane. In other words, they used speed, not finesse, to be able to fly. Because of that, along with an elementary level guidance system, they were quickly redesigned."

"So, it can't hurt us?" Katherine asked, a little unsure of what he meant.

"Oh no, it can definitely kill us. It has amazing firepower. I'm just glad it's not one of the newer drones. I feel we have at least a fifty percent chance of surviving this."

"How can you look so calm, at fifty percent?" I shouted at him.

"With the other drones, I'd give us less than a one percent chance."

We were maneuvering through town at more than eighty miles an hour, so I wasn't able to give him the dirty look I wanted to. About that time, Robert informed me it was coming back. Before I could respond to him, the drone fired a shot at us.

Catching it in my side mirror, my reflexes seemed to automatically take over. I turned sharply to the right as a

125

small missile took out a pizza parlor to the left of us. At about the same time, the drone shot past us and was once again out of sight.

I was glad this thing was a bad shot. It hadn't just blown a hole in the side of the building; it leveled the whole place and most of the building next to it.

"I don't think it needs to be a good shot!" I yelled over at Cornelius. "It just needs to get one close to us."

I had to slow our speed to about fifty miles an hour through the last section of town. For some reason, the bodies had been removed, but cars and trucks still blocked most of the street.

I tried not to slow too much, but I had to be careful. Twice, I clipped vehicles as I went by them. I looked up ahead, and it appeared that the road was clear once again. Cautiously, I increased my speed as we made a long sweeping left. Just as the corner straightened, the drone reappeared in my mirror. Instantly, I saw the flash as it released another missile.

I shoved both my feet onto the brake and the truck slid sideways off the left shoulder of the road. We slid out of control, hitting a large fir tree, tearing the driver's door from the truck, and shattering my left arm. At the same time, the missile exploded directly in the middle of the road just ahead of us.

Still out of control, the truck bounced off the tree and was now heading back to the right, straight through the cloud of dust created by the explosion. I could feel the front wheels drop into the crater it made as we came to a stop.

Dazed and confused, I sat still for a moment listening to the moans from the others. The explosion had been close enough to cause our ears to ring but not close enough to inflict damage. As the dust settled, I realized the front wheels were now a good ten feet above the bottom of the hole.

With no time to waste, I stuck the truck into reverse and stepped on the gas. I could hear the tires on the pavement and felt it trying to back up, but nothing happened. I tried it a second time with the same results. My mind raced, trying to figure out what was wrong. I knew it was only a matter of seconds before the drone came back. If we didn't get moving, there would be almost no chance of it missing us.

With seconds clicking away, everything suddenly became very clear to me. I shoved my foot onto the brake, and at the same moment, with my left arm hanging by my side, I released the steering wheel and put the truck in four high. From the corner of my eye, I caught a glimpse of the drone as it released another missile. Letting go of the brake and pressing on the gas, I felt the front of the truck rise out of the hole.

There was a bright flash as dust and rock pummeled the truck, breaking the windshield and passenger windows. Instantly, I put the truck in drive and once again headed for the dam.

Chapter 8

SACRAMENTO RIVER

Seconds before the drone took the last shot, something in me changed. I felt as if a curtain had lifted. Everything was clearer: my vision, my sense of smell, and even my hearing.

Not only were my senses heightened, but my movements had also become extremely fluid. I was aware my arm was broken and the flesh ripped open exposing the bone, yet I felt no pain. Just moments earlier, the discomfort had affected my ability to focus. Now it felt as if a low voltage of electricity flowed through my arm. It tingled but nothing more.

With my new sense of clarity, I also no longer feared the drone. In its last three shots, it had shown a pattern. It fired where it anticipated us to be. If I made some movement to the left, it shot left. It did so no matter how slight my movement was. If I made no movement in either direction, it shot straight on. I was sitting still the last time it fired, and the missile hit nearly in the same spot as the previous one. Any movement I made after the missile fired did nothing to change its trajectory. As long as I waited to react, I could easily avoid being blown up.

I figured I had nearly a minute until the next shot and took the time to check on the others. Robert and Katherine held each other tightly in the backseat. They'd changed positions at our last stop, and Robert was now sitting behind me. A great deal of blood covered his left side, and at first, I thought he was injured. Taking a second look, I realized it was my blood on him. Regardless, the two of them looked as if they were at peace with the situation. Cornelius, on the other hand, continued to stare at me with a childlike grin.

"You feel it, don't you?" he asked as I turned towards him.

"Feel what?" I questioned, hoping for an explanation.

"The nanites," he said happily. "I saw your expression change just before the drone fired that last time. They detected your stress level as a flaw and corrected it. In time, the nanites will bring you to a complete state of equanimity — at least in theory. For some reason, it never fully takes effect. You may have moments of clarity and then go right back to the way you were."

"You're weird, you know that," I said, giving him a little wink.

A second later, the drone came into view and fired on us. Almost as if it were second nature, I effortlessly avoided the missile and continued on our way. No longer doing eighty mph, I found the truck's maneuverability to be much better at around thirty-five to forty.

"What are we going to do once we reach the dam?" Cornelius asked.

"According to Josh's directions, we drive across the dam to the other side and follow the road all the way to the river."

It was about that time that we rounded the last curve at the top of the hill, exposing the three Shastas. The view was amazing. The sun was beginning to set, making the water behind the dam look almost as if it were on fire. It wasn't like the small lakes we were used to back home. From where we were, it seemed to go on forever, only ending as it reached the base of Mount Shasta.

Robert and Katherine both leaned forward. "Wow!" Katherine said. "Josh wasn't lying about how beautiful the view is."

Rising up as far as he could, Robert peered out over the left side of the hill, trying to see the view below us.

"There it is!" he shouted joyfully. "I can see the river."

He threw his arms around Katherine and pulled her to him, kissing her on the cheek. After a few seconds, he released her. Then he placed both hands on my shoulders and shook me.

"Good job, Steve. We're actually going to make it," he said triumphantly.

Before I could respond, we found ourselves face-to-face with the drone. It had been following the road we were on from the opposite direction. For a split second, we were caught off guard. Fortunately, the drone was just as unprepared to see us. It fired its missile harmlessly into the hillside above us and then rapidly disappeared from our view.

With a sudden burst of adrenaline, I picked up my speed. As we rounded the next corner, the road opened up to a large parking lot. Off to our left was a three-story concrete building with dozens of large windows. Directly across from us, on the other side of the parking lot, was the entrance to the road across the dam. I pointed the truck straight for it and held the pedal to the floor. Cornelius had a death grip on the dashboard as we flew towards our destination. Then, with just a few hundred feet to go, I slid the truck to a stop.

We all stared. The entrance across the dam was blocked off — not by some abandoned vehicles or debris, but by some kind of mechanical roadblocks. Smack dab in the middle of the road blocking our path was a guard shack. To either side of that were steel barricades.

"What do we do now?" Katherine asked, almost sounding defeated.

I quickly looked around, hoping to find an alternate route down to the river. There just had to be some other way to get there in a vehicle. The drone may not have had the greatest guidance system, but on foot, we could never outmaneuver it. Even if we did somehow manage to make it there, we couldn't just jump in. Whoever was controlling the drone needed to think they'd actually killed us. That was going to be difficult enough using the truck; without it, we had no chance.

"Hold on, everyone!" I yelled, spinning the truck back around. "There was another road running along that building we passed."

Racing back, we saw that it too was blocked off. However, instead of using an impassable steel barricade, it used a metal gate. I didn't bother to slow down.

"Do you even know where the road goes?" Robert yelled as we closed in on it.

"I can't say for sure, but I hope it goes down to the river."

Still holding the pedal to the floor, I drove straight into the center of the gate. It wasn't nearly as explosive as I thought it would be. Instead of ripping the gate from its posts or tearing it in two, the gate just flung open. The chain they'd used to secure it was either unhooked or made of the cheapest steel they could find. It really didn't matter to us why it hadn't held; we were just glad to make it through.

Once on the other side, we could see that it did indeed head to the river. I could see a few tight turns off in the distance, but other than that, there didn't appear to be any more obstacles to keep us from reaching the water.

Looking at my side mirror in the passenger door, I watched for the drone to reappear. I figured it should be showing up any second. That's when I decided to have a little fun.

"Watch this," I hollered as we passed the first building, the one with all the windows.

I held the truck to the right side of the roadway, keeping a close eye on the mirror. Then as soon as the drone appeared, I shot left, straight at the second building. Seeing the flash from the drone as it fired its missile, I turned back to the right and accelerated.

"Holy shit!" Robert screamed as the building exploded and fell into itself. "That was awesome! Did you really cause the drone to do that?"

"Damn right I did. I just made that drone my bitch!"

"The hell with trying to trick it!" Robert exclaimed. "Let's just have it follow us and blow more shit up!"

"Don't worry," I laughed. "Once we lose this thing, there will be plenty of stuff to blow up to keep you entertained."

I did my best to calculate my speed with the distance to the water. I wanted to make sure we'd get there at the exact same time the drone fired again. I could then steer the truck into the water, giving the illusion we crashed. Now that the sun was dropping over the horizon, the only way the drone could see us would be with its infrared cameras. Once our body temperatures dropped, we'd appear dead.

"OK, everyone, this is it," I yelled as we made the last turn. "Make sure you don't take your seat belts off until after we hit the water. After the truck is fully submerged, undo your buckle and swim away. By then, the drone will be past us; it'll be safe to inflate your life vest. Make sure you don't forget your bags."

We were running parallel to the river, about forty feet from its edge, when the drone appeared. I held my line perfectly until I saw the flash from the drone and then turned sharply towards it. The missile hit less than thirty feet behind our truck, lifting the rear tires off the ground. It wasn't enough to turn us upside down, but it made for a good show as we entered the water. Within seconds, the truck sank below the surface, allowing us to get out undetected.

The plan seemed to go perfectly, except we underestimated the effects the water would have on our muscles. We figured the water temperature should be around fifty-six degrees for this time of the year. This would've been cold enough to carry out our plan and still sustain us for nearly an hour if needed. It became apparent quickly that the water was much colder than that — possibly as low as forty-seven to forty-eight degrees. At that temperature, the risk of shock was as much of a factor as hypothermia.

When the truck first came to rest in the river, I quickly assessed the others. I could tell Katherine was in trouble. The sudden rush of cold water had literally taken her breath away. I undid my seat belt and tried to make it into the backseat. Robert stopped me.

"You and Cornelius, get the hell out of here!" he yelled. "I'll grab Katherine."

Fear raced through me as the fast-moving water engulfed the pickup and rolled it over under the surface. Pulling myself free through the missing door, I glanced back at the others. Robert had gotten both of their seat belts off, but as the water covered her head, Katherine became combative. Confused and in a panic, she was still trying to breathe, almost oblivious to the fact she was underwater. Each time Robert grabbed her, she'd claw at him and pull away. Unable to hold his breath any longer, Robert pushed free of the truck and swam to the surface. Taking in a deep breath, he tried to locate the pickup.

Getting a glimpse of the truck on an underwater ledge, he had to act fast. The swift moving water rapidly moved the vehicle from the shallow edge of the river to the center.

If it made it out there, the water's depth would be greater than twenty feet. The possibility of making it back to the truck at that point would be nearly impossible.

Fighting the current, he dove down and grabbed the truck's fender. Inch by inch, he pulled himself along the body of the truck and into the cab.

Cornelius and I could barely make out the outline of the events unfolding beneath us. Several times, we tried to fight the current, diving down to try to reach our friends. Each time we did, however, we found ourselves further downriver.

After what seemed to be an eternity, the drone flew over, so close to the surface of the water that it created a wake. Then, in a split second, it was out of sight.

With less than a minute until its next pass, I had to act quickly. Scrambling onto the shore, I ran as fast as I could to where we first entered the water and dove in. By then, the sun had vanished behind the hills, taking with it any chance of ever seeing the truck again. Still, I dove down, hoping against hope to locate them. I was no match for the current and once again found myself too far downriver. With nothing to show for my efforts, I waited for the drone to pass over a second time and again pulled myself onto the shore.

This time before I jumped in, I found the biggest rock I could hold with one hand. Then, doing my best estimate where the truck might be, I reentered the water. The heavy rock quickly pulled me to the bottom. Trying to hold the rock in my right arm, I frantically started reaching out in all directions with my feet. Again no luck. Releasing the rock, I realized I wasn't heading towards the surface, but that I was now caught in an undertow. I've never been able to hold my breath for even a minute, so I knew I was in trouble.

As a current pulled me down into the deeper water near the center, I got an idea. The emergency life vest we put on not only went over our head but also fastened around our chests. Because of that, the swift water hadn't pulled it off. Reaching up with my right hand, I found the ripcord and pulled. With a sudden rush of excess air, the device rapidly inflated, dragging me with it to the surface. Coughing and choking, I called out into the twilight for the others.

"I'm over here!" Cornelius yelled out.

Straining my eyes, I made out his silhouette against a log protruding aimlessly out of the water. Letting myself go with the current, I drifted within a few feet of him. Then, using nearly the last of his strength, he reached out, grabbed me, and pulled me to him. Grabbing the log, I again called out for the others.

"I can't find anyone," Cornelius stuttered through shaking teeth. "I'm so cold."

Adrenaline pumped through my body so quickly I was nearly oblivious to the cold. Trying not to face the grim reality of what just happened, I pushed us away from the log and pulled Cornelius onto the shore.

I'd lost my bag during the ordeal, but fortunately, Cornelius still had his tied to his wrist. My fingers on my one good hand were slightly numb, making it difficult to untie the string. Finally, I slid the knot open and grabbed a dry towel out of the bag for him. As he did his best to dry himself off, I pried the lid off the thermos and handed it to him. He quickly guzzled down half of its contents and then offered me some.

I was focused on trying to figure out a way to reach Robert and Katherine and declined his offer. They'd been under water for several minutes, but I wasn't ready to give up.

I took a moment to get my wits about me. It was then that I realized that not only had the drone quit coming, but I'd also started to regain the use of my left arm — an arm that less than ten minutes ago was limp and broken at my side. Making my way back to where I figured the truck should be, I studied the miracle the nanites had performed. With two good arms to work with, I was sure I could make it there this time. I was just about to enter the water when I heard a cough.

At first, I thought it might've been Cornelius. Then hearing it a second time, I nearly fell into the river. It was Robert! He'd somehow floated past us.

I raced past Cornelius, stumbling over rocks and bushes along the way. I could hardly see where I was going; I just knew I needed to get there. I was still at a full run when I tripped over Robert. He'd somehow freed Katherine and after floating downstream, managed to pull them both from the water. Katherine was lying on her back with her head softly resting on her life vest. Robert had pulled the towel from her pack and was trying to dry her off.

"Oh my God, you're alive!" I said as I grabbed him. With pleading eyes, he pushed me aside.

"Please, help Katherine," his voice was low and weak.

With the last of the fading light, I could see that both their lips had turned dark blue. I figured it had to be from the cold.

"Cornelius!" I yelled. "Get over here!"

The first thing on my mind was to get her warmed up. Grabbing her bag, I pulled it open and rummaged around until I found a few items to start a fire. She didn't have a lighter or matches, but she did have a flashlight and a pack of gum. About that time, Cornelius made his way over to us and knelt over Katherine. As he did, I took his pack from him and pulled a dry shirt and some paper from it.

I shredded the paper into tiny strips; then, using the shirt, I created what appeared to be a small bird's nest. After filling it with shredded paper, I removed the batteries from the flashlight and opened a stick of gum. The piece of paper adhered to a thin piece of aluminum foil keeps the gum fresh. I carefully tore the gum wrapper into the shape of an hourglass, thinner in the middle, for the ignition point, but not too thin. Then I placed the ends on the battery — one on positive and one on negative. The foils shorted out and caught the paper connected to it on fire. I quickly placed it into the nest I made, igniting the paper strips. When the fire spread to the shirt, I added sticks and brush until it was a hot blaze.

The whole time I worked on the fire, Robert and Cornelius diligently tended to Katherine. Finally, cold and exhausted, Robert collapsed to the ground.

"She's dead," he said softly.

He wasn't speaking directly to either one of us. I felt he was saying it more to convince himself. That's when I noticed Katherine wasn't breathing.

Between the hot soup and fire, Cornelius was beginning to regain his dexterity and cognitivity. He placed his head against Katherine's chest and pressed firmly on her belly. Then, raising his head, he floored us both.

"She isn't dead," he said with a look of relief.

"What the fuck do you mean?" Robert growled at him. "She drowned right in front of me."

"That's just it!" Cornelius said more forcefully. "The water in her lungs caused her to lose consciousness, but it didn't kill her — at least not yet. The frigid water slowed her metabolism and stopped her heart, but her brain is still alive."

With that, he leaned down, pinched her nose between his fingers, and then pressed his lips to hers and gave her two deep breaths. Robert immediately slid over next to him and started chest compressions. For nearly ten minutes, the two of them worked in unison, one working her heart and the other her lungs. Undaunted by the cold chill running through their own bodies, they steadily carried on.

By then, the day had succumbed to night, with a cold, empty, moonless sky. The only light was from the fire's glow. Its radiance illuminated the eerie scene before me, nearly breaking my heart. Katherine lay there motionless; her limp, lifeless body seemed so empty and cold. Her beautiful, long, chestnut hair no longer flowed gently over her shoulders, but instead lay flat against the ground, soaking wet and full of dirt and twigs. Her warm, olive-colored skin and soft, pink lips were now a mild shade of gray and blue. Even her fingers appeared dark and rigid.

Robert and Cornelius were at the point of exhaustion when Katherine finally coughed up some water and took a labored breath. Nearly collapsing on her, Robert pressed his body close to hers. He did this not only to express his love, but also to help warm her. She wasn't yet out of the woods. We had no way of knowing for sure just how low her body temperature had dropped; we just knew we needed to bring it back up.

"We need to get her off the ground!" Cornelius shouted as he grabbed some dead branches. "We can make her a bed out of brush and lay her on it. Then you can use your own body heat to help warm her."

"What about her hands and feet?" Robert asked. "Should we massage them to heat them up?"

"No!" he replied. "Not until we bring her core temperature up. Otherwise, we run the risk of her having a heart attack."

For nearly an hour, we did all we could think of to warm up Katherine. Everything from feeding her hot soup, to warming rocks with the fire and placing them under her makeshift bed. We felt the worst had passed and that we were gaining ground. She lay there cuddled up with Robert, faintly talking with him, and even laughing at times. Then, without warning, things took a drastic turn for the worse.

At first, we thought she was just trying to cough up some more water. She coughed two or three times and then started to dry heave. Robert quickly pulled her into a sitting position to keep her from choking when her body began to convulse slightly. He held her gently in his arms until she softly requested he lay her back down. By then, her breaths were becoming labored, and we knew we were about to lose her.

"Can't you do something?" Robert asked, pleading with Cornelius.

Cornelius stared blankly at him for a moment. We were all so cold and tired that even simple tasks, like decision-making, had become challenging. Finally snapping out of it, Cornelius reached for his bag.

"I almost forgot about the nanites!" he said excitedly. "Robert, I need you to grab them for me while I stabilize Katherine."

Cornelius didn't really need his help. He just wanted to give Robert something quick and easy to do to keep his mind occupied.

To protect the glass jars from breaking, Cornelius had transferred the vials from his small bag to a wooden box. Over and over, Robert fumbled with its clasp, to no avail. His fingers were so numb and swollen from the cold that he couldn't work the tiny mechanism. Finally, out of frustration, he set the box on the ground and went to smash it with a rock.

"What the hell are you doing?" I yelled, putting my hand on top of the box to absorb the blow.

"I'm trying to get the damn box open," he said, sounding bewildered. "Why did you stop me?"

"Don't you remember what Cornelius told us this morning? If you break a vial of nanites this close to us, we'll all suffer a horrific death."

My hands weren't affected by the cold like Robert's were, so I carefully opened the box and filled a syringe for him.

"I'm sorry," he said as he reached for it. "I'm so cold I can't think straight."

After several attempts to hold the syringe in his hand, he got frustrated and held his hand out.

"You have to do it," he said, handing it back to me.

"I don't care who brings it to me, but would you please hurry up," Cornelius said in frustration.

I made my way over to Cornelius and gave him the syringe. He held it up to the firelight and confirmed I had the right amount. Then, as Robert cradled Katherine's head in his lap, Cornelius placed the needle against her neck. Reaching up, Katherine put her hand on Robert.

"No, Rob," she said weakly. "I want to give you a baby."

Trying his best not to cry, he gently took her hand in his and pressed it against his heart.

"I would love for you and I to have a baby," he said, giving her a gentle smile. "I'm OK if we can't, but what I can't take is losing you. I love you."

Before he had finished talking, Katherine closed her eyes and was gone. In a panic, Robert looked up at Cornelius.

"Are we too late?" he asked, his eyes filled with tears.

"No, we still have time, but I'm not going to give her the shot."

"Why not?" Robert asked, totally confused.

"It's not my place, Rob. Katherine doesn't want the shot, because if she gets it she won't be able to give you a child. It's up to you to give it to her."

Reaching up, he took the syringe from Cornelius. Forgetting all about his numb fingers, he held it firmly in his hands. Then, bending down, he softly whispered in her ear, "Please forgive me, my love," and injected the nanites into her neck.

He handed Cornelius the syringe and placed his head on her chest. After a few seconds, he raised back up.

"She doesn't have a heartbeat. Does that mean she's gone?" he asked, on the verge of breaking down.

"Normally, yes," Cornelius answered, "but as long as there is brain activity, the nanites can bring her back. The brain doesn't die right when the heart stops; it can go on for seconds, or even minutes. There's no set timeline. Once the nanites reach their destination, they'll restart her heart and lungs and bring her back."

"How can the nanites possibly get where they need to go?"

"Trust me, Rob," he said softly. "They'll get there."

Chapter 9

GONE FISHING

Robert felt helpless sitting there next to Katherine's lifeless body. He'd gently stroke her arm and caress her hand, hoping against hope that she'd respond. He trusted Cornelius and had already seen what the nanites could do. Still, this seemed different. Katherine quit breathing before receiving the injection. I wouldn't say Robert was feeling optimistic. He'd lost too much in his life to believe in miracles. Still confused by the whole thing, I turned towards Cornelius.

"How long until she's better?" I asked.

"It varies, from minutes to hours. It all depends on the individual and how much damage was done. We just need to be ready to give her the second shot as soon as she comes to."

With that, he retrieved the box and loaded a second syringe.

"Would you mind?" he asked, handing it to me. "There's no chance of you dying from the cold, but Robert and I need to get warmed up."

"I was meaning to ask you about that," I said, moving over to Katherine's side. "How did my arm heal in minutes, when it took Ben several hours? Not only that, but it wasn't even painful."

I'll try to simplify it as much as possible," Cornelius said. "Before you get injected with the nanites, your body is pure — genetically, that is. The first round does an inventory of your entire system and starts to rebuild it. They read your DNA and build a completely new set of blueprints for your entire body based on what they find. For some reason, though, they always end up wanting to destroy everything at once and start over. The second shot of nanites destroys the first round and carries on.

"Try to picture wanting to remodel an old home. The first group goes in and figures out how the place looked in its heyday. The first thing they do is create a set of plans to follow and then begin the work. They soon decide it would just be easier to knock the place down and start over. The second group goes in and focuses on the remodel. Since they didn't have to recreate the blueprints like the first group did, they're more willing to fix the issues rather than start over. When it comes to broken bones, blood would normally clot around the break. Phagocytes clean the bone fragments and kill the germs. Afterwards, a small callous made mostly of collagen..."

He went on for several minutes explaining in detail how the nanites do a lot of the work the blood would normally do, and how there's a difference between DNA and RNA. To be honest, I never fully understood what the nanites did, even after he explained it, but I didn't really care to know. I was just happy they worked.

Cornelius and I took turns during the night keeping the fire hot. With the sun beginning to clear the horizon, we could already feel the cool night air warming to greet the day.

Except for Katherine, we were still wearing just our underwear. Robert and I had both managed to lose our bags in the river. I also used Cornelius' shirt to start the fire, while Katherine was wearing his pants to help keep her warm.

I admit things looked sketchy from the outside — three grown men wearing nothing but boxers hovering over the body of a young woman. I was just grateful we had the fire and didn't need to cuddle to keep warm.

Rising up from my bed on the dirt, I made my way to a standing position.

"How are you doing, Rob?" I asked as I stretched my arms and arched my back to help loosen my muscles.

He watched me for a second. "I think I'm doing OK. Katherine still hasn't taken a breath, but her color is almost back. I just don't get it, though; don't you need to breathe to stay alive?"

"Not according to Cornelius. He told me I could've breathed in all the water I wanted last night and it wouldn't have made a difference. I didn't really understand all the mumbo-jumbo he said about the way these things work, and I'm sure as hell not going to try and breathe underwater."

"I didn't say you could breathe underwater," Cornelius stated as he stood up to join us. "What I said was that it wouldn't kill you. The nanites supply your body with the oxygen it needs to sustain life. You wouldn't actually breathe the water; your lungs would just fill up with it. Then, after you were back on dry land, your body would naturally force it out of your lungs and you'd start breathing again."

"What if I were underwater for a week?" I asked sarcastically.

"Then you would be dead, and the fish would eat you," Cornelius snapped back sarcastically. "Speaking of which, I'm starving."

"Rob, if you're OK here alone taking care of Kat, Cornelius and I will go locate a car and hopefully some food."

"What do I do if she wakes up?" he asked, his voice strained with fear. "I don't want to give her the shot at the wrong time and kill her."

Cornelius took a long look at the two of them together, her hand clutched tightly in Robert's.

"Don't worry, Rob, you'll know when it's time. Just remember she may be confused, in pain, or maybe both when she comes to. When she does, just do your best to comfort her after you give her the shot. It doesn't matter where you stick her with the needle; just do it quickly, and then let her sleep."

He said his good-byes to us as we left without ever removing his eyes from Katherine. He'd seen firsthand the pain Ben went through when he came to and swore to himself he would limit her pain as much as possible.

As Cornelius and I worked our way back up toward the dam, it became apparent just how lucky we were. From our perch some twenty feet above the river, it was obvious that the swift, turbulent waters should've taken us all to our graves — or at least those of us without the nanites. It wasn't just the speed or temperature of the water as much as the undertow. In fact, after locating the truck, we could see where the current had actually pulled it upstream, into a deep crevice.

Shaking off the chills from the view, we continued toward the parking lot. We hoped the visitor center we passed on the way down would have a souvenir shop. If they did, we might be able to get some clothes and hopefully a snack. We were just reaching the remains of the lower building, the one the drone destroyed, when Cornelius stopped me.

"How are you feeling today?" he asked.

"I'm worried about Katherine, but other than that, I've never felt better," I replied. "Why do you ask?"

"You look a little younger and more full of life than you normally do. As far as Katherine goes, you have nothing to worry about. Once she receives the second injection, she'll be better than ever."

I knew firsthand how effective the nanites were and believed Cornelius when he said not to worry. I was curious, however, what changes he'd seen in me.

Reaching the visitor center, we walked past a row of offices with one-way glass. The tinting gave a nice mirror effect, allowing me to see my reflection. I slowly made my way up to the building and raised my hand to touch the glass. I couldn't believe I was really looking at myself; there had to be some mistake. My once thinning hair was now full and dark, while my unshaven beard and mustache resembled that of a young man. Even my body seemed fit and muscular.

I've always been told our eyes never change, but I saw a spark in them that hadn't been there for a great many years. For a moment, I stood in front of the glass, flexing my muscles and trying different poses.

"Holy shit!" I said excitedly as I turned to see my rear in the reflection. "Michelle is going to love this."

"Easy there, big guy," Cornelius laughed. "Let's get you covered up before you excite yourself."

"Oh my God, this is just so cool," I said, reaching for the door a few feet away. "I look better now than I did in my twenties."

"I'll take credit for that," Cornelius said, following me into the building. "We were doing a lot of amazing things in the field of cell regeneration. I just can't believe they bastardized my work the way they did. I could've made the whole world young."

"I guess there really is a yin for every yang," I said. "The universe just doesn't allow it any other way."

"I know," Cornelius said sadly. "I just never thought that creating the fountain of youth could cause so much death."

We didn't speak any more about it that day. Dwelling on the things we couldn't change would just tarnish the life we were trying to create. Our past would never be forgotten, and we'd just do our best not to repeat the vile things that others had done. Today, however, was a new day — one that had never been seen before, nor would ever be seen again. It was up to us to make this the best day ever.

Looking around, we noticed this building wasn't just a visitor center. It was also a museum of sorts on the history of the dam. We found many photos taken during its construction, including the towns the lake had consumed. There was also a brief history on the events that created the need for such a project. Hidden off to one side of the room was a large display case exhibiting the various minerals discovered in the process.

With all the things in this room, one thing really stood out, and Cornelius was the first to notice it.

"Hey, Steve!" he shouted from across the room. "Come take a look at this display case."

I made my way over to where he was and looked in.

"So," I said, sounding a little disappointed as I looked in at more rocks. "Is this really the type of thing that gets you excited?"

"Look closer, smartass!" he shot back.

"Holy shit!" I said, sounding surprised. "You and Robert can no longer hang out together; you're getting to be a regular potty mouth. Now, let's see what's so impressive in here."

Trying to pay more attention this time, I slowly studied the rocks. I saw limestone, obsidian, several different colors of quartz, and even some fool's gold. Yet nothing really stood out.

"OK, I'm still not sure what's so impressive," I said, beginning to get bored.

"Look at the quartz. Isn't it beautiful the way they have the light reflecting off it?"

Taking one last look, I figured I would just act excited to placate him. Then I noticed what he was trying to show me. It wasn't the rocks at all; it was the fact that the light in the display case was on.

"What in the world!" I exclaimed, truly surprised. "How can they have power here?"

"It may be possible that all the breakers in the system haven't been tripped," Cornelius stated. "There's also a chance that this place is getting its power directly from the substation below the dam. Regardless of why it's still on, I just feel good knowing we can restore power if we ever need to."

"That may be very beneficial when we begin to rebuild," I agreed. "My first concern, however, is to find some food and clothes. Then we need to locate some type of vehicle and get back to Robert and Katherine. I'm not overly comfortable leaving them alone down there."

"Are you worried the drone may come back?" Cornelius asked.

"No, I just don't trust those two alone together. I think Katherine might've been faking all this just so they could fool around."

Cornelius stared blankly at me. Then it finally sunk in, and he realized I was making fun of his drone response.

"Smartass!" he laughed as he walked away.

I followed him as he made his way to the second floor. It was there that we came upon a small gift shop, containing t-shirts, jackets, and even some sweatpants. As we were getting dressed, I noticed the glow from a vending machine across the room. While Cornelius grabbed some extra clothes for the others, I put myself in charge of getting snacks. I'll admit I'd always wanted to break the glass out of one of those things.

After loading a box full of cold drinks and goodies, I met back up with Cornelius. He'd finished his shopping and was looking out one of the windows facing the parking lot.

"Looks like slim pickings out there," I said, walking up next to him.

"I'm sure you'll find something fun to drive," he replied. "You always do."

We carried our boxes downstairs and made our way outside. Finding a vehicle didn't go smoothly, though. The first two we came to were locked, and the third vehicle had a dead battery. Cornelius suggested swapping batteries, but without tools, it turned out to be a daunting task. After wasting nearly twenty minutes, we gave up on the idea.

Going back empty-handed wasn't an option, so we decided to take off walking. A road sign near the edge of the parking lot pointed us in the direction of the boat ramp. Since we hadn't passed any other vehicles for nearly a mile the night before, we opted to head that direction.

We'd only walked a few minutes before reaching another parking lot. A sign at the entrance said Fisherman's Point. Cornelius instantly set his sights on an old Volkswagen van covered with peace symbols and flowers. Being that it was an older vehicle, even if it didn't have keys we could at least hotwire it. All the other vehicles had been too new to do that. Besides having locking steering wheels, the newer cars all had some other type of antitheft device.

Climbing inside, I instinctively reached above the visor. I figured the person who owned a van with daisies and peace symbols painted all over it still had trust in their fellow man. I was right; gathering up the keys, I stuck one in the ignition and hoped for the best. I pumped the gas pedal and the motor sputtered and came to life.

Cornelius had been checking out a Chevy pickup that was nearby, just in case, when he heard the motor start. Running up to the side of the van, he slid the side door open and froze in place. There in front of him where the seats should've been were four psychedelic-colored bean bag chairs.

"Somebody pinch me," he finally said after taking it all in. "This is the coolest van ever."

I looked back at him, hoping he wasn't serious, but at first glance I knew it was true. He looked like a young child at Christmas, wide-eyed, full of wonder and excitement. Shutting the door behind himself as he climbed inside, he flopped into one of the bean bag chairs, his eyes fixated on a Bob Marley poster.

"Oh my God!" he exclaimed, running his hands over it. "It's actually signed; that means Bob Marley himself has touched this poster."

I laughed to myself as I backed out of the parking space and took off towards the others. Looking at Cornelius with his taped-up glasses and bowl haircut, you instantly thought nerd or bookworm. Truthfully, that was an accurate comparison, but something about him changed the second he entered the van.

"You know," he said, now sitting on his knees between the front seats, "my grandfather met Bob in person in 1966. He'd just moved to the U.S. and was working with DuPont. He was going by a different name at the time, but he confided in my grandfather that his real name was Bob. My grandfather had just graduated and was working for DuPont. They were either lab techs or something like that.

"Anyhow, my grandfather said the two of them used to hang out after work and play music. Some nights they stayed up so late that my grandfather would end up being late for work. Bob was only there for a short time, and then he went to some auto manufacturer and they lost contact. It was probably a good thing, though, or I think my grandfather would've lost his job."

He was so passionate about his story that the drive back seemed way too short. I could tell by his enthusiasm that his grandfather had really taken a liking to the man. Shoot, by the way he was talking, it was almost as if he were the one who knew him.

Pulling to a stop about fifty yards away from Robert and Katherine, I slowly looked around at the beautiful scenery.

"What do you say we go fishing?" I unwittingly blurted out, as my mouth made the decision without me.

"Could we really?" Cornelius asked excitedly, just as wide-eyed as before. "My grandfather used to take me all the time."

Realizing I was in too deep to back out, I shot him a reassuring smile.

"Let's do it. That is, if Katherine is safe and feeling up to it. If so, I think it would do us all good to spend the day at the lake."

The more I thought about it, the better the idea seemed. We could spend a few hours not thinking about drones and bad people, but actually relaxing. Robert would finally get to sit still and fish for a while without interruptions, and Cornelius could join him. It would also offer Katherine some downtime to recuperate further. Then, as a bonus, we might have a nice fish dinner to cap it off.

Cornelius and I were pumped up about the idea as we made our way towards the others. We could see Robert was still sitting on the ground, Katherine's head in his lap. Her eyes closed as he ran his fingers through her hair. He watched her intently, with a soft smile on his face. The smile was all I needed to be reassured everything was OK.

"What's up, guys?" Robert asked, looking up at us.

"We're going fishing!" Cornelius happily informed him.

"Are you serious?" he asked, looking towards me, his eyes now as bright as Cornelius'.

"Sure, why not," I answered back. "I think we've earned a day off just to play."

"Yes!" Robert exclaimed, pumping his right fist to his side. "I've wanted to get some fishing in ever since we first got to the lake."

"Well, today you'll get your chance," I assured him. "How's Katherine doing?"

"It was a little rough shortly after you left. She woke up fighting me, and I almost dropped the needle. I finally just stuck her in the butt with it, and she calmed right down."

"Do you feel like carrying her a little ways?" I asked. "We have a van at the end of the road about a stone's throw away."

"Just show me the way," he said, gently lifting Katherine into his arms. "Man, you have no idea how badly I wanted off this ground. I think my ass actually fell asleep."

Laughing at Robert's remark, Cornelius picked up his and Katherine's bags and then followed us to the van. He was still a few steps behind when Robert got his first look at it. He turned towards me with a disapproving look in his eyes.

"Really, Steve?" he asked, not sounding amused. "That's not a van; it's a freaking hippie mobile."

"Calm down, Rob. It's the only thing I could get running. Besides, Cornelius thinks it's the best thing since sliced bread."

"Are you shitting me? Nerd boy is actually a hippie?"

"Not a hippie," Cornelius answered, catching up to him. "I like to think of myself as more of a free spirit."

"Whatever, nerd boy," Robert said with a smirk. "Just don't try any of that love-in shit with me!"

Feeling his oats, Cornelius took both bags into his left hand and slapped Robert on the butt with his right.

"No promises there, big boy," he said, quickly getting beyond his reach.

"You little son of a—"

Robert didn't finish what he was saying as he chased Cornelius all the way to the van. He still held Katherine in his arms. She was tired but awake, and I could tell by the smile on her face that she was happy to be part of our crazy little group. The spectacle the three of them made caused me to laugh aloud. It made me feel good to see everyone safe and happy together.

With everyone loaded up in our little hippie mobile, we made our way back up to the visitor center. Once there, we unloaded and made our way back inside. Robert opted to use a few of the bean bags from the van to make Katherine a bed. Cornelius took a turn by her side, while Robert and I checked the rest of the building. We were able to locate the break room, complete with another set of vending machines and an employee shower. I took some fruit that still looked edible out of one machine and returned to Katherine and Cornelius.

Robert stayed behind to take a shower and freshen up. He grabbed some fresh clothes and a towel that Cornelius gathered for him from the gift shop. The idea of a long, hot shower was more than appealing. It had been a long, cold night filled with worry and anticipation. Now that Katherine was out of the woods, and would soon be her old self again, Robert could finally relax.

Cornelius slowly ate the apple I gave him. With the amount of calories we'd exerted in the last twelve hours, I figured he would've eaten it much more ravenously. The idea of eating was pleasing to me, but I was far from being hungry. I was beginning to realize that the nanites were changing more than just my broken bones.

When I'd seen my reflection earlier, I just assumed the lack of food along with plenty of exercise had gotten me back into shape. After giving it some thought, it dawned on me that the nanites probably played a much bigger role than starvation. That was the only way to explain my hair getting darker and thicker.

I was just about to say something to Cornelius when Katherine decided to sit up. She turned her head, looked around the room, and smiled at me. Then she gently sighed.

"Other than the two of you, everything smells so fresh. Especially those apples and oranges you brought us."

I knew what she meant; that was the first thing I noticed after receiving the nanites also. Everything seemed to be so much more fragrant. Unfortunately, that sense seemed to come and go at times.

Robert entered the room as she finished talking. As they made eye contact, a huge smile lit up her face.

"You, my dear, smell the best," she said, holding her hand out for him.

"I bet you say that to all the guys that save your life," Robert said as he reciprocated the gesture.

"Not really," I said, interrupting them. "Cornelius helped save her, and she basically said he smelled like shit."

"Dick!" Cornelius responded as he threw his apple core at me. "We're going to be getting stinky and dirty anyways, so what do you guys say we go fishing now and clean up later?"

"That all depends on Kat and whether or not she's up to it," I reminded him.

"To be honest," she said, "I feel pretty damn good."

"Well, that settles it," I said as Robert helped Katherine to her feet. "Let's go find some gear and make a day of it."

"I saw some poles and tackle boxes in that pickup back at Fisherman's Point," Cornelius stated.

"Not so fast," Robert said, glancing at the apple cores on the ground. "I'm starving; what's there to eat?"

"Here," I said, handing him an apple. "We still have three apples and two oranges left, not to mention a box full of junk food in the van. I had them on the floor near the front seat. I guess I got sidetracked earlier and forgot to tell you."

"That will work for now," Robert said, taking a bite of his apple, "but I think smoked bass would taste a lot better."

"Well then, let's get a move on," I said, heading toward the exit.

Cornelius was so excited he shot past me and out the door.

"I call shotgun!" he yelled, halfway to the van.

"Seems like somebody's starting to loosen up a bit," Katherine said with a slight laugh.

"There's definitely something different about that boy," Robert said as he held the door open for Katherine. "He doesn't seem anything like he did when we first met him."

As we got to the van, Robert again opened the door and waited for Katherine to get inside. Cornelius, on the other hand, was already sitting in the passenger seat, squirming around like a little kid.

"We forgot the bean bags," Robert stated as he entered the van. "Do you want me to run back in and grab them?"

"Don't worry about it; we still have two," Katherine said as she pulled Robert down on them next to her.

Glancing back at them, I couldn't help but smile. Katherine might've been a little rough around the edges, but in so many ways, she reminded me of my Michelle. Always doing little things to make the one she loves feel special. After everything Robert had told me about his past, it was nice to see him fall so deeply in love.

We were at our destination in just a few minutes. Cornelius was out of the van almost before it came to a complete stop. Racing to the pickup, he excitedly grabbed the two poles in the back and a tackle box.

Robert and Katherine exited the van and joined Cornelius at the truck. Spying a cooler, Robert reached into the bed and pulled it out.

"What do you say we take a peek?" he said hopefully.

"Be careful," I warned him. "Anything in that cooler has been there a month. If it had any type of meat or dairy, it may smell pretty rancid."

"Good point," Katherine said, stepping back a little. "For some reason, everything smells much stronger today. I really don't want a direct shot of rotting food."

Robert didn't care; he just loved getting into things. If there was even the slightest chance the cooler contained beer, nothing was going to stop him.

"Jackpot!" he yelled, pulling the lid off. "The only thing the guy had in here was Coors light."

"Extremely warm Coors light," I reminded him.

"No problem," Robert said. "I saw two bags of ice in the freezer back there in the break room. I'll run back and grab it while the rest of you get set up."

Before anyone could answer, Robert had the cooler in the van and was gone. I turned to make a comment to Cornelius about it, but he was halfway down the path heading towards the lake.

"Do you think they're a little excited?" Katherine asked me as she pulled a blanket from inside the truck.

"I did kind of get that impression," I laughed.

Making our way towards the water, we met up with Cornelius. He had one pole already in the water and was getting ready to cast the second. It was odd to see him act like that. He wasn't the staunch scientist we made him out to be. He actually had other likes and interests.

While Katherine spread the blanket out and took a seat, I set out to explore the area around us. This new world of ours fascinated me. At times, I felt somewhat like an explorer studying an ancient land. Even though this was the world I grew up in, very little was the same. Not to mention it was fascinating to me to see what people were doing when they died. I figured a thousand years from now, people would be doing the same thing. I was just getting a jump on them.

The temperature here was much warmer than I was used to back home. It wasn't even ten a.m. yet, and already it was in the eighties. Other than a small thunderhead way off to the southwest, the sky was clear. The lake looked amazing; with little to no breeze, the water was like glass.

Making my way around the small bend, I could see a boat ramp and parking lot up ahead. Heading towards it, I came upon two men lying next to some fishing equipment. Some small remnants of arrows were left in them. Their bodies were still intact, a few feet from the lawn chairs they'd been sitting in. They didn't appear to be mutilated in any way, but they'd begun to shrivel like dried prunes. Curious as to whom they might've been, I removed a wallet from one of the men's pockets.

Pulling out his driver's license, I read his name, Clarence Woods. As I studied it, I noticed he was also from Oregon, and was born in 1941. He must've been retired by now, I thought as I pulled an old faded picture out of one of the card slots. It was two people, a man and a woman, panning for gold. Turning the picture over, I could barely make out the faded writing on the back: *Gliela and I, French Gulch 1981*. Taking another long look at the picture, I tried to remember back that far. It seemed like a million years ago.

Feeling empathy for them, I carefully returned both of them back into their lawn chairs. Then, just for good measure, I stuck the fishing poles in their hands. I don't know why it affected me so much, but it just seemed from the time that picture was taken until now was too short.

We grow up with all these dreams and ambitions, but before we know it, our bodies become broken and worn out. By the time we finally do get to retire, we're no longer able to do the things we once loved. I took one last look at them sitting there. "I hope that they had more happy days than sad days," I thought to myself, and then I turned and walked away.

I finished making my way to the boat ramp and studied the vehicles around the parking lot. There must've been a lot of chaos here at the time of the attack. Cars, trucks, and trailers all intertwined together on the narrow road leading in and away from there. A large four by four was resting on top of a boat trailer that had been pulled by a gorgeous motor home. It was evident none of the bodies had been moved from this area. The bloody drones had killed many people. All of those appeared to either have been eaten or drug off by animals, leaving just the ones that were killed by the arrows.

Looking into a car that the bloody drones had attacked, I spied what was left of a half-eaten body. For a moment, I felt a little uneasy. It dawned on me that the animals that ate these people had gotten a taste for man. What was stopping them from coming after all of us?

I was studying the landscape around me, looking for possible threats, when a noise coming from inside the RV startled me. It wasn't the sound of an animal or something being knocked over; it was the sound of a gas burner coming on. As I made my way over to it, I could see the heat radiating off an exhaust port on its side.

"The refrigerator!" I excitedly said aloud.

I made my way into the RV and quickly located it. It was a large double door unit, much larger than any I'd ever seen in other RVs. Opening the freezer compartment, I was overjoyed to see several packages wrapped in white freezer paper. One by one, I pulled the packages out and set them on the table. There were eight total, all of which were marked T-bone. Rummaging through the cabinets and drawers, I grabbed a couple of empty boxes and filled them with the meat, canned goods, a can opener, pots, pans, and utensils. I even found some clean socks and a handgun; I needed both since losing mine in the river. I also found one special item that I placed in my pocket for later.

Exiting the RV, I carried the boxes down towards the water. There, tied to the dock, was a beautiful red and white twenty-one foot open-bow Seaswirl. It looked like it might've been an older boat, but it was in excellent condition. I placed the two boxes on to the dock and then dropped into the driver seat and turned the key — nothing. Then I remembered they usually have a shut-off switch for the batteries. Looking around, I located a dual battery switch. It was in the off position. I turned it to engage both batteries and returned to the driver seat to try again. The inboard motor instantly came to life. While it warmed up, I retrieved the boxes from the dock and untied the boat.

The motor purred as I backed away and turned the boat around. The sound of the motor cut through the silence as I made my way back to the others. It took only a couple of minutes before I could see them. All three stood near the edge of the water watching me. At first, they weren't sure who it was. All they knew was that a boat was making its way towards them. As I got closer, we made eye contact. Recognizing me, Cornelius ran into the water and held up a large bass tied to a homemade stringer.

"Nice job!" I said, sliding the nose of the boat up onto the shore next to them.

"You stole a boat?" Robert said, ribbing me. "I swear, I just can't take you anywhere. Here, have a beer."

"Not just yet," I said, picking up one of the boxes. "I'll save mine to help wash down my steak dinner."

"Bullshit!" Robert yelled as he grabbed the box.

Setting it on the ground, he pulled a package out of the box and read the writing.

"T-bones! Are you serious? Where the hell did you find frozen T-bones?"

"There's a twenty-four hour mini-mart right around the corner. The sign said 'always open,' so I took a chance."

"Really!" he exclaimed with a gullible look.

"Seriously, Rob, you dumbass," I said jokingly. "Do you really believe there's a store open anywhere?"

"You never know with those little mini-marts," he said, looking serious. "I saw one half destroyed in Eureka years ago after an earthquake. That little bastard was still open."

"Right," I said skeptically. "Anyhow, I was walking next to an RV when I heard the refrigerator kick on. I took a chance and checked it out."

"Nice job, genius!" Katherine said. "I suppose we'll let them thaw out and eat them raw?"

"Sounds good," Cornelius said happily. "That leaves more fish for me."

"That's one option," I said, reaching for the second box. "Or we could build a fire with the lighter I found and put the steaks in this here frying pan."

Katherine reached over and grabbed the box from me. Going through it, she gave me a huge smile.

"You actually brought a frying pan and vegetables!" she squealed with delight as she unpacked the box.

"You must really be hungry," I said, reaching into my pocket.

"I'm actually not hungry at all," she said. "I just wanted to make you guys a home-cooked meal to thank you for saving my life."

"Don't thank us," I laughed. "Thank the na—"

Robert cut me off mid-sentence.

"I told you, honey, you don't have to thank us," he said, giving me an odd look. "We did it because we all love you."

He signaled me with a nod of his head while he spoke. Having a sudden inkling that I almost said the wrong thing, I removed my hand from my pocket and made an excuse to pull Robert to the side.

"I believe I saw some wild berries earlier. Care to give me a hand with them, Rob?"

"Glad to, buddy," Robert said as he followed me.

I turned to him when we were a safe distance away.

"What's up?" I asked.

"She was talking earlier about how grateful she was that we saved her without using the nanites. Steve, she was very adamant about us not using them."

"She's going to find out sooner or later. You know that, right?" I questioned.

"Sure, I know. I just don't have the heart to tell her right now."

Reaching back into my pocket, I took out a small box.

"There!" I said, handing it to Robert. "I found this in the RV. It's an engagement ring. I know you love Katherine and figured you might have a use for it. Don't worry about the nanites. That girl loves you to the moon and back. Trust me, it will all work out."

Staring at the ring in the box, Robert reached out with his right arm and pulled me in for a hug.

"I don't ever want to do anything to hurt her," he said in a somber tone. "I'm just worried I'll somehow fuck this up too."

I could tell he was envisioning his past by the tone in his voice. It was the same as when he told me about losing his fiancée.

"This is a whole new world, Rob," I said calmly. "We all have a clean slate."

With that, we turned and headed back down to the others.

"Where are the berries?" Katherine asked as we reached them.

"I guess I was mistaken," I answered back.

"No worries," she said happily. "I can still make you guys an amazing meal. Why don't the three of you enjoy your fishing while I start a fire?"

"Sounds good to me," I said, grabbing one of the poles. "I could use a little downtime with my family."

Robert and Cornelius had just taken a seat next to me when a large rock suddenly splashed in the water next to us.

Chapter 10

A VISITOR

It had been a refreshingly peaceful and calm day on the lake. Without even the slightest hint of a breeze, the water was as close to glass as it could be. Other than ourselves, the only sounds we heard were the birds singing in the trees or an occasional deer coming down to get a drink. Our minds focused on relaxing and spending time together.

When the rock hit the water, the sound it made sent a wave of fear through the four of us. We were so caught up in the moment that we'd completely let down our guard. The realization of our carelessness tore through each of us; we suddenly felt naked and vulnerable

I could feel the rise in my body temperature as adrenaline pulsed through my veins. Every ounce of my being told me to run, yet I was frozen in place. I wasn't frozen from fear for myself as much as I was for the others. If any of us made a sudden move, there was no telling how our unknown visitor would react.

The others must have all felt the same, and for a moment, we remained motionless. Then slowly, in unison, we all turned our heads to face the source of the disturbance.

"Josh!" Robert called out. "What the hell are you doing here?"

"Something told me that if I weren't around, you would all just goof off. So I figured I'd sneak up and see what you were doing — and here you are!"

"Very funny, asshole," Katherine said with a big smile. "We're just glad it's you."

"Seriously! Why are you here?" I asked, a little upset.

It wasn't that I didn't want him there. It was just that I was counting on him to deliver my letter to Michelle.

"You guys are all the family I have left."

"We could tell by the statement that he'd found the answer he was looking for.

"Are you OK?" I asked, feeling a little guilty about my earlier tone. I sometimes forgot that even though I'd lost a lot in the attacks, most had lost everything.

"I'll make it," he said somberly.

His head was down as he did his best not to make eye contact. Still, we could tell the moment we saw him that he'd been crying and probably hadn't slept. He even had some cuts and bruises on his face and arms.

"Come on down and join us," Katherine said warmly. "Steve found us some steaks and canned veggies."

We all watched quietly as he made his way to us. Taking a seat on a rock next to Katherine, he finally looked up at us. It was obvious he wanted to share his story, so as Katherine continued cooking, the rest of us took a seat close to him.

"Just for future reference. A little gas goes a long way. When that place exploded, I thought for sure I was a goner. After I shot out the window, I took off running deeper into my hiding spot. It was a good thing I did; the stove landed right where I'd been standing."

Josh continued his story, telling us that after the explosion, he stayed in the storage unit until he heard the drone fly by.

"There was debris everywhere, so it took a little longer than I'd planned to get out of there. Once outside, I tried to see if I could locate you, but because of all the smoke, I found that to be impossible. I could hear the drone every now and again, and occasionally I even heard some explosions. I continued sitting there a good thirty minutes without hearing anything and figured it must be over.

"The sun had already set, and there was just enough daylight left to grab a boat and make it back to Ben and the others. Let me tell you, that boy is sure crazy about that girl we saved. I gave him the letters and then went back to the boat ramp where we first arrived. I know I said I was going to find my family first and then join Ben, but after you left, I got scared. That was when I decided to change the plan. I made sure Ben would take the letters to Michelle before looking for my family. Then, regardless of what the outcome was, I was going to locate all of you."

We all sat quietly as time to time he paused, trying not to break down. Finally, with tears flowing, he tried to go on.

"I pretty much knew my wife and son were gone, and I couldn't stand the thought of losing you guys too."

Katherine stopped cooking and sat down next to him, wrapping her arms around his neck. Josh looked softly at her.

"You know the really odd part?" he asked.

We all shook our heads.

"For the most part, the whole neighborhood looked exactly as it did when I left. Going back, it felt as if I were in some other dimension. You know, like the twilight zone."

"Well, we're just glad you're back safe with us," I told him.

"That still doesn't explain how you found us," Robert quickly spoke up.

"I took a chance you might still be in the area. I figured on looking down by the river, but as I came over the hill, I heard everyone talking. The sound carried on the water, so it was difficult to tell exactly where you were. I checked the boat launch first, and then figured you must be over closer to the dam."

"That's odd," I responded. "You could hear us talking, but we couldn't hear your vehicle."

"That's because I rode a bicycle."

"Why the hell would you do that?" Robert asked, giving him a dumb look.

"Oh yeah, I almost forgot," he said. "After I got to my house, I got angry and broke a bunch of stuff. Then, to cool off, I went for a walk. I was planning to go back to grab some pictures and personal items when I came upon another group of slaves and drones. That was when I grabbed a bike and came looking for you. I was afraid they'd hear a car."

Everyone suddenly came alive with questions.

"What! Are you sure they were slaves?" I asked.

"Where did you see them?" Robert chimed in.

"Did you actually see the drones?" Katherine asked.

Even Cornelius seemed to be excited about the news of more survivors.

"Are you sure they were slaves?" he asked suspiciously. "You said the neighborhood looked like it did when you left. Why would they be in an area that's already been cleared?"

His question made sense. If they were slaves doing cleanup, Josh would've seen bodies somewhere along the way. I could see the wheels turning as he thought about it.

"You know," Josh finally said, "they were in pretty good shape for being slaves, and I believe they were all dressed the same. I didn't actually see any drones; I just assumed they were there."

There was a little more discussion while we tried to make sense of it.

"One thing is for sure," Robert said as he reeled in his line. "We need to find more firepower; everything we had ended up in the river."

"I have a handgun I found in the RV," I informed him.

"I don't think that'll be enough," he said. "If these aren't slaves, then they could be more guards. Josh, do you know where any gun stores are around here?"

"I believe there's one back the way you came," he said. "If not, I definitely know where there's a pawn shop. They had a whole bunch of guns the last time I was in there."

"That won't work," Robert told him. "Most pawn shops don't carry ammo — just a few weapons."

"What about the police station?" I ask hopefully.

Robert's eyes lit up. "Holy shit!" he said excitedly. "I never even thought of that."

I turned back to Josh. "Can we make it to the police station without passing the area where you saw them?"

"Easily," he said. "The state police have a station alongside the freeway. It's located between my house and here."

"That's it," I said. "Let's load up and go."

"Bullshit!" Katherine said angrily. "I made food for everyone and I expect it to be eaten."

"We can eat in the van!" Robert said excitedly.

Katherine glared at him. "I didn't go to the trouble of cooking just to have you scarfing it down on the road. We're going to sit here and actually enjoy our food."

Robert sat back down reluctantly, as Cornelius moved over next to him.

"You know, Rob," he said nonchalantly, "back in my lab, I have equipment that could help us locate your balls."

Before Robert could react, Katherine smacked Cornelius on the back of the head. "Keep it up, and I swear even your fancy equipment won't be enough to locate yours."

Robert smiled and winked at Cornelius. "Welcome to the club, old buddy."

We all got a good laugh and felt more at ease as we enjoyed our meal. We were ready to load up and go by two o'clock. Cornelius reluctantly released his fish and gathered up his pole. Robert grabbed his from where he'd laid it and picked up the tackle box.

"One of these days, I'm going to actually get the chance to just sit and fish," he said as he took up the rear.

Josh was out in front a few yards as we reached the parking lot. Heading straight for the Chevy pickup, he yelled out, "Shotgun!"

"You're going to be awful lonely sitting there all by yourself," Katherine ribbed as we got in the van.

For a moment, Josh stood there giving us a strange look.

"Are you serious?" he called out as I backed up the van.

"Afraid so," I said, stopping next to him.

Opening the side door, Cornelius stuck his head out, grinning from ear to ear.

"You're gonna love it. They took all the seats out of the back, so we can just sprawl out."

"You go ahead and sprawl; I'm going to sit in a seat," Josh said, opening the passenger door and hopping in. "Is there a reason you picked this over the truck?" he asked, glaring at me.

"Believe me," I said sheepishly. "This wasn't my first choice."

Cornelius was on his knees between us, staring out the front window. "See, isn't this great!" he exclaimed.

Josh shook his head. "I don't think we should let Skippy here pick out our rides anymore."

I gave him a reassuring nod as we headed away from the lake. Josh stopped me when we reached the intersection we'd passed on the way there.

"Don't go that way," he said. "Interstate Five is impassable from this direction. Make a right here and we'll go in on a back road."

We headed down Lake Boulevard. It was nice having Josh back; there was something about his personality that really rounded out our group. Cornelius, on the other hand, had done a complete one-eighty. No longer the subdued intellect, he was spunky and full of life. It was a pleasant change that we all enjoyed, but none more than Cornelius himself.

"Take a left here!" Josh suddenly blurted out as we drove past the side road.

Slowing the van to turn around, I shot Josh a dirty look.

"You do know where we're going, don't you?" I asked suspiciously.

"Sorry, Steve," he answered. "I was lost in my thoughts for a moment. I've been on this road a thousand times, yet it doesn't feel like I've ever been here before."

Turning onto the side road, I nodded at him. He was right; even the mundane things, such as cooking, driving, and bathing, seemed almost unfamiliar. It was slowly sinking in that no matter what we did, this world would never again be the world we once knew.

"Stop the van!" Robert yelled from the backseat.

The urgency in his voice caused me to slam on the brakes, almost skidding off the road. Unaware of the reason for his sudden outcry, I thought it best to obey as swiftly as possible. It might not have been one of my better ideas, as Robert and Katherine both flew forward on top of one another, striking the back of my seat. Josh reacted quickly enough to get his hands on the dash and hold himself in place. Cornelius wasn't so fortunate. Because he'd been on his knees between the front seats, nothing was there to protect him. With the sudden stop, he flew forward, striking his head against the windshield. The dull thud quickly gave way to the sound of breaking glass and a low, deep moan.

"Cornelius, are you OK?" I yelled out.

Quickly sliding out of my seat, I moved him to the back and set him up. I couldn't see any visible signs of injury, but he was a little upset, nonetheless.

"Dumbass!" he said, almost happily. "First you try to kill me, and then you try to paralyze me. You should never move someone after an accident, until you know the extent of their injuries."

I was a little confused. He was chewing my ass; yet at the same time, he was damn near laughing.

"Why the hell are you so happy?" I demanded. "Do you have some sort of brain injury?"

"No, I'm all right. It's just that..." He paused for a moment, contemplating whether he should finish what he was thinking.

"Well, spit it out," Katherine said, sliding up to us. "What is up with you lately?"

"My grandfather only took me fishing twice — both times within a mile of the laboratory. I know it may seem odd to all of you, but this has been the happiest trip I can ever remember."

We all suddenly understood Cornelius better. He wasn't employed to work in the lab as much as he was a slave to it. For the first time in a great many years, he was a free man. My mind suddenly shot back to Robert.

"Dude! Why did you need me to stop so badly?"

"Oh yeah!" Robert exclaimed, as if he'd forgotten. "I thought I saw someone back there in the bushes."

Everyone turned to look out the back window.

"Shouldn't we go look?" Josh asked after a few seconds.

"I don't know, guys," Katherine hesitantly answered. "We really don't have any way of protecting ourselves if we're attacked."

"I have to agree with Kat," Robert reluctantly said. "If it is some sort of ambush, we're sitting ducks."

For what seemed like an eternity, we all stared out the window, unsure of our next move.

"I do have a handgun," I pointed out.

"That's hardly enough to protect all of us," Robert said, shaking his head. "There's just too much that could go wrong."

"It doesn't have to protect all of us," I said, turning to Cornelius. "How sure are you about these nanites?"

"You've seen what they can do," he responded. "I promise, unless you get shot in the head, you're virtually invincible."

"Oh hell no!" Katherine said, putting herself between the door and me. "They may be able to heal broken bones and such, but that doesn't mean they can bring you back from the dead. They can still kill you."

"Yeah, but you heard Cornelius; it would have to be a direct head shot. As long as my brain stays intact, I'll be OK."

"That's bullshit!" Katherine yelled. "What if you get shot in the heart and bleed out? There are no guarantees; it's just too risky."

"You have to trust me," I said somberly. "I've seen what they can do."

"I said no!" Katherine said angrily. "You've seen them heal a minor flesh wound or some broken bones. That's all."

"We've seen more," Robert said as he put his hand softly on her shoulder. "We've seen it bring someone dead back to life."

"What are you talking about? When did you see more?" she asked, giving him a confused look.

As Robert stared into her eyes, she began to cry.

"No, Rob, no!" she sobbed. "I was supposed to have our baby. I've never wanted a family till you. ... Please, no."

As she fell into his arms, he held her tightly.

"Go," he told me. "We'll be OK."

I felt guilty as I left the van. By saving her, we took from her the one thing she wanted most — to give Robert a child, so they could be a family.

Making my way back to where Robert had yelled out, I did my best not to focus on Katherine's words. I could live through most things, but there was still a chance of dying. Not to mention that if I'm shot or taken prisoner, it could put all the others at risk. I needed to stay focused and not do anything foolish. I stared intently at the bushes as I covered the last few yards. Suddenly, I felt a hand on my shoulder.

Turning around quickly, I found myself face-to-face with Katherine. Robert, Josh, and Cornelius were just a few feet behind her. I was standing there bewildered when she put her arms around me.

"Robert reminded me that we already have a family, and family sticks together."

Looking over her shoulder, Robert gave me the thumbs-up. Pulling back, I gave Katherine a bewildered look.

"Don't worry," she said, flashing me a smile. "You and I will take the lead."

A sense of peace came over me. Even with the threat of death looming all around us, they stuck by my side. Time and time again, we'd faced uncertainty, and through it all, we held together. Feeling a new burst of courage, I turned and made my way straight at the bushes.

"Stop!" a voice called out. "I have a gun!"

Hearing the fear in his voice as he spoke, I could tell it was a young man and that he wasn't a threat.

"I'm sure you do," I said calmly, "and I don't blame you. The world has become a scary place."

"What do you want from me?" he asked.

"I just want to make sure you're OK. That's all.

"Then you'll leave me alone?"

"If that's what you want, I promise we'll leave you be."

"Can you tell me what happened?" he called out again in a shaky voice. "Where is everyone?"

His questions caught me off guard. He had to know what had happened; there was no way not to know.

"Do you have amnesia?" I asked, not really believing him.

"No, I don't believe so."

"What's your name?" Katherine asked in a soothing voice.

"It's Kyle, ma'am," he responded after a short pause.

His voice no longer sounded frightened; somehow just hearing her helped him relax.

"How did you do that?" I mouthed quietly to her.

Giving me a sly look, she winked and then continued talking to Kyle.

"You know, Kyle, I'd feel a lot better if you came with us. I promise in time we'll answer all your questions. For now, we're not safe here and we need to keep moving. So, please do me a favor and come with us."

As he slowly came out from behind the bushes, we got our first real look at him. He was dirty from head to toe and about as skinny as a man can get. He was dressed in a torn hospital gown and still had the band on his wrist. Katherine put her hand out to him.

"Come on," she said softly. "You're among friends now."

She and Kyle took the lead while the rest of us followed.

"You were scared of that?" Robert asked sarcastically and laughed. "What a pussy!"

"What do you think happened to him?" Josh asked.

"Could be from a mental institution," Robert stated.

"Not likely. He's wearing a purple medical bracelet," Cornelius pointed out.

"So what does that mean?" Josh questioned.

"He's a DNR. For some reason, he wanted them to just let him die if he quit breathing or his heart stopped."

"That's stupid!" Robert shot back. "Hell, he can't even be thirty years old. Why the fuck wouldn't he want to be brought back?"

He wasn't looking for an answer; he was actually feeling sorry for the guy. To be so young and give up on life told of a painful existence. Robert had been there before; his pain was emotional and not physical, but regardless, it was still enough to make him want to die.

With everyone loaded into the van, we continued over a hill that blocked our view. Just as we crested the top, the plane crash came into sight. It was about a quarter of a mile ahead of us. From the looks of it, the plane had hit just on the other side of the interstate and continued across it. Debris was scattered as far as the eye could see. Bringing the van to a stop, I turned to face Josh in the passenger seat.

"Well, what now, Hoss?"

"Go back to the road we just passed. It should get us close to where we need to go."

I turned the van around and took the first left. I could hear the other four talking quietly in the back. They were too quiet for me to hear over the motor, but spying on them in the mirror, I could tell it was going well.

We were heading through a small neighborhood when suddenly everyone became quiet. Slowing down to about five miles an hour, we all stared out the windows. Before us lay a small city park. It was a grim reminder of just how quickly everyone had died. There were three strollers lined up in front of benches, all facing the playground. Toys and balls lay right where they'd dropped and numerous bicycles were strewn all about. Even the remnants of a dog leash hung loosely from a nearby fence post.

"Where did they all go?" Kyle asked, pressing his face against the glass.

"They died," Katherine said softly. "Didn't you know that?"

"No, I wasn't sure what happened. I woke up in my hospital bed about a week ago. My nurse was lying on the floor next to me, so I started yelling for help. A man came into my room and stared at me for a minute. Then he told me to be as quiet as possible until nightfall. When it was dark, I was to leave town or he'd be back to kill me.

"Then he dragged my nurse out into the hall and put her on a cart with several other bodies. I was scared, so I did exactly as I was told. After it got dark, I made my way out of the hospital and tried to find my way home."

"Where's that?" Katherine asked, trying to keep him talking.

"Just outside of Lovelock."

"I've never heard of it," she responded. "Is that here in California?"

"California!" he exclaimed. "How did I get here?"

"I'm not sure," she replied. "I don't even know how you ended up in the hospital." She gave him a quizzical look. "You're so young; why would you have a do not resuscitate armband?"

"I'm in the last stages of cancer and the pain gets to be unbearable. I just figured if it's my turn to die, there's no sense in prolonging it."

Cornelius slid over to him and poked him in the arm with his finger.

"You don't look like you're in pain. Shoot, you don't even look sick."

Kyle sat there in silence for a moment as he thought about it.

"You know," he said, sounding confused, "I haven't felt any pain since I woke up. I've never even thought about it. The only thing on my mind was trying to figure out what was going on."

Intrigued, Robert jumped into the conversation. "So, you say you don't know where you are, how you got here, and absolutely nothing about the drone attacks?"

"Drone attacks?" he asked, puzzled. "What harm could a drone do?"

Robert went on to fill him in on all the details. It was an interesting conversation, to say the least. Kyle had pretty much decided he'd already died, before we came along, and had somehow ended up in hell. Even though he was saddened by the news Robert shared, he still felt a sense of relief.

We were nearly to the police station when Cornelius moved back between the front seats.

"Haven't you learned your lesson yet?" I asked him, motioning towards the windshield.

"Don't hit the brakes," he pleaded. "I just want to fill you in on this guy."

"I could hear some of it," I told him, "but the motor is too loud to catch it all."

"Did you hear that he still thinks this is December? From what I gathered, he was at home waiting to die and his parents were taking care of him. They just started opening presents when the pain became so severe that he felt like he was going to pass out. The next thing he knew he was waking up in a semi-dark room with a dead nurse."

"How is he taking the news?" Josh asked, looking back to see him.

"Better than most would have, but considering where he thought he was, this is a blessing."

"What could possibly be worse than this?" I asked, a little perplexed.

"Hell!" Cornelius abruptly said. "He actually thought he was in hell."

"Bullshit!" Josh shot back. "I can see why he'd think that if he'd woken up somewhere else. Like maybe Fresno, but Redding is awesome."

"We can all hear you," Katherine yelled up to us.

"Good!" Josh yelled back. "Tell him if he doesn't like it here, he can get out and walk."

He sounded serious, but we all knew he was kidding.

Just to clarify things, Robert interjected, "Now, now, Josh. He didn't say he didn't like it here. He just said it reminded him of hell. Face it, if you went to sleep and it was twenty degrees outside, and you woke up in Redding, you'd think you were in hell too. I mean, seriously! Do you ever have days under one hundred degrees?"

"Sure we do," he chuckled. "We call it winter."

Their banter seemed to help Kyle relax. It was hard enough on all of us, and we knew what happened. I couldn't imagine just waking up to it, and being alone.

Cornelius' mouth dropped open as we pulled into the parking lot of the state police.

"Oh, Steve," he said, almost in disbelief. "Can we change cars and take that instead?"

His eyes were fixated on an all-terrain assault vehicle. It had to be one of the ugliest things I'd ever seen. It was a pasty yellow and nearly twice as long as your average pickup truck. The tires were at least four feet tall and a good foot and a half wide. Instead of having just two axles, this thing had four, two in the front and two in the rear. It had seven windows, which all appeared to be made of bulletproof glass. Five of them were placed like most vehicles, two on the front, two on the side, and one on the rear. The last two were at a forty-five degree angle between the front and sides. There was also a gun turret on top. The weapon was missing, but the mount for it was still there.

Overhearing Cornelius, Robert slid forward to look.

"Holy shit!" Robert hollered. "That is one ugly ride. We're taking it, right?"

"Damn straight!" I said. "We're going to have some fun with this thing."

"What do you mean by having fun?" Katherine demanded.

Robert and I both looked at the vehicle, and then back at Katherine. Almost as if on cue, we both answered, "We're going to run shit over!"

"Oh yeah!" Cornelius responded as he tried to slide past everyone to get out the door.

"Hold tight, Skippy," I said, taking hold of his arm. "First things first. Let's go inside and see if we can locate some decent firepower."

Everyone exited the van, and we made our way to the front doors. Cornelius followed, but he didn't take his eyes off the beast until we were inside the building.

Chapter 11

A Soldier's Story

I'd been expecting the inside of the police station to be dark, but thankfully, they had solar backup lighting. The problem was finding the guns and the ammunition. I figured it would be like the movies and there would be a rack of guns they could choose from. That wasn't the case, at least not out in the main section. The door leading into the back was solid steel, including the framing. The locking system seemed nearly impenetrable, but that didn't matter to Robert and me.

"Well, gentlemen," Katherine said sarcastically, "any other bright ideas?"

Robert and I turned towards each other. "You thinking what I'm thinking?" he asked.

"Hell yeah!" I answered. "We need to find those keys."

"What keys?" Katherine asked. Then it hit her. "Oh no, you don't! Are you guy's crazy?"

"Oh come on, Katherine," Cornelius said excitedly as he rummaged through a drawer. "You know this will be fun. Almost as much fun as blowing up that station wagon."

"OK, but I get to drive this time."

Josh and Kyle stood back and watched as the rest of us ransacked the room, looking for the keys.

"You all right, Kyle?" Josh asked. "You look confused."

"It's just a lot to take in; so far nothing seems real."

"I can understand that; this would be difficult for any of us to wake up to. Trust me, though; just follow their lead. They may seem like they're not playing with a full deck, but they've managed to keep us all alive."

"I get that, but it doesn't make sense going to such extremes just to get a couple of guns. Why don't you all just stay put and enjoy the fact you're still alive?"

Josh gave him an odd look. "This isn't over, you know. There are still people being held as slaves, and if we don't free them, who will? Besides that, until we eliminate whoever is behind this, nobody is safe."

"The best part is it's wicked fun," Robert hollered as he ran past them to search another desk.

Kyle paused for a second, still unsure about the lot of us. "Have you actually saved anyone?"

"Yes, yes we have. How many, I don't know — maybe thirty or forty. It's not so much about the numbers, though. We'd do it even if there were only one."

"Why would you risk your life for just one person?"

Josh put his hand on Kyle's shoulder. "Because it's just the right thing to do."

"I've got them!" Robert yelled as he exposed a wall of keys that were hidden behind a picture.

"Which one is it?" Katherine asked, studying them.

We all scanned the board, looking for anything that stood out. The keys were tagged with names and numbers. We figured the numbers on the keys matched the numbers on the vehicles. The names, however, threw us off: Donut King, Girl Magnet, Speed Racer, and Tricky Dick. We figured that one must have belonged to one of the detectives.

"There it is," I said triumphantly, grabbing a set of keys and showing the others.

"I'm confused," Cornelius said, staring at the keys.

"The Family Truckster #1983 — that doesn't sound like the name of such an awesome machine."

"Oh, you poor child," Katherine laughed, giving him a smile. "You've lived such a sheltered life. The Family Truckster was the car they used in 'National Lampoon's Vacation.' It was a movie from the eighties."

"I still don't get it. This thing is much tougher than any car."

"Trust us," Robert said as I handed the keys to Katherine. "The Truckster was not your daddy's car. That thing was nearly indestructible. When all this is over, I'll locate the movie for you."

"Can you get Kyle and me a copy too?" Josh asked. "I think we have a bit of a generation gap here."

"Fucking kids!" Robert exclaimed. "Sometimes I wonder what they were actually taught in school."

We took a moment to study the door one last time before heading back outside.

"You should really let me drive," Robert insisted.

"Not a chance," Katherine said. "You and Steve both have the habit of overdoing things. This takes finesse. Too little and we don't get inside; too much and you destroy everything on the other side. Trust me, boys; this is a job for a girl."

Josh opted to wait next to the van with Kyle. Until we knew more about him and his cancer, we didn't want to risk putting him through any undue stress. He already had enough on his plate. The rest of us loaded into the Truckster and belted in. It had enough seats and seat belts for thirteen people — two upfront, five on either side, and one in the turret right in the middle.

Katherine studied the instrument panel for a minute and then fired up the beast. It was easy to tell this wasn't some little gas sipper. There was a muffled growl through the whole interior from the roar of the motor.

"You sure about this?" Robert asked her one last time.

"Just hold onto something," she said, shifting it into gear and releasing the clutch.

Katherine pulled out of the parking lot and across the street into an open field. The wide-open space gave her a chance to feel how it handled before attacking the door. We had a ball. That dang thing turned on a dime even at high speeds, and not once did it feel like we might turn over. We even caught air once or twice without shaking our bodies like a bunch of rag dolls.

After Katherine was satisfied with the way it handled, we shot back across the road and reentered the parking lot. She stopped about twenty feet from the front of the building and looked at the controls. Then, reaching down to the floorboard, she shifted it from rear-wheel drive to all-wheel drive and shoved the pedal to the floor.

That made a huge difference in the way it felt to us. Instead of being quick and smooth, it became rigid and staunch. Not only that, but it also changed the lighting and airflow in the cab. The whole interior filled with an eerie red light, and a cool breeze blew gently from the vents.

It was hard to tell whether Katherine was enjoying herself. She had a tight grip on the steering wheel and her eyes glued on the front door of the building. Her teeth were clenched so tightly together that if she'd closed them any tighter, I swear she would've broken her jaw.

Just as we hit the door, Robert, who was sitting next to her, yelled out his approval. I couldn't really tell what he said, but it was obvious he was excited. I sat with my head up in the turret right until impact. Ducking down at the last second, I did my best to watch through the windshield.

It truly was a thing of beauty. Anything in our path was either crushed by our massive weight or tossed about like a child's play toy. Before reaching the steel door, Katherine slammed on the brakes, locking up all eight tires. Sliding the last few yards, we crashed through the doorway, ripping down most of the concrete wall with it. Then, after the vehicle finally came to a stop halfway into the next room, Katherine put it into reverse and backed up just far enough to gain access.

"That's how it's done!" she yelled as she turned off the motor and undid her seat belt.

Undoing his seat belt, Robert grabbed her and pulled her into his arms.

"Holy shit, baby, you did it!" he exclaimed.

As we exited the vehicle, Josh and Kyle cautiously stuck their heads into the large opening that was once the front doors.

"Everyone OK?" Josh asked as he made his way to us.

Kyle came a short ways into the building, turned a chair upright, and took a seat.

"I'll just wait here while you guys do your business."

"I'll sit with you," Katherine said, visibly shaken by the ordeal but still quite amused. "That was a kick in the pants, but now I just need to rest for a bit."

As we first peered into the opening, it was apparent we'd found what we were looking for.

"Tell you what, Rob," I said. "This is your area of expertise. Why don't you and Josh get what we need while I have a word with Cornelius."

While Robert and Josh set off to pillage through the weapons room, Cornelius and I stepped outside to talk in private.

"Is everything OK?" Cornelius asked, feeling a little unsure about me wanting to speak with him alone.

"Yes, I'm just curious about something. I was hoping you might have some insight that would help make sense of it."

"I'll do what I can. What seems to be bothering you?"

"It's Kyle. He claims that he knew nothing of the attacks and his last memories were of Christmas. What do you make of that?"

"Well, it's possible that he was in a comatose state and somehow something was triggered, causing him to wake up."

"I'd considered that, but two things are really eating at me. The first is he was a DNR. Why would they have him on life support if he didn't want to be kept alive? The other thing that bothers me is a claim he made about being in the final stages of cancer. That was nearly six months ago, and other than being skinny he looks totally healthy."

"I've been pondering it myself," Cornelius said, sounding bewildered. "I have a hypothesis, but it's highly speculative."

"English, please," I said, hoping for a clear answer.

"I'm sorry," he said, giving me a strange look. "I was just saying that I have a possible idea, but it'll almost be impossible to prove it under our current circumstances."

"Got ya. So there's a chance he's telling the truth?"

"Yes, but like I said, it's not very plausible. When he lost consciousness, his parents took him to the hospital. As long as he wasn't put on life support, they might still have opted to tube feed him. Now, that doesn't totally go against his wishes. In the unlikely event he'd been drinking water beforehand that had the mutated nanites in it, there's a possibility they somehow attacked his cancer. This would've been done before the addition of the inert gas. At some point during his hospital stay, his heart could've stopped and against his wishes someone used electric shock to restart it. That would've killed the nanites before he was one hundred percent healed but also before the inert gas was added. He would've been tube fed right up to the time of the attack. When his body was just about to shut down due to severe dehydration, it sent a signal to the brain and woke him up. At some point during all of that, he would've had to have been transferred to the hospital here."

"I get what you're saying," I told him confidently. "There ain't a snowball's chance in hell he's telling the truth."

"To put it in a nutshell, yes."

I started walking back into the building when Cornelius stopped me.

"If we can get his medical transcript, we could either disprove his explanation or show it has reasonable merit."

"That settles it then; our first stop will be at the hospital. I need to know if this guy is on the up and up."

When I made it back to the others, Robert was just exiting the vehicle.

"Perfect timing," he said. "We're all loaded up and ready to go. We even found the gun that hooks to the turret."

"I need to have a quick talk with everyone first."

They all gathered around me, including Kyle.

"As you all know," I said, raising my voice to sound authoritative, "Kyle has an amazing story about waking up three weeks after the attack. Normally, stories like his would've been met with some skepticism and then dropped. Unfortunately, we don't have that option. Trust me, Kyle; this isn't anything against you. A lot has changed in the world, and for the safety of everyone, including yourself, we need to confirm as much of your story as possible."

"Yes! Thank you," Katherine exclaimed with a sigh of relief.

"How can you do that?" Kyle asked, sounding hopeful.

"Well, we'll never be able to fully explain everything that's happened to you. What we can confirm is your hospital stay. Do you know what hospital you were in?"

"No, I don't." He suddenly had a scared look on his face. "I didn't even know I was there until the day I woke up."

"I know this town quite well," Josh said, giving him a reassuring smile. "Do you remember anything at all about the outside of the building?"

Kyle stood there thinking for a moment. "It was dark, but I recall seeing a large cross on the front of the building. Oh! I also remember being grateful that I was walking downhill after I left."

"Perfect!" Josh said triumphantly. "That's Mercy Medical. I know right where it is."

Since Josh was the one who knew the city, we elected to let him drive. He took his place in the driver's seat while the rest of us found a spot to sit. For the first time, Robert and Katherine hadn't sat together. I guess he figured girls weren't as much fun as machine guns and strapped himself in at the turret. I took my seat next to Josh, in hopes of learning the city a little better.

I'll admit watching Katherine drive made it look easy — Josh, on the other hand, not so much. He was doing his best to back through the hole she'd made in the center of the building, but he kept getting hung up. After the third attempt, he took advantage of the all-wheel drive and just forced his way out. That ended up being not only more fun, but also necessary, due to the fact we were burning daylight.

Once on the main road, he disengaged the all-wheel drive, making the vehicle handle a lot smoother. For the most part, we managed to travel at a good clip. It wasn't until we left the freeway that we started running into obstacles. Cleanup hadn't been done in the same way as it had been back home. Cars and trucks clogged nearly half of the streets, and some even had bodies left in them.

The further we entered the city, the worse it became. There were a lot more wrecked cars and damaged buildings than we'd seen anywhere else. It almost appeared as if everyone knew what the drones were going to do and did their best to outrun them. Vehicles of all types were lodged into the storefronts of countless businesses.

In one section, we even spotted a bus stuck halfway into the side of a convenience store. Josh slowed as we went by it so we could all get a better look. Several large holes in the back told us that the bloody drones attacked this bus. Bodies remained inside it.

The birds and critters had been feeding off their remains for quite some time. They were mainly skeletons, which actually made it a little easier to take in. We had no real way of distinguishing age or sex.

"Damn, Steve," Robert called out. "These guys did a pretty shitty job removing the bodies here."

"You're telling me!" I answered back. "Just look at that." I stopped talking and took a good look around. "Oh shit! Josh, get us out of this section, and do it quietly. I don't think this area has even been touched yet."

Robert slid out of the turret and made his way to where I was sitting. "We didn't plan for this," he said quietly. "Do you still think we should head up to the hospital?"

Turning my head so I could spy on Kyle out of the corner of my eye, I answered him so only he could hear.

"More than you know, Rob. The guy's story doesn't make sense. He could very easily be one of the guards, and if that's the case, we're not safe."

Robert stayed next to me all the way to the hospital. We shared a little small talk, but at that moment, both of us were feeling a little uneasy. Not only did we have our doubts about Kyle, but also, the fact that the cleanup hadn't been done meant the drones were still around.

"This is it," Josh said, pulling up to the front of the hospital. "Does anyone have a flashlight?"

"No worries," Robert informed him, grabbing a box he had sitting on one of the seats. "I found a bunch of them back at the police station, and these things are bright."

As we exited the vehicle, Robert handed each of us a flashlight and a handgun — everyone, that is, except Kyle. Until we could confirm his story, we couldn't risk arming him.

"Do you know what floor you were on?" Josh asked as we reached the front doors."

"I believe it was the third," Kyle responded.

Kyle was definitely a hard man to read. Every instinct I had told me he was lying; yet he stayed perfectly calm as we entered the hospital. His whole demeanor told us he was on the level and all this was just a waste of time. Still, I couldn't shake the feeling that something just wasn't right.

Robert was correct about the flashlights. They definitely lit up the hallways nicely. It also helped to have plenty of windows that let in the natural light.

When we opened the door leaving the stairwell, we were directly in front of the entrance to the ICU. The bend in one of the doors was evidence that they'd been forced open. The last hospital we'd been in looked clean and orderly compared to this one. A computer lay on the floor; its screen was shattered. Paper was scattered clear across the entire wing, and several windows were broken. All this would've made sense considering the damage the bloody drones could do, yet there was no blood anywhere.

Robert and I took a quick look around to make sure the floor was secure. When we returned to the group to give them the all clear, Cornelius pointed out something odd.

"What do you guys make of these broken windows?" he asked, pointing to one of them in the room next to us.

Entering the room, we all studied it.

"Oh shit!" I exclaimed. "Somebody broke the glass from the inside. Do you think they were trying to get away from the drones?"

"That would make sense if there were some sign that the drones had gotten in," Cornelius stated. "All the damage around here tells another story, though. It just isn't consistent with the damage we've seen other places."

Looking out the window, I could see what I assumed to be the object someone had used to break the glass. There on the ground three floors below us was a wheelchair. One wheel had bent underneath it from the force of hitting the ground from this height.

"I don't get it," I said, turning to the others. "What happened here that was so different?"

Still having more questions than answers, we had Kyle lead us to his room.

"This is it," he said, stepping inside. "I was in that bed when I woke up and saw the nurse's body."

Cornelius walked past us all and grabbed the chart on the end of the bed. He studied it for a few minutes, carefully reading each page. After he finished, he handed me the chart and filled us all in.

"It says his name is Kyle Drake, born July 2, 1987. Current residence is Lovelock, Nevada. He has stage IV bone cancer and has been in a coma since December 24. According to this, he was removed from life support two days before the attacks and had a previously signed DNR. His wife fought the DNR, but his parents got a court order to go against his wife's wishes. I know it sounds unlikely, but he appears to be telling the truth."

"Now that you all believe me, can I be part of your group?" Kyle asked. "I feel a little uneasy being the only one without a weapon."

"What do you think, Steve?" Robert asked. "He appears to be on the up and up."

"I'll tell you what!" I said, pulling out my handgun and putting it to Kyle's head. "You tell me your wife's name, and I won't blow your fucking head all over the room."

Surprised by my reaction, the others all drew their weapons and pointed them at Kyle.

"What the hell is going on?" Katherine demanded.

"Take a look at the picture next to the bed," I told her.

There on a small table next to the bed was a Christmas card and a picture of Kyle and his bride. The inscription on the frame said, *"forever in love, Kyle and Sarah Drake, June 2, 2014."* The problem was that the Kyle in the picture was blonde and had a scar above his eye. This man had dark hair and no scar.

Fear instantly filled his eyes as he looked down at my barrel. Trying to put distance between him and myself, he fell backwards and landed on the bed.

"Please don't shoot!" he yelled. "My name is Matthew Campbell. I'm with the National Guard. I separated from my unit a week ago. I swear I'm telling the truth!" he yelled, pulling his dog tags out from under the pillow.

He'd already lied to us once; what would stop him from doing it again? Robert placed the tip of his barrel against Matthew's temple.

"I say we just shoot him now and move on."

"Oh God, please no!" he begged. "I can prove it to you. There's a pair of pants across the hallway in the other room; my wallet is in the pocket."

"So, big deal," I told him. "You could've found that earlier and memorized the information the same way you did Kyle's."

"My driver's license! Inside the wallet is my driver's license; you can look at the picture."

Josh had already left the room to retrieve it, before I said a word. When he returned, he was holding Matthew's license.

"He appears to be telling the truth," Josh calmly said as he handed me the license and wallet.

Holstering my gun, I went through his wallet to see if I could find anything else that would be helpful. I found a couple of pictures, a bank card, a little cash, and a second piece of identification that confirmed his latest claim. It was his military ID. I placed most of the items back into the wallet and gave it to Robert. I kept one picture.

"I want the whole story," I told him as I handed him the picture of himself and another man in army fatigues. "For your sake, I hope your memory is a lot better than it has been.

He could tell from my tone that I meant business, and his life depended on a full disclosure.

"My name really is Matthew. My hometown is Malta, Montana. I finished my tour of duty in Afghanistan on July 17 and came home with an honorable discharge. I had a difficult time adjusting to civilian life and found myself in trouble with the law on multiple occasions. Because of my military background, the judge gave me two options. I could spend the next six years locked up, or I could do six years in the National Guard. I picked the latter.

"My best friend was sent home a year ago after finding out he had cancer; that was Kyle. He and Sarah got married while he was on leave back in 2013. I tried to contact him after I got out, but I was told he was in a coma here in Redding. That's when I started getting into trouble. The recruiting officer gave me a list of bases that were shorthanded, and when he told me they had a base here, I jumped at it.

"I visited him every chance I had. Then, after the attacks, he was the first person I thought of. My sergeant declared we were at war and confined us to base to await further orders. Only eleven of us were left alive on base at that time, and we had no word from the outside world."

"What were you doing at the time of the attacks?" I interrupted him.

"There were about thirty of us doing training for crowd control. We were learning about non-lethal weapons and their effects on the body. Earlier that day, we all got a dose of mace to see how it felt. They made us try it on ourselves first so we'd use discretion before using it on someone else.

"We were about halfway through the Taser demonstration when we got word of an attack on U.S. soil. Several of us were still out of commission after getting tased and left behind. By the time we were able to rejoin the others, everyone was dead."

He paused as if he were trying to put the pieces together.

"I never did see any drones around our base, and none of the bodies we found showed any indication of how they died. We figured it must've been some type of chemical warfare, and for some reason the room we were in protected us."

"It was the combination of gas and nanites that was already in their system," I told him. "However, it wasn't the room that kept you alive. It was the electric shock. Somehow, they were able to infest everyone with nanites. Then they used an inert gas to activate them. The electric shock you received killed off the nanites in your body before the gas was dispersed."

"How could they possibly infest everyone?" he asked, trying to fathom such a large-scale maneuver.

"We believe one way was in the water supply. There must've been other ways of doing it as well, but we're still unsure how," I said. "We do know they used drones as a backup in areas they felt would have the most survivors."

"How did you end up in a hospital gown?" Robert asked, still having some reservations.

"After about three weeks with no word from the outside world, I decided to go AWOL. I was worried about Kyle and decided it was up to me to make sure he was OK. It took me a full day to make my way to the hospital. The first part of the trip, I passed hundreds of bodies. Then as I got into town, I noticed fewer bodies and the roads were clear. It was like something out of the twilight zone."

"Yes, we've been told that before," I said, looking at Josh.

"Well, as I got closer to the hospital, I discovered a few sections that were still covered with the dead and vehicles still blocked the roads. It was then that I figured out someone or something was removing them. My first thought was that aliens must've been behind it; nothing else made sense. I reached the hospital with about an hour of daylight left. There was no electricity, so I took the stairs up here. At first, I was scared, but I was relatively calm. That changed when I found I couldn't open the door. I know they use magnets to lock the doors, but with the power off, the magnet should also be off. In a blind rage, I forced my survival knife between the doors and pried them open until I could get my fingers in there. Then, I ripped the door open. Once inside, I could see that somebody had jammed a metal bar through the mechanism at the top of the doors, basically locking them together.

"I was still in a rage when I found Kyle's body. I started breaking things. Then, when I threw the wheelchair out the window, I got my first look at a drone. Some of them were hovering around a flatbed loaded with the dead that was coming up the road. I panicked and tried to make a run for it. I ran back downstairs, but another group was already at the door. I figured I was a dead man and I wanted to say good-bye to Kyle one last time. Therefore, I went back upstairs and into his room. I sat down next to him and told him how sorry I was and that I would be seeing him soon. Then I got an idea; if they thought I was dead, I'd be safe. I removed Kyle from his bed and put scrubs on him. Then I got undressed and tossed my clothes in the room across the hall. Before I got into bed, I removed Kyle's hospital bracelet, put it on my own wrist, and put on a gown."

He told us that he lay there for a half hour before he heard someone coming down the hall.

"I could hear him in another room as he dragged the body out into the hallway. There, one or two other people joined him. It's hard to say how many, since nobody ever spoke. I did my best not to move or make any noise. My eyes were open just a crack, but I never did see the drones. I could hear their buzz out in the hallway, but for some reason they never made it this far. Suddenly, one of the men walked into the room. He smelled so rancid — like a mixture of body odor and rotting flesh. I almost threw up when he walked over to me and pulled my covers off.

"My eyes shot open. We stared at each other a few seconds, and then he bent down and whispered in my ear. He told me to stay as quiet as possible and then as soon as it was dark, I was to get as far away from here as I could. After that, he grabbed hold of Kyle and dragged him out of the room.

"I did exactly what he said. When there was no more hint of daylight left, I took off. I hid during the day and walked at night. The only water I drank was out of a creek when I ran across one, but I was too scared to go looking for food. It was slow going, because I hid every time I heard a noise and I couldn't tell where I was. Then, about two or three days ago, something started flying around not far from here. At that point, I just stayed hidden in pretty much the same spot until you found me."

"Why didn't you just tell us the truth when we found you instead of making up that story?" Robert asked.

"I figured since pretending to be Kyle was what kept me alive at the hospital, it was best just to stick with it."

"How many more survivors did you say there were at your base?" I asked.

"Eleven," he answered softly. "You're not going to send me back, are you? They'd court-martial me for desertion."

"No, Matthew, they wouldn't," I informed him. "Due to the current circumstances, they're no longer in charge. In fact, unless we find a working government still in place, we'll be policing ourselves. That means we'll take charge of any situation we feel has a significant importance to our survival and prosperity. We're going to locate them, however. We need all the help we can get."

Chapter 12

HILLBILLY

Now that we knew the truth about Matthew, it was time to locate the others from his unit. I had a good idea they were the men Josh had seen near his home the day before. If that were the case, we'd need to act fast. There were still slaves working in this area, and eventually their paths were bound to cross. According to Matt, nobody left in his unit had encountered these drones before. Because of that, they'd have almost no chance of knowing how to survive against them. Not to mention that they would inadvertently get the slaves killed as well.

Before leaving the hospital, Cornelius put together a large batch of gadolinium and gathered a box of syringes. While he worked on that, the rest of us loaded first aid supplies into the assault vehicle. Between the weapons and supplies, it was beginning to get cramped in there.

Loading back into the vehicle, we all retook our seats, including Josh. Even though he wasn't the greatest driver, he still knew the area better than any of us. I figured Robert and I would get our chance behind the wheel soon enough. Until then, Robert was content operating the machine gun.

After leaving the hospital, we confirmed the spot we passed earlier had yet to be cleared. This would be where we'd set up our surveillance after locating the others from Matthew's unit.

We reached Josh's old neighborhood just after five o'clock. That gave us a little more than four hours of daylight in which to find them. Once it got dark, we'd have to wait until morning. There was an increased risk of being fired upon if we made contact with them after the sun had set.

Street by street, we made our search. Our eyes peeled for any signs they'd been there. It was difficult on us to see so many homes sitting vacant, knowing there would never again be families to fill them. A sense of loneliness overcame us. For a while, nobody laughed and we barely even spoke. We quietly drove through each neighborhood trying to comprehend all that had been lost. It was Katherine who'd eventually get us motivated again.

We carried out our search until about an hour before sunset with no luck. It wasn't from lack of effort, though. In fact, the only time we stopped at all was to stretch our legs and go to the bathroom. Not wanting to be out after dark, we decided to stop and gather some canned goods from a grocery store we passed. Robert, on the other hand, grabbed several cartons of cigarettes and some lighters.

After leaving the store, he opened the hatch on the roof of the vehicle and spent most of his time sticking halfway out of it. I'd occasionally climb out onto the roof and join him. I could feel everyone slowly giving in to depression. It was then that Katherine saved us all.

She found an iPod full of music back at the store and began to sing to us. She didn't do it in such a way that we were in awe of her talent. No, she did it in true Katherine style. She sang off-key and changed every word she could to make each song as dirty as possible. She soon had us all nearly in tears with her antics. It didn't take long before everyone joined in, and it seemed we were laughing harder than we ever had before.

Matthew moved to the front seat to help Josh keep a lookout for trouble. The two of them were a little more conservative but continued to sing along the best they could. Even Cornelius seemed to be enjoying himself. He laughed and sang the whole time he gave us all booster shots of gadolinium. Then, after the festivities died down, he kept busy writing in a journal.

"OK, Josh," I said as darkness fell. "Let's find a place to bed down for the night."

"Anywhere in particular?" he asked.

"Yes, let's find an RV park or someplace like that. I'd like to spend the night in something with a generator and propane. I could go for a hot shower and a soft bed."

"Now you're talking my language," Katherine said, sliding off her headphones.

Josh thought for a second and then his eyes lit up. "I know just the place."

Turning up the next street, he caught the main road and turned left. Then, after climbing a long hill, he turned right and pointed out a large water slide off to our left.

"There's a campground a few blocks from the water park; we should be able to find something in there," he stated.

I was glad it was so close by. We still had just enough daylight to find an RV and get situated. The park had already been cleared of bodies, so we didn't have to worry about any unwanted guests during our stay.

It only took a few minutes for us to locate the perfect setup: two beautiful coaches with slide outs parked side by side. We pulled up next to them and unloaded from the assault vehicle. Robert and Katherine claimed one for themselves, while the rest of us took the second one.

After settling in, Robert gave everyone a crash course on the weapons we'd picked up. I opted to miss his class and went through a few of the campsites looking for some things I felt we needed. They were finishing when I returned.

It was now pitch-dark in the park except for our little campsite. The generators on the RVs were running and the outside lights were on. Robert and Katherine joined us in ours for a bite to eat. It was also a good time to clean up from the day's activities.

Since Matthew had gone the longest without a shower, we let him go first. He'd changed back into his own clothes before leaving the hospital but still didn't smell very good.

"Here, Matt," I said, handing him some fresh clothes and deodorant I'd found. "We all thought it would be nice to get you a present."

"Now, you'll be a little more pleasant to travel with," Josh grinned.

"Wow. Thanks, guys. That was very nice of you."

The gesture didn't offend him. In fact, he was truly thankful to have the opportunity to finally take a shower and change out of what he was wearing.

"Well, guys, if you don't mind, I think Katherine and I will slip off to our RV and get some sleep," Robert said, stretching out his arms and yawning.

"OK, good night, you two." I winked at him.

Everyone else said good night as they left.

"You should all get some sleep too," I told the others. "I have a feeling tomorrow is going to be a very busy day."

"I've got the bed," Josh called out. "If anyone plans on sharing it, just remember, no spooning and keep your damn pants on."

"I don't know, Josh," I smirked. "We all get pretty lonely at night."

"Here," he said, throwing a large stuffed teddy bear that was lying on the bed at me. "Just pretend that it's Michelle."

"OK, but it's going to get awfully wet in the shower."

"Here, give it to me," Cornelius said. "I guarantee you, I've been the longest without a woman."

"Be gentle," I said, throwing it to him.

Matt stared at us, unsure how to react to our banter.

"You'll get used to us in time," Cornelius told him as he cuddled up with the bear on the recliner.

While the others were settling in and falling asleep, I went to take my shower. It felt good to relax under the warm spray and reflect on everything. I kept trying to remember what life had been like before the attack. It had only been a month, yet already many of my memories were becoming hard to recall. The one I couldn't forget was the one of Michelle as we said good-bye the last time I saw her. There was so much fear in her eyes. I could still see the trust she had in me that everything would be OK. I was hoping Ben had made it back with the others by then, so she'd know I was still alive.

As the hot water began to run out, I turned and let the spray continue on my back. Being that it was still over eighty degrees outside, the cold water actually felt refreshing.

After my shower, I dried off and got dressed. I could hear the other three snoring away, but I didn't feel the least bit tired. Stepping out of the RV, I took a seat at a nearby picnic table. A thunderhead had formed earlier, and I could smell the scent of rain off in the distance.

The night before, we had a moonless sky. Tonight, however, a small sliver was present, giving just enough light to make out shapes of things close by. Everything off in the distance was still lost to the darkness.

The sound of a door shutting surprised me. I quickly turned to see a figure exiting the motor home next to ours. I couldn't tell if it was Robert or Katherine, so I quietly called out.

"Hey, over here."

"Steve, is that you?" It was Katherine. Her voice was much softer than usual, as she was doing her best not to wake Robert.

"What are you doing out here?" I asked as she took a seat across from me. "I thought you and Robert had other plans tonight?"

"So did I," she said sarcastically, sounding more like her old self. "I went in to take a shower and get freshened up, but when I came out, Rob was asleep."

I laughed quietly and then apologized. "Sorry, I guess when he said he was tired, it wasn't code for 'let's go fool around.'"

"Yeah, no shit!" she said. "I kind of got that."

"Do you want to go for a walk?" I asked.

"Sure. Where to?"

"I want to check out the water slide. I haven't been to one of those since I was a kid."

"That sounds like fun. I can't seem to sleep anyhow."

"I think it has something to do with the nanites," I told her, trying to make conversation. "Ever since I got injected, I don't seem to get real hungry or sleepy anymore."

"Oh man, it's going to suck if that's the case," she said bluntly. "Those are two of my favorite things."

"Don't worry. I've seen Rob eat. He can do that for the both of you."

She giggled softly. "Yeah, that boy sure likes his food."

We talked idly back and forth for a while. It was nice to spend time alone with her. I was able to share my feelings about how deeply I missed my wife more openly than I could with the guys around. She also shared some things about herself with me. Personal stuff that she hadn't even been able to share with Robert yet.

"When I was just fifteen, I got pregnant by a boy I'd known my whole life," she told me. "He always talked about the life we'd share together and all the places we'd go. Then, on the day I gave him the news, he told me there was someone else in his life and that I needed to abort the baby."

She started to cry and then stopped herself.

"My parents all but disowned me and sided with him to get me to have an abortion. I ended up changing schools after that and became cold and bitter. To help hide my pain for what I'd done, I blocked anyone from getting close to me. I never told anybody the truth about my past, and I never let myself fall in love again. That is, not until I met Robert. He's been the only person I ever let in. I truly believed he was my one chance at having a family."

"Now I understand why you were so against the nanites."

"I guess I just wasn't meant to have children."

"I'm so sorry you went through that, but you really should tell Rob."

"I want to, but I'm afraid I'll lose him if I do."

"Has Rob ever shared anything about his past with you?" I asked, trying to decide how much to share with her.

"A little, but nothing that told me he'd understand what I went through. Why? Do you know something?"

By that time, we'd made it to the main entrance of the water park. In the middle of the parking lot was a lone car. The gate was unlocked, indicating to me that even though the park was closed at the time of the attack, someone had been in there. The body may have been missed when they cleared this part of town. Either that or they went to the trouble of latching the gate after retrieving it. I kept an eye out, just in case. As we entered, Katherine stopped me.

"Steve, if you know something, you have to share it with me. Please!"

I'd never seen Katherine like this before. Her voice was so full of pain. She seemed so frail and vulnerable.

"I really wish you'd wait to have Robert tell you," I said as we walked up the path leading to the top of the slide.

"I can't even hardly face him right now," she admitted. "The reason he didn't sit next to me earlier today was because I asked him for some space. I thought I'd let my past go, but after what Cornelius said about the nanites making a woman unable to have children, it's all I think about."

Reaching the top, we took a seat and peered out over the park. The outline of the entrance was barely visible.

"I hope this doesn't cost me my friendship with him," I said, giving in to her.

"Oh, thank you!" she said happily, throwing her arms around me.

For the next hour, I shared everything I knew about Robert and did my best to put her fears to rest. She really wasn't the hardass she pretended to be. The more we talked, the more she softened up. After some time, I could see just why Robert had fallen for her. There's just something about the two of them that told me they'd always be together.

"Did you see that?" she asked, jumping to her feet.

"Shhh, quiet," I said, pulling her back down. "Yes, I saw it too."

Off in the distance, someone had struck a match. The flame effortlessly pierced the dark; a soft glow afterward told me that someone had lit a cigarette. It was repeated a second later, indicating to me that more than one person was out there. The wind had kicked up from the impending rain and kept them from hearing us as we talked.

"What should we do?" she asked, her voice full of both excitement and fear.

"Let's head back to the others and wait there until morning. There's no sense in waking everyone yet; unlike us, they still need their sleep."

As we headed back towards the front gate, the thunderhead let go and it started to pour. We opted to wait it out in one of the small buildings along the fence line. We made our way from door to door, each time finding them locked. I'd just about given in to the idea of getting totally soaked when Katherine gave one door a push and it creaked.

"This one is open!" she called out quietly.

I quickly made my way over to her, and we went inside. Leaving the door open, we tried to let in as much light as possible, which wasn't much. For the next few hours, we sat on the floor in the doorway, watching it rain and talking about our lives. She enjoyed my stories about Michelle and even admitted she was a little jealous of our pet names for each other. She'd tried that with Robert a few days ago, but it just seemed weird calling him anything sweet.

"Robert's not a bad guy," she said thoughtfully. "He's just a little rough around the edges."

"I know what you mean. I truly think he'd be more comfortable with you calling him asshole, rather than honey, babe, or pooky."

"Pooky?" She laughed. "Who would call you pooky?"

"That's my wife's pet name for her little girl."

"I guess that's OK for a little girl, but could you imagine me calling Rob pooky?"

We both laughed at the idea. We were really beginning to have a nice time when we saw a bright flash of lightning. I instantly started counting the seconds to determine how far away it was: one.... two.... three.... four.... boom! The crack of thunder rolled from a nearby canyon.

"Are you OK?" I asked Katherine as she slid inside a little further.

"Yes, I'll be fine. I don't usually mind thunder or lightning, but something inside me tells me not to screw with it either."

I slid in next to her, and we quietly watched and listened as the storm grew more violent. After several more flashes of lightning, it became evident they were hitting extremely close to us. I tried to count after one particularly bright flash, but before I could react, the roar of the thunder shook the building.

Moving into the building even further, Katherine turned her head in anticipation of the next flash. She didn't have long to wait; the whole room lit up, and simultaneously the thunder shook it right down to its foundation. Even through the ominous roar of thunder, I could hear Katherine's scream.

I figured that last bolt of lightning was too close for her and quickly turned towards her. Then, with the next flash, the true cause became apparent. As the room filled with the bright light, Katherine buried her face in my chest. There on the floor next to her was the body of a man whose car was out front. We'd seen plenty of bodies in the last month, but this one even made my skin crawl. The nanites had kept his body from decaying, but they didn't keep a rodent from making a nest out of his skull. Staring at us from inside the eye socket was a fat brown rat. Another one was peeking out through the sides of his cheek.

Gathering Katherine up in my arms, I carried her in the pouring rain to the car out front. Finding the doors unlocked, I carefully set her in the passenger seat and made my way to the driver's side. Taking a seat next to her, I could tell she was visibly shaken. She looked at me with tears in her eyes and then slowly shook her head.

"Seeing him like that just brought back all those feelings from the day of the attack."

"I know, Kat. It seems that no matter what we do, nothing will ever be able to erase that from our memories. I can promise you, though, that in time it won't hurt nearly as bad as it does now."

I wrapped my arms around her as she leaned up against me. Soon after, the thunder and lightning passed by us and was now clear off to the west. Still, we stayed there quietly watching the rain. It was a little after three a.m. when the last of the storm passed by us, allowing the small sliver of moon to gently illuminate our surroundings.

Still cuddled up in the front seats, we were oblivious to the dark figure of a man walking towards the car. Reaching my door, his shadow reflected off the windshield, catching our attention. I quickly reached for my door lock, but I was too late. The door flew open and the cold, dark figure leaned into the car above me.

"Really! I fall asleep one time, and you run off with another man!" Robert exclaimed, staring at us.

"Oh shit!" I said, grabbing my heart. "It's only pooky."

"You scared the hell out of us!" Katherine shot back, smacking him on the arm.

"Wow, really! I catch the two of you fooling around, and I'm the one who gets hit and called names. Just move over, asshole. I want in there with you guys." Robert pushed his way into the car, sliding me over closer to Katherine. "I hope you know the two of you scared the hell out of me. I've been looking for you for well over an hour."

Leaning across me, Katherine kissed him on the cheek.

"Now that you found us, would you care to join us?" she asked seductively.

"I'm out of here!" I said, forcing myself past Robert. "I already told you, Katherine, it's me or him, but you can't have us both. She's all yours, buddy."

"Really!" Robert laughed. "Just like that! Hell, if I'd known you were going to give up so easily, I would've just waited back at the RV."

"Whatever," Katherine said, wrapping her arms around him as she moved in for a more passionate kiss.

"Don't forget," I said, interrupting the two of them, "I want us to get to their camp right at sunup."

"Hold on!" Robert said, grabbing me so I couldn't leave. "What are you talking about? Whose camp?"

"We're not sure," I told him. "We spotted two small flames off in the distance earlier. I figured it might've been a couple of guys from Matt's unit lighting cigarettes."

"Let's go!" Robert said, trying to slide out of the car.

"Not so fast," I said, pushing him back towards Katherine. "The two of you need to have a little talk first. Just be back before sunup."

I shut the car door, leaving the two of them there, and made my way back to the others. Cornelius and Josh were already awake, waiting for me at the picnic table.

"Good morning, Steve," Josh said as he sipped a cup of coffee. "We need to stay here more often; this place has everything. Not only did I find some cheap coffee, but I also found some Danishes that were only slightly moldy."

"Don't get used to it," I said. "We can't afford to live this extravagantly all the time."

"Did Robert find you?" Cornelius asked.

"As a matter of fact, he did. He actually had the audacity to interrupt Katherine and me while we were trying to cuddle over at the water park."

"Cool!" Josh smiled. "It's about time she started taking care of all of us and not just Robert. I get her next."

"What about you, Cornelius?" I asked. "Do you want some special alone time with Katherine too?"

"I'm good," he said, facedown against the table. "I'm kind of in a committed relationship with that teddy bear."

"That's awesome! I'm happy for the two of you. Oh, by the way. I believe Katherine and I found those men we've been looking for."

His head shot up from the table, and his eyes were wide open.

"When? Where?" he asked excitedly.

I filled them both in on the details while sneaking a sip of Josh's coffee. He was right; that stuff tasted awful.

Robert and Katherine came striding back, holding hands, just as the first hint of daylight entered camp. Hearing the chatter from everyone, Matt crawled out of his warm bed and joined us.

"Good morning, Matt," I said cheerfully. "There's a good chance we've located the rest of your unit. Grab yourself a cup of coffee and Katherine will fill you in on the way. Everyone else, have your weapons at the ready, but leave your safety on. There's no telling how this will go, and I don't want anyone discharging their firearm prematurely."

A sense of nervous energy ran through the group. We'd never engaged with other survivors before; it had always been the actual enemy. Even though we'd do our best to make contact peacefully, there was no way of knowing how they'd react.

Everyone loaded up, but this time I took the wheel. I had a good idea where they were located and was hoping to sneak up on them. Josh took a seat at the turret while Robert rode shotgun. The others sat in the back and talked quietly amongst themselves.

The night before, Josh had pointed out that he'd discovered the assault vehicle had a silent mode. As we got to within about a quarter of a mile from where Katherine and I spotted the flame, I tested it out. A nearly inaudible hum replaced the low roar of the motor. Unfortunately, the power had also gone away.

No longer was this large V-8 diesel pushing us along; instead we had a small electric backup motor. It still seemed to drive nicely, but it no longer had the same feel as before. That thing wasn't designed to be a hybrid; the electric motor was strictly for sneaking into places a short distance away. That was evident by the battery indicator that came on when I engaged it. The meter showed a full charge, yet it also had a countdown timer that only showed twenty-seven minutes.

Robert and I were scanning both sides, hoping to spot Matt's unit before they spotted us. Glancing in my side mirror, I tried to judge the distance we were from the water slide compared to the flame Katherine and I had seen. Getting to the general area, I slowed down even more. We were barely creeping along when I caught sight of a rifle leaning against a tree.

"I believe we found them," I called out to the others.

I turned the vehicle towards the brush near where the rifle was located. I continued driving until we were within about fifty feet of my mark, turned slightly left, and shut it down. For nearly a full minute, we just sat there. Everyone watched out different windows looking for any sign of movement.

"There, to the left of the rifle, something just moved," Katherine informed us.

Robert slid off his seat and went to the box that had contained the flashlights. Returning a second later, he had two pairs of binoculars. Handing me one pair, he gave the other to Katherine. I gave Robert a dirty look.

"Why didn't you tell me about these last night?" I asked as I looked through them.

"Sorry, asshole," he responded sarcastically. "I was a little preoccupied with what was going on with you two. You don't usually walk away from the group without letting us know where you're going."

"Yeah, what was going on?" Josh called down from the turret.

"None of your damn business," Katherine shot back at him.

Then, as she adjusted her binoculars, she caught sight of something.

"There," she said, pointing towards the tree. "You can see someone's foot in that tall grass. From the looks of things, I would say they're still asleep."

Taking a closer look, I could make out a leg and a boot.

"Good eye, Katherine," I said softly. "Is everyone ready?"

"Steve, can I see your binoculars for a minute?" Matt asked, still staring towards the tree.

"Sure, what do you see?" I inquired, handing them to him.

"It's that rifle. I don't know if it matters or not, but that's not a standard-issue rifle. It looks more like a 30-06."

Taking the binoculars from him, Robert took a look and concurred.

"What do you make of that, Steve?" he asked.

"I'm not exactly sure," I said, grabbing my own rifle and opening the door. "I'm going to find out, though."

Everyone else followed suit and joined me outside. Robert and I took the lead while the others fanned out behind us.

"Now would be a good time to turn your safeties off," Robert quietly reminded everyone.

With about twenty feet to go, we all spread out to cover the area better. I could still see only one person, so I took a quick look all the way around for more. I couldn't see anyone else, but I did see a red Chevy van about thirty yards away, near the freeway off-ramp.

"I know there's at least two of them," I whispered to Robert. "When I wake him up, keep a close eye on the van. If you see anyone raise a weapon, take him out. The rest of you get down on the ground and don't fire unless they fire first."

Raising my rifle to the ready, I stepped forward until I was even with the tree.

"Good morning," I said, just loud enough to get his attention.

The man slowly stirred and opened his eyes. Then seeing me, he jumped to his feet and tried to grab his rifle.

"Not so fast," I said, pointing mine straight at his head. "We're not here to harm you; we just want to make sure you're not with the drones."

"We ain't with no dang drones!" the man said belligerently.

"I guess we won't have any problems then," I smiled. "Just to be on the safe side, why don't you call the others out? Oh yeah, make sure you do it real calm like, so they don't get spooked and do something foolish."

"There ain't nobody but just me and Billy," he said calmly, finally understanding the gravity of the situation.

"Hey, Billy!" he called out. "Get on out here!"

It sounded like someone was wrestling in the van. Carefully, Robert took aim and waited. We could hear someone in the van cursing as he opened the door.

"Gall dangit, Ronald!" he yelled. "I don't be disturbin ya when it be your turn."

He had his head down as he stepped out, still trying to pull his pants on. Looking up, he saw me and dove back towards the open door. Robert fired a warning shot over the man's head, stopping him in his tracks.

"Wwwhat do ya'll want with us?" the man stammered. "We ain't done nottin wrong."

"I never said you did," I assured him. "I just need to have a talk with you and your friend. Who was inside there with you?"

"I told y'all!" the first man said, raising his voice. "We ain't got nobody else. It just be the two of us, ain't that right, Billy?"

"Yes, sir," the other man said as they stared at each other. "We just tryin to find someplace safe to get us some shut-eye."

"Is it Billy, you say?"

"Yes, sir," he answered. "I'm Billy, and that there be Ronald."

"Nice to meet you, Billy. Why don't you come on over here and you and Ronald take a seat?"

They both did as they were told as I handed my rifle off to Robert. Taking a seat a few yards from the two of them, I gave them the once-over.

"Like I said, all I want is to ask you a few questions. Then we'll leave you alone, or you can come with us. Can you tell me a little bit about the attacks and how the two of you managed to survive?"

"We heard about them thar attacks on the buzz box," Billy said, eyeing us suspiciously.

"What's a buzz box?" I asked.

"Ya know, that there box the police jabber through," Billy replied.

"Do you mean a scanner?" I asked.

"Heck, I reckon that what it be called. I don't know all them thar fancy words."

"So how did you keep from getting killed?"

"We ain't done nottin!" Ronald growled. "We just stayed put and minded our own business."

"He ain't lyin," Billy added. "We was just sitting thar when we heard em talkin bout some kind of drone attack. We seed em flying over us, but they ain't bothered us none."

"What were the two of you doing when that happened?" I asked, a little perplexed. "Did you hide from the drones?"

Billy gave me an odd look. "Shucks, mister, why would we hide from em? We ain't bothered em none."

"Good point," I said.

These two were a few cards short of a full deck, so trying to explain it to them would just be a waste of time.

"Where did you say you were when they flew over?" Robert asked.

"We was up thar in them hills makin our shine," Billy said proudly.

By that time, the others came over and stood by Robert. After telling the two of them to continue sitting, I picked up Ronald's rifle and joined the others.

"What do you guys think?" I asked.

"Could be lead-lined equipment they're using," Cornelius answered. "If they've been drinking from it long enough, it may have contaminated their system with lead."

"Yes, that does make sense," I said, looking back at them. "It would actually explain a lot of things."

Katherine looked over at them and then back at us.

"If you want my opinion, I'd almost guarantee those two have eaten a lot of paint chips."

The way she said it was so matter-of-fact that it made all of us laugh aloud. It was a good thing too. We had so much adrenaline pumping through us expecting a fight that we were in need of something to lighten the mood. As I walked back over to the two men, I called back to my group.

"Katherine, why don't you and Robert take a quick peek in the van?"

Both men jumped to their feet.

"Y'all don't need to be getting nowhere near that thar van!" Ronald called out. Then the two of them got between the van and us.

Before I could say a word, Katherine raised a rifle towards them. I could tell something had set her off. Even with as much dumb stuff that Robert and I did, I'd never seen her so upset.

"I swear to God, I will shoot the two of you right here and now if you don't sit your asses back on that ground!" she commanded. "If they move, shoot them!" she yelled, walking past them as they sat down.

Seeing the way the two men reacted had me concerned about what we might find in there. Robert was feeling the same and hurried to join Katherine. Ronald and Billy were staying put, but the closer Katherine got to the van, the more agitated they became. They were looking back and forth between her and me, trying to figure out their next move.

"Just calm down," I said, bringing my rifle up in front of me.

"This just ain't right," Billy said nervously. "We ain't done nottin to y'all."

Katherine paused at the side door of the van. All the windows had blankets over them, so she couldn't see inside. Taking a deep breath, she grabbed hold of the handle and quickly pulled the door open. We all watched in anticipation as she and Robert climbed inside and disappeared from view.

Once they were inside, the two men sat motionless, waiting for what was next. Katherine suddenly reappeared in the doorway and stepped out of the van. Her eyes fixated on the two men sitting on the ground in front of me. She walked straight to them.

"OK, you two, what gives? Why the hell didn't you want us in your van?"

"Cuz I ain't finished my turn yet," Billy said, sounding as if he might cry.

"Your turn at what?" she demanded.

"On that thar air mattress," he answered. "Ronald got himself a longer turn than I did."

"Are we all in trouble for taking it?" Ronald asked nervously as Robert left the van and walked over to us. I glanced at Robert. He grinned and shrugged his shoulders.

"No," I said calmly. "You guys aren't in any trouble. Like I said, we're just out looking for drones and the bad men who control them."

"See, mister," Ronald said with a big smile, "I told y'all we ain't with no drones."

"Well, I'm very glad to see that," I said, handing his rifle back to him. "Just try to stay safe and keep yourselves out of trouble."

"What about that thar air mattress?" Billy asked with a concerned look.

"You keep it," I told him. "In fact, you can help yourself to anything you need."

"Anything?" Billy asked excitedly.

"Yes, anything," I said, "as long as you promise not to hurt anyone to get it."

"We promise, mister!" both men exclaimed as they raced back towards their van.

We all had a good laugh and watched them drive away.

"Why didn't you see if they wanted to join us?" Katherine asked.

"I got the feeling these two are happiest when it's just the two of them," I said thoughtfully. "What do you say we go back to the RV and fix some breakfast before heading out to find Matt's unit?"

"Now you're talking my language," Robert said, taking off towards our vehicle.

We'd just reached the door when we heard a noise off in the distance. It wasn't in the same direction that Billy and Ronald had gone; it was coming from the freeway. Turning to see what it was, we watched as three military jeeps made their way down the off-ramp.

Chapter 13

CONCEPTION

Finding Ronald and Billy wasn't what we were expecting. We'd arrived at their camp early, hoping to have the upper hand when confronting Matt's National Guard unit. Now, unfortunately, that was no longer the case. As we watched the jeeps coming towards us, it was they who had the upper hand.

With only seconds to figure out our next move, I sent Robert and Cornelius into the assault vehicle. Robert was to staff the machine gun just in case things got ugly. As for Cornelius, well, he was too valuable now to risk.

"What about Katherine?" Robert asked, not wanting her caught up in a possible gun battle.

"Don't worry, Rob. Even if things go awry, the nanites will keep her from getting killed."

"I'm OK," she said, kissing him on the cheek. "Besides, with a woman out here, they're less likely to be on the offensive."

In theory, she was correct. Seeing a woman in the group should've helped put their minds at ease, but it didn't. I doubt if they even noticed her until they were right on us. What they did notice was a group of heavily armed insurgents standing in front of an assault vehicle. If that wasn't bad enough, we were also harboring the deserter they'd been seeking. Hindsight being what it is, we may have had a better outcome if Mathew had gone inside also.

Pulling to within a hundred feet of us, the three jeeps came to a stop and nine men got out. Instead of trying to question us, they simply opened fire and tried to advance.

Trying to get the others safely out of harm's way, Katherine and I used our bodies as shields. We could hear the bullets flying overhead and bouncing off the Family Truckster. Everyone was safely behind our vehicle before I noticed that I was hit.

Thankfully, Robert was able to end their onslaught by spraying the ground in front of them with bullets. Not wanting to get shot, they made a hasty retreat to the other side of their jeeps. It was then that I noticed Katherine had been hit. She'd taken two bullets in her right leg, while I'd taken one in the back of my left shoulder.

"Are you OK?" Josh asked, frantically trying to pull Katherine's pants off to get to her wounds.

"I'm fine," she hollered as she lay on the ground. "Now leave my damn pants alone before I sick Robert on you!" Pulling herself into a sitting position, she tore open the back of her pants to get a better look. "It really doesn't hurt much at all."

"What about you?" Josh asked, lifting up my shirt.

"Josh! Relax, I promise you we're both OK," I said, pulling my shirt back down. "Just give us a moment. The longer the nanites are in us, the quicker we mend. I should be good in a minute or two."

Pulling my shirt up, I showed them the spot the bullet entered. New skin had already closed up the hole, and I could feel my strength returning to my arm. Matt and Josh stood back in disbelief as our bodies quickly healed right before their eyes. Josh was just about to reach up and touch my shoulder when someone started hollering over a bullhorn.

"This is Sergeant Phillips with the California National Guard. You are harboring a wartime criminal. Drop your weapons and walk towards us with your hands in the air."

"I'm sorry I got you into this," Matt said apologetically. "I never planned on any of this. I just wanted to see my friend."

"Don't worry," I said, looking at the three of them. "I've got this; just stay put."

Pulling my handgun from its holster, I stuck it into the back of my pants and stepped out into the open.

"Sergeant Phillips," I yelled out. "We're not the ones you're at war with. In fact, we're currently pursuing the people responsible for all of this."

"Quiet!" he yelled. "You are not to speak unless spoken to. Now, the rest of you, come out or I will kill your friend and then come after you as well."

"Screw you, dickhead!" I yelled back. "If you don't calm your ass down and talk to me about this rationally, I'm going to have my friends shoot every last one of you."

There was a moment of silence as he considered the gravity of the situation.

"Send out Private Campbell and we'll talk," he finally yelled back.

I was a little past the point of being pissed off. This man didn't know anything about us, yet he had no problem trying to kill us. To me, he seemed no different from the cowards who'd started this war.

"Tell you what. Why don't you come here instead, and I'll kick your ass for shooting me, you little pussy."

"You have till the count of five!" he called to me. "After that, we'll take you out. One, two, three..."

A lone shot somewhere from off to my left interrupted his countdown. I didn't know who'd taken it, but it blew the rifle right out of the sergeant's hand. The rest of the soldiers were preparing to shoot, when Robert opened fire, riddling their jeeps. Taking advantage of the situation, I made my way back to the others as quickly as possible.

"Well, that didn't go as I planned," I said, looking around for the shooter. "Did any of you see where that came from?"

"I just know it didn't come from any of us," Josh said. "Thank God, you're still alive. I actually started to worry that asshole might shoot you in the head."

Suddenly, a voice came from the trees across the road behind us. "Hi, ya'all."

"Holy shit!" Katherine yelled. "What are you two doing here?"

Billy and Ronald stepped out from their hiding spot. As they crossed the road, Billy called out to us, "We heard a ruckus and figured we'd best be check'n on y'all. We done parked the van over yander and hoofed it through them thar trees."

"Right good thing we did," Ronald added. "Them thar boys looked as if'n they were fit to give ya'all a woopen."

"Yes, I believe they were," I said. "We really appreciate the help."

"Awe, it weren't nuttin," Ronald replied. "We shur do enjoy a good fewd every now and again. Billy brung y'all a little shine if'n ya' wanna do it up right."

"Thanks, Billy," I said, peeking around the edge of the vehicle at Matt's unit. "I think we'll just stay sober for this one."

"Speak for yourself," Josh said, sticking his hand out to them. "I would love a drink; it might help calm my nerves."

"So what ya'all do to rile them boys up anyhow?" Billy asked, trying to look concerned.

"Hard to say for sure, but I believe they're not real clear on who the enemy is, so they're looking to fight everyone.

Ronald pointed up at the turret. "Shucks, ya'all got that big ole gun up thar; just waste em."

"I was hoping to talk with them and tell them everything we know about what's going on. I don't think they have a clue about what's really happening."

"Shoot," Billy said, "just start talkin. Ya'all don't need ta be up in each chother's business for them ta listen. Jus make sur ya talks real loud, so as he can hears ya."

Suddenly, a little door on the side of the vehicle opened up. It was only about a foot square, but it was enough for Robert to stick his head out.

"Holy shit, guys, I've been yelling to you. Is everyone OK?"

"Steve and Katherine got shot!" Josh exclaimed.

Trying to shove his whole body through the hole, Robert started looking around frantically. "Are you OK, honey?" he yelled.

Katherine climbed up on the side of the vehicle and gave him a kiss. "Aw, you called me honey," she said, blushing. "I love you, pooky. I'm OK. The nanites already fixed everything, and all that's left are a couple of soft spots."

Gazing into her eyes, he started to tear up. " I love you too. Now I'm going to kill those fuckers."

"Whoa, Robert, just hold on a minute," I said. "Let's give them the benefit of the doubt and assume they're just dumbasses. Once we fill them in with the details, they should calm down a bit. If not, then we'll shoot them."

"Just do it quickly," he said. "I'm highly pissed off right now, and shooting one of them would sure cheer me up."

I couldn't tell if he was serious or not. Robert had a strange way about him that made me feel he might be a little unstable at times. It wasn't a bad thing, though. I always knew he had our backs.

Moving to the edge of the vehicle, I got ready to holler to Matt's unit when I heard Sergeant Phillips yell out.

"Stop right there and lie facedown on the ground. I want to see your hands out to your side."

"Oh shit," I thought to myself, quickly looking around. "Where the hell is Matt?"

My mind raced wildly. Matt had decided he was the cause of this and it was up to him to end it. While the rest of us were focused on Robert and Katherine, he snuck away to give himself up.

"Oh God, Steve, they're going to kill him!" Katherine cried.

"Not if I can help it," I said, taking off in a dead run.

Coming around the corner, I could see Matt facedown on the ground. Sergeant Phillips stood over him with a handgun pointed at his head. He was rattling off the charges for which he was about to execute Matt.

He'd just about finished his speech when I dove through the air and knocked the sergeant to the ground. Unfortunately, I had too much momentum and continued on past them.

"You're going to pay for that," the sergeant said coldly.

I'd just gotten to my feet to face him when I heard the report from his handgun and felt a burning in my chest. By that time, the others from my group had come out into the open. Watching as I got shot, Ronald raised his rifle to retaliate.

"Not so fast," Katherine said as she pushed the barrel of his rifle towards the ground. "This should be good."

Ronald gave her an odd look and then turned his attention back to us.

Everyone else on both sides stood back and waited to see how it would all end. The sergeant had just turned back to Matt and asked him if he had any last words.

"You have some real serious issues, asshole," I said, pulling the gun from my waistband. "If you shoot me again, I swear I'm going to kill you."

In disbelief, he turned back towards me. He could tell by looking at my torn shirt that I wasn't wearing a vest.

"Why won't you die?" he yelled as he emptied the last four rounds out of his magazine into my chest.

I dropped to my knees, putting my left hand on the ground in front of me. I leaned forward and held myself there for a second. I could hear him reloading the magazine as he prepared to shoot me again.

"Stupid fucks!" he exclaimed. "I'm the one in charge here, and nobody is going to undermine my authority."

He'd just finished reloading his magazine and was about to insert it back into his gun when he looked up. His face turned white when he saw me standing a few feet from him.

"You're just a bad person, and I warned you not to shoot me again."

In disbelief, he slammed the magazine into the butt of the gun. At that point, I decided enough was enough and put one shot between his eyes, dropping him to the ground. Quickly turning to the other men in Matt's unit, I yelled out to them, "You need to quit shooting us! All you're going to do is piss us off and end up dead! Now, can we please just talk?"

Before I'd finished talking, everyone from my group had made it over to me. Katherine helped Matt off the ground while Josh tried to check out the holes in my chest. Robert, Cornelius, and our two hillbilly friends kept their rifles fixed on the other guardsmen.

Slowly, they all started putting their weapons down and came out from behind the jeeps. Unsure of what to do next, they knelt down, placing their hands behind their heads.

"What the hell are you guys doing?" Robert asked, lowering his rifle.

Looking up, a young man about twenty or so years old answered him. "I guess we're surrendering," he said, looking around at the other men kneeling next to him. "We've never done this before."

Robert gave me a strange look. "We're not taking prisoners, are we?" he asked, a little confused himself.

"Hell no!" I said. "We need you guys to help us; we're not the enemy. The only reason I killed your sergeant is because he wouldn't quit shooting me."

"That's not really our sergeant," the young man said as they got back on their feet. "After we found everyone else dead, he just appointed himself to that rank."

"What was he before?" I asked.

"To put it bluntly, sir, he was just some asshole on base with us. About two days after everything happened, he decided we were at war and needed a leader. He seemed fine at first, but the longer this went on, the crazier he became. Then after Private Campbell left, he totally lost it."

"Why didn't you just put him back in his place and elect a new leader?" Katherine asked, walking up to the young man.

"Like I said, he was crazy. Private Moore tried to stand up to him, and the sergeant stabbed him and laughed as he died."

"My name is Katherine," she said, reaching out to shake his hand. "I'll admit, our leader is a bit of an asshole too at times, but he truly looks out for us. As she spoke to him, she turned slightly towards me and winked.

"I'm Private Daniels," he said, returning the gesture.

"Not with us, you're not. What's the name your parents gave you?"

"Ma'am, can I just go by Daniels then?"

"Why?" Katherine asked." Don't you like your first name?"

"It's not that I don't like it. I just find it easier to use my last name."

"His name is Jack," another man called out as he walked up to him. "I'm his twin brother, Charlie."

"No shit!" Katherine said with a laugh. "I don't see any problem with those names. They're actually kind of cool."

"Dang, kids," Billy said, walking up to us. "Them thars names you can be right proud of."

"It's a new world, kid," Katherine said, putting her hand on Jack's shoulder. "Be proud of the name you've been given. The past is over; it's up to you to make that name mean something."

Both groups came together, and we all got to know one another for a while. I told them how we happened across Matthew and why Katherine and myself seemed impervious to bullets. However, I left out the part that they could still kill us by shooting us in the head. I didn't think that was information they needed to know.

I don't know if they believed everything I told them, but they were more than willing to listen. A few of us took turns sharing our experiences on the day of the attacks. I was about ready to turn the floor over to Cornelius so he could explain everything in more detail, when I heard a familiar hum off in the distance.

"Have any of you been using a cell phone or two-way radio?" I asked.

Everyone just shook his head. Then one of the men stepped forward; his name was Joel. At thirty-two, he was the oldest of their group.

"I don't believe any of us have cell phones, but I did activate the distress beacon in my jeep. I did it out of habit after hearing the first gunshot earlier."

"What jeep?" I asked frantically.

He turned and pointed to one closest to us.

"Quick, Cornelius!" I yelled. "Get all of these people into the assault vehicle. I need you to start giving all of them the gadolinium. I'm going to get this jeep out of here and try to lure them away."

"It's too late!" Josh yelled. "I see them."

We all made a run for the door. Robert got there first and hopped inside. One by one, he was pulling everyone to safety when the drones opened fire. I'd nearly forgotten how swift and ruthless they were. With the arrows striking all around us, Josh and Charlie dove under our armor-plated refuge. The drones weren't able to see those from my group; it was the others they were coming after. Unfortunately, the arrows weren't biased, and soon thousands of them filled the air. Katherine and I could feel them striking our bodies as we did our best to protect the others.

Thanks to the nanites in us, the arrows did little more than irritate our skin. That put us in a position where it was our duty to act as shields.

With Robert helping to pull people inside, we were able to get most everyone to safety rather quickly. It just wasn't quick enough. Six of us were still out in the open as the drones began to pass over the top of us. Because of the angle of the arrows, we could no longer effectively shield the others. With safety just out of arm's reach, three of the four dropped helplessly to the ground. The last one had lost consciousness right in the doorway. Robert pulled him inside and went right to work on removing the arrows.

When the last of the drones flew past, it allowed us a few seconds of clear air. Josh and Charlie each pulled a body under the vehicle with them and attempted to remove the arrows as quickly as possible. Katherine and I grabbed the final victim and pretty much threw him through the doorway.

As quickly as possible, we went to work helping Robert pull the arrows from the two men inside with us. While we did that, Cornelius took charge of inoculating the others. A stunned silence surrounded Matt's group. They weren't sure what was going on and watched blankly as we hurried around them.

"I take it this is your first encounter with the drones," Cornelius said to Jack as he stuck the vein in the side of his neck with a needle.

"I had no idea," he said, almost in shock. "Is that how everyone was killed?"

"Not hardly!" I growled, feeling the anger starting to build inside me again. "Those were just some of the lucky ones."

"What do you mean, the lucky ones? Are you saying those stories you told us were true?"

"Every damn word! Unless that gadolinium shit takes effect rather quickly, I'm pretty sure the bloody drones will be here next."

Joel had been watching intently as Robert, Katherine, and I removed the last of the arrows from the two men. We then removed them from each other.

"We're safe in here, right," he said softly.

I couldn't tell if he was asking a question or just trying to comfort himself and the others. Stopping what I was doing, I turned towards him and looked directly into his eyes.

"I wouldn't bet on it, and to be totally honest, if they did get in here, the rest of you are better off than Katherine and me."

"What do you mean?" Jack asked, a little confused by the statement. "You can't die."

"Yeah, I know," I said, glancing over at Katherine.

"Oh shit, I'm so sorry," Jack said after he realized we'd remain alive even after being torn to shreds.

"Don't worry about it. If they do show up, you guys are on your own. The rest of us are going to make a run for it. They can't see us."

"It should be OK in a second," Cornelius said as he got ready to stick Billy. "I'm injecting the gadolinium directly into their bloodstream rather than having them drink it. Once I get the last man taken care of, it should only take about a minute or two until we're all safe."

"Hey, I ain't need'n no dang shot," Billy said, pushing the needle away. "Me and Ronald ain't got no issues with em. Besides, we ain't put'n nut'n in our bodies les'n we made it ourselves."

"Sorry, Billy," I said. "Either you get stuck, or you have to go. I can't risk the others."

"Well, shucks, Billy and me jus cum along to help ya'all. We ain't plannen on stickin round none."

"I do appreciate the help," I said, "but I guess this is where we part ways. You two, be safe out there."

"Don't fret none bout us," Billy said, moving towards the door. "We in God's country."

With the last of the other men inside taken care of, I carefully opened the door to let the two of them out. The first wave had passed by us, so now only time would tell if the bloody drones would show up. I followed them outside just as Josh and Charlie were coming from under the vehicle.

"They didn't make it," Josh said somberly.

"I think we lost one inside also," I told them. "They were just hit too many times."

Cornelius quickly gave Charlie a shot and then directed him to sit with the others.

"What ya'all plan on doing wit dem bodies?" Ronald asked softly.

I was thrown off by his question and gave him an odd look.

"I'm jus say'n Billy and I can bury em proper like if y'all wanna be fix'n to get a move on."

"I would really appreciate that, Ronald. You two really are good men."

"We ain't nuttin special, we just us, now y'all git!" Ronald said, flashing me a near toothless smile. Then he and Billy pulled the two men out from under the vehicle. Josh helped pull the other man's body from inside, and then he hopped back in and headed straight for the driver's seat. I stood in the doorway and watched as they carried the men off. Nothing was said, but I felt a great admiration for those two, and I truly think they felt the same about us.

Shutting the door, Josh hollered back, "Does anybody have a clue as to where we're going?"

"Stop!" I yelled at him. "I think I hear the other drones coming. Just don't shut the engine off."

"Shouldn't we try to outrun them?" Josh asked.

"Only if they attack," I replied. "Right now we need to know if the gadolinium is working on the others."

"Steve, do me a favor," Robert said. "Take Katherine away from here until we know it's safe."

Understanding the risks she and I would face if we didn't get away from the others, Katherine didn't argue. She kissed Robert good-bye, and then we jumped out of the assault vehicle. We ran about one hundred yards away and then turned to watch. The hum of the drones increased as they came into view.

Standing out in the open, we watched as the drones flew over the jeep, straight at the others. Adrenaline started surging through my veins.

"Oh God! I think they can still see them!" I yelled to Katherine.

"Go, Josh, go!" Katherine began screaming as she ran back towards the others.

I chased after her and stopped her about halfway back to them. Turning to face me, she covered her ears and buried her face against my chest. I closed my eyes and wrapped my arms tightly around her, pulling her close to me. Hoping to drown out the screaming we were about to hear, I sang "Amazing Grace" just as loud as I could.

"What the fuck! Seriously, dude, either go back home and get Michelle, or find your own damn girlfriend; just quit cuddling up with mine!"

I quit singing and looked up. "Oh my God. You're alive!"

Letting go of Katherine, I raced over and threw my arms around him, lifting him into the air.

"Hey, I said a girlfriend, dumbass!"

I was just about ready to set him down when Katherine knocked us to the ground. The three of us were still wrapped together when Josh poked his head out of the doorway.

"Dog pile!" he yelled, leaping out the door. Cornelius was hot on his tail. The others quietly unloaded and watched as Josh and Cornelius joined the pile.

"Man, we were really scared for you guys after the drones turned straight for you," I said, trying to contain my excitement.

Katherine didn't say anything; she just clung tightly to Robert.

"They turned?" Josh questioned. "I wonder why."

"I think it was just our imaginations getting the better of us," I said, looking back towards the jeeps. "They were probably honed in on the signal Joel sent out. We just assumed it was all of you they were after."

As everyone turned towards the jeeps, we caught sight of Billy and Ronald. They were nearly a half mile away, but we could plainly see the drones hadn't fazed them in the least.

"What do you make of that, Rob?" I asked.

"Maybe it's like Billy said. Why run; we ain't bothered em all none."

"That must be it," I laughed. "Come on, let's get out of here."

"Once again, where to?" Josh asked.

"Take us back to the RV park," I said with a smile. "I believe these gentlemen would appreciate a hot shower."

"And a bar of soap," Katherine added. "They smell worse than Matthew did."

Everyone loaded back up and we turned around to head for the campground. The two hillbillies had already finished up and were now nowhere to be seen.

"Man, those guys are quick," Robert said.

"Tell me about it. I just can't believe that while we were all cowering from the drones, they just casually continued what they were doing."

"Speak for yourself, Steve," Katherine said defensively. "I only got out to get a better view."

Everyone broke out in laughter and started engaging in conversation again. When we pulled into the campground, Josh pointed out the swimming pool and convenience store. He was just saying something about getting some pepperoni sticks when Katherine doubled over in pain.

Holding her stomach, she turned to Robert with tears in her eyes. "Something is wrong. I hurt so bad all of a sudden."

"What's going on? Is it cramps or something?" Robert asked, not really sure how a woman's body works.

"No, it's nothing like that. I feel like my insides are gonna explode."

Cornelius quickly moved over to her. "Katherine," he said softly, "I need to raise your shirt a bit. I have to see your belly."

"I don't care. Just do it! ... Holy shit, I thought the nanites were supposed to stop pain."

As Cornelius tried to raise her shirt, she let out a loud scream and doubled over again. Giving her a few seconds to relax, he tried a second time. With her shirt up, we could see her belly was starting to swell.

"What's causing this?" Robert asked Cornelius after he'd finished examining her.

"Josh, stop here," Cornelius said, trying not to show his concern. "I need you to step outside with me, Rob."

His voice was soft, like that a doctor uses before giving someone devastating news.

"Bullshit!" Katherine forced out. "This is my body; don't you dare keep something from me!"

"OK, I promise I'll tell you exactly what I believe it to be. You're pregnant."

"How the hell can that be?" Robert asked, frustrated. "You said that nanites would cause her to be barren."

"Yes, that's true. That means she would've already been pregnant before I injected her with the nanites."

"That's not possible," Katherine said weakly. "The only person I've been with in years is Rob. We only had sex one time, and that was this morning in the car. There's no way I can be pregnant."

Screaming again, she slid onto the floor. Robert quickly knelt next to her and gently raised her up, resting her in his lap.

"There's the possibility that you were ovulating when I gave you the shot. The lone egg may have been floating around untouched by the nanites. It's a long shot, but I truly have no other explanation."

"If I had gotten pregnant, it would take weeks or months to show. Just look at me!" Her voice was weak and she appeared to be getting worse.

"I'm so sorry," Cornelius said, looking at the two of them. "There are a few flaws in the nanites we hadn't been able to fix. This is probably the worst of them. If we inject a pregnant woman, the nanites find their way into the uterus and accelerate the baby's growth rate. In time, all the nanites will leave you as they try to fix the baby. They see the fetus as a broken human. We have to abort the pregnancy, and quickly. By tomorrow, the baby will have torn through the uterus and end up killing her."

"Can't you take the baby out of me to finish growing?"

"Even if that were possible, the baby still wouldn't survive. It's growing so quickly that the brain never receives it's programming, and essentially it ends up being brain dead."

Katherine nearly rolled out of Robert's arms, screaming and writhing in pain. "I don't care! Please, Rob, save our baby," she cried.

Cornelius turned towards Robert. "You know she isn't thinking straight, Rob. There's just no way to save the baby, but I can save her."

"Do what you have to. I can't lose her," Robert said as tears filled his eyes.

"Josh, get us back to the hospital. NOW!" Cornelius ordered.

Chapter 14

DR. CORNELIUS

We couldn't recall ever hearing such panic in Cornelius' voice before. He always seemed so sure of himself and it showed in his demeanor. Just about the only time we'd seen him scared or unsure about anything was the day we attacked him and the others at the mill. The drastic change in his tone was enough to convince us all that Katherine was in dire straits.

Josh pushed the assault vehicle to its limits. Topping out at nearly 90 MPH, that heavy beast handled more like a sports car than a tank. Everyone was securely fastened in except for Cornelius and Robert. The two of them seemed almost glued to Katherine. Robert held her firmly but lovingly to help keep her comfortable, as Josh nearly slid around the corners.

Hoping to lessen her pain, Cornelius tried to slowly inject morphine through a needle stuck in a vein on her arm. It was a difficult task, to say the least, due to Josh's radical driving. He didn't have him slow down, though; there wasn't time.

"There's a risk to using any type of painkiller on her," Cornelius informed us. "It has to do with the reaction they may cause in the nanites. Normally, it would make no difference either way. The morphine would just pass harmlessly through her system. The problem is her being pregnant. The nanites are shifting from her to the fetus, and as the morphine hits her system, it causes a chemical change in her blood. If it changes too quickly, they consider her a threat to the fetus and attack. If they do, it will leave Katherine completely paralyzed. Once that happens, there will be no reversing it."

"Then why the hell are you giving her morphine?" Robert asked, glaring at him.

"I need to take the edge off her pain. If I don't, she'll eventually end up in cardiac arrest. If I inject it slowly enough, the change will be so gradual it won't alert the few nanites left in her. You see, by now ninety-nine percent of the nanites have left her and are now in the fetus. Her body is almost totally unprotected, but there are still enough in her to harm her — just not enough to keep her alive."

"I thought the nanites were a good thing," I said, watching the three of them intently.

"They are, but like I said, there are still some flaws in them. That's why I only use them as a last resort."

Katherine kept her eyes closed and remained quiet nearly the whole trip to the hospital. We could tell she was still in a great deal of pain by the way her body tensed up at times. Still, she did her best to hide that, and her fear, from us.

We were nearing the hospital, and so far, under the circumstances, everything seemed to be going smoothly. Then Katherine let out a loud scream and arched her back. The baby was growing so rapidly that Katherine's body wasn't able to adjust quickly enough. We heard a loud crack, followed by Katherine's scream, and what sounded like her hips breaking from the extreme pressure pushing them outward.

Now in a panic, Josh opted for a shortcut through a part of town he knew hadn't yet been cleared. It could shave nearly two whole minutes off our trip, but he feared the road might be blocked. As we rounded a long curve leading up to the hospital, his fears became a reality. Several vehicles, both cars and trucks, had the road completely closed off less than half a mile ahead of us. With the hospital just coming into view, Josh yelled back to me, "Steve! The whole road is blocked. What should I do?"

My mind raced wildly as I looked at all the people who were counting on me to make the right decision. Resting my gaze on Katherine, I saw her eyes slowly open and she smiled faintly at me. In that instance, I knew everything would be OK.

"Ram them!" I yelled, undoing my seat belt and moving over next to him. "Give it all she has and hit those two on the left."

We were on a small two-lane road with sidewalks on either side. Only a few feet beyond it on the left was a row of doctors' offices. On the right was a nice grassy area filled with a few trees. Normally, the grass on the right would've been the clear choice, but that space was currently occupied.

A flatbed pulling a load of steel had flipped over, creating an unsurpassable wall. It covered both lanes as well as the entire area to our right. That only left us with one option — we had to drive through a Honda Accord that was tangled up with a small Geo Metro. Both cars were turned sideways up over the sidewalk, between the wrecked semi and the buildings.

"Hold on, everyone!" Josh yelled as he accelerated straight at the two vehicles.

Cornelius quickly removed the needle from Katherine's arm and grabbed hold of the empty seat next to her, where I'd been sitting. Moving his body directly in front of Katherine, Robert tightly gripped the back of her seat and pulled his body into hers, hoping to lessen the blow.

There was a loud crash and violent jolt as our vehicle collided with the others. The impact sent the Honda sailing through the air and through the front of one of the offices.

The smaller Geo didn't fare as well. It folded up like a tin can, caught between us and a metal pole used to protect a doorway. Bouncing off the crumpled remains, we shot back across the roadway, just clearing the overturned flatbed, and struck the side of a minivan the bloody drones had torn into. With minimal damage to the assault vehicle, Josh continued on.

"Is everyone OK?" I asked, pulling myself up off the floor.

"I think so," Robert answered as he released his grip on the back of Katherine's seat. "Just please hurry!"

Moving away from her, Robert froze as her body went limp and collapsed lifelessly in her seat.

"Cornelius, help her!" I hollered as I dove towards them.

Robert appeared lost and in a daze as he gently undid Katherine's seat belt and pulled her into his arms.

"Is she gone?" he asked softly, his eyes pleading with us to tell him otherwise.

Putting two fingers against the artery in her neck, Cornelius found a pulse.

"She's still alive, but just barely."

Then he reached for a handgun that had landed on the floor in front of him. Holding the gun by the barrel in his right hand, he pushed his left hand between Robert and Katherine.

"You need to move back a little, Rob," he said firmly.

Pushing her upright into the seat, he struck her leg just below the knee with the butt of the gun. An involuntary twitch of her leg reassured us that she wasn't paralyzed.

"Go ahead and hold onto her, Rob," he said, relaxing. "I believe the stress and pain caused her to pass out. She's all right for now, but I'm afraid her body won't take much more. We need to get that fetus out of her."

"We're here!" Josh yelled, coming to a stop in front of the ER. I quickly pushed the door open and then turned to assist Robert in carrying Katherine inside. Matt had taken off ahead of us in search of a gurney. He mentioned he'd spotted one on our previous trips there. Josh and Cornelius followed him inside to locate a room.

By then, everyone was out of the vehicle, helping in any way possible. They held open the door and made sure we had a clear path into the hospital. We'd barely made it to the entrance when Matt showed up pushing the gurney.

"Cornelius needs his bag and something to light the room with!" he yelled as he came to a stop. "Also, I have some medical training, if you need some extra help."

"Check with Cornelius. He'll be the one in charge of saving Kat," I said and then turned and raced back outside.

Entering the assault vehicle, I grabbed his medical bag and two of the large flashlights we had. When I reentered the emergency room, I realized I had no idea what room they were in. I was in a near panic until I heard all the commotion at the end of the hall.

By the time I got to the room, they already had Katherine set up on a hospital bed. She'd just regained consciousness, and Robert knelt beside her, praying. I quickly set up the flashlights and handed Cornelius his bag. He and Matt gathered up the items they would need and discussed the procedure.

"Please, Rob," I heard Katherine say weakly, "do me a favor."

"Anything, baby, just name it," he said, getting back to his feet.

"Let me go, and save our baby."

"I can't, love!" Cornelius said. "The baby would grow too rapidly, and the brain wouldn't get programmed, or something. The baby doesn't have a chance, but you do. Please trust me."

Turning her head away from us, she stared out the window and softly cried. The little bit of morphine Cornelius gave her seemed to ease the pain in her body slightly. It was the pain in her heart I was worried about. We all have something in our live we never seem to get over. Katherine already had hers. To make her repeat it might be enough to kill her, at least emotionally, if not physically.

I stood back and watched the two of them as Cornelius walked over and removed the sheet. She didn't appear overly huge, but that was because of the location of the baby and its position inside her. Instead of pushing her belly out, it was actually spreading her side to side.

Carefully, Cornelius and Matt mapped the best place to make the incision with a marker. Due to the location of the baby, they had to work quickly. For some reason, her entire uterus had dropped down nearly in between her hips. A normal abortion was also out of the question. The baby had already matured to the size it should be in the second trimester, and neither Matthew nor Cornelius would have any part of that.

They were finishing up getting her prepped when Charlie and Jack wheeled over a large generator and placed it outside the doorway. Joel followed close behind with a stack of clean linens and some towels. As if they'd done it a thousand times before, the men from Matt's unit worked side by side flawlessly to power up the monitors. Cornelius left the room momentarily and then returned with a breathing mask and a tank of anesthesia gas.

"Normally, we'd use an IV or oral medication for pain, and to put her to sleep. The gas would work as a backup to keep her under. Because of the nanites that may still be in her system, we can't risk that. I'll give her a topical for the pain, which will help some. I'll also need to give her a larger dose of gas to get her to sleep. Unfortunately, she may end up with a terrible headache from it."

Robert and I both nodded. We didn't really understand everything Cornelius told us; we just wanted Katherine safe.

"I love you, Kat," Robert said as he gently stroked her hair.

She didn't make an effort to look at him. Her heart was so broken, nothing mattered to her anymore. Not the drones, the slaves, or us. I don't think she even cared about her own life. I almost felt as if her life would end the second Cornelius took the baby.

Fighting him as he tried to put the mask on her, she reached down and felt the baby inside her one last time. Then she closed her eyes and succumbed to the fate of herself and her unborn child.

After about ten minutes, Cornelius checked her and decided she was under far enough to operate. He and Matt thoroughly cleaned her with iodine and coved her from the neck down with clean sheets. The only spot not covered was where they'd actually cut her open.

"Steve, before we go any further, could you get me the defibrillator?" Cornelius asked. "I saw a portable one a few rooms back as we came in. It's best to have it handy in case her hearts stops during surgery."

"What does it do?" I asked, heading towards the door.

"It shocks her heart and hopefully restarts it."

Making my way down the hall, my own heart was breaking knowing what Katherine had already gone through. I couldn't imagine what she and Robert were feeling at that very moment. They were both being torn in opposite directions due to their pasts.

Robert had lost the mother of his child and now couldn't bear to lose Katherine. She, on the other hand, had been living with regret for having an abortion. To her, the baby's life was more important then both of theirs combined.

Spotting the machine, I walked into the room and just stared at it for a moment. My mind was going a thousand different directions, and I was on the verge of breaking down. Then, suddenly, I had a moment of clarity as I thought through the situation. I grabbed the defibrillator and ran back to Katherine's room.

Except for the doctors and Katherine, Robert and I were the only ones allowed in her room. The others all waited patiently in the hall. They all must've thought I was crazy as I ran past them like a man possessed. I burst through the doorway and yelled for Cornelius to stop.

"What is it?" Robert asked nervously. "Are the drones back?"

"No! I just want to know why we don't shock the nanites and kill them like Hayley did with us?"

Cornelius set the scalpel down and pondered the idea for a moment. "I don't know if it would work. I could shock Katherine and kill the nanites in her. However, it wouldn't be enough to kill the ones in the fetus. I'd need to use a much higher voltage to kill them. That in turn would most definitely electrocute Katherine."

"What about if you shocked them separately?" I asked.

We could see Cornelius was working everything out in his head. The fact that he had to stop and think about it gave Robert and me some hope that it might just work.

"Tell you what. You two go and get me a second defibrillator, two small electrodes, and a pen and paper. You can find the electrodes in the OB/GYN wing." Seeing the blank looks on our faces, he slowly shook his head. "Maternity ward. That's where the babies are born."

"Oh yeah, got it," Robert said as he and I rushed back out to the hallway to gather the others.

There was an instant buzz of excitement as we informed the others of our plan. With no time to spare, everyone broke off into two groups. One group would track down a second defibrillator, and the second group would head to the maternity ward. We needed to locate the electrodes.

Needing flashlights, I went back into the room where Katherine was to grab the two I brought in earlier. Now that the generator was running the lights, I knew they wouldn't need them.

As I opened the door, Cornelius turned towards me and yelled.

"Damn it, Steve, don't come in here without a mask on."

His tone was cold and firm, which really surprised me. After all, I was the one who decided not to shoot him.

I grabbed a mask and quickly put it on. Then I went over and retrieved the flashlight off the floor next to them. Securing the flashlights, I looked up to see what they were doing. That was a mistake. Cornelius was just running the scalpel across Katherine's abdomen.

"What the hell are you doing? I thought we were going to save them both?"

"We are, but I still need to remove the fetus from her hips. Not to mention, if this doesn't work, we'll have to go back to plan A."

I felt myself getting pissed off.

"Let's get a few things straight, Cornelius," I said gruffly. "First, I don't want to hear you call it a fetus again; it's a baby. Second, plan A is to save both of their lives. Until I tell you otherwise, that's the only plan we'll be going with. Do I make myself perfectly clear?"

Cornelius nodded his head and quickly turned back to Katherine. I didn't want to come off like an ass, but I was a little concerned he'd take the baby while we were getting the items he'd requested. To him, it wasn't even a real baby yet. The reason we were fighting this war in the first place was to make the world safe for our children. What good would that do if we didn't fight to save them also?

"What was going on in there?" Robert asked as I closed the door and removed the mask.

"Nothing. Just setting a few things straight."

Robert put his hand on my shoulder. "Dude, you were loud and scary sounding. Thank you."

I could tell he had a good idea about what had taken place. If there was any chance of saving both Katherine and the baby, we'd take it. Even if it meant the risk of losing both of them.

I split us all into two groups, Jack and Charlie in one and the rest of us in the other. We did it that way because we figured finding the electrodes would be far more difficult than trying to find another defibrillator.

Making our way down a dark corridor, Robert turned on the flashlight. It was as different as day and night. That darn thing seemed to light things up better than having the power on.

Spotting a map of the hospital on the wall, we stopped quickly to get our bearings. Luck was on our side; we were just one hallway over from the maternity ward. With Robert leading the way, we all took off running.

The idea of actually being able to save the baby had the group feeling hopeful and alive. After spotting the double doors just ahead of us, we picked up the pace even more. When we reached the doors, we pulled them open and prepared to make quick work of finding what we needed and getting back to Katherine.

That nearly changed in the blink of an eye. Until that point, we hadn't seen any real signs of the bloody drones in the hospital. Rushing through the doorway into the maternity ward, reality once again slapped us in the face.

A hundred or more of those wretched things must've torn the walls open. All the bodies had been removed, but it did very little to hide what had happened in there.

Flies and maggots still covered the blood-soaked walls and floors. Then, as we passed the nursery, the men who'd recently joined our group practically broke down crying. The devastation we saw tore at us even more than finding the school bus. I don't believe even the most cold-hearted person alive could've seen that without being scared for life.

"Was there anything you've told us about the attacks that wasn't an exaggeration?" Joel asked, trying not to believe what he was seeing.

"No, sadly, it's all true," I told him. "This has happened all over the world, and as far as we know, only those responsible made it through unscathed."

"Unscathed for now," Robert added. "I swear, eventually we will kill every last one of those heartless bastards."

Joel shook his head as he looked around the room. "I didn't know what to make of you guys at first, but now I get it. If you want my help, I promise I'll give my very soul to help rid the planet of these awful beasts."

"You can count on us also," the other two men said as they stepped forward.

"Thank you. We truly need all the help we can get. For now, though, let's try not to focus on all of this and get back to the task at hand."

With Katherine and her baby both depending on us, we blocked everything else out of our minds and carried on. The holes the drones had torn into the walls let in enough natural light that we no longer had to rely on the flashlight. Separating, we all went room by room, going through cabinets and drawers.

"I've got them!" Joel called out, running back into the hallway.

"Good, now let's get them back to Cornelius," I said, heading to the double doors.

"What about the pen and paper?" Josh asked.

"Really?" I said, pulling a pen and paper from my pocket and giving him a dirty look. "What have I been telling you since we met?"

"That Robert's an asshole," he replied, grinning at me.

"Screw you!" Robert said, smacking him on the back of the head. "You're just jealous that Katherine likes me, and she thinks you're just a computer nerd."

"Hey, wait a minute, she's a computer nerd, too," Josh reminded him.

"Yeah, maybe, but she's hot and you're just ... well, you know, you!"

"Come on, you two," I said, trying to get them back on track. "Let's focus on getting her safe, and not on worrying about her poor choice in men. Besides, we all know the real reason why she picked you, Rob. It was because Ben was too young, and Josh and I were already spoken for. I mean, let's face it, at the time she thought you really were the last single man on earth."

"It doesn't matter why she chose me," Robert said cheerfully. "I'm just glad she did."

With the flashlight illuminating the dark hallway, we got back to the others in record time. Taking the electrodes from Josh, I put my mask back on and prepared to enter the room. I grabbed the door handle and then stopped.

"Do you want to come in too?" I asked Robert, not wanting to leave him behind.

"I can't," he said, tearing up. "Just promise me you'll keep her safe."

"As if it were Michelle," I said, disappearing behind the door.

"How was it out there?" Cornelius asked as soon as the door was closed.

"The worst so far," I said, placing the electrodes next to him.

"I was afraid of that. The type of nanites they were using never would've made it to the fetus. Even if they had, the air in the nursery is so filtered that the inert gas never would've gotten in there."

"Trust me, when I find the people who did this, I'll make sure it will be a slow and painful death."

"I know just the way to do it," Cornelius said, giving me a wink. "We'll give them a taste of their own medicine."

"I hope you mean injecting them with the same nanites you put into me and Katherine."

"Yes! The very same, and with nobody there to give them the second shot, it's going to be extremely painful."

"I like it, but doesn't that mean we're going to have to capture each one to inject them?"

"I might just have a way around that," he said with an evil tone.

"OK, Cornelius. I think we're ready," Matt said as he popped his head out from under the sheet.

"Thank you," Cornelius replied. "Let's just take a quick look."

I couldn't see what Matt had been doing, because they'd put a cover over Katherine's open incision. It wasn't removed while they worked on her; rather, they'd duck under it.

"That looks good," I heard Cornelius tell him. "Now I need you to hook the electrodes here and here."

Coming out from under the cover, Cornelius stuck his hand out to me.

"I need that pen and paper now also," he said.

"What's it for?" I asked, handing it to him.

"I don't want to cook the fetus — I mean baby. So I estimated his weight and measurements, and now I can calculate just how much voltage to use. Some of these damn things are preset, and you can't adjust them. Fortunately, the first one you brought me can still be dialed down."

I hadn't heard half of what he said. I just stood there with a shit-eating grin on my face.

"Are you feeling OK?" Cornelius asked, giving me a funny look.

"It's a boy," I said happily.

"Yes, Steve, it's a boy," Cornelius laughed. "Now do me a favor and get the hell out of here while we work. I promise, as soon as we're done, I'll update all of you."

Turning around, I quickly walked out the door, closing it behind me.

"What's going on?" Robert asked apprehensively. "Is everything OK?"

"They hadn't started yet. Cornelius wanted me out of the room so he and Matt could work."

"Damn it! I really wanted you in the room to make sure nothing goes wrong."

"I'm not the doctor, Rob. I'm sure Cornelius and Matt will bring Katherine and your son through this safely."

"A son!" he yelled excitedly. "I'm having a boy."

"No, Katherine is going to be having a boy. You already did your part, you ole dog."

"Oh wow, a boy. I can't wait to take him fishing."

"You get to do a lot more than that," Josh added joyfully. "You get to change diapers, get up at all hours for feedings, and now that we don't have a school system, you get to homeschool him. Face it, the only chance you'll have to go fishing is after he's old enough to join you. I guess what I'm trying to say is, I'm happy for you, and you'll make a great dad."

"Thanks, Josh," Robert said, smiling from ear to ear. "That really means a lot to me."

Everyone came over and took turns shaking Robert's hand and congratulating him. After what we'd seen that day, the hopes of seeing a new baby brought into this world gave us all hope for the future.

"Well, Rob," I said. "Sadly, you and I will be splitting ways here shortly."

"What do you mean? I want you all to be a huge part of our baby's life. Especially when it's time to change diapers."

"For us, the war isn't over yet. You and Katherine will need to head home when we leave here. Where we're going is no place for a baby."

Robert dropped his head and walked out of the hospital without saying a word. He'd wanted a wife and child more than anything in the world, but he felt it was his obligation to finish this. He felt the same as the rest of us. Until this war was over and the people responsible were put to death, none of us would ever be safe.

"You need to go talk to him," Josh said, looking me in the eyes. "You're the only one besides Katherine who can make him realize this isn't his battle alone. We'll finish this; you just need to assure him everything will be OK."

Doing as Josh said, I took off after Robert. To be honest, at that moment I was more afraid of him leaving than he was. Since the start of this, we'd fought side by side. I didn't want him to go, but in no way would it be fair to have him stay.

I was also a little jealous. Robert had found love and had gotten to spend practically every moment with her. I, on the other hand, yearned just to hear the sweet voice of my beloved bride and to see my children raise their families. To add to it, he and Kat were about to have a child and head home. Even though I couldn't have been happier for them, my own loss was beginning to consume my thoughts.

"Hey, Rob, is everything OK?" I asked as I made my way closer to him.

"Yes and no," he said quietly. "I'm happy about the baby, and I couldn't love Katherine any more than I do. It's just..." He stopped there and took a seat on the hood of a Prius parked on the street. I could tell he was deep in thought. "You know, Steve, I just don't feel worthy of having a family."

"What the hell would make you say that? You and Katherine are amazing."

"She is, but I'm just a piece of shit!"

"Whoa, buddy, you are not a piece of shit. You deserve a family just as much as anyone. In fact, more than most."

"I had a family once, remember? It's because of me we didn't get a chance to stay one."

"No, Rob, it's not because of you. Sometimes bad things just happen. It's your ex-in-laws-to-be that didn't deserve to have a family. They attacked you at your lowest, instead of helping you when you needed them the most. Anyone can stand by you in good times. It's the ones who stand by you at your worst that matter in life. As far as I'm concerned, they are pieces of shit. They had no right to steal your child from you."

"They didn't steal him. I gave him up."

"That's bullshit, Rob. They took advantage of your pain and forced you out. Even as men, we still grieve. With them attacking you the way they did, it's a wonder you're even still alive. I can only imagine the pain you must've gone through with absolutely no one there to lean on."

"Do you really mean that?" he asked.

"You're damn right I do. I also believe Katherine is going to need you more than ever after this. She's had just as rough a life as you have, and if she starts feeling unworthy of a family, she may just bolt on you. Take my advice and leave the past in the past. You three have the chance of possibly being the first family created in this new world. Make it count."

"You're right. I currently have the greatest life on the planet. Let's go see if my son is here yet."

As we made our way back inside, I noticed Robert had a little more spring in his step. It was nice to see the change in him. He'd always seemed to be carrying so much extra baggage that at times, I began to wonder if anything could change him.

"Nice to see you, Rob," Josh said as we made our way over to the others. "How are you doing?"

"I'm doing great, Josh. I just needed to get a fresh perspective on things. Any word yet on how they're doing?"

"Nothing yet. We've been on pins and needles waiting to hear a baby cry."

"Well, you're not going to hear one today," Cornelius said as he opened the door.

"Oh God, no!" Robert yelled, dropping to his knees. "What went wrong?"

"Robert, it's OK," Cornelius said, rushing over to comfort him. "Katherine and the baby are doing great. The reason you don't get to hear a baby is because she's still with child."

"What? How can that be?" Robert asked, jumping back to his feet. "You said if the baby stayed in her they'd both die."

"True, that is what I said. That was only because I'd never even considered killing the nanites with electric shock. I had to shock both mother and child simultaneously but separately. That's why I needed the second defibrillator and electrodes. I'll explain it all to you later. Right now, you need to be in there when she wakes up."

Katherine was just beginning to stir as Robert walked into the room. The rest of us followed right behind him. With her eyes slowly beginning to open, she reached down and felt the stitches on her abdomen. She started to cry instantly.

"It's OK, love," Robert said, taking her hand. "Cornelius and Matt were somehow able to save you both."

"I don't get it, Rob," she said weakly. "How is that possible?"

"I'm not sure. He said he'd tell us later."

"So, I'm going to be a mother?"

"Yes," Robert said, letting go of her hand and reaching into his pocket. Then dropping down on one knee, he held out a ring. "Would you care to be a wife too?"

Chapter 15

Murphy's Law

Katherine lay still on the bed, not saying a word. She gently closed her now tear-filled eyes as she moved her hand back down over her baby. Silently, we all stood near the doorway, waiting in anticipation for her answer. Her response thus far had surprised me almost as much as Robert's proposal. I was beginning to think she hadn't heard him.

"Are you OK, Kat?" Robert asked softly.

"Yes, I'm all right. I'm just scared to wake up."

Getting back to his feet, Robert leaned over her and gently kissed her lips.

"Please, baby, you're scaring me," he said as he gently ran his fingers through her hair. "I need to know you're still you."

"So, I'm not dreaming? I'm really going to be a mama."

"Yes, I promise. This isn't a dream."

Katherine slowly opened her eyes and gazed lovingly at Robert.

"If it were a dream, it would be the best dream ever. Yes, Rob, I would love to be your wife."

As they embraced, we gave them a quick round of applause.

"Katherine needs her rest," Cornelius said as he ushered us all from the room and back into the hallway.

"I'm not going anywhere," Robert said firmly, giving him a defiant look.

"I'm sorry, sir, but only family is allowed in right now."

"I am family," Robert said, turning back towards Katherine. "I'm going to be her husband."

"Yes, I know," Cornelius thoughtfully said. "We were all beginning to wonder what on earth you were waiting for. I'll see you both in an hour or so."

Shutting the door behind him as he left, Cornelius dropped to a sitting position on the floor. He slumped over with his head nearly between his legs. Josh and I rushed over and knelt down in front of him.

"Is something wrong, or are you just worn out?" I asked.

"I almost killed their baby," he said, looking up at us. "I've been so damn fixated on those nanites all these years that I saw the baby as the problem, not them."

"How do you see them now?"

"I'm not sure what you mean," he said, giving me a bewildered look.

"Do you now see the nanites as being the problem?"

"No, not at all. Nanite technology is amazing. They have so many uses, they can really benefit mankind. The problem is with our own thinking."

"There you go. Nanites were created to help us, not replace us. You just need to remember not to put your creation ahead of God's. Now, come on; let's go outside and get some fresh air."

Josh and I helped Cornelius to his feet, and we all headed out to enjoy the sunshine. The others were several steps ahead of us and found a nice spot to sit in the grass. Off in the distance, we could smell the sweet fragrance of lilac.

It felt good just to sit and relax with our new friends and idly pass the time. We'd just started discussing the day's events when a small deer walked nonchalantly down the road towards us. Soon, several more followed. Paying no attention to anything around them, they stopped a few feet away to nibble on the grass.

"Wow, have you ever seen anything like this before?" Joel asked.

"Actually, we've seen a lot of animals acting this way lately," Josh replied calmly. "We figured they just didn't see us as a threat anymore."

"Do any of you know why that is?" Cornelius asked.

"Is it because there are so few people left that the animals don't think we're still at the top of the food chain?" I asked.

"Not hardly," Cornelius laughed. "It's just one of the side effects from the nanites and the gas that activated them. Many of the animals around larger cities and towns had been getting their water from the same source that the people had. If you go out beyond where man has polluted everything, you'll find the animals act the same as they always have."

"What about the buck we ran into right after the attacks?" I asked. "He wasn't scared of us but got spooked by a dog that happened by."

"It affects each animal differently," he explained. "It depends on the amount they ingested compared to their size and gender. The males seem to retain certain fears the females don't. A lot of the smaller animals lose their fear altogether, yet may still act skittish. I read one study where a herd of rabbits sat grazing while a wolf ate them one by one. Even as he held them to the ground, they made no attempt to get away."

"Are you saying we could butcher one of these deer and the others would just continue eating?" Jack asked suspiciously.

"Like I said, not all animals react the same, but in theory, that's exactly what they'd do."

"You know, Steve, it wouldn't hurt to get some fresh meat for everyone," Josh said, almost salivating at the idea. "We could even jerky some to have for later."

"Tell you what, Josh," I said. "I'll take a few men with me to get some briquettes and drinks. The rest of you can build a fire pit and get some meat ready. Just make sure you only kill what we can eat today or turn into jerky. I don't want you doing it just for sport, and I don't want any of it wasted."

"It's a deal!" he said excitedly. "We'll have everything ready by the time you return."

"I need you to do me another favor. Locate some cell phones and have them reprogrammed to kill more drones. The drones may not be able to see us, but I have a feeling we might end up locating a slave camp around here within the next day or so."

"It's a good thing I can still remember the code I wrote. How soon until you'll be needing them?"

"I was hoping to have them ready by sunset. I'm in the mood to do a little hunting tonight myself."

"That shouldn't be a problem, but I'll need you to get me a SIM card from a drone. I don't have one, and I'll need it to overwrite their code with mine."

"Thanks, Josh. I don't know how I'll find one, but I'll figure something out."

I motioned to the two men I hadn't yet gotten to know. "You two will be coming with me."

They both seemed excited to have been chosen.

"Do we get to take the assault vehicle?" one of them asked.

"Nope, we're going to walk the first part. Somewhere out there is a car or truck with our names on it. By the way, what are your names?"

"I'm Craig," the first man said, sticking his hand out to me.

He was about six feet one and built like a beanpole, tall and skinny, with long, lanky arms. The other man introduced himself as Doug. He had a similar build but was shorter, probably five feet six or seven. Neither of the men appeared to have shaved for at least a month, yet their clothes were in relatively good condition. I figured they must've had extra clothes back at their base — just no water with which to bathe or shave.

Nobody said a word as we took off walking. Doug broke the silence after about a quarter of a mile.

"How will we know the right vehicle when we find it?" he asked, still unsure of this new world he found himself in.

"That's easy. It'll be large enough to carry all of our supplies, have a full tank of gas, and most of all, it has to look cool. I don't want to drive around in some beat-up pickup, or worse yet, a hippy van."

I didn't want to tell them we already did that. I wanted them to believe we actually had a higher standard.

"We don't need to worry about gas," Craig said, wanting to join the conversation. "If we can find a hardware store, we just need to grab bolt cutters and a twelve-volt pump with plenty of hose."

"You sound like you've done this before," I said, giving him a suspicious look.

"Well, maybe once or twice, but not since I was a teenager."

"In that case, we just need to focus on finding a nice truck. Once we find a hardware store, we can get some gas cans to fill as well. I want to make sure we have plenty of fuel to keep the generator running."

Over the next mile, we saw all kinds of cars and trucks but nothing that really stood out. I wanted a truck that made your heart skip a beat just by the looks of it. Besides, I was rather enjoying the walk and the three of us were having a nice time shooting the breeze.

By the second mile, I could tell the other two were starting to get a little warm. We were walking uphill and the temperature was well into the triple digits. Doug was dripping with sweat when suddenly he spotted a garden hose hanging on the side of a house. Running over to it, he turned the faucet.

"Hey, look!" he yelled. "The water here is still working."

He eagerly brought the nozzle to his mouth to take a drink.

"You don't want to do that!" I yelled, getting his attention.

"But I'm hot and I need to quench my thirst," he replied.

"Yes, and we'll get you some bottled water as soon as possible. If you drink that, there's a good chance you'll be dead before you can even taste it."

"Are you telling me they poisoned the water supply?"

"It's not poison; it's nanites. They're just slightly different than the ones Cornelius injected into Katherine and me. We believe they put them in the cities' water supply, and that's how they infested everyone with them."

"I didn't think that mattered since we all got tased and Cornelius gave us that shot."

"The shot was just to make you invisible to the drones. As far as getting tased, that killed the nanites that were already in you before you were gassed. If you add fresh nanites, the fact that you killed the first ones won't do you a damn bit of good."

"I've been drinking water straight from a hose since the attacks, and nothing has happened so far."

"City water?" I asked, slightly confused.

"No, it was pumped from a well before we lost power and kept in a holding tank," Craig stated.

Realizing the difference, Doug took one last look at the water coming from the hose and walked back over to us.

"How exactly do they kill you?" he asked.

"Once they're activated, they literally drain all the fluids from your organs. They do it so quickly that you die before you even know anything is wrong."

"Get out of here!" Craig said, looking at me as if I were pulling his leg. "There's no way something as small as a nanite could absorb your fluids so quickly."

"Tell you what," I said. "Let's grab the first car we see with someone still in it and I'll show you just what they can do to a person's organs."

Intrigued by the idea, Doug forgot all about his thirst. I was no longer searching for the perfect ride; I just wanted something that would start. Just like back at the lake, I was having a problem finding a car without a dead battery. For some strange reason, whoever was moving the cars off the road had a habit of leaving the keys in the on position. We were on enough of a hill that if I'd found a car with a manual transmission, I could've just pushed it to start it.

I finally found a car that had a good battery on my third attempt. It was an older Toyota Camry. One of the tires was a little low, and it had enough dust on it to grow a garden. After a month of sitting, all the cars were covered in dust. This one, however, looked as if it hadn't been cleaned in years. Its once metallic blue paint was missing most of the clear coat. The interior smelled of dirty old gym socks — which, to be honest, wasn't much worse than Craig and Doug smelled.

Hearing the engine fire, the two men came running. It was funny watching them decide who got to ride up front. They didn't just call it or take it; they stopped right there next to the car and played rock, paper, scissors. After playing the best three out of five, it was Craig who ended up getting the front seat.

"Do you guys make all your important decisions that way?" I asked smugly as they took their seats.

They didn't say a word. They both just gave me a silly ass grin.

Finding a body to examine wasn't a difficult task. Besides the fact that the cleanup was done rather poorly, I knew of a whole section that was still untouched. I wasn't overly concerned with running into drones at the moment. We saw no signs that the slaves would be coming back any time soon. In fact, other than wondering if the POS we were driving would make it that far, the drive over to it was uneventful.

"This is it," I said, bringing the car to a stop. "In a few minutes you'll see just how powerful those little nanites really are."

Getting out of the car, the two of them followed me into an office building. We'd barely made it through the doorway when we spotted a middle-aged man who'd died at his desk. He didn't look quite the same as the first bodies we'd encountered after the attacks. Little by little, the bodies were beginning to shrivel up like old rotting apples.

"Oh my God!" Craig exclaimed as he ran his hand over the dead man's skin. "It's almost like touching a dried-out prune."

"You should've seen what they looked like the first couple of days after they died."

"We did," Doug quietly said. "Everyone on base had only been dead a short time when we discovered them. At first we thought they were just unconscious. We never could figure out what had actually killed them."

"It was the same thing that would've killed both of you if you hadn't been tased beforehand."

"We heard all of you discussing that this morning," Craig said, still examining the man's skin. "It just seemed so far-fetched."

"So, did the government do this?" Doug asked, looking around the room for some other type of destruction.

"Not exactly. A large number of computer geeks and scientists who'd been working for several different governments from around the world did this. I guess the whole thing began back in the late sixties to early seventies. Cornelius was unwittingly a major player in the attacks. It was his technology they used to create the nanites."

Doug gave me an odd look. "Then why on earth would you trust him?"

"It's a long story. In fact, I almost killed him in the beginning, but over time he's proved to us that he wasn't one of them. He was trying to create a cure for all the world's illnesses; it was the government that turned it into a weapon. Come on, I'll show you why I brought you here."

I pulled out the pocketknife I found at the lake and opened the blade. The two of them watched intently as I opened the dead man's shirt. Leaning him back in his chair, I stuck the knife in just under his belly button and drew it up to his chest. Then with my left hand, I took hold of his internal organs, including his heart, and used my knife to cut them free.

Craig and Doug stood there speechless as I placed everything on the desk and closed my knife. It wasn't the same effect as the first time I saw this done. Even with the organs only about a third of their normal size, it was enough to convince Doug to never drink from a hose again.

Craig reached over to the desk and touched the man's organs.

"Wow! They look all dried out, yet they're still soft to the touch. How's that?"

263

"I don't know for sure. I just know it kills you so quickly that most people didn't have a clue that anything was even wrong. Those that the nanites didn't kill had to face the drones.

"I've seen enough," Doug said, turning away from the desk.

"Yeah, me too," Craig added. "Let's get out of here. This place gives me the creeps."

We'd just started making our way towards the door when we heard a vehicle coming up the road. With no time to run, we stood there motionless.

Soon, several drones followed by a pickup truck cruised slowly past us. At first I thought it might keep going and that we could sneak back to our car. That wasn't the case. Stopping just a few doors down, they shut off the truck and got out.

"What do we do now?" Doug whispered.

"That depends," I said, trying not to look as frightened as they were. "We can hide in here until they leave, or we could go out and face them."

"What, are you nuts?" Craig asked as he grabbed my shirt and pulled me away from the doorway.

I watched as the slaves disappeared inside the building next to us, and then I turned towards Craig.

"Watch this," I said, breaking free of his grip and stepping outside.

I made my way over to their truck, the whole time keeping an eye out for the slaves. I was nearly to the front of it when Craig and Doug caught up to me. I could tell they didn't care much for being out in the open with the drones around. When I pointed out the bloody drones connected to the hood, they nearly ran off.

"Hold on, you two," I said just above a whisper. "We're not in any danger. That shot Cornelius gave you this morning made you invisible to them. Believe me, they don't mess with you when they can't see you."

"Then why are we trying to keep so quiet?" Doug asked, still eyeing them suspiciously.

I pulled my knife back out of my pocket and began pulling the covers off the two drones.

"It's for the safety of the slaves. If they see us, they may yell out or react in a way the smaller drones don't like. If that happens, they start shooting little arrows everywhere and alert these two bastards here on the hood. Once these two wake up, things tend to get pretty bloody real quick."

"So, what is it you're trying to do with your pocketknife?" Craig asked, moving a little further away from me.

"I'm getting Josh a little gift," I replied, holding out the SIM cards for them to see. "He needs these to turn a cell phone into a weapon."

I could tell they had no idea what I was talking about, and judging by the looks on their faces, they didn't care to stand around and discuss it either. Both men stared intently at the door the slaves had gone into.

"If it makes you two feel any better, we can go now."

I didn't need to tell them a second time. Both men shot past me and jumped into the backseat of the car. Shutting the door behind them, they slumped down into the seat.

Taking my position behind the wheel, I turned towards them.

"Do you guys want to play a quick game of rock, paper, scissors to see who gets the front seat?" I asked, poking fun at them.

"No, we're good," Doug nervously said. "Can we please just get out of here now?"

The entire time, he and Craig kept an eye on the doorway, waiting for the drones to appear.

"Not just yet. I need to see if the slaves come out first, or if the drones do. That'll give me some indication of how we can free them."

"I was kind of hoping you'd say that," Craig said, beginning to sound a little more relaxed now that we were in the car.

"What about you, Doug?"

"To be honest, Steve, I'm scared as hell right now, but I won't let you down."

"I appreciate you guys being willing to step up to the plate like this. I promise you'll be totally safe from the drones."

We sat there in the safety of the car, watching and taking mental notes for nearly half an hour. Repeatedly, the slaves entered and exited the buildings, retrieving the bodies. Each time they did, they were always a good two to three seconds ahead of the drones, and they always carried the bodies together.

Feeling secure with the pattern we'd seen, we exited the car and made our move. The plan was a simple one. As the drones followed the two slaves into the building, I'd go over and wait outside the door. Then, when the slaves came back out with a body, I'd simply shut the door, trapping the drones. When the arrow-shooting drones could no longer get to the slaves, they'd simply power down.

At that point, Craig and Doug would drive over to me and I'd put the slaves in the backseat. Then all we'd have left to do was to drive away. Nothing could be easier.

It started out just how we planned. The slaves entered the building, with the drones a good five to ten feet behind. I got out of the car, made my way over to the building, and hid just outside the door. Our well laid-out plan turned to shit about two minutes later.

It started when two more pickups half-loaded with bodies came rolling in from the opposite direction. In a panic, thinking that I hadn't seen them, Craig made the decision to honk the horn to warn me.

Now, I'll admit, that was partially my fault. I'd told both of them earlier that the drones weren't affected by the noise we made. What I apparently hadn't conveyed to them correctly was that the slaves would be.

Just as Craig was hitting the horn to warn me, one of the slaves came out all alone carrying a body over his shoulder. All alone, that is, except for the drone that was practically right on top of him. As if hearing the horn wasn't enough, he also caught sight of me and the other trucks all about the same time. Up until that point, every slave we'd ever come across appeared half-starved and completely sleep-deprived. That definitely wasn't the case here.

Believing he was about to be added to the truckload of bodies, he opted not to go down without a fight. Raising the body he was carrying high into the air, he threw it at me, knocking me to the ground. Then he took off like a bat out of hell, straight at Craig and Doug.

I pushed the body off me as quickly as I could and jumped back to my feet. I realized then that deactivating the two drones on the hood of the pickup wasn't going to make a whole lot of difference. Not only had the drone following him gone into attack mode, but so did the twenty or so that were with the other slaves. With all the drones revved up to kill, the other slaves went into panic mode.

With the bloody drones no longer secured to their vehicles, the drivers in the other trucks took off like a bullet. They shot past me and almost ran over the man who'd taken off running. The driver in the first truck did his best to avoid him but ended up hitting the Camry head on.

Fortunately, just before impact, the two of them made the decision to leave the vehicle and attempt to tackle the slave before he got past them. Seeing the first truck crash and block their escape, the driver of the second truck turned sharply and slammed on his brakes. Instantly, they went into a barrel roll, sending all the bodies flying through the air.

The smaller drones converged on the runaway slave just as Craig and Doug got to him. They fired thousands of arrows, but none of them managed to reach their intended targets. All three of the men now lay protected under a heap of previous victims. However, the bloody drones weren't far behind.

Hearing the screams from the second slave, a woman, I turned and rushed inside the building. Following her cry for help, I made my way to a small office in the back. Entering the room, I quickly spotted her. She was crouched under a desk, using the body she'd been carrying as a shield. The drone was between us, with its back to me. Relentlessly, it fired thousands of arrows at its intended victim.

It almost seemed comical as I plucked the small drone from the air and shoved it into an open file cabinet. Then, slamming the drawer shut, I turned and rushed back outside to try and help the others.

The image I saw as I cleared the front door stopped me in my tracks. There among the wrecked vehicles and countless bodies lay twenty or so dead drones. I stood there flabbergasted, my mouth hanging open in disbelief. Then, from the other side of the carnage, Scott and Ray appeared, followed by an army of former slaves.

"Rough day, Steve?" Scott called out as he made his way towards me.

"You know," I replied. "Same shit, different day."

Scott was a unique individual; ever since I met him, I'd yet to see him wear shoes. He just seemed to be more comfortable with bare feet.

I stuck my hand out to greet him. "So, what brings you to my little neck of the woods?"

"Ben showed up at camp a few days after we arrived, with a bunch of women and children in tow. He mentioned to us that you and Robert were vacationing down this way, doing a little fishing. Ray and I decided we liked fishing and thought we might as well come join you."

"Well, my friend, I'm glad you did. How is it you were able to locate me right when I needed you most?"

Ray stepped up and shook my hand.

"Let's just call it dumbass luck," he said, looking around. "We were actually following those two pickups, and they led us right to you."

"I'm glad you were. Those damn things nearly ruined my whole day."

"We figured as much," Scott said, surveying the mess. "We'd just taken a side road to cut them off when I spotted you near the doorway. It was obvious you had no idea what was coming your way. Then, when we heard the horn, our team went into action to disable the drones. To be honest with you, in all the extractions I've done, I've never seen anything quite so crazy."

"Pretty bad, wasn't it," I said sheepishly.

"Don't take it the wrong way," Ray said, almost grinning. "We've had some sketchy rescues ourselves, but damn, that was definitely one for the books."

We finished talking and I led them both into the building where I'd left the woman under the desk. She was still there with the dead man's body covering her. Shaking and scared, she peered out at us. Since I was pretty much having an off day, I thought it best to let Scott approach her first. He slowly made his way towards the desk, talking softly as he did.

"You two seem to have gotten really good at freeing slaves," I told Ray as he and I watched Scott.

"Yes, you might say that. Unfortunately, we've also had our fair share of losses. Two weeks into this, I lost nearly my entire crew. One of the guards caught wind we were in the area and set us up. I did all the usual reconnaissance and didn't notice anything out of the ordinary. I made the call to move in, but when my extraction team entered the camp, the whole place went up like the fourth of July. We lost seven team members and twenty-three captives that day."

"Oh my God, Ray! I'm so sorry."

"Yeah, me too. I damn near called it quits after that. Then Scott reminded me that they weren't killed because of something we did. It was because of who did this. It's not up to us to save everyone — just everyone we can."

"How's that been going so far?" I asked, anxious for him to give me some clue about Michelle.

I knew he'd found her, but nothing had ever been said about whether or not she was alive. I just told myself she was, so I'd have something to hold onto.

"We've freed three hundred eighty-seven souls to date and have lost fifty-two."

"Ray, what about Michelle?" I asked nervously.

"Don't worry, Steve. She's back at base safe and sound. In fact, she's the reason we're here. When Ben showed up early yesterday and told us what you were up against, Michelle sent us after you. I truly thought this was going to be a recovery mission. I never dreamed we'd find you alive."

"Believe me, if it hadn't been for the nanites, I'd have been dead clear back in Coos Bay."

"Ben mentioned something about nanites. I just figured he was talking about the ones in the water."

At that point, Scott was escorting the young woman out from under the desk. She'd made it through the most recent drone attack only getting hit twice by arrows. The body she'd used to cover herself, on the other hand, looked like a human pin cushion.

"Her name is Julie," Scott said as he walked her over to us. "She's still a little apprehensive about talking, in fear that the drones might retaliate against her. She did, however, want to express her gratitude for rescuing her."

"It's nice to meet you, Julie. I'm Ray and this is Steve. He's the reason you're now free."

"Thank you," she said through tear-filled eyes as she wrapped her arms around me.

I gave Ray and Scott both a confused look.

"I didn't do this. You and your team are the only reason this mess didn't get us all killed."

"Follow me outside and let me show you something," Ray said, taking the lead.

With the young woman still clinging to my arm, the three of us followed Ray out of the building.

"Take a good look around, Steve. This is just a small portion of the resistance you started. If you and the others hadn't taken it upon yourselves to fight back and free the people you did, none of this would be possible. That little band of misfits, as you called yourselves, set in motion a force that has been growing exponentially since you saved the first slaves.

"As of two days ago, we had seven units heading east, continually adding more survivors to the resistance. That doesn't even count what Shelly has been doing. I'm not privy to her missions, but I've been informed she has units flying into other countries."

What Ray said surprised me. As I slowly looked around, I saw a group of fifty plus men and women tending to the slaves and disassembling drones.

"Holy shit, Ray!" I exclaimed. "How do you guys keep hidden as you're traveling? It must take a small fleet just to get you from place to place."

"I'll let Scott fill you in on the details. After all, it's because of him so much of this is possible."

"It's really quite simple," Scott stated. "We don't hide. Thinking we were hidden only gave us a false sense of security. After we lost so many lives during that disastrous rescue attempt, I set out to make a new plan of attack. Now, instead of hiding, we make our presence known. That literally causes the drones to not only show themselves but the slaves as well. It seems to be much more effective. Not only does it take us less time, but it also draws the attention to us and off those we're trying to help. The drones here today are a prime example. They were fleeing us when they led us to you."

"I'm curious. How do you get the drones to notice you, not to mention run from you? Aren't you all taking gadolinium to be invisible to them?"

"Yes, we are," Ray proudly said. "They don't actually see us. What they pick up on is the signal from a drone of our own. It sends out several different types, depending on what we want the other drones to do. We can either make them run from us or we can make them chase us."

"How on earth did you guys figure all that out in such a short amount of time?"

"It just so happened that three of the people we rescued have engineering backgrounds. I stuck them together with a couple of young computer nerds and they came up with all kinds of goodies. We also currently have access to three full military helicopters, a fighter jet, and thousands of surface-to-air missiles."

"What about the drones here? You didn't use missiles on them."

"No, we used a modified laser that has some of the technology Josh created. We can take out a single drone from nearly a mile away, or multiple drones from as far as two hundred meters."

"Damn! Things really have changed in a very short time. It makes what we're doing here seem so miniscule."

"Oh, God no, Steve!" Scott said excitedly. "That's not even remotely true; everyone feeds off the energy your team puts out. You should've heard the uproar back at camp when Ben showed up with news of what you've been doing. Even though most of the people have never met you, you're a regular folk hero to them. Not to mention everyone considers you to be the person in charge. The instructions you laid out for us still govern every unit out there."

"Thanks, guys. That really means a lot to me."

Spotting Craig and Doug, I excused myself and started heading over to them. The young woman was still holding tightly to my arm. She nervously watched several drones on the ground as we passed them.

"What did you say your name was?" I asked, gently moving the hair out of her eyes with my free hand.

"It's Julie," she replied meekly, with a soft smile.

It seemed most of the slaves that we freed that day were only in their twenties or thirties. Julie was no exception. I put her somewhere in her mid-twenties. Her long blonde hair was matted up around her face, and a large section was stained red from blood. I couldn't tell if it had been from her or from that of the bodies she'd been forced to carry. She was so fair-skinned that her face and arms had blistered from long exposure to the sun. Even her bare feet were callous and swollen. Still, there was a sense of beauty and youth about her, and her smile could brighten a dark room.

"There's no need to fear the drones. Isn't that what you said to us?" Craig asked, giving me a dirty look as we got closer to him.

"Excuse me!" I exclaimed. "Let's not start whining about having to put forth a little extra effort. I don't see either one of you with as much as a pinprick from those arrows."

They both laughed.

"So, is this what we can expect from all of your rescue attempts?" Doug asked sarcastically.

"Of course not," I answered, wrapping my free arm around his shoulder. "Sooner or later, something is bound to go wrong, and then we'll really be in trouble."

There was a slight pause as both men glanced around and gave me a dirty look.

"I'm only kidding, you two. I'm very sorry about the way things went. Unfortunately, there are no guarantees or sure things in what we're doing. What we do have is a personal responsibility to help all those we can. We no longer live in a world where it's acceptable to look the other way, in hopes somebody else will make it right. Every single abled-bodied person needs to not only be prepared to do their own part, but be prepared to do for others as well."

"We're all done here," Scott said as he and Ray walked up to us. "Would you four care to catch a ride with us back to home base?"

"We can't right now," I informed him. "The others are waiting for us to return with supplies. We were on our way to get them when we happened upon the slaves doing cleanup here."

"That's great news!" Scott replied. "We were afraid to ask if anyone else made it."

"Thanks to Matt and Cornelius, we're all still alive. In fact, we just found out Robert and Katherine are going to be having a son in the near future."

"How can that be?" Ray asked, loud enough to get everyone's attention. "I thought the two of them just met. Was Katherine pregnant before the attacks?"

"It's Rob's baby, and the ironic part is they didn't actually have sex until early this morning."

"OK, now I know you're just messing with me," Ray laughed.

As we made our way over to their convoy, Doug and Craig shared with them the events of our day thus far. We could tell everyone either thought we were screwing with them or we were just plain off our rockers. The idea of nanites being able to do everything we'd just told them was beyond their realm of thinking.

"I'll admit, you do seem to look a lot younger and healthier than the last time I saw you," Ray said skeptically. "Still, the idea of bones healing in minutes or of babies growing in less than a day is, well, you know... crazy."

I could tell they all thought I was out of my mind. Most of these people had never even met me before, and even those that had looked at me as if I were in need of a padded room. The only two that didn't give me an odd look were Doug and Craig. They were the only ones that weren't questioning my stability; even Julie let go of my arm and moved closer to Ray.

Quietly, Craig whispered something in my ear and then waited for my response. Looking around at the others, I could tell none of them believed a word I said. If I couldn't prove myself to them now, there'd be no way to get them to follow me in the future.

"Go ahead and do it, Craig," I said, turning so everyone could see.

With that, he removed his handgun from its holster and fired three rounds point blank into my chest.

Chapter 16

A Redneck's Dream

Pulling myself to a sitting position, I could see Craig lying next to me, his eyes full of fear. We'd figured shooting me would prove to the others that we were telling the truth about the nanites. We just never counted on the crowd responding the way they did.

Instead of watching in awe as I recovered from the gunshot, the crowd attacked Craig. As they forced him down next to me, Scott drew his own weapon and prepared to kill him.

"If you shoot him, he'll more than likely die," I said as I worked my way back to my feet.

Scott dropped his gun and stumbled backwards, knocking himself and two others to the ground as well.

"What the hell is going on here?" he demanded from a sitting position.

I walked over and helped Craig up, before turning my attention to Scott and the others.

"We tried to tell you, but none of you cared to believe us." They could all tell by my tone that I was more than a little pissed off.

"If you people plan on being a part of my group, you will need to trust everything I say or do. In return, I will do the same for you; my whole team will. Often, we find ourselves in situations where one member of the team may see or hear something the others missed. He or she won't always have the time to stop and prove it to you. You have to have trust! Now, I really don't enjoy getting shot. Not only does it hurt, but it also tends to ruin whatever I'm wearing. Do you all understand?"

"I'm sorry, Steve," Ray said as he made his way near Craig and me. "Neither myself, nor Scott would allow anyone to question what we told them. We should've given you that same respect."

Ray helped Scott off the ground and turned back towards me, his eyes fixated on the three holes in my shirt.

"May we take a look?" he asked, still dumbfounded by the whole idea.

"Go ahead," I said, calmly removing my shirt.

Ray and Scott examined my chest as the others squeezed in to take a closer look. All that remained were three quarter-size dimples where the bullets had entered.

Ray ran his hand over the indentations. "Holy cow! You can hardly see where the bullets entered."

"Yes, and in a few minutes there won't be any indication anything ever happened."

"What happens to the bullets?" he asked, sounding more confused than ever.

"The nanites consume them. I'm not exactly sure how. What I do know is the darn things can eat nonstop and never shit. It's amazing."

"You need to inject us all!" came a voice from the crowd.

Pushing his way past the others, a large man about six foot six with a full beard made his way over to where I was. Glaring at me, he voiced his opinion again.

"You need to put those nanites in all of us!"

Not really sure of his intent, I tried to answer him as calmly as possible.

"At the moment, we don't have enough to go around. If we feel someone is in dire straits and about to die, then we'll use them. Until that happens, nobody is going to be injected with the nanites."

"That's bullshit!" he yelled, getting right up in my face.

Reaching up for the big man's throat, I grabbed hold of him. At the same time, I swept my right leg, taking his out from under him. Slamming him to the ground, I dropped to one knee and brought my face to within inches of his.

"This will be the only time I say this to you. Don't you ever fucking get in my face again! Do you understand me?" My tone was forceful, yet I spoke only loud enough for him to hear and no one else.

"Yeah, I understand you," he said, pushing my hand away from his throat. "You think you're hot shit because you have those things protecting you."

As he turned and made his way back into the crowd, I gave Ray a strange look.

"What's up with that guy?" I asked while I put my shirt back on.

"Sorry, Steve. He was one of the first guys we saved. I don't care much for him and would just as soon not have him as part of my team."

"Then why on earth did you bring him?"

"I didn't really have a choice. If you think he has a problem with you, you should see how he treats women. It was either take him with us or leave him back at base with Michelle."

"In that case, thank you for not making Michelle have to deal with him. I'm sure she has enough on her plate as it is."

"That's for sure. The last thing she needed was to deal with Mr. Douchebag."

"Does Mr. Douchebag have a name, or is that it?"

"It's Jason," Scott said, wanting to add his two cents. "The guy is major trouble; we're just not sure what to do about him."

"Let's just keep an eye on him; maybe he'll mellow out in time. Right now we need to focus on getting supplies and making it back to my group."

"What kind of supplies do you need?" Scott asked. "We have pretty much anything you can think of."

"I want to get some canned vegetable, spices, and a few bags of charcoal briquettes. The guys were planning on having venison for dinner."

"In that case, we've got you covered," Ray said happily.

"Did you bring it from home?"

"Yes. Why do you ask?"

"I'm just curious how you got around that mess on the freeway in Medford."

Ray gave me a wink and grinned. "Trust me, Steve, Medford was nothing compared to some of the shit we've seen. I'll tell you a few stories tonight over dinner."

After the incident with Jason, everyone else had begun heading back to their vehicles. Craig and Doug stayed next to me until it was time for us to join them. I'd only seen the two trucks they'd been putting the drone parts into. It wasn't until we rounded the corner about a half block away that I truly realized just how these people traveled. They had large military transports full of supplies, two assault vehicles not a lot different from the one we had, two four-wheel drive jeeps with 50mm machine guns, and a handful of other very impressive cars and trucks.

The one that really stood out was a deep red Ford F-450 club cab. It had a six-inch lift, oversized tires, and a massive front bumper. There were nerf bars on the sides of the truck that were way too high off the ground to use as steps, not to mention enough LED lights to turn night to day.

"See, guys," I said, turning to Craig and Doug. "This is what we were looking for. When I see this, my heart damn near skips a beat."

"Whose truck is it?" Craig asked.

"Don't look at me," Ray said, getting into his jeep. "That truck says redneck all over it."

"That would be mine," Scott said, holding his hand out to me. "Care to drive?"

He opened his hand and showed me his key fob that was all lit up with purple LEDs.

"I'd love to, Scott, but with the type of day I'm having, I'm thinking we'd both be better off if I just rode shotgun."

"No problem," he said, making his way to the driver's side.

I looked for the handle on the passenger door but couldn't find it.

"How do you get in this thing?"

"Press the button under the body," Scott called out.

I located the button and gave it a push. Even down there, it was still a reach. It didn't open like I'd expected it to. Instead, an electric motor came on and slowly raised the door up like the ones on some of those fancy sports cars. As it did, a set of steps lowered from beneath the body, extending below the nerf bars.

"See, what did I tell you," Ray called out. " It's definitely a white boy's toy. I'll let you two take the lead — that is, if you can manage to even see out of that thing."

"Come on, you two, follow me," I said, climbing up into the cab.

Craig pushed the button under his door and watched as the process was repeated.

"You coming, Doug?" he asked.

"Not on your life," he said, turning towards the others. "I think I'm better off a little closer to the ground." With that, he walked over and hopped into the jeep with Ray. He was a little afraid of heights and really didn't care much about having to climb steps just to get inside.

Settling into my seat, I realized Ray was right; we sat up so high that we lost sight of anything too close to us.

"How do we close the doors?" I asked, trying to reach up for it.

"There's another button on the side of each of the seats," Scott replied. "They're located just behind the controls."

I found the button and gave it a push. Once again, the electric motor kicked on, slowly lowering the door. A second later, I heard the steps rise up and lock into place. Scott flipped a switch on the dash and the entire cab glowed purple. Looking around, I saw more switches and buttons than I'd ever seen before in a vehicle.

"Holy shit, Scott," I said, checking out all the gadgets. "This thing must draw a lot of juice. Just how often do you have to put fuel in it?"

"Only once so far," he grinned. "But it does hold eighty gallons."

He pressed a button on the dash that was glowing red. The truck shook slightly as the large diesel motor came to life. It was surprising how quiet it was in the cab. I could barely hear a little noise from the engine.

"Where to?" Scott asked as he shifted the transmission into first and released the clutch.

"Just take this street to the end and then turn left. We'll follow that road for about a mile or so. When you see the hospital up on the hill, just take any road you can to get to it."

We had a great view from our seats, but I wasn't overly impressed with how uncomfortable the ride was. I guess to make a truck look that radical you had to make some sacrifices.

A few minutes later, the hospital was in sight. With only a few blocks to go, Craig had us stop. After whispering something in my ear, he opened his door and climbed out. We watched as he made his way back to the jeep Ray and

Doug were in. They all spoke for a minute, and then the three of them made their way over to one of the transport vehicles. Ray spoke to the driver, and then Doug and Craig got in and they drove away.

"What's going on?" Scott asked as he watched Ray get back into his jeep.

"You'll see soon enough," I grinned. "Let's head out."

We pulled up the long hill and made the final turn towards the emergency room. I saw the cars we'd smashed through earlier and I could even see the Family Truckster. What was missing, however, were all the people.

With the caravan of trucks behind us, we pulled up near the entrance. There were two medium sized deer hanging from a tree in the middle of the grass but no sign of anyone. It appeared as though they'd bugged out, for some reason.

"Have everyone wait here!" I called out to Scott as I jumped from the truck. "I want to see if everything is safe."

I made my way over to the doors leading into the building and cautiously looked in. Then, as I slowly pushed the doors open, I saw the barrel of a rifle sticking out of a nearby room.

"Really! How many times do I need to get shot today?" I asked, hoping my voice would reassure them they were safe.

"Holy shit, Steve, is that you?" Robert asked as the barrel disappeared behind the door.

"Yes, it's me. Why in the world are you so spooked?"

"Things have been crazy around here," he responded. "In the last couple of hours, we've had drones fly over us three different times. About half an hour ago, we heard some loud noises coming from off to the north. Then, just before you got here, we heard what sounded like a whole convoy coming this way."

"The noise you heard a while ago was because of me. I had some trouble back in town, but it all worked out. Scott and Ray showed up to save the day, bringing with them nearly half the population. You've got to see this! They have more troops and firepower than we've ever had."

Robert came out of the room and took a look outside.

"That explains the noise, but what about those drones? They weren't the normal ones we've been dealing with. These things looked more like the drones we killed back on the interstate. You know, the ones with cameras on them."

"Tell you what, Rob. Let's gather up the rest of our group, and then we'll see what Ray and Scott know about them."

"That's not going to be so easy. With everything that was going on, I had the others take Katherine into hiding. I have no idea where they are."

"Are you OK, Rob? You seem a little nervous."

"I'll feel a whole lot better once she's safe back home."

"Come outside with me. I'll have Scott and Ray fill you in on everything that's been going on. Once you get a look at the army they brought and the new weapons, I know your nerves will calm down. Then we'll set out to find Katherine and the others."

I led Robert outside and gave everyone the all clear. Ray was the first to make it over to us. He couldn't wait to share the story with Robert of my somewhat comical rescue attempt.

While he was telling the story, Scott came over to join us. He'd already given orders to everyone else to set up a temporary camp. The two of them filled us in on their updated weapons and extraction techniques.

"Where's the mother-to-be?" Ray asked after the tour was over.

"I'm not exactly sure," Robert told him. "I sent her and the rest of our team off into hiding about ten minutes before you showed up."

"Tell you what, Rob. I have a new toy we found that I think you'll find pretty impressive."

Ray calmly walked over to his jeep and pulled out a laptop with some type of sonar hooked to it. Aiming it towards the hospital, he turned the screen toward us and made a few adjustments.

"There they are, Rob. Third floor, between the stairwell and a drinking fountain."

It was amazing. The screen showed so much detail, it was almost as if the walls had been removed, and we could see exactly what they were doing. Ray made a few more little adjustments and we could hear part of what they were saying as well.

"Wow, that is one scary piece of equipment," I said, shaking my head.

I stood there staring at it for a good minute, completely dumbfounded that such a thing even existed.

"There was no way around this, was there?" I asked somberly.

The three men gave me a blank look. Then Scott spoke up.

"We're a little confused, Steve," he said softly. "No way around what?"

"You know," I said, shrugging my shoulders, "all this death. It just seems that man was bound and determined to become God. If it hadn't been this group killing everyone off, another group was bound to do it. Hell, with all this technology, I guess we can consider ourselves lucky. One of the other bunch of crazies might've just blown the whole damn planet up."

"Are you seriously defending those assholes?" Robert asked angrily.

"I'm not defending anyone; I'm just beginning to understand them a little better. They saw firsthand all the different weapons man created. If I'd been in that situation, what would I have done?"

"For one thing, you wouldn't have killed nearly every last person on the planet, keeping only a select few alive."

"I don't know, Rob. If we worked out all the numbers and realized the planet was about to die, who would we save?"

"I would've figured out a way to save everyone."

"Hell, even the powers that be knew we couldn't save everyone. We were already sending life to a far-off galaxy just to preserve our species. We've done so much damage to our planet in the last two hundred years that something had to give."

"So, are you telling us that you don't want to fight this war anymore?" Ray asked, sounding surprised.

"No, I want to be part of this," I said, taking the gadget from Ray. "What I'm saying is I want more answers. There's so much of this stuff out there that any schmuck can get his hands on it and do the same thing. I want to do everything in my power to make sure we learn from this and that it never happens again."

"I agree with you wholeheartedly," Scott said, looking at the piece of technology I was holding. "I just believe all of this can be put to good use. We don't have to let things get out of hand again."

"Regardless of who did what," Robert said angrily, "we can't let those pricks who orchestrated this massacre get away with it."

"Trust me, guys," I said. "When this is all over, those responsible will be dead. For now, let's get the others and enjoy the fact that we're still here."

With that, the four of us took off into the hospital. As we exited the stairs onto the third floor, Robert called out to Katherine. Cornelius was the first to greet us. I could tell he was apprehensive about the newcomers, but after we introduced them, he seemed to relax a little. Then he quietly led us into the room where Katherine lay sleeping.

She looked so peaceful lying there, almost as if she didn't have a care in the world. She definitely didn't have to worry about being attacked in her sleep. Every man from our group that hadn't gone with me was sitting on the floor next to her keeping watch. Each and every one of them was ready to lay down his life for Katherine and her unborn son.

"Hey, Steve," Jack called out as I walked in. "Is everything OK?"

"Yes, Jack," I smiled. "Things are better than OK. For those of you that don't already know them, this is Scott and Ray. They've been part of our team since shortly after this all started. They came here today with reinforcements to help us take San Francisco."

"San Francisco?" Charlie asked excitedly. "Is that where we're heading?"

"Yes," I answered. "According to intel, that's where we should find the men who started all of this. Tonight, however, we're going to celebrate. That is, if Katherine is up to it."

Katherine opened her eyes. "Oh, I'm up to it, whatever it is. Cornelius did a little something with the nanites, and I feel great."

Surprised, I turned to Cornelius. "I thought nanites would be bad for her since she's pregnant."

"They are, but I gave her just a small amount directly into her incision. The blueprint the previous nanites left behind is still in her, so there wasn't any break-in period. Once the nanites had repaired her body after the surgery, I gave her a small isolated current and eliminated them."

"Thank God we have you here," I said gratefully. "If not, I honestly don't think we could administer them correctly."

"I'll admit that there's an art to these things," he said, sounding a bit cocky. "If they're not done just right, things can go bad in a hurry."

Hearing a noise behind us, we all turned to see Jason standing in the doorway.

"Can we help you?" Ray asked.

I could tell Ray didn't trust this guy. There was just something about his demeanor. He looked normal, but the way he spoke and looked at people put off a strange vibe.

"I just wanted to see if anyone wanted vegetables with their dinner." He was talking to Ray, but his eyes were locked on the bag Cornelius was carrying.

"Everyone can serve themselves," Ray answered. "For now, you need to be outside with the others."

Jason continued standing there, his eyes still fixated on the bag.

"Can we help you with something?" I asked calmly.

"Is that where he keeps the nanites?"

"You don't need to worry about the nanites, son," Cornelius said, moving out of his view.

"I'm not your son!" Jason snapped back. "I think it's bullshit that you think we're all so far beneath you! You have no right keeping something like that from us."

With that, he turned and slammed a food cart in the hallway onto its side. We could hear him swearing as he stormed off back down the stairwell.

"What the hell set him off?" Katherine asked as she slid out of the bed.

"The boy just has some issues," Ray said, staring at her. "Holy shit, Steve was telling the truth. You are pregnant."

"Yes, I'm only one day along, but my small frame just makes it stand out more," she said with a little laugh.

"How much longer 'til you pop?" Ray asked, putting his hand on her belly.

The rest of us all turned towards Cornelius and Matt. We'd been so focused on everything else that day that none of us had even bothered to ask.

"I'm putting her right at twenty-two weeks, judging by the size of the baby," Cornelius said. "She has roughly four months until she pops, as you put it. She's a very lucky lady to be alive. The nanites that caused her baby to grow so rapidly also kept her body from growing with him. He ended up cracking her pelvis; the nanites repaired it and then he cracked it again."

"Oh shit, that sounds painful," Scott said. "I'm so glad I'm a guy and don't have to go through that."

"I bet," Katherine said sarcastically. "You guys are such pussies that the mere thought of getting pregnant would scare you away from sex forever."

Everyone in the room had to agree with her. The idea of trying to force a baby through such a narrow opening was painful just to think about. Not to mention all the work involved afterward. One thing was for sure; if the shoe were on the other foot, there never would've been such a population problem.

Hearing footsteps in the hall, we all turned, expecting to see Jason again. This time, however, it was Doug and a woman I hadn't met. Her name was Shy'Anne. She had a large box in her hands, while Doug was carrying two large bags.

"Sorry to bug you guys," Doug said, "but we need everyone except Katherine to leave the room."

"What's going on?" Robert asked, taking Katherine's hand.

Just then Craig appeared behind Shy'Anne. He had another large bag in his hand.

"You get to come with me, Robert," he said with a smile. "You're not supposed to see your bride on her wedding day."

"Oh my God!" Katherine cried out.

With tears in her eyes, she quickly ushered everyone out of the room. Stopping Robert and me at the doorway, she gave him a big kiss. Then she turned towards me.

"Steve, thank you so much for all of this," she said, beaming with excitement.

"Don't thank me; it was all Doug and Craig's idea," I replied as we left the room and made our way back down the stairs.

I could feel the buzz in the air as we stepped outside. Two men were just finishing up mowing the lawn, while several others were setting up chairs and building an arbor. The others were all busy with the food and wrapping gifts. They'd turned the whole common area into a beautiful park-like setting for the wedding. They'd even picked flowers to make bouquets.

Everyone was doing his or her part to make this the perfect wedding. Everyone, that is, except Jason; he was nowhere to be found. A few others informed us that he'd stormed out of the hospital earlier and took off on foot. He'd stopped at Ray's jeep and grabbed a bag before leaving.

I offered to help Ray locate him, but he declined. He was hoping some time alone would help Jason get his head on straight. If not, they'd probably be forced to leave him behind.

We went back to work, helping the others. In just over an hour, the whole place had been transformed. The fresh-cut green grass offset the new arbor nicely. There were seven rows of chairs, ten in each. An aisle for the bride to walk down split them right down the middle.

At the edge of each row of chairs was a large bouquet of flowers, everything from roses to daisies. The bride's bouquet was made with asters, purple flowers with yellow centers. They were similar to sunflowers in shape, but the colors were much more vibrant.

They had gotten the tables out of the cafeteria and covered them with clean bed sheets to form the reception area. The chairs for both the wedding and the reception also came from the cafeteria. The centerpieces were made from items found in the gift shop.

On the food end of things, everything looked just as impressive. Two of the men Ray brought with him had been cooks in their former lives. With help from several others from the group, they built an oven in the fire using rocks and bricks. They used it to make the dinner rolls and to bake the wedding cake.

For aesthetic purposes, the one put out for display was a faux cake from a nearby bridal boutique. It had three tiers beautifully decorated in pink and blue, with the bride and groom on top. The cake we actually got to eat was more of a large flat cake with white frosting. It was a little boring looking but served its purpose well.

The meal itself consisted of canned and fresh vegetables, mashed potatoes, the homemade dinner rolls, along with the most amazing BBQ venison I've ever tasted. The whole setup, including cooking all the food and transforming the grass area near the parking lot, took roughly two hours. That had to be some kind of world record.

With about a half hour to go, Doug came down to check on things. He also instructed Jack on ring sizes and sent him back down the road to retrieve both a man and woman's wedding band. As it turned out, the one I found at the lake was only an engagement ring. After that, he caught up to Ray, and both men each brought me a surprise.

Doug informed me Katherine had asked that I give her away. He presented me with a nice black suit. It was my size, except for the pants, which were a tad loose. I was speechless; the idea that Katherine cared enough about me to give me that honor meant the world to me.

Then it was Ray's turn. Walking me over to his jeep, he pulled a letter out of his duffle bag. It was from Michelle.

"I wanted to give this to you earlier, but I didn't think the timing was quite right. You're one lucky man, Steve. I've never seen a woman love someone so much or have as much faith as Michelle has in you."

Ray handed me my letter and walked away. There I was, all alone, a suit in one hand and a note from my own bride in the other. For several minutes, I stood there motionless.

Every memory I had of Michelle seemed to flood my mind. One memory in particular I couldn't shake was the day of the attacks. If I was such a great husband, why the hell didn't I keep her with me after work that day? I knew something wasn't right, yet I still let her take that woman home without me.

As I stood there, almost angry with myself, a gentle voice spoke to me: "There's a reason for everything."

That's all I heard, but it did the trick. I wasn't sure if it was a real voice, or if my mind was playing tricks on me. Regardless, it lifted my spirits and let me release my guilt.

For some reason, Michelle and I were apart during the attacks. If we hadn't been, it's doubtful either of us would've survived. Chances are the outcome for every one of us would've been different.

"Yes," I quietly said to myself. "There is — a reason for everything."

With that, I turned and headed inside to change my clothes. Finding a nice private room with plenty of sunlight,

I put on my new suit and freshened up a bit. Then, after I felt I was clean enough to be worthy of such an honor as I was bestowed, I sat down to read Michelle's letter.

"My Dearest Love, as I sit here next to the creek where we spent so much time together, I can't stop wondering. Are you OK? It feels like forever since I saw that smile — the one that melts my heart. There are so many people here to help me feel safe, yet I still feel so alone. Just last night I was looking up at the stars and wondered if you might be looking at them too, at that very moment. I know in my heart you're still alive, but I can't shake the feeling something bad is about to happen. Please my love, come home to me.
Love, Your Princess Bride

I sat there just reading her letter over and over, trying to picture in my head her loving face. I was reading it for the fourth time and could almost hear the sweet sound of her voice when I heard Robert call out. I quickly folded up my letter and stepped out into the hallway.

"Oh good, there you are," he said as he hurried over to me. "Dude, I'm scared shitless right now."

He held out his hands, and I could see they were shaking uncontrollably.

"I was never this scared fighting the drones," he said, staring at me wide-eyed.

"It's going to be OK, Rob," I said, my voice calm and quiet, trying to comfort him. "Remember, this is what you've always wanted."

"Hell, that's just it. I've never gotten what I wanted before. I don't know how to react to it."

I laughed at him and slapped him on the shoulder. "Trust me, after today you never will again either."

"Oh, thanks, asshole," he said with a nervous smile.

"Come on, Casanova, let's go put you out of your misery," I said, giving him a soft push.

We walked side by side towards the doors that led outside, sharing small talk along the way. As we reached the doors, they opened, and several people we'd never met started shaking our hands and introducing themselves. It was so odd; even though we'd never met any of them, it still felt like we were surrounded by family. Slowly, the small group parted and we saw a familiar face.

It was Scott. He wasn't dressed in the ratty clothes we'd always seen him in. He was actually in a black suit, sporting a priest's collar.

"What the hell is this, Scott?" Robert blurted out.

"Well," he said, "do you remember the day we met and I didn't seem much into fighting? This is why. I've spend the last eight years as a priest and just couldn't get my head around the idea of taking a life."

"What changed?" I asked, taken aback by the whole thing.

"I prayed about it, and I truly believe God spoke to me. He told me I wasn't taking lives, but saving the lives of his children. Ever since then, I just do whatever I need to do to save his people."

Suddenly, Ray grabbed Robert and me from behind.

"Believe me, gentlemen, I was just as surprised as you are when I found out. Trust me, though, when I tell you Scott has been my greatest asset. He stood by me when things were their darkest. I couldn't have asked for a more loyal friend to do battle with. Besides, it never hurts to have God on your side."

"Now, enough talking," he said firmly. "We need to get this show on the road."

Scott and Rob took their place under the arbor. Josh was standing next to Robert as his best man, along with

Ray and Cornelius. There were three girls on Katherine's side as bridesmaids. They each wore light pink summer dresses with purple accents.

I was admiring them as I waited patiently at the door for Katherine.

Suddenly, the door flew open and Shy'Anne pulled me inside. Katherine was standing next to her, and she looked amazing. She had on a beautiful white sequined wedding dress, with a long train flowing effortlessly behind her. Her hair was braided and wrapped up in a bun held in place by a diamond-studded tiara. She was smiling so hard that it damn near made my jaw hurt.

In that instant, she went from being one of the guys to being my little girl. My eyes teared up as I took her arm in mine.

Shy'Anne stepped outside first and cued the music. Then, as she held the door open for us, Katherine turned to me and smiled.

"Thank you," she said softly.

With tears of joy in her eyes, she turned back towards Robert, lowered her veil, and we stepped out.

Chapter 17

JASON'S INDISCRETION

As the doors opened, images of my own wedding day danced happily through my head. Michelle had been such a beautiful bride. Instead of the traditional white dress, hers was a deep purple (her favorite color.) Her hair was done up in an elegant bun; a small wisp of hair in a tight curl flowed softly against her left cheek. She truly was my princess.

We'd been online friends for several years before finally meeting in person. I'd fallen in love with her long before I'd ever laid eyes on her. She was my best friend, and one of the bravest women I'd ever known. On our wedding day, however, she looked terrified.

With a tight grip on her father's arm, she made her way slowly down the aisle. She seemed to stagger like a drunk heading for the bathroom. I remembered laughing to myself and thinking, "That's why the bride walks with her father down the aisle. It's not so much that he can present her to the groom as it is to keep her from falling on her ass."

My mind was a million miles away when the sound of Scott's voice and laughter from the others suddenly got my attention.

"What's that?" I asked, giving him a confused look.

Making sure he had eye contact with me, Scott repeated himself. "I said, who presents this bride to her groom?"

I turned to Katherine and went to give her one last hug. She grabbed hold of me and wrapped her arms around my waist, holding me as tightly as she could. For the first time in my life, I got to experience both the joy and the pain a father feels on his daughter's wedding day. We slowly let go of one another, and I reached out for Robert's hand. As I placed her hand in his, I turned back towards Scott.

"I do," I said proudly.

I took my seat, watching and listening as Robert and Katherine shared their vows with each other. These weren't written sentiments that they'd long thought out, but rather, straight from the heart. Katherine promised to love Robert and to teach their son all the things they valued most. Things like love, family, honesty, and trust. Robert promised to love her and resolve issues that might arise between them with love and understanding. He also swore he'd fight to protect her and their son from any harm. If need be, he'd even lay down his own life to preserve theirs.

Scott said a prayer over them to bless their marriage and offered hope for peace. He prayed they could live their lives without fear and raise their son with the same love that had brought them together. After he'd finished, he asked if anybody wished to object to the marriage. There was no chance of that ever happening, but Scott wanted to have a little fun with it. So, as he asked, he opened his vest with his left hand, revealing an old style Colt 45. Everyone laughed. Hearing no objections, he closed his vest and carried on.

"Robert, do you have a ring for Katherine?" he asked.

Both Robert and Katherine gave Scott a timid look.

"I'm already wearing it," Katherine said softly.

"No, that's an engagement ring," Scott informed them. "Before I can marry you, a ring has to be given to show your never-ending love for one another."

Robert had a blank look on his face. I couldn't tell if he knew Scott was messing with him or if he was about to snap and shoot Scott with his own gun. Either way, it didn't matter; Shy'Anne walked over and handed each of them a small box.

"The sizes are just a guess," she said before returning to her seat.

The two of them opened their boxes in disbelief. Robert looked up at Katherine and then over to me.

"How?" he mouthed.

"Craig and Doug," I said, quietly motioning over to the two of them seated in the row adjacent to mine.

Robert pulled the ring out, but instead of giving it to Katherine, he walked straight over to them. He stopped just short as the two stood up. Robert looked down at the ring and then back at his bride. Returning his gaze to the two of them and slowly shaking his head, he leaned forward and embraced them both.

"You have no idea what this means to us," he said, fighting back the tears. "Thank you so much."

With a huge grin on his face, he returned to Katherine and slid the ring onto her finger. Bawling like a baby, she threw her arms around him and pulled him to her.

"I love you so much," she cried.

"Kat, do you have a ring for Robert?" Scott asked.

"Yes, oh God, yes!" she said, quickly sliding his ring onto his hand.

"By the power vested in me by..."

It was too late. Robert and Katherine were already kissing each other repeatedly. They were both so happy and excited that they could no longer wait for Scott to say the words.

"I'm married!" Katherine called out to all of us, holding up her left hand.

"Yeah, you married Robert!" Josh yelled back to her. "How do you know you wouldn't have liked something a little south of the border even more?"

Robert held up his left hand to Josh.

"All mine, baby," he said happily.

The two of them kissed one more time before joining the rest of us as husband and wife. The whole ceremony took only a few hours to put together and lasted less than ten minutes. Still, it was one of the nicest weddings I'd ever attended. The amazing part was when this day first started, the idea of a wedding was probably the farthest thing from any of our minds. Not to mention, finding out Katherine and Robert were going to have a son. To be honest, I'd thought she was still making him wait.

Robert and Katherine made their way through the crowd thanking everyone, never once releasing each other's hands. It seemed as if for some reason they were both scared to let go. Katherine later told me she was afraid. She feared if she let loose of his hand she'd awaken and find it was all just a dream. Robert, on the other hand, was afraid Josh would try to run off with her. It didn't matter what their reasons may have been, those two were made for each other.

From the first person they thanked to the last, Robert glowingly proclaimed to each one that Katherine was his wife. He didn't do it to be a braggart; he did it because to him there was nothing more noble than the accord a marriage symbolizes.

While he and Katherine were enjoying their first gathering as husband and wife, Craig and Doug started dishing out the food for everyone. As an extra surprise, they also managed to round up some champagne and beer. It wasn't as cold as everyone would've liked, but nobody complained. It had turned out to be a near perfect day.

It was nearly 7:30 p.m. when the two of them finally sat down to enjoy their meal with the rest of us. Katherine still had a glow about her as she raised her glass for the first toast.

"Hello, everyone," she began. "As many of you know, my name is Katherine. The wonderful man seated next to me is my husband, Robert." She paused for a moment and looked at him. "When the attacks first happened, I was at a point in my life where nothing mattered anymore. I had pretty much lost faith in everyone I'd ever known and felt life just wasn't for me. In fact," she said as she began to cry, "just that morning I started to write a note telling the world good-bye. I didn't have any real friends, and my family had all abandoned me. The only reason I even came into work that day was to get some of the poison we'd been using to kill rats."

Robert reached up and took her hand in his. Katherine turned to him, and with tears streaming down her face, she continued.

"I noticed Rob when he first walked through my door at work. Oh, for those of you who don't know, I worked at a mini-mart. Anyhow, when he walked in, I swear I felt my heart skip a beat. He had a lost look on his face, and my heart went out to him. Normally, I avoided making direct contact with people due to my own insecurities. That day, however, I didn't care. I walked right up behind him and was about to literally throw myself at him when the first wave of drones attacked. I'd never been so scared in all my life. It was during the first attack that I realized I didn't want to die; I just wanted someone to share my life with. With that said, I want to make this first toast to my husband."

Looking into his eyes, she said, "Robert, I can honestly say I loved you from the moment I first laid eyes on you."

There wasn't a dry eye amongst us as Robert arose from his chair and held Katherine close to him. As they stood there holding each other, I decided it was a good time for me to share a little about the couple I'd grown to love. I slid my chair back from the table and stood up.

"Everyone, if I can have your attention, please," I said, tapping my glass. "There's no sense in waiting for these two to let go of one another before we go on with the stories. From what I know about them, that may take a while."

As I spoke, I made my way over to the two of them.

"Now, Katherine may claim that she fell for Robert right off. Believe me, she didn't just throw herself at him like she'd planned. Don't get me wrong. We could all see the connection the two of them had right from the start, but she was anything but easy. And Robert! Oh man, that boy doesn't know the meaning of refined. Sticking his cigarette butt in his empty beer can was his idea of cleaning things up. Yet, for two people who at first glance seem so totally different, the two of them truly share one heart. This toast is for two of the greatest people I've ever met. I love—."

"I bet you all think you're pretty fucking invincible, don't you?" a voice suddenly yelled out over the crowd.

We all turned to see Jason standing next to one of the transport vehicles.

"Everyone else is dead, but since you have nanites, you get to go on with life and have parties. I want to see just how invincible you really are."

With that, he pulled a camouflage knapsack out from behind him.

"What the hell are you doing with that?" Ray demanded.

Jason gave him a psychotic look and reached into it, pulling out a grenade.

"I just figured these little babies would give me some trading power."

"What is it you want?" Ray asked, bringing his tone down and trying not to upset him.

"I want that bag that doctor guy has."

"You want my bag?" Matt asked, stepping forward.

"Not you! That other guy. The one with the nanites."

"You're not getting them," Ray said firmly. "Those are for people who are seriously injured or on the verge of death. There just isn't enough to give to everyone."

"I don't give a shit about everyone else. I want the nanites for myself, and if I don't get them now, somebody is going to die."

I watched as Scott reached under his vest for his handgun while Jason spoke. At the time, he was the only one still carrying. The rest of us had put our weapons away before the wedding started. Figuring Scott was the only one who could take him out, I did my best to distract Jason.

"If we give you the nanites, will you promise to just go away?" I asked, slowly walking towards him.

"Show me the nanites first, and then we'll talk."

"Fair enough; just let me get them out of my truck, and I'll give them to you." I knew Cornelius still had the nanites with him, because he rarely went anywhere without them. My objective was to draw Jason's attention away from the others long enough to give Scott a clear shot. So far, everything was going smoothly. Jason's eyes were locked on my every movement and Scott was nearly in position.

"Hold it right there!" Jason yelled at me. "You can go back to the others. I'll get the bag myself."

I'd just started to turn around when Scott squeezed off a shot, striking Jason. That should've been the end of it, but it wasn't. The bullet had only grazed him and he quickly sought cover behind one of the jeeps a few yards away. Without any more hesitation, he pulled the pin from the grenade and threw it into the crowd.

Doing what he could to keep Katherine safe, Robert moved forward to block Jason's view of her. His heart nearly stopped as he watched helplessly while the grenade soared over his head and landed only a few feet from his bride. In an instant, his past flashed before his eyes. This time, however, instead of waking up in a hospital and being told about it, he'd have to witness it.

Katherine froze in place. Her mind screamed at her to run, but her legs wouldn't listen. She turned away and caught sight of Robert. Almost as if she were saying good-bye, she gave him a reassuring smile and closed her eyes. The explosion sounded nearly muffled as the grenade sent shrapnel tearing through flesh. All hell seemed to be breaking loose around him, and he no longer had sight of her. The screams from a few of the women in the crowd pierced Robert's ears, bringing him to his knees. He too was about to scream out when he heard her voice.

"Robert! Where are you?"

Robert sprang to his feet and pushed through the crowd.

"Katherine, is that you?" he yelled.

"Yes, I'm over here. Please hurry,'" she called back to him.

As he made it around the last person, he saw Katherine. She was on her knees in front of a body lying on the ground. Robert rushed over to her and pulled her up into his arms.

"Oh my God, I thought I lost you!" he cried.

"He saved my life," she said, sobbing into Robert's chest.

With his heart still pounding, Robert gently released her and turned his attention to the person lying before him. He reached down and turned the body over. It was Craig.

He and Doug had been carrying the wedding cake over to them just as Jason called out. Remaining motionless, the two of them watched as the events unfolded. Craig's eyes fixated on the grenade in Jason's hand. Almost as if it were his destiny, he watched and waited. Then, spying it flying through the air, he sprang into action. Letting the cake drop to the ground, he sprinted past Doug and dove through the air, landing on the grenade.

Katherine's eyes had remained shut until she heard the scream. Confused that she wasn't in pain, she slowly opened her eyes and saw the body lying before her. Instantly realizing the sacrifice that had been made, she dropped to her knees and called out for Robert.

All the people had blocked my view, so I couldn't tell where the grenade went off. What I could see, though, was that Jason wasn't finished yet. As everyone scrambled for cover, he fired two shots into the crowd with a handgun. Then, pulling out a second grenade, he stepped back out into the open.

"I told you people would die! Now give me those damn nanites!"

I quickly scanned through the crowd as they scattered. There was no sign that anyone was taking the offensive, nor were they in a position to. Figuring all I could do was rush him, I made my move.

"Hold it, Steve!" I heard Cornelius yell. "Let's just give him the bag and end this thing."

I really didn't want Jason to have access to them, but it was better than more blood being shed. I gave Cornelius the go-ahead and stayed put as he walked the bag over to him.

"You know, these things are extremely deadly if you don't use them correctly," Cornelius cautioned.

"You let me worry about that," Jason said, placing the gun against his temple. "Set the bag on the ground, and then take two steps back and stay there."

Cornelius did as he was told. Jason picked up the bag and stepped back behind the jeep. Setting the knapsack and grenade up on the hood, he pulled the bag open.

"What is this bullshit?" he screamed at Cornelius. "There's nothing in here but some jars and needles. Where the hell are the nanites?"

"That's them," Cornelius calmly answered. "They're kept in liquid so they can be handled. All you do is draw a small amount into a syringe and inject them into your body."

"Do I need to do it into a vein?" he asked.

"No. It doesn't make a difference if you hit a vein or not. They'll get where they need to go."

Doing his best to keep one eye on Cornelius, Jason filled a syringe nearly to the top. That was way more than I'd ever seen Cornelius use. I almost said something, but then decided against it. I remembered what Cornelius told us. He said an overabundance of nanites preserve the nervous system as it eats most everything else. Even if he didn't take too much, the same thing would happen without a second shot. If anyone deserved such a fate, it was that asshole.

Nearly everyone stopped and watched as he stuck the needle into his shoulder and pressed the plunger down. After it was empty, he pulled it out and dropped the syringe to the ground. He slowly scanned the crowd before picking up the grenade.

"None of you are worthy of such a gift!" he yelled. Then he raised his gun, pointed it at Cornelius, and fired several shots into his chest. He then pulled the pin on the grenade and stuck it in the bag with the nanites. I panicked at first, fearing he was going to throw it into the crowd. If that happened, the explosion would send what was left of the nanites over anyone standing nearby. Thankfully, he turned and threw it out past the parked vehicles.

I'd just taken off in a full sprint towards Cornelius when I heard Jason start screaming. The sound sent chills through my whole body. It wasn't like I'd never heard someone scream in pain before — I'd just never heard it sound like that. The sound caused me to momentarily forget about Cornelius. I stopped and watched as the nanites dissolved flesh, bone, and organs, while at the same time preserving his entire nervous system.

Little by little, I watched Jason's form change. At first, I thought it was my mind playing tricks on me. His face seemed to droop and his arms hung loosely at his sides as if he had no shoulders. It didn't take long before I realized that what I thought I was seeing was really happening.

I quickly rushed over to the assault vehicle and retrieved my handgun from inside. "The only way to stop the pain he's going through is to put a bullet in his head," I thought to myself as I headed back to him.

These things almost seemed biblical. On one end you had eternal life, free from pain and harm, and on the other end you had eternal damnation — an eternity of pain and suffering, unable to cry out or do anything about it. The thought nearly made me sick to my stomach.

Scott had moved towards Jason while I was getting my gun. Even though he'd attacked all of us and had done so only for his own benefit, Scott still couldn't help feeling compassion for him. Slowing my pace, I watched as Scott emptied his revolver, hoping to end Jason's pain.

His wailing subsided, but it wasn't because he was dead. It was because of the combination of the nanites eating away his insides and Scott's bullets tearing through his lungs. Jason was far from dead; he just no longer had air to scream with.

Seeing that he was still alive, Scott moved in closer, hoping to figure something out.

"Stay away from him, Scott!" a voice called out.

It was Cornelius.

"When those nanites finish eating through his flesh, they're going to want a new host. As long as we're not too close, they'll end up in the soil and eventually just die. If you do happen to get too close... Well, you see what happens."

Scott quickly jumped back and turned his attention to Cornelius.

"How is it you're still alive?" he asked.

"All in due time. For now, let's end this poor bastard's suffering."

"I'm on it!" I said, stepping forward and raising my gun towards him.

"Now remember, Steve," Cornelius said, "you must hit him directly in the head. You may want to take several shots. He's past the point of being able to tell if he's still alive or not."

He was right. Jason no longer resembled anything I'd ever seen before. What was left of him lay in a bubbling pile on the ground. At first glance, it nearly appeared as if he'd been turned inside out. The parts of him that his clothes covered now looked more like jam being forced through a strainer. His eyes, teeth, and skull had completely dissolved, and only a small patch of hair-covered skin now lay over his exposed brain.

Taking a deep breath, I fired round after round into the gelatin-like mass. Each time I did, tiny bits of brain matter and molten flesh splattered against the jeep he'd been standing near. Finally, hearing the click of the firing pin against the empty chamber, I quit pulling the trigger.

My whole body shook uncontrollably as I let loose of my gun and dropped to my knees. Leaning forward, I put one hand on the ground to steady myself. Almost as if on cue, everything I'd just eaten came hurling out of me. The nanites may have been able to fix gunshots and broken bones, but they did absolutely nothing for my stomach. The combination of seeing and smelling Jason as he turned to mush was beyond anything I'd ever experienced before.

My mind suddenly raced back to the first grenade. I knew Jason threw it in the vicinity of Robert and Katherine, but I didn't know the outcome. Had everyone gotten out of the way? What about the ones Jason shot? I jumped to my feet and raced through the crowd.

"You and I need to have a talk," I told Cornelius as I shot passed him and Scott.

Matt was already working on one of the gunshot victims, a young woman. Her wound appeared to be superficial but still very painful. The bullet had pierced the back of her calf muscle and continued on through her shin. It would've been much worse, but the bullet never mushroomed. We made eye contact and I paused momentarily, trying to recall her name. She was one of the people Ray brought with him to help us. I'd only met her briefly then. As she smiled at me, her name popped back into my head.

"Don't worry, Sara," I said, returning the smile, "Matt will take good care of you."

I moved to the next person, which was Charlie. His brother, Jack, was doing his best to keep pressure on the bleeding. The bullet had entered his left butt cheek but there didn't appear to be an exit wound. I mentioned this to him and received a dirty look in return. Then, carefully rolling himself over, he removed a bloodied rag from his groin.

Seeing that it missed any vital organs, I chuckled. "Good thing it was hanging to the right and not the left, or we'd have to call you stubby," I ribbed him.

Jack gave me a wink. "Between the two of us, you might say he got the short end of the stick."

"Screw both you assholes," Charlie moaned as he put a fresh rag against his wound.

"Don't worry, Charlie. We're just giving you a hard time," I assured him. "Cornelius or Matthew should be with you shortly."

Several people had gathered near the area where Katherine and Robert had been seated. Heading in that direction, I could feel my heart rate increasing. Forcing my way through the crowd, I was afraid of what I might find. The idea of anyone being killed was bad enough, but I really wasn't sure what I'd do if it were the bride or groom. I was passing the last of the bystanders when Josh grabbed my arm.

"Who is it, Josh?" I asked, seeing Doug cover a body with one of the linens from a table.

"It's Craig," he said softly.

A sudden sense of relief flowed through me. I felt bad that Craig had paid for Jason's greed with his life, but at the same time, I was grateful that only one body lay there.

"Find Ray," I told Josh. "Get him over here to help Doug with Craig's body. I want you to find Scott also."

"What do you want Scott to do?" he asked.

I glanced down at Doug sitting there on the ground.

"I just need Scott to be there for him. In fact, I need Scott to make himself available to everyone. We've all suffered a lot of loss this last month, and I want someone available to help us grieve. I don't want to see anyone else so broken and lost that they do the same thing Jason did."

"What about you?" he asked. "What are you going to do?"

"I'm going to go home and say good-bye to Michelle," I answered bluntly. "Then I'm taking anyone who'll go with me to San Francisco and kill those bastards that are responsible for all this."

"Just make sure that you take me with you."

"For what part?" I asked.

"All of it," he said, sounding nervous. "I've lost everything and everyone I've ever known or loved. Without the four of you, I'm afraid I'd just give up."

Without waiting for a response, he turned and slowly walked away. All Josh wanted was for our little group to always stay together — nobody leave and nobody die.

Spotting Robert and Katherine, I quickly made my way over to them and pulled them both to me. I felt the same as Josh. Many people were sure to come and go over our lifetime, but there was just something different about the five of us.

"It's over for the two of you," I said as we stood there holding onto each other. "You need to go home and focus on being a family."

"You're partially right," Katherine corrected me.

"What do you mean?"

"Robert and I already spoke. We figured you wouldn't allow us to go with you, but to be honest, it's not your decision. So this is how we see it. You come home with us and see Michelle. Then you and Robert can come back here to rejoin the group and finish this. I'll stay with Michelle, and she can help me with the pregnancy."

"It's not that easy, Katherine," I said. "Too many things—"

"We know the risks," she said, cutting me off mid-sentence. "It's not about us anymore; it's about our baby. The two of us have lost pretty much the same things in life. If the only reason we lived through the attacks was to have this baby, then we're OK with that. In fact, we're better than OK; we're blessed."

"It's a deal," I replied, "but on two conditions."

"What are those?" Robert asked.

"Number one, we take anyone that isn't up to this back with us."

"Fair enough," Robert agreed. "And number two?"

"We find out the truth about Cornelius."

"What are you talking about?" Robert asked. "I thought he'd been totally up-front with us?"

"Apparently not so much," I said. "Jason shot him three times and he got right back up."

311

"Are you saying he has nanites in him?" Katherine asked, not sounding overly surprised.

"Shoot, if it were just the nanites, I wouldn't even bother bringing it up. I mean, why would you create something to make man nearly immortal and not use it yourself? No, it has more to do with a look he gave me when I found out about them. There was just a little too much guilt in that look to be just nanites."

We all turned to look for Cornelius. When I spotted him, it was obvious he'd been watching us. He quickly diverted his eyes and turned towards the assault vehicle. It was almost as if he were considering running. Finally turning back towards us, he took a deep breath and started walking our way.

Chapter 18

A GREAT GRANDPA

If I had learned one thing over the past month, it was to expect the unexpected. We couldn't let setbacks keep us from achieving the good we set out to accomplish. Cornelius was still an intricate part of our plan, and regardless of what had just happened, I still trusted him with my life. I just had a strange feeling there was more to his story than he'd shared with us. I couldn't really blame him for not being more forthcoming about having been injected with nanites. Hell, I would've been a little tight-lipped myself, considering the circumstances in which we met. Sometimes we feel we need our secrets to protect ourselves. Still, with so much at stake for everyone, secrets were a luxury none of us could afford.

As Cornelius made his way over to us, Robert's eyes kept going back and forth from me to Cornelius. He hadn't seen the look Cornelius gave me earlier, and in some way, he was hoping he might see it for himself. Regardless, he knew I'd ensure it was dealt with before moving on, whatever it was.

Cornelius hadn't noticed the way Robert kept looking at him. His eyes were fixated on Katherine.

"I'm sorry your wedding day was ruined," he softly said as he stood before us.

"Don't blame yourself," she responded. "There was no way anyone could've seen that coming. Besides, Rob and I have both been through much worse — we all have. I'm just a little concerned about you."

"I'm fine. I'm just afraid I let you guys down."

"Why would you say that?" Katherine asked.

Cornelius turned his head down toward the ground. I could tell he didn't have the heart to look either Robert or me in the eyes. We stood there quietly watching him as he nervously bit the side of his lower lip.

"Can we go for a walk?" he asked, still not wanting to look up.

"What's wrong with this spot?" Robert asked, trying to get Cornelius to face him. Instead of looking at Robert, he turned his gaze to Craig's lifeless body just a few yards away.

"To be honest, Rob, I have so much guilt built up inside me right now that I just can't stay here anymore. Besides, it's going to be hard enough to tell the three of you what I have to say. I don't think I can do it with everyone listening."

"What are you talking about? Nobody else is listening," Robert said.

At first it appeared he was correct. Everyone was either doing some sort of cleanup or tending to the dead or injured. A more careful observation, however, revealed that just wasn't the case. They might've seemed busy, but almost everyone was heavily engrossed in our conversation.

"OK, now I see what you're talking about," Robert said, embarrassed that he hadn't noticed it earlier. "I don't have a problem taking a little walk; how about you two?"

"I'm good with that, " Katherine said, trying to sound upbeat.

"What about you, Steve?" Robert asked, raising his voice slightly to get my attention.

"Oh, yeah. I don't have a problem with that either," I said, still staring at the others.

"Hey, Ray, can you handle things here, please?" I called out. "Cornelius is pretty shaken up right now, and we feel it's best to let him walk it off."

"No problem, Steve. Just do me a favor and bring me up to speed on everything when you get back."

"You go it," I answered, not really hearing what he said.

The four of us took off walking, and nobody said a word for nearly ten minutes. Cornelius had the lead, with me less than half a step back on his right side. Robert and Katherine were directly behind us. Not wanting to pressure Cornelius, they refrained from talking and instead focused on each other. Holding hands as they walked, they didn't need words. The way they looked at one another said everything they wanted to say.

I, on the other hand, was lost in my own thoughts. I couldn't put my finger on it, but something didn't seem right back there. No matter how hard I stared at the others, I couldn't figure out what seemed out of place. Was it that I had just seen a man stay fully conscious while being dissolved from the inside out? Maybe it was the idea that we went from having a wedding to having a murder? Whatever it was, it sure caused me to feel uneasy inside.

Reaching a small house nearly a half mile from the hospital, Cornelius came to a stop.

"Would you mind if we sit on the porch for a bit?" he asked as he turned toward me.

"I don't see why not," I answered. "Go ahead; we'll follow you."

The house was one of those little one-bedroom places that you'd expect a little old couple to have. The old wood siding was painted a cheerful light blue, with white trim. Both of the front windows had flowered curtains that were pulled back to let the light in. There was even a large covered porch that went from corner to corner. That seemed nearly as inviting as the flower-lined path that led up to it.

Cornelius made his way up the path and took a seat on the second step. Then, as the three of us sat down near him, he began to speak.

"My wife and I used to have a little house just like this," he began. "During the spring and summer, we'd spend nearly every evening out there sipping sweet tea and reading to our grandkids." He paused for a moment and took in the confused looks on our faces.

"Don't worry, you heard me right. Mildred and I had two beautiful granddaughters and one of the most rambunctious grandsons I'd ever set eyes on. They were my whole world, and if I could go back in time, I never would've left that old porch. I would've stayed retired and somehow dealt with the death of my wife. At least then I could've been there for my grandchildren."

It was as if a light went on in my head, and I began to see both the good and the bad of nanites more clearly. It wasn't just the side effects that could inflict pain. Even more painful was to lose the ones you loved while you yourself faced immortality alone.

"Cornelius," I said softly. "May I ask how old you are?"

"Let's just say I've seen the turn of the century twice in my lifetime. In fact, the first time I ever rode in an automobile was after my wife and I got married."

"That doesn't make any sense," Katherine said as she got to her feet to face him. "When we met you, you told us you were twenty-five. I even thought that was a stretch. Not to mention you wear glasses and have scars. According to everything you've told us about the nanites, your eyes and skin should be nearly flawless."

"I added some flaws to my own DNA to create the scars. I've also learned to act more like everyone else just to fit in. Like back at the river, while Robert and Katherine were nearly frozen. I wasn't cold at all, but I did my best to convince you I was. As for the glasses," he reached up to his face and pulled them off, "I've been wearing these dang things for nearly fifty years, just so I could fit in easier. Every now and then I get new ones to keep closer to current styles. I can see fine with them on, and without them my vision compares to that of some birds."

"Bullshit!" Robert blurted out. "I'm sorry, Cornelius, but that just isn't possible."

"I know how this all sounds. That's one of the reasons I've never had the guts to tell you the truth. Until you actually experience it for yourself, there's just no way to comprehend it.

"I've got an idea!" Robert said, jumping to his feet. "I picked up a dime earlier. I'm going to go across the street and hold it up for you. If you can tell me the date on it, I'll believe everything you have to say without question. "

Robert quickly ran up the path and out into the street.

"This should do!" he yelled, pulling the coin from his pocket.

Holding the coin by its sides, between his thumb and forefinger, he held it out in front of him for us to see.

"Now, Cornelius," he said haughtily, "all you have to do is tell me the date on my dime."

Straining my eyes, I could barely make out he was holding a coin at all, and I considered my vision to be better than ever. I could tell by the way Katherine was squinting that she too was trying her best to see it.

With a soft smile on his face, Cornelius slowly shook his head. "Sorry, Rob. I can't tell you the date on your dime."

"Ha! See, you're full of shit, just like I thought."

"Maybe if you held up a dime instead of a penny, I'd be able to answer your question. However, if it makes you happy, your penny was minted in 1943. Unfortunately, due to my poor vision, I can't tell you where it was minted."

"It can't be a penny," Robert insisted as he stared at it. "Pennies are made of copper."

"Not in 1943, sonny boy. Except for a few that may have slipped through, they were all made of steel. Copper wasn't used for coins in that year, just bullets."

Still staring at his penny, Robert walked over and retook his seat.

"It might be easier to understand if I just go back to the beginning," Cornelius said. "The year was 1935, and my wife and I were both molecular biologists at Caltech. We were only in our forties, but we were already considered two of the brightest minds in our field. It was that year that the U.S. Government approached us to do research on the effects radiation had on DNA. At the time, we felt it was a huge honor for such a task. What we didn't realize was the high cost with such an assignment."

He told us that by 1940, his wife was diagnosed with bone cancer, caused from exposure to the radiation. The following spring, he too was diagnosed.

"In 1942, the university suspended our research and let us both take an early retirement," he said. "We knew there was no hope for survival, so we bought a little house near the air force base where our daughter and her husband were stationed. Our plan was to spend every minute we could with our grandchildren.

"The next several years, we were treated with several experimental drugs. It wasn't so much to kill the cancer as it was to prolong life a little longer and keep the pain at bay. Nearly every day was spent out on our porch reading to our grandchildren and reminiscing about our lives together. Then in 1946, exactly one week before our grandson's sixteenth birthday, my beloved Mildred passed away. I was no longer willing to accept my fate and decided to do something about it.

"She died on a Wednesday and was buried on Sunday. Monday morning, I was on my way to a secret research facility in Wendover, Utah. My lab was a mile underground in the middle of what once had been a missile test site. I never saw my children or grandchildren again."

Cornelius explained that during his first year there, his main focus was just trying to stay alive. Then, in 1947, he discovered a link in his own DNA and the cancer inside him. He instantly began work creating something small enough to destroy single strands of DNA instead of large bodies of cells. He'd managed to prolong his own life, but development was painstakingly slow, and his confinement was beginning to take its toll. However, on April 7, 1953, his entire world changed forever.

"I was having breakfast when my commanding officer showed up with a little kid in tow," he recalled. "As fate would have it, I was this child's last living relative. My granddaughter had died a month earlier, and her husband, whom I'd never known about, died before the baby was born. It turned out that I'd lost my son, his wife, and all three of my grandchildren in less than five years.

"Not wanting me to raise a child underground, the powers that be moved my research to the private sector. I spent every moment that I wasn't doing my research with my great-grandson. He loved the stories I told him and tried to share with me the ones he could remember his mom telling him. His favorite was the story about the first gentile to convert to Christianity, whose name was Cornelius. Yes, that's how I eventually got my name. My great-grandson gave it to me. We continued to learn together, and he actually understood all my research."

In 1959, Cornelius had a major breakthrough in his work, thanks to another scientist. Richard Feynman was a theoretical physicist at Caltech a few years after he and his wife left.

"His work on nanotechnology changed my way of thinking, and soon after that, I had the catalyst I needed to alter DNA. Over the next several years, we made change after change, but the outcome was always the same. The nanites would destroy all the bodily fluids containing the DNA before reaching its destination. In 1965, the government caught wind of what we were doing and shut down the company I was working for, taking control of my research. They didn't intend to use it for the same purpose we had. Instead, they wanted to try it in chemical warfare. I refused to take part in such a heinous endeavor, so they removed my great-grandson and me from the premises."

Cornelius told us that at fifteen, his great-grandson had such a vast knowledge of microbiology and molecular chemistry that he wowed the chemists at DuPont. Despite his age, he was asked to join their R&D team. He met Bob Marley soon after that.

"No longer doing our own research, the two of us moved into a small apartment in Wilmington, Delaware," he said. "He worked all day, and at night he continued working with nanites in private. The government had taken everything we had on nanites, but they couldn't take our love for them.

"Finally, in 1972, my cancer took over again. The doctor told me I had about two weeks to live. It was then that my great-grandson approached me and told me what he'd been doing. He hadn't gotten all the bugs worked out, but it was close. He'd figured out a formula where the first round of nanites created a blueprint and the second round stabilized the first. He was still trying to perfect the time frame between the two, but the variable kept changing. Due to the fact that time was not on our side and we had no other options, he injected me with them.

"It was about a month later that we realized the nanites' true capabilities. Not only had they cured my cancer, but they also actually reversed the aging process. I was getting younger! We were excited by this latest breakthrough and stepped up our research. Unfortunately, we weren't the only ones taking note of my sudden change. Some government officials started poking around, so we decided to go into hiding. That's when I started going by Cornelius; before that I had always gone by Clifford."

They stayed hidden until the spring of 1987. That was when his great-grandson decided it was time to share their discovery with the world.

"Mind you, there really wasn't a world wide web back then, but he could still use phone lines to transmit information between computers. At eight o'clock in the morning, Pacific Standard time, on April 27, he started sending our files to the American College for Advancement in Medicine. By noon, with about only half the files sent, we received a knock on the door. It was a federal marshal.

"At that point, we were detained by the government and spent the next month as prisoners at Guantanamo Bay. During that time, they decommissioned the naval facility at Coos Bay and turned it into a research laboratory. In exchange for our freedom, we agreed to live there and continue developing our nanites for them."

"Didn't they question who you were?" I asked. "I mean, it's the government. They're not going to just have you do work for them without a background check."

"Back then, things weren't quite as complicated as they were just a month ago. My great-grandson and I had already created our new identities, including birth certificates, school transcripts, and even service records. I was to be known as Cornelius Rutherford, a twenty-five-year-old science major. My great-grandson was now my father, Gerald Rutherford, a theoretical physicist and amateur inventor."

"When we met you, you told us he was your grandfather," I said, still taken aback by his whole story.

"Every so often they'd replace the staff and guards at the base. I hadn't aged, but my great-grandson had. So, during one of the changes in 2005, we altered our paperwork to show him as my grandfather instead of my father. Nobody really seemed to care enough to check into it. They were just there to babysit us. It wasn't until 2012 that the base changed from being strictly military run to being run by more of the computer nerd types. The only military personnel on the base were the ones handpicked by our new commander."

Cornelius went on a little longer, telling us about how they started using the nanites to create new, smaller, more efficient nanites. He also told us that he and his great-grandson had a falling out because his great-grandson refused to be injected with them. It was quite the tale. By the time he'd answered all of our questions, the sun had not only set, but it was also nearly midnight when we finally made it back to the others. I could see Ray sitting alone near the campfire. While the others found a nice spot to sleep, I went over and joined him.

"Well, how did it go?" he asked, handing me a cold beer.

"It was actually quite interesting," I replied.

I filled him in on everything Cornelius shared with us. I also let him know about my intentions of heading home for a day or two. He was very receptive to the idea of a couple days R&R. There was no telling what this next battle of ours would curtail, so a few days to relax first would be nice.

On the other hand, he wasn't overly sure what to think about Cornelius. The idea of nanites being able to rapidly repair our bodies was confusing enough. It just seemed too unbelievable to look at this acne-scarred kid and accept that he was nearly a hundred years older than any of us.

The two of us pondered why Cornelius would fabricate such a story. We also imagined what life could be like if he were actually telling us the truth. Either way, the nanites had already proven to be both beneficial and deadly. The fact that Cornelius was the only one who truly understood them made him a valuable asset to have on our side.

As the night wore on, the two of us discussed a suitable spot to rendezvous. We wanted a location that gave him and his men ample coverage as well as visibility. It also had to be a spot we could easily locate so we wouldn't unwittingly bypass them when we returned.

Ray and I still hadn't decided on a location when the morning light began to make its way over the horizon. We had spent most of the night checking and rechecking our maps, trying to find a suitable spot, when Josh came over to join us.

"Good morning, gentlemen," he said, taking a seat next to us. "Have you guys been up all night?"

"Yes," I replied. "We can't seem to agree where to meet up after I visit Michelle."

"Do you mind if I add my two cents to your conversation?"

"Not at all," Ray responded. "We could use a fresh perspective."

"What have you come up with so far?" Josh asked.

"Well, Steve was thinking either the airport or the mall. The airport doesn't conceal our vehicles very well. Not only that, but it's also not directly in view of the interstate."

"Does it need to be right on the freeway?" Josh asked as he looked at our map.

"No, not necessarily. I just don't want him and his group to somehow drive right past us. I was thinking more along the lines of the stockyard," Ray said, pointing at the map. "That would give us a place to park our vehicles under cover. It's also on a frontage road next to the freeway, allowing us better visibility to watch for them."

"What do you think, Josh?" I asked. "You know this area quite well."

"I'll admit I like the idea of the stockyard, but there's one spot that will work even better for you," he said. "Have you considered using the CHP checkpoint?"

"No," Ray answered. "To be honest, I don't even know what that is."

"It was one of the weigh stations along I-5. The highway patrol used it to inspect trucks."

"Don't those things just have little shacks that the guys doing the weighing sit in?" Ray asked, still wanting to use the stockyard.

"Not this one," Josh responded. "It has offices and enough indoor parking to accommodate every vehicle you have. It also has access damn near right on the freeway and a clear view in every direction. If for some reason you need to hide out, I heard from a friend that there's a bomb shelter under the office space. I've never seen the shelter myself, but regardless, it would make a great meeting point."

"Can you show us where it is on the map?" I asked Josh.

"Sure," he replied. "It's right here just a few miles past the stockyard."

The three of us studied the map for a while. From everything he'd told us, this would make the ideal spot to reconvene. There was no way for Ray and his men to miss us if we tried to drive by. Nor would we wonder if we were in the wrong spot if they weren't there.

"Looks to me like we finally have someplace we can agree on," Ray said happily.

"In that case," I said, "let's get breakfast made for everyone and find out who all is going with me."

I was in a great mood as we cooked breakfast. For the first time since we'd been separated, I was actually going to see my wife. In my mind, it was almost like we'd never been apart. I could still feel her warm kisses on the side of my neck and hear the sweet sound of her voice. She'd held a special place in my heart from the moment our hands first touched.

I thought back to one of our first dates together. We were both nearly penniless, but she wanted to do something special for me. I showed up at her apartment to find she'd prepared a picnic lunch for us. Then, using the last little bit she had on her credit card, she filled the gas tank in her car.

I had no idea where she was going to take me. As it turned out, neither did she. Each turn we made was decided by her asking me to choose, right or left. There was no set destination; that wasn't what the trip was about. In her eyes, it was just about spending time together. That, and to let me know that no matter where life took us, she wanted to be there with me.

Even though we hadn't been together very long, by the end of that date I knew she was my sole reason for existing. From then on, it didn't matter what we were doing; we were inseparable. I shared my love for the outdoors with her, and she shared her love of concerts and movies with me. She was much more than just the girl I loved; she was my best friend.

I could've spent the rest of my days basking in the memories of the love we shared. I could have, that is, if it hadn't been for Jason. I'd been making my way over to one of the transports to wake up those still sleeping when I nearly stepped into his remains. The vision of that gooey mess lying on the ground snapped me back to reality.

Most of the body had turned into some type of foamy gelatin. The nanites had preserved his nervous system up until his brain had been killed. Now that they had nothing to preserve, they were lying dormant in what was left. Cornelius assured us they would die in time, but until then we needed to avoid touching any of the gooey mess. If someone or something did come in contact with it, they too would share the same fate as Jason. Even worse, if nobody was around to destroy their brain.

I asked about killing them with electric shock, but he couldn't give me a definitive answer. He claimed that due to the excited state they were in, the introduction of electricity could actually charge their particles, making them airborne. I wasn't really sure what he was talking about, but nonetheless, I chose to leave them alone.

With my mind no longer in the clouds, I began to worry. What if Michelle and I had changed so much that the spark we once shared was gone? What if she decided I'd become a cold-hearted killer, void of empathy? I'd done so many things this last month that I myself felt cold and merciless.

Reaching the transport vehicle, I forced the negative thoughts out of my head and woke the others.

"Good morning, everyone!" I called out cheerfully. "Rise and shine."

"What's that smell?" Scott asked as he lifted his head off the floor.

"Fresh coffee, scrambled eggs, and a whole mess of flap jacks," I replied.

"What! No bacon?" came a voice a little further back. It was Charlie Daniels.

"Nope. Sorry, Charlie," I said deviously. "Now, get a move on; I want to be on the road in an hour."

It was nearly seven by the time everyone was up and fed. There was little to no talk about what had happened the night before. It was still there in the back of everyone's minds, but this was a new day. The past was merely a marker in time, a thing we could learn from or even reflect on. It was the basis for the stories we'd someday share with our children and our children's children. It wasn't a place, however, where we could afford to dwell.

As I kicked back with Robert and Katherine out on the lawn, Josh busied himself getting some medical supplies. He made three trips between the hospital and the assault vehicle with his arms full. It wasn't until after he felt we had enough bandages and antibiotic ointment to last a lifetime that he took a seat next to us.

The four of us sat and listened as Ray went over the game plan for the next couple days. He painted a picture in everyone's minds about how much fun this group was going to have. How they could loot the mall and hook their generators up to run the projectors at the cinema. He also promised to butcher a few steer and have a BBQ party in the middle of the civic auditorium.

Afterwards, he talked about my group heading back into Oregon. He talked about how much fun we'd have scavenging for food and fuel. He said the trip would be long and tiresome, but we could all look forward to a rewarding nap when it was over.

I'll admit, Ray was one hell of a salesman. By the time he finished, even my group had second thoughts about leaving. In fact, if it hadn't been for Michelle and Katherine, I'm convinced our trip would've been canceled.

"What about the two people Jason shot?" I asked.

"I already spoke with them," Ray assured me. "They both believe they can continue on."

As it was, only the five of us from our original team opted to go home. That was just fine with us. We'd all been together since day one, and that made it seem more like a family vacation. The hardest part was knowing that both Katherine and Michelle would be left behind when we took off again.

Ray had a few of his men refuel our vehicle, and we were on our way by eight. I felt like a little kid going to Disneyland for the first time. Josh was behind the wheel, and I was riding shotgun. Well, at least I was supposed to be. I kept going from my seat to the back, and then to my seat again. I was sharing stories of adventures Michelle and I had together. At first, everyone was more than willing to listen, but by the time we got to Medford, they were ready for some new entertainment.

The assault vehicle had a stereo with a CD player, so we stopped at the mall on the north end of town to get some music. That was an adventure in itself. The glass on the doors leading into the mall had been broken out, letting every type of animal you can imagine in there. A herd of deer was bedded down in the food court, along with several families of raccoons. At one point, I thought I spotted a bear entering JCPenney, but since I don't trust bears, I didn't go inside to confirm that.

I was amazed at the amount of natural lighting the mall offered. Even with the power off, the main section was lit up enough to easily see everything. As the others went into the music store, I separated from them and went to Kay Jewelers. I hadn't seen my bride in so long that I thought it would be nice to get her a little gift for our reunion.

As I entered the jewelry store, it brought back a flood of memories. Michelle and I had gone to the one in Roseburg during her lunch hour years ago. It was then that she realized how serious I was about marrying her. Back then, however, I couldn't afford the ring she'd fallen in love with. We had to settle for something a little smaller and with a lot less flash. Today, however, the sky was the limit. Not only did I find the ring she originally wanted, and in her size, but I also got her earrings and a beautiful necklace to match.

I met up with the others as they finished their shopping. Each of them carried a stack of CDs and a few DVDs to watch when we got home. Glancing at their selections, I could tell it was going to be an interesting trip. Josh was into some new music I'd never heard of, including things like the Catalyst and Burning in the Skies. Robert seemed to like the rock bands from the eighties and Katherine was into country. I liked both rock and country, but to me the stuff Josh had really didn't sound that good. Cornelius, on the other hand, only had two CDs I recognized; both were Bailey & the Boys. The others were some big band stuff from the twenties.

We all had a nice time together, singing along when we could and making fun of Josh's stuff when he played it. A few songs of his, however, started to grow on us a little. By the time we hit Roseburg, we knew most of the words. Other than listening to the music, there was nothing really eventful about the last part of our trip.

It was 4:05 p.m. as our tires left the pavement and started down my long dirt drive. My heart felt as if it would rip through my chest, it was beating so hard. I was excited and nervous at the same time. In a matter of moments, the greatest love of my life would be standing in front of me. I had no idea how I should react. Should I sweep her off her feet and into my arms, or should I wait and let her take the lead?

I jumped from the vehicle before it came to a complete stop. My mind was still spinning wildly as I made my way past the tree line and started heading towards the entrance of the shelter.

Then, off to my right, I saw her. She was facing away from me, sitting on the ground in front of the memorial

Justin had made. As I got closer, I could see she was tending to some flowers someone had planted. I was quietly walking over to her when she picked up a picture of us and started to cry.

Chapter 19

GIRLS AND GUNS

All my fears of how Michelle would react disappeared the moment I saw her sitting there. Her long chestnut hair gently flowed in the breeze, and I could smell the soft fragrance of her perfume. She had lost a lot of weight, but she didn't appear to be overly frail.

"Hello, beautiful," I said softly as I walked up behind her.

Dropping the picture from her hands, she quickly jumped to her feet and spun around. For a moment, she stared at me with a lost look. Her soft cheeks were moist from her tears, and her mouth was slightly open. I could tell she wanted to say something but couldn't.

Then, as her tears started to flow again, I wrapped my arms around her and held her tightly. For nearly a minute we just stood there, neither one of us saying a word. It was as if we were trying to erase all the things from our minds that had pulled us apart. Fighting back the tears, she pulled me closer.

"I was afraid I'd never see you again," she softly said.

"I had that same fear myself," I said, my voice cracking a little. " I'm so sorry I couldn't make it back to you sooner."

"You're here now. That's all I care about."

I had totally forgotten about the others until I heard Robert's voice.

"So, are you going to introduce us, or do we just get to stand here and look stupid?"

"Sorry, Rob," I said, releasing my hold on Michelle just enough to turn towards him. "I can't change the way you look."

"Very funny, asshole," he said as he moved in to hug both of us. "I'm Robert. It's a pleasure to finally meet you."

The other three also joined in the hug, introducing themselves as they did.

Giving Michelle a soft kiss on the lips, I released her momentarily and gave them all a proper introduction.

"I've heard so much about all of you that it seems like I already know you," Michelle said as she greeted them.

"Yes, I can imagine that once Ray found you, he had plenty to share," Katherine said, pulling Robert into her arms.

"Actually, it was before I ever met Ray. I started hearing about all of you pretty much the moment I was picked up. One of the men guarding us questioned me about a group of rebels who had killed some drones. Without thinking, I told them that was my husband and he was coming to save me. That could've been why I was treated differently. There were strict rules on speaking — I mean strict to the point the drones would kill you. Yet, they never seemed to bother anyone I spoke to or me. They just listened in. More and more stories floated around the guards about all of you for several days. Then one morning, they forced several other people I'd been talking to and me onto a train. The next day they dropped us off at a different camp, but they didn't make us clean up any more bodies. They just locked us inside a warehouse and kept an eye on us.

"I wasn't totally sure if it was Steve they had been talking about until Ray and the others found us. He asked all of us to tell him our names and took notes. When he got to me, I told him my name and he looked really serious. Then he called some other people over and asked my name again. I was really nervous at first, thinking he was there to kill me. Then when I said my name again and told them where I was from, everyone got excited. They rushed me outside and put me in a pickup all by myself. Several men with guns stood guard around the truck as I sat there. Then finally, Ray came over and got into the truck next to me. He asked me if I knew Steve and when I told him I did, he told me what was going on. I don't think I stopped crying until we were back in Oregon."

Michelle quit talking for a moment and wrapped her arms around me. She started to cry again as she turned her head to gaze into my eyes.

"I just can't believe you're really here with me," she said as she pressed her lips to mine.

Michelle and I enjoyed the feel of one another a little longer as the others looked over the memorial Justin had started.

"Who made this?" Katherine asked, trying to steal our attention.

"Justin did," I replied. "The day we all took off for Coos Bay. He made it for his parents, but it looks as if it's grown a bit."

"Everyone who comes through here tries to add a little something to it," Michelle said. "I think it helps to have some place special where we can remember those we've lost."

"Wow! I think that's beautiful," Katherine said, kneeling down in front of it. "That sure is one strong little boy."

"Yeah, he is," added Michelle. "When I first got home, I almost lost it. Not only was my husband missing, but also my home was completely destroyed. It was Justin that gave me the strength I needed to keep going."

"We're so sorry," Katherine said, giving Michelle her best puppy dog eyes.

"Don't worry about it," Michelle smiled. "I heard all about the ordeal with a certain someone wanting to put a post on Facebook. I'm a bit of a romantic myself and loved sharing everything about Steve and me. Everyone said the two of you had just met and were head over heels for each other. It looks as if Robert's getting a baby in the deal as well."

"Yes, it's a little boy," Robert said proudly. "I was so surprised when I found out I was going to be a father."

"Oh my God! You think you were surprised," Katherine exclaimed. "I thought Cornelius had lost his freaking mind. It just didn't seem possible."

"Wow, so you never knew you were pregnant until after the attacks?" Michelle asked, sounding surprised.

"Actually, Michelle, I didn't even get pregnant until after the attacks. Two days ago I was as skinny as you."

"OK, now I know you're messing with me," Michelle laughed. "There's no way you get a bump like that in just a few days. I figure you're at least four months along."

Robert reached over and placed his hand on Katherine's belly. "It's a long story, but she's telling you the truth. She's only been pregnant for a few days, but she is roughly four months along."

Michelle turned back towards me.

"Honey, are they making fun of me?" she asked softly.

"No, my love, it's just one of the many things I need to tell you about. Well, not me, so much as Cornelius."

"Thanks, Steve!" Cornelius remarked sarcastically.

"Hey, what are friends for," I said. "Now let's go inside and greet the others."

As we started walking towards the entrance to the shelter, Michelle reached over and grabbed my left hand.

"I don't know why you left this behind," she said, placing my ring back on my finger. "I just hope it wasn't because you quit loving me."

"No, princess," I thoughtfully said. "It was because I quit loving myself."

"Good," she replied playfully. "I was afraid I might have to kill you."

I reached down and tickled her sides. Michelle squealed and ran past everyone. She was already down the ladder and halfway through the tunnel before I caught up to her. I was just about ready to tickle her again when I heard someone call out my name as I was knocked to the ground.

"You're here! You're really here!"

It was Justin, and I think he might've been more excited to see me than Michelle was. He held my hand as he led me into the shelter.

"You have to see the pictures I drew. Michelle said they were really good, and she hung them up in the playroom."

"We have a playroom?" I asked, looking towards Michelle.

"I thought it would be a good idea for the kids to have a place to play," she replied happily.

I walked into the living room, amazed at the transformation that had occurred since we'd been gone. The place looked more like a giant day care than a shelter. A half dozen or so kids were sprawled out on bean bags, either reading books or drawing pictures. I didn't see digital games of any kind, just old school dolls and toy trucks. A large bookshelf was on the adjacent wall. Next to it were several small drawing boards along with paper and colored pencils.

"Right now it's study time," Andrea said as she brought the kids some fruit from the kitchen. "The kids all read for a while and then draw pictures of what they've read. It's amazing that they can all read the same book, yet each one gets something totally different from it."

Looking around the playroom, I could see dozens of pictures the kids had drawn. Andrea pointed out that in the earlier pictures they always added family members to their drawings. Now, not even a week later, the pictures had more to do with what they were reading.

Justin had a section all to his own. He had a few pictures of his parents and a few from the books he'd read. The majority, however, were with the original six of us: Robert, Katherine, Ben, Josh, Justin, and myself. Justin had on a red cape and was holding a cell phone up at the drones.

"See!" he said excitedly. "I drew pictures of the way we saved everyone."

"Yes, you did," I responded while picking him up, "and you did an amazing job too. I bet those old drones will think twice before messing with you."

"Especially now that you're here!" he said excitedly. "Michelle said when you got here we could be a family, and you two would take me to the park together."

I stood him up on the edge of the sofa near the bean bag chairs. His remark caught me off guard, and I needed to make sure he understood what he was saying. To me, the idea of raising him as our own was amazing. Michelle and I had often discussed adopting another child, and I couldn't think of a more wonderful addition to our family than Justin.

"Are you sure you're ready for a new family?" I asked him as we faced each other eye to eye.

"Oh yes!" he said cheerfully. "If you and Michelle become my new mom and dad, I won't have to go to any more foster homes."

I gave him a puzzled look. "I thought that you said those were your parents that died in the attacks? Wasn't that your dad that put you in the refrigerator?"

"No, that was my foster dad. His name was Larry. I lived with him and Brenda since Christmas. They didn't like me to call them by their names, so I just go used to calling them mom and dad. I really did love them; they just weren't my forever family."

"What happened to your real mom and dad?" I asked.

Justin shrugged his shoulders. "I don't know exactly. Larry said they were killed when I was little, but I don't even remember them."

"In that case, Michelle and I would be honored to be your forever family."

"Yeah!" he yelled, giving me a big hug. After he released his grip on me, he went over and held onto Michelle.

"I see the children, but where are all the adults?" I asked.

"It was beginning to get a little crowded, so most of them have relocated to other homes right around here."

"Is anyone in town?" Robert asked.

"Not anymore," Andrea replied. "There was one older gentleman, but it didn't work out well for him. Ben found his body yesterday. It appears the dogs got to him."

"I was hoping the nanites were out of their system by now," I said, saddened by yet another unnecessary death.

"What are nanites?" Andrea asked.

"It's a little complicated. We need to gather up all the adults so Cornelius can bring everyone up to speed at one time."

"If you want to follow me, I'll show you how to alert everyone," Andrea said cheerfully.

I followed her into the video room, which according to the sign above the door was now the control room. Andrea made her way over to the video monitors and showed me a large dial with a button next to it. The dial had four settings: meet at bunker, meet in town, all clear, and under attack.

"It's pretty self-explanatory," she said, turning the dial to meet at bunker. "You just make your selection and press the button."

Instantly, a loud siren went off. It wailed for a few seconds and then made three loud, quick chirps. It repeated the process three times before shutting down.

"Who in the world hooked this up?" I asked as I studied the switch.

"I did," I heard a woman say as she entered the room.

I turned around to see Hayley coming towards me.

"Well, hello there, stranger. How have you been?" I asked as she walked over and hugged me.

"I'm doing great," she said, taking a step back. "Wow! Look at you; that California sun did you some good. You look ten years younger."

"Well, thank you, young lady. I've been watching what I eat lately. You know, no fast food or things of that nature."

"No, I'm serious. You really do look a lot younger."

"According to Cornelius, I'll keep not only looking younger but also getting younger, thanks to the nanites he injected me with."

She gave me a strange look. "What the hell are nanites, and who is Cornelius?"

"Cornelius is that kid we found at the mill. You know, the one with the broken glasses?"

"Do you mean that weird one who was one of the guards or something?"

"Yeah, that's him. Anyhow, he invented some type of nanites that repair your body and make you younger."

"Well, they seem to be working," she laughed. "So did Kenny come back with you?"

I nearly froze. She and Kenny had a special bond and Hayley felt very close to him. I'd assumed since Ben arrived several days ago, he would've at least updated everyone about how Coos Bay went.

"Has Ben told you anything?" I asked.

"Oh, God no. He's been so head over heels with Amy that we hardly even see him anymore."

"So, where is he now?" I asked, hoping to change the subject.

"Amy wanted some new clothes, so Ben took off to town."

"Alone?" I asked, sounding surprised.

"Are you kidding? No way. He has Artemis and a couple of guys Ray brought back with him. So, how about Kenny?"

I took a deep breath and filled her in on the whole ordeal. Hayley was visibly hurt by the news, but she did her best not to cry. I walked over and held her for a moment to help ease the pain.

"So, was Kenny the only one to die, or did we lose others?"

"As far as Coos Bay goes, we lost Kenny and Travis both. Ben and I were almost killed, but the injections Cornelius gave us saved us. We lost a few more people in Redding, but not anyone you'd know. It was four guys we'd just met and some wackadoodle Ray brought with him."

"Do you mean Jason?" she asked, sounding almost happy.

"Yeah. Why? Do you know him?"

"No, he was just the crazy one Ray brought back with him. He wanted to leave him here, but your wife wouldn't allow it. That guy was really weird. So, was he really the one who got killed?"

"Yes, and it was pretty brutal too. His body was basically eaten from the inside out."

I was going to tell her the whole story but Michelle called out to me from the other room. When I went to check on her, she once again threw her arms around me.

"I love you, daddy," she said, tightening her grip on me. "I don't ever want to be apart from you again."

"I know, princess," I said softly. "What do you say we take Justin to the park and enjoy some family time?"

"What about Cornelius? Didn't you say he was going to share some news with us?"

"Don't worry, love," I said. "I'll make sure you're up to speed on everything Cornelius tells them."

That wasn't the truth, however. He was going to share some information with the others that I preferred Michelle didn't know about. At least not right then. She and I had already been apart for a month. If she knew I was going to be leaving in two days, it might ruin the time we did have together. I wouldn't spring it on her at the last second, but I didn't want to do it on the first day either.

I informed Robert and Katherine what we were up to. I figured it was the right thing to do so they wouldn't worry. I was pleasantly surprised when they asked to join us. Not only were they family in my eyes, but I wanted Michelle to get to know them as well. It also gave us a babysitter for Justin, so the two of us could have a little time alone.

With the bunker quickly filling up, the five of us made our way to the surface. It was already almost six p.m., but there was still plenty of daylight left to create some new memories.

"Are you ready to go to the park?" I asked Justin as we started making our way towards the tree line.

"Oh boy, really?" he exclaimed excitedly.

"You betcha," I said as I picked Michelle up and cradled her in my arms. "We get to have a family day."

Michelle squealed and wrapped her arms around my neck.

"Thank you so much for coming home to me," she said as she laid her head on my shoulder. "I was so lost without you."

I gave Michelle a kiss as I glanced over at the others. Justin was a few feet ahead of us, dancing around happily.

Katherine watched as the two of us held tightly to each other and then turned to Robert.

"Aren't you going to carry your new bride also?" she coyly asked.

"Oh, hell no!" Robert exclaimed. " Do you have any idea how much weight you've put on lately?"

Realizing at the last second what he'd just said, Robert did his best to get away. It was to no avail. Katherine knocked him to the ground and jumped on top of him. He was now on his back, with Katherine sitting on his chest, bouncing up and down on him.

I set Michelle back on the ground and we both watched and laughed.

"So, I've gained too much weight for you to carry me? Is that what you're saying?"

"No, no," Robert laughed as he tried to breath with her bouncing on him. "I just meant you're kind of fat compared to Michelle."

"You asshole!" she screamed, pinning his arms to the ground. "Let's see how you like this."

Bending down so her face was directly in front of his, she began licking him. The two of them were both laughing so hard, Michelle couldn't tell if she was upset or just playing. She turned to me with an inquisitive look.

"Don't worry, angel," I said, hoping to reassure her. "Katherine just gets this way sometimes. It seems no matter how nicely a guy calls a girl fat, they just seem to take it the wrong way."

Katherine stopped licking Robert and glared at me.

"Don't think just because your wife is here I won't kick your ass." With that, she jumped up off Robert and started after me. I took off running with her in hot pursuit. Not wanting to be left out, Justin dove into me, wrapping his arms around my legs. As the two of us tumbled to the ground, Katherine pounced on us and smacked me alongside the head. Then she and Justin held me there and tickled me.

I was wiggling around trying to break free when I noticed Robert standing next to Michelle with his arm around her. Katherine and I both stopped what we were doing and sat up to face them. Justin was still lying on the ground laughing.

"Are you really putting the moves on my wife?" I asked, trying my best to sound upset.

"Sorry, Steve; just deal with it. The way I see it, I'm allowed one freebie with her to make up for all the times I caught you with Kat."

"OK, but just one," I said, giving him a serious look. "Technically, she was only your girlfriend at the time."

Michelle didn't know what to do. She was sure the two of us were just fooling around, but we had gotten so serious that she began to worry. With Robert still holding onto her, she just stood there nearly frozen. Katherine stood up, walked over to them, and socked Robert in the chest.

"Leave the poor girl alone. Can't you see she's been through enough with the drones? She doesn't need to add to it by being hit on by some gray-haired old man."

"What do you mean, old man? I'm much younger than her husband."

As Robert and Katherine put their arms around each other, Michelle loosened up a bit.

"Justin told me the three of you were a lot like the three stooges. I never quite understood what he meant until now. Are you always this way together?"

"I'm sorry, Michelle," Katherine said respectfully. " I love Robert to death, but sometimes the two of them act like a couple of kids. At first I thought they did it just to piss me off. However, I've learned it's actually a great way to deal with all the stress. If it bugs you, I promise we can tone it down."

"Oh no, don't do that," Michelle said happily. "It just caught me off guard. I think it's amazing how well the three of you get along."

Michelle stopped for a second, her eyes going back and forth between Robert and me.

"I hadn't noticed it until Robert said something, but why do you look so young?"

"I'll explain it to you on our way to the park," I told her. "For now, let's get going so we can have time once we get there."

We made our way through the trees and out to the assault vehicle. Michelle would've preferred a nice car or truck, but Justin thought it was awesome. He ran around the vehicle twice before stopping at the door to get in.

"Wow, it has a machine gun and everything! Can I shoot it?"

"You bet," Robert said. "That's if it's OK with Steve and Michelle."

"Oh, hell ya!" I answered excitedly. "I bet we can find some cool stuff to shoot along the way."

Michelle slowly shook her head.

"What is it with boys and guns?" she asked, looking over at Katherine.

"I used to feel the same way," Katherine grinned. "Just try it once, and I promise it will all make sense."

We loaded into the vehicle. Robert took the driver's seat, with Katherine next to him, while Michelle and I sat towards the back. Justin didn't waste any time finding himself a seat at the turret. Then, as we left the driveway, Robert called Justin up to him. His little eyes lit up when Rob put him on his lap.

"OK, I'll do the pedals and you steer. Can you handle that?"

"You should probably ask first," Katherine suggested.

"Oh, right. Justin, do you want to drive?

"I sure do!" he shot back.

"I meant Steve and Michelle."

"What for?" Robert asked. "If I'm going to be his Uncle Rob, it's my duty to do shit like this."

Katherine shot us a quick glance to see if we looked upset. Seeing that we were more into each other than Robert's driving class, she sat back and relaxed.

I knew Robert wouldn't get too crazy with Justin at the wheel, so I focused my attention on my bride. We held each other and shared bits and pieces about what we'd gone through. Michelle actually had it far better than any of the other slaves I'd talked with. Her first few days were hell, but by the time they loaded her onto the train, she was already being given special treatment. She was allowed to use the restroom and sleep without the fear of being killed.

I don't know if there was something special about her, or if they wanted to cause unrest with the other slaves. I had a strange feeling they wanted the others to kill her, causing us to abandon our fight to free them. Regardless of why they did it, I was just grateful she hadn't endured the same treatment the others had.

I'd just started to tell her about how I'd gotten shot and how Cornelius had injected me with nanites when Robert stopped the vehicle.

"Hey, Steve!" he yelled out. "How do you feel about shooting a couple police cars?"

I turned to Michelle as if to ask for permission.

"Go ahead," she sighed. "You boys do what you gotta do."

"Come on and join us. It's a lot of fun."

344

"I think I'll just hang out with Katherine," she said as she let go of me.

"In that case," Katherine hollered back to her, "you're going to be shooting police cars. I'm not going to miss out on this."

"See, honey," I said, taking her by the hand, "even girls like to shoot things on occasion."

"It just seems wrong to go around shooting cars. Won't we get into trouble?"

"Oh, come on, girl," Katherine said as she came and took Michelle's other hand. "We can do anything we want without getting into trouble. This includes blowing up resorts and shooting police cars."

Michelle gave her an odd look.

"Trust me," she said. "Steve will tell you all about the resort incident later. For now, let's teach you how to be a bad girl."

The three of us stepped outside of the assault vehicle while Robert and Justin took a seat in the turret. The police car was about fifty yards away. Not too far that we couldn't do some serious damage, but not so close that we risked injury from flying debris.

"Are you ready?" Robert yelled down to us through the open door.

I figured they'd fire one or two shots into the thing. What was I thinking? Round after round tore through the first patrol car, nearly ripping it in two.

After they quit shooting, Justin ran out to survey the damage he and Robert had caused. It was great to see him so happy. He laughed and ran all around the car.

"Can we do another one?" he pleaded. "That was so much fun!"

"Sorry, little guy. It's the girls' turn now," Katherine said as she pulled Michelle inside with her.

Robert gave them a quick lesson on how to fire the weapon before stepping out to join me.

"This should be good," he said with a devious laugh.

We could hear the girls talking things over before they shot. At first it didn't seem like it was going to happen, since they were talking so long. Then the girls finally took their first shot. A lone bullet tore through the rear door of the second car. There was a slight pause, and we could hear giggling coming from inside the assault vehicle.

Suddenly they let loose. Bullets riddled the car from one end to the other. They didn't stop there, however. Soon they were shooting a nearby pickup and anything else that was even close to our vicinity. I didn't think they were ever going to quit. Finally, we heard a clicking from the gun as they exhausted their supply of bullets.

"Hey! What the hell!" Michelle yelled down to us. "Why did the gun quit? I still want to shoot more stuff."

"Easy there, Rambo," I hollered back. "We need to reload it first, and then it's my turn."

Sliding out of the turret, Michelle dove out of the doorway and into my arms.

"Oh my God, that was fun," she exclaimed. "Can we really blow up some buildings too?"

"This is the whole reason guys don't like to take women shooting," Robert said bluntly. "Once they figure out how much fun it is, they just go crazy wanting more."

"Well!" Michelle said, grabbing Robert's shoulders and shaking him. "Then give us more."

"Tell you what, Rob," I said. "I'll drive while you reload. I think I know just where to take these girls for a little target practice."

Everyone hopped back inside and we were off again. Soon, Robert had the gun reloaded and came up front to join me. Justin was in the back with the girls sharing stories about what they'd just done.

Robert gave me a dirty look. "You do realize we won't get to touch the gun anymore, except for maybe reloading it."

"Yeah, I kind of figured that out. At least the girls are having a good time."

A few minutes later, I pulled into a large, open gravel lot. On the far end were a couple of brightly polished tanker trucks.

"What are those?" Rob asked, sounding worried.

"Don't worry, buddy," I said reassuringly. "It's just milk."

"Oh good. I was afraid it might be fuel or something."

"Oh come on, Rob. What do you take me for, an idiot? I'm saving the fuel trucks for us."

"Oh good," he said again and grinned. "For a second I thought you'd totally lost it."

Chapter 20

SOUR MILK

It was amazing to actually be home again with Michelle. I was beginning to realize what the man meant when he told Cornelius they were bringing back the Garden of Eden. Life wasn't about all the stuff we could acquire; it was about having the time to spend with those you love and the freedom to be yourself. We still had a long road ahead of us, but in the end, we'd be much happier than we'd ever dreamed possible.

I was in the middle of daydreaming about the future when I heard the gun begin to fire once again. I quickly turned my attention to the tanker, expecting to see milk come pouring out of the holes. At first it was disappointing. The unpasteurized milk had spent a month out in the hot sun. Now, instead of seeing milk flowing from the tanker, it looked more like a mixture of cottage cheese and yogurt. Fortunately, the breeze pushed the smell in the opposite direction.

The three of them continued firing as Robert and I looked on. We were just about ready to find a new target when the tanker suddenly split in the middle. The weight of the milk inside caused it to bend at the top as the belly ripped wide open. The contents, somewhere between a liquid and a solid, came rushing out of the tank. It did so with such force that it consumed a car parked a few yards away. At first, it just shattered the car's glass, but a second later, it picked it up off the ground and rolled it over.

We could hear the three of them laughing hysterically as they quit firing and quickly exited the vehicle.

"Steve! Steve! Did you see that?" Justin yelled as he raced over to me.

I didn't have time to answer as he jumped into my arms, wrapping me up in a huge hug.

"Thank you so much!" he said, holding me tightly. "This has been the best day ever."

"So, I take it you like shooting things with the big gun?" I said, throwing him into the air and catching him.

"Not just that!" he exclaimed. "I have my very own family to do things with."

"Yes, you do," I said, giving him another hug.

Jumping from my arms, he ran to greet Michelle as she made her way over to us.

"Mom, did you see how high Dad threw me in the air? That was awesome."

Hearing him call us mom and dad caught me off guard for a moment. We had lost our children in the attacks and had done our best not to think about it. Everybody who was still alive had lost someone, yet somehow it was different than it normally would've been. Before the attacks, death was more personal. We'd anguish at the loss of a loved one. Since the attacks, however, it wasn't death we focused on as much as it was life — preserving our own as well as those around us.

Hearing Justin call us mom and dad brought on a feeling of guilt. It was only for a brief moment, but it reassured me that even though my children were no longer in my life, they'd always be a part of it. I watched as Michelle knelt down to his level and held him by the shoulder at arm's lengths.

"That was awesome!" she exclaimed. "We really need to shoot something else."

"I have an idea," Katherine said. "Why don't we go shoot up the old mini-mart where I used to work."

"I've got an idea too," I said, acting excited like them. "Why don't we give the gun a rest and go to the park?"

"That would be awesome!" Robert yelled, dancing around, totally overselling it.

The two of us danced around together like idiots, whooping and hollering. We didn't care how stupid we looked; it was just wicked fun to mock the girls.

"Really? Is that how the two of you want to play?" Katherine asked, giving us the evil eye.

Robert and I were still too busy dancing around acting silly to notice Katherine take off towards the tanker. She had a devious plan to get even with us. As she approached the curdled goo, she retrieved an old paper cup lying on the ground. Filling the cup to the top, she returned to us, and as we danced around, she poured it over our heads.

For a moment, Robert and I just stopped and stood there. The foul smell of sour milk filled our nostrils as the slime made its way from our heads down to our feet. Then, looking over at me, Robert gave me a shit-eating grin. I knew exactly what he was thinking and gave him the go-ahead nod.

"Oh, it's on, baby!" he yelled, grabbing Katherine.

She tried to fight him until I moved in and grabbed her legs. We had to be somewhat gentle so we wouldn't hurt their unborn child. She screamed and cursed at us as she realized what was about to happen, but to no avail. Robert and I carried her over to the thick mess and carefully rolled her around in it.

Justin and Michelle stood back and watched at first. Then, realizing they were missing out on all the fun, they rushed over to aid Katherine. Soon, the five of us were covered from head to toe. That had to be the stinkiest food fight I'd ever gotten myself into. It lasted nearly ten minutes before Robert and I finally called a truce.

We had to be the ones to give in. If not, those girls would've continued the battle until they either passed out from exhaustion or Katherine gave birth. There's just something about women that makes them take things too far.

As we lay there on the ground, laughing and talking, a family of raccoons caught the scent and joined us. They really seemed to be enjoying the taste of the spoiled milk, and us as well. One of the younger raccoons instantly took a liking to Justin, making it his duty to give him a thorough cleaning. No matter how much Justin squirmed or how loudly he laughed, the little thing never got skittish.

In time, more animals started to show; soon, there was everything from deer to chickens joining in on the feast. At one point, even a bull elk started making his way toward us. Robert and I were focused on him, while Michelle and Katherine were more interested in the smaller animals. With the elk now just a few feet from us, he snorted and darted away. A second later, all the animals ran for cover.

"What's going on?" Michelle asked. "Why did he scare all the animals away?"

"I don't think it was the elk that scared them," I said, jumping to my feet. "We need to get back to our vehicle, and quickly."

I could tell Robert and Katherine were on the same page as I was. We'd seen this behavior before. The first time was with the buck shortly after the attacks, and then again over on the coast.

"What scared them then?" Michelle asked, puzzled by our response.

"Dogs!" I said as I picked up Justin and held him in my arms.

"Well, why would we be scared of..." she stopped mid-sentence as she recalled what she'd heard about Jesse being killed a few days earlier.

We were about halfway back to the assault vehicle when the pack of dogs showed themselves. There were three of them, all mutts but all fifty pounds or better. They weren't directly in our path, but close enough that we knew there was no way we could make it the last thirty or so yards unscathed.

Turning towards Michelle, I handed Justin off to her. I did it slowly, trying my best not to set off the dogs.

"Don't set him down," I warned her. "With him being so much smaller than us, they may pick him out as a target."

"What are you going to do?" she asked, her voice shaky from fear.

"I'm going to buy you some time," I calmly said.

"What do you want me to do?" Robert quietly asked.

"Just get them inside safely. Oh yeah, and I need you to get a gun and shoot these damn things. Just remember, don't shoot me in the head."

"I'll try not to shoot you at all," he said, trying to lighten things up.

Almost as if they knew where we were going, the dogs moved between our vehicle and us. A low growl rumbled from deep inside them. Their teeth were fully exposed and foam dripped from their jowls. I knew it was time to make my move.

In a full sprint, I took off to the right, as if I were heading for the nearby tree line. All three dogs went into a frenzy and were hot on my trail. Michelle screamed and in a total panic, nearly dropped Justin. Fortunately, the dogs were so consumed by the thrill of the chase they paid no attention to the others. Robert grabbed Justin from Michelle, while Katherine pulled her to safety. She did her best to break free, wanting to save me from what she feared to be certain death.

I had barely made it thirty feet before one of the dogs got ahold of me. As he sank his teeth into my left arm, I could hear Michelle off in the distance screaming. That was my cue to fight. Turning quickly, I caught the second dog by surprise. As he lunged at me, I wrapped my right hand tightly around his neck. I could feel my flesh ripping away while the first dog attempted to pull me to the ground. It was a futile effort on his part. I barely paid heed, tightening my grip on his friend's neck and snapping it like a twig. Then, dropping the body, I readied to face dog number three, a little too late. I had barely made the turn towards him when I felt his sharp teeth sink into my neck.

I'd seen just what nanites can do and how rapidly they repair things, but this had me a little worried. Blood poured from my throat like water from a hose. The sheer sight of it alone was like something from a horror flick. Reaching up, I tried to slide my fingers into its mouth, hoping to loosen the grip. That's when the first dog released my arm and sank its teeth deep into my chest.

I didn't feel pain — I got angry. I was just about to strangle the little shit when everything went quiet. I was aware of the commotion around me, yet the sound was completely muffled. I calmly watched as Robert pushed his way past Michelle and fell from the doorway. Trying to break his fall, he stuck his hands out in front of him, dropping the handgun as he did. I was so at peace that for a moment nothing seemed real. Everything was playing out in slow motion. I could hear Michelle's screams and Robert yelling, but it seemed so surreal and far off. Even the growls from the dogs as they chewed deeper into my flesh seemed distant.

I calmly watched as Robert retrieved the handgun and came running towards me. I even laughed to myself as he tripped over his own two feet and nearly crashed a second time.

STEVE WOODS

Then, in the blink of an eye, everything sped back up as both dogs dropped to the ground, writhing in pain. Standing there, I watched as they convulsed violently. Instantly realizing what was happening, I yelled for Robert to stop. I'd seen this before, just last night with Jason. The nanites had entered the dogs through my blood as it poured into their mouths. Just like him, they too were being consumed from the inside out.

With the dogs still flopping around, Michelle took off running towards me, tears streaming down her face. Robert grabbed her and stopped her from getting any closer. Screaming and kicking at him, she tried to get free from his grip.

"Michelle, stop!" I yelled, getting her attention. "You can't come any closer to me."

"What the hell are you talking about?" she yelled, still trying to get free.

"You and Robert need to get back inside. It's not safe for you out here."

"What about you?" she cried. "You're bleeding! I can't just stand back and watch you die!"

"Please, princess," I said softly. "You just have to trust me. I promise everything will be OK."

Walking backwards as Robert escorted her to the assault vehicle, she kept her eyes locked on mine. Then sobbing uncontrollably, she turned and climbed inside.

"Throw me your gun!" I yelled to Robert as I stepped past the dogs.

Turning, he threw his handgun towards me and stared for a moment before entering the vehicle. Stepping over to where the gun had landed, I picked it up and switched the safety off. Cautiously, I made my way back over to the pile of flesh that just moments ago had been my attackers. They were no longer moving, but I knew without a doubt they were still alive. Their brains and nervous systems still fully intact and functional, pain was now the only thing they knew.

"Not even a bad dog deserves to die like this," I said as I raised the gun towards them.

With two quick shots each, it was all over. I even shot the first dog just in case. Content with knowing they were no longer in pain, I walked towards the vehicle and took a seat on the ground about ten feet away. Robert had shut the door to be safe, but Michelle's eyes were still glued to me from the window.

Robert and Katherine never saw what happened to Jason. They'd been focused on Craig's body, with their view blocked by the others. Still, they could tell by his screams and the stories they heard that it truly was a fate worse than death.

It only took about five minutes before my body fully healed from the attack. There wasn't so much as a scratch on me. I didn't rejoin the others right away, though. I wanted to make sure all the nanites were either safely back in my system or dead on the ground. Then, after nearly an hour passed, I felt it was safe to rejoin them. Before doing so, however, I stripped down to my underwear. I didn't want to take the risk that some of them may still have been in the blood on my clothes.

As I entered the vehicle, the four of them stared at me. Michelle and Justin were sitting next to each other in the back, while Robert and Katherine seemed to be discussing something in the front.

"Isn't anyone going to say anything?" I asked as I glanced around at them.

"I'm not sure what to say," Robert said quietly. "I've never seen anything like that before."

"You know I have the nanites in me, Rob."

"I know, Steve, and I thought I had seen all the crazy shit they could do."

He paused for a moment, slowly shaking his head while looking towards the ground. Then, as he looked back up, he continued. "What I saw out there scared the shit out of me."

"I can't say as I blame you. Watching the way they ate those dogs freaked me out a bit too."

"Hell, Steve," he said, giving me a strange look, "it wasn't the dogs that freaked me out. It was seeing what they did to you."

"What are you talking about?" I asked. "You've seen me heal before."

"Damn it, Steve, those things didn't just heal you — they took your whole body over. Just before the dogs dropped off, everything changed. I honestly think I could see right through you."

Nearly floored by what he'd just said, I turned towards Michelle and Justin.

"Are you guys OK?"

"What's going on?" Michelle asked, tearing up again.

"I don't honestly know," I answered, taking a seat near the door. "I thought I was doing a good thing by saving your lives."

"You did a great thing," Katherine said, sitting down next to me. "We can't thank you enough for what you did. The problem is we don't know if you're really you or not."

"What kind of dumbass comment is that?" I asked, beginning to get annoyed. "Who else would I be?"

"It's not that, Steve," Robert said, putting a hand on my shoulder. "We're just concerned for your safety as well as ours."

Michelle and Justin came over to get a closer look. Justin hopped onto my lap and wrapped his arms around my neck.

"I was scared those dogs were going to eat you," he said as he held me. "If those nanite things did save you, then I'm glad you have them."

"What about you, Michelle? How do you feel about all of this?"

Squeezing next to Justin on my lap, she too wrapped her arms around me.

"I've spent every day for the last month scared that I'd never see you again. I'm not exactly sure what Robert saw, because I was crying so hard. Right now, I really don't care either. Just promise me we won't ever be apart again."

Holding her tightly in my arms, I glanced up at Robert. I could tell from the look he was giving me that he wasn't real happy that I hadn't told Michelle yet.

"I can't make you that promise," I said, bracing myself for her reaction.

"I didn't think you could," she said sadly. "I was just hoping."

She let go of me and gave me a warm smile as she looked into my eyes. "Can you promise me you'll come back?"

Before I could answer her, she pressed her index finger against my lips. "I know the answer," she said, "but please just promise it anyway. I need to have some type of hope to keep me going."

"I promise, there is nothing that could ever stop me from returning to you. I love you, princess."

With her tears flowing, she wrapped her arms back around me. "I love you too, daddy!"

We never did make it to the park that day. Robert was still unable to come to grips with what he'd seen. It wasn't because he feared I was turning into some type of beast. He was afraid that someday Katherine and his son might. Cornelius had re-injected her with a small amount of nanites to help her heal after the surgery. He said it was no big deal, but other than Cornelius, none of us knew anything about those things.

I spent the whole next day alone with Michelle and Justin. We didn't discuss the dog attack or even the nanites. Instead, we focused on being a family. Michelle carried on like a schoolgirl when I gave her the necklace and earrings, but she wouldn't take the new wedding ring. She told me to hold onto it and when I returned, we'd renew our vows. Until then, the ring I gave her when we got married would be the only one she'd wear.

Later that evening, we returned from our walk and enjoyed a nice home-cooked meal. Afterwards, everyone still living at the bunker gathered for a movie and popcorn. The kids were in one room watching "Ninja Turtles." The rest of us watched our movie in another. I thought Robert's choice for the movie was a bit ironic: "Seeking a Friend for the End of the World." Whether it was in poor taste or not, it didn't matter. He thought it would be fun, considering the circumstances, and we all really kind of enjoyed it.

When the movies were finished, we tucked all the kids into their beds and went outside for a bonfire. It was the first time since getting home that we really discussed what had happened. As we each shared our experiences, Josh took notes and snapped pictures of everyone on an old cell phone. He thought it would be nice to create some type of history book for future generations.

I'd already heard most of the stories told that night. It wasn't until Michelle started telling us her story that I truly understood what she'd gone through.

She'd been taking the woman home when the first attack happened. They'd barely gotten out of town when the drones blocked out the sun. At first, everyone around them seemed intrigued and stopped their vehicles to get out for a better look. Michelle also stopped, but she never got out; she only rolled her window down. She didn't remember much about the first attack other than getting stuck in the face with several of the little arrows. She tried to drive away but blacked out just as someone ran in front of her.

When she regained consciousness, some guy in a ball cap was carrying her into a small mobile home. She screamed and he dropped her. Several other people tried to tell her she needed to get inside, but she insisted on leaving to find me. She told us she wasn't feeling right and kept getting dizzy as she tried to make it back to her car. When she got there, she found the car wrecked. In a panic, she scoured the car for her purse and retrieved her cell phone. She figured the best thing to do would be to call me.

After several failed attempts to get a call through, Michelle said she took off walking. Then, going about one hundred yards or so, she remembered the survival kit I'd made for her. Going back, she stuffed several items from it into her purse.

About that time, she flagged down a pickup heading towards town. The cab was full, so she and another woman rode in the back. Hoping to avoid all the bodies and vehicles, the driver opted to take an old dirt road next to the river. They'd only gone a mile or two when the second wave of drones hit. Michelle remembered one of the drones crashing into the truck and ripping a hole in the cab. The truck swerved off the road and rolled over the embankment, throwing her into the river. The cold water kept her from feeling as dizzy and the drones didn't seem to notice her. She stayed in the fast-moving river and floated for what seemed like hours. The entire time, she made as few movements as possible in fear the drones would return. Then, when she realized where she was, she pulled herself out and walked to my work.

It wasn't until she was nearly there that she realized she still had a death grip on her purse. Unzipping it, she pulled out her cell phone. It was relatively dry and appeared to be working fine, but the calls still wouldn't go through. She was cold, wet, scared, and there were bodies everywhere. She even found Clancy dead right outside the door at my terminal.

Michelle spent the entire night alone, hidden in the corner. It was so dark in there with no electricity that she dared not move. Then, when the first rays of light filled the office, she wrote me two notes before heading for home. She put one on the mirror and one in my cubby.

She made it nearly halfway when a black SUV pulled up and forced her in. Two others were already being held in there. The men who abducted her asked her a few questions about some rebels before taking the three of them to the mill. Once there, they were put into groups and given instructions. They were told to follow the drones, pick up the dead, and then return. It was very basic, and just to prove how serious the men were, they had the drones kill several people right in front of them.

It was shortly after the men in the SUV left that she first started hearing stories about us. A few of the guards were talking about a group of survivors they were trying to track down. She started telling everyone I was one of them. Not because she knew I was, but because she needed a little hope to hold onto.

I felt as if I could cry by the time she finished telling her story. I never dreamed this woman I loved so dearly would ever go through such a horrifying ordeal. To look at her, you'd swear she had an easy time of it, but we all knew she too had scars that would never heal.

I hadn't had to rest but a few hours here and there since being injected with the nanites. That night, however, I held her in my arms and just let sleep take me.

Michelle woke up before me and prepared an amazing breakfast for everyone. Bringing mine into me, she set it next to the bed and began to sing "Good Morning Beautiful." It felt like a wonderful dream as I lay there and listened. The sweet sound of her voice brought as much joy to my ears as she had to my heart. My eyes opened to find her sitting on the edge of the bed gazing lovingly at me.

"Good morning, my love," she said, covering me with kisses. "How did you sleep?"

"It was incredible," I answered, taking her into my arms. "You and I were on the beach in Maui and the waves were lapping at our feet."

Michelle giggled and turned towards the foot of our bed. "That's because Artemis snuck in and was licking your toes."

I looked down at my feet to see Ben's dog wagging his tail.

"Well, good morning to you," I happily said to him. "Are you glad to see me again?"

Artemis jumped up on the bed and tried to squeeze in between us.

"He just hasn't been the same since we left you in Redding," said Ben, who was standing in the doorway.

"Well, hello, stranger. Where have you been keeping yourself?"

"I've been out on patrol," he answered proudly. "We take turns securing all the properties around here, looking for rabid dogs. After Jesse was killed the other day, we decided it made more sense to find them before they found us."

"Did you see any?"

"Not yet, but they seem to be our biggest threat at the moment, so I figured it's best to be ready for them."

"Good call," I said, rising to a sitting position. "I'm just about to get up. Why don't you take the bed and get some rest?"

"I can't," he answered. "A little birdy informed me we're going into battle today. I plan on being right in the mix of things with you and Rob."

"What about Amy and her daughter?"

"They're safe here with the others. My place is out there with you. I remember a while back you telling me nothing was more important to you than family. I figure if you're going, it must be to keep yours safe. I want to make the same sacrifice so Amy and Calista will know just how much I love them."

"Ass kisser!" I said as I got up and grabbed my breakfast. "The only reason I'm going is to get out of doing a whole month's worth of chores I'm behind on."

"You wish it was just one month," Michelle said as she made the bed behind me. "Now that you've lost your job, that list has doubled. I took it easy on you before only because you brought home a paycheck."

"See what I mean?" I said as I took a seat at a small table in the room. "There's no way I'm sticking around here with such a tyrant."

"Oh, poor baby," Michelle said, giving me a kiss on the top of my head. "Just do me one favor and have a talk with Justin. You may not know this, but that poor kid is a total wreck when you're not here — we both are."

She and Ben left the room to let me eat in peace. Michelle knew better than anyone that there were certain times I just needed to be alone.

My mind replayed the events of the dog attack over and over again. I should've been thinking about the battle to come, but I just couldn't. The image Robert told me he saw was stuck in my head. Could I have really disappeared for a moment as the nanites did their repairs? The whole idea seemed pretty far-fetched, but any more, far-fetched didn't mean impossible. We'd figured out that there were just some things our government had that they kept a secret.

Cornelius wasn't much help either. Robert had shared his concerns with him the moment we got home but never got a straight answer. Cornelius had several theories on the subject but nothing ironclad. He couldn't even tell us why these nanites killed the dogs while the others made them rabid.

As I finished my breakfast, Justin came in to say his good-byes. We spent about twenty minutes talking to each other, trying to ease the pain we were both feeling. Then, getting an idea, I once again removed my wedding ring.

"Do you believe I'll come back now?" I asked.

Staring at the ring, Justin got a big grin on his face. "Now I know you'll be back. But won't Mom think you don't love her?"

"No. Mom knows it's not the ring that makes a marriage. It's not even that little piece of paper. Marriage is about the vow you make with a person that promises them you'll always be theirs."

Giving me a hug and kiss, he left the room. I quickly changed clothes and then grabbed my dishes before making my way to the kitchen. By then, everyone else except Michelle was outside. They did that to give the two of us a few final moments alone together.

Wrapping our arms around each other, we stood there without saying a word. We could always tell not just what the other was thinking, but also what they were feeling. Finally letting go of one another, we went up top to join the others. Little did I know, but I would never again set foot inside the bunker.

Once outside, we quickly said our good-byes and loaded into the assault vehicle. There were eight of us:

Robert, Cornelius, Josh, Ben, three others, and me. Ben took his usual place behind the wheel.

Then, as I watched Justin and Michelle from the window, we drove away.

The trip back to Redding seemed to go much quicker than the trip home. There were no stops along the way to find CDs or little gifts for those we loved. Most of us just spent our own time quietly thinking about all the events that had gotten us there. In fact, other than Ben, who passed the time driving, Josh was the only one who did anything.

Page by page, he went through all the notes he'd taken the night before. Every now and then he'd open a journal he'd brought, jot something down, and then return to reading his notes.

My mind was on Michelle and Justin. The two of them trusted every decision I made. They knew the only reason I'd left was to ensure their safety. Still, something inside me didn't feel right about the trip. I couldn't tell if it was just my fear of the unknown or the emptiness I felt not being near them. No matter what it was, I was sure the others were feeling it too.

"I think this is the place!" Ben called back to us as the weigh station came into view.

I took a quick look out the windshield and then down at my watch. "Wow! Not bad, Ben; you made great time getting us here. It's only 11:13."

As we cut across the freeway to the weigh station, I saw Ray and Scott driving over to meet us.

"Glad you're here!" Ray shouted anxiously from his jeep as I got out. "We had a run-in with some drones about an hour ago. They were only surveillance drones, so nobody got hurt, but I believe we may have lost the element of surprise."

"Well then, grab your men and let's do this thing."

"No need," Ray said. "They've already left and air support is on its way. Scott and I stayed back to wait for you. We were able to hone in on the signal between the drones and whoever is controlling them. You were right; it appears the signal is definitely coming from somewhere around San Francisco."

The others had gotten out of the assault vehicle and were hanging on his every word.

"Robert, you come with us!" I yelled, motioning towards the jeep. "I want the rest of you to ride with Ben."

With that, I jumped into the front seat, with Ray taking the wheel. Robert and Scott took their seats in the back. Ben and the others were right on our heels as we tore through the parking lot and back across the freeway.

Except for a few animals or debris from an occasional downed airplane, the road had been completely cleared. Still, I feared we would never reach the battle — at least not in one piece. Ray seldom dropped below eighty mph. It wasn't until we neared the city that he began to slow down.

With just a few miles left to go, we began to see the drones and hear the sound of gunfire. It wasn't just an occasional shot from a rifle; it was an all out assault. As we made the last turn leading to the San Francisco-Oakland Bay Bridge, I got my first taste of what we were getting ourselves into.

Our troops were spread out along the roadside, attacking the drones from any hiding spot they could find. They weren't surveillance drones or even the ones from the first couple attacks. They'd taken out those with the weapons they'd created. These were more like the one we encountered by the lake. The only difference was there were dozens of them. We were only about a hundred yards from the rear of the battle when one of the drones appeared over the bridge.

Ray slowed the jeep even more, and we were only doing about thirty mph when we saw the flash as it fired a missile. In my mind, I could see us easily getting around such a predictable adversary. However, I wasn't the one driving.

The missile hit only a few yards off to our right. The blast caused Ray to swerve the vehicle onto the left shoulder of the road, hitting a tree. Ben wasn't so lucky. As a large chunk of asphalt shattered his windshield, he drove nearly head-on into an abandoned car. The assault vehicle careened wildly out of control and rolled down the embankment. Jumping from our wrecked jeep, we looked towards the bridge just as a second drone appeared.

Chapter 21

BETRAYAL

For a second, I watched helplessly from the passenger seat of our wrecked jeep. The drone was now past us, and I knew from our previous encounter with one what to expect. It would take several seconds at best before it could make the turn and get back to us. What I didn't know, however, was how many of these drones had targeted us.

That question seemed to be answered as soon as we exited the jeep. A second drone appeared on the bridge following nearly the same path as the first. This one, however, had a different target in mind and sailed harmlessly past us.

Thankfully, our speed was so slow when we hit the tree that nobody got hurt. As the second drone flew past us, we grabbed any weapons we could get our hands on. We quickly made our way over to Ben and the others. The assault vehicle didn't look badly damaged, but it was lying upside down about forty feet over the embankment.

Scott raced back to our wrecked vehicle and retrieved a rope while the rest of us slid down the hill. Reaching the wreckage, we forced the door open and started pulling everyone out. Most of them only had minor injuries, but it appeared to us that Josh and another man had lost their lives. Reaching inside, Robert pulled the first man out. We confirmed his condition as Robert turned to go back in for Josh.

Suddenly, a missile hit about sixty yards away. We all turned to see where it came from and noticed two more drones way off in the distance heading our direction.

"We've got to go, Rob!" I yelled.

"What about Josh?"

"I checked him already!" Ben nervously replied. "I think his neck was broken."

I grabbed Robert and pulled him back out to us.

"Damn it, Rob, we have to go! Now let's get a move on!"

Scott tied off one end of the rope and threw the other end to us. With everyone working together, we were able to quickly maneuver the hillside. Reaching the top, we took off running as another missile shot over our heads. It struck a building not far from us, almost leveling it.

We didn't run far before taking shelter in a small ravine. Once there, Ray pulled out his device to locate the signal controlling the drones.

"Here, Cornelius," he said. "You can probably read this better than any of us."

Locking in on the source, Cornelius popped his head up out of the ravine. "It appears the signal is coming from the other side of the bridge, somewhere in the city. According to my readings, we're only about a mile from the source. If we can shut it down, it would eliminate the drones, allowing our troops to move in and kill those responsible."

About that time, one of our planes came into view. We watched as it locked onto a drone, blowing it out of the sky. Figuring the extra firepower would allow us to make it across the bridge, we took off running. We were nearly to the front line of the battle when the plane we were counting on exploded in midair. In a flash, the drone responsible for its destruction shot through the burning debris as its remains fell towards the water.

STEVE WOODS

"There's no way we're getting across that bridge!" Scott yelled.

"We don't have a choice!" I called to him. "Our main priority here is to get into the city and destroy that signal. Now follow me!" I ordered them as I ran towards a burning building.

"What the hell are you doing?" Ben asked.

"Only the top floors are burning," I told him. "We can use the heat from the fire to temporarily camouflage ourselves from the drones. That will buy us time to figure out a game plan."

Once inside, we dropped everything we were carrying and gathered around an office desk.

"OK," I said. "The way I see it, the bridge is going to be impassible. Using it to get into San Francisco would be suicide. With no place to hide, such a long stretch out in the open would make us sitting ducks. We need to figure out a way to sneak in."

"Maybe we could take a boat across," Ray suggested.

"Only as a last resort," I said. "That's a lot of open water to get across without being seen."

"I've got an idea," Robert said excitedly. "We can head back a little ways into Oakland and use the BART tunnel."

"The what?" I asked.

"It's a tunnel between the two cities," he explained. "It actually goes across the bay, under the water."

"Yeah, yeah! I've heard about it," Ray added. "We could take it right into the center of the city."

"That is, if it wasn't destroyed by the quakes," I reminded them.

Several months before the attacks, the largest quake ever recorded hit the area we were now in. Both cities were in ruins, and only a select few were allowed in to start rebuilding.

That probably had a lot to do with them using San Francisco to head up the attacks. The use of drones for doing the surveying had become so commonplace that the military pretty much quit paying attention to them. Not to mention that in an effort to speed things up, overseas deliveries were no longer being fully inspected. A person could do virtually anything he wanted and stay totally off the government's radar.

Leaving the cover of the building, we ran into several men from Ray's team. They filled us in on the casualties and their plan of attack. Ray let them know the game plan we had for accessing the BART tunnel.

Of the three men who had tagged along when we left home base, only two were still alive. They'd been relatively new to the team and felt a bit skittish about our idea. Something about being in a tunnel under the ocean scared them even more than facing drones. Honoring their wishes, we let them join the others in battle.

As Ray's team took off with the men towards the bridge, we made our way to the train line. Once on the tracks, it was only a matter of minutes until we reached the entrance to the tunnel. When we got there, we nearly scrapped the idea of getting into the city by that route. The first hundred feet or so had collapsed onto a commuter train. At first glance, it appeared getting into San Francisco that way would be impossible.

Knowing we were quickly running out of options and resources, we split into three groups. It was a long shot, but somehow we needed to find a way through. Robert and I looked for an opening inside the train itself, while the other two groups tried from the outside. For nearly a half hour, we checked out every little crack and crevice. With the ceiling crushed nearly to the floor in the least damaged areas, it didn't take long for us to realize why the drones weren't securing this entrance. Nobody had even made any real attempts to remove bodies from it since the quake.

Their main focus must've been the bridge and areas more easily accessible. I began to worry. Even if we made it through on this end, we had no guarantee the tunnel wasn't flooded. Not only that, but if we did manage to make it to the other side, there was a good chance it too would be collapsed. Still, we pushed on, moving both bone and metal to make our path.

We were just about ready to call it quits when we heard Scott and Ray call out. It sounded like they were on the train but further up ahead. There was too much debris between us to make out what they were yelling. Then, after a few minutes, we heard someone tapping. Keeping as still as possible, we were able to make out the signal. It was an SOS.

It had taken us nearly a half hour to get as far as we had, yet only about two minutes to backtrack the same fifty feet. Once outside, we met up with Cornelius and Ben.

"Did you guys hear that too?" Cornelius asked. "I think Scott and Ray are in trouble."

Confirming we were all on the same page, we went to save our friends.

The four of us quickly located the entrance the two of them had used. Lying flat on our bellies, we squeezed through a small opening under the train and followed it. At times, we could feel the jagged metal from the train cutting into us. We were nearly pinned as we shimmed under a thick piece of steel. The metal was laid in such a direction that once past it, there was no way to make it back.

Finally, with the last person through the tiny hole, we were able to stand up. Looking around, we found ourselves in one of the train cars. The last opening we pushed through was actually a gap where the car had been torn apart. One half was upright, while the other half was crushed and twisted onto its side.

The remains of one of the passengers were split between the two pieces. His legs from the hips down were on one side, while the upper part of the torso appeared crushed inside the other. The odd part was no other bodies were anywhere else in the entire car.

Ray suddenly appeared in the doorway ahead of us.

"What the hell are you doing here?" he demanded. "I said it was too dangerous, and we were trapped."

I looked questioningly at the others. "All any of us got was SOS. We couldn't figure out what else you were saying."

"Oh. I couldn't remember how to do all the codes, so I tapped quietly. I guess that one is on me."

"It doesn't matter. We're all here now, so we might as well push ahead," Robert said. "How does it look further up?"

"It's hard to say. Scott is still checking it out, but I can tell you the tunnel is at least partially flooded."

I shut my flashlight off and stuck it in my waistband. "There's no turning back, so we'll all need to conserve our batteries and share flashlights."

Everyone else shut his off except Ray. Since he'd already ventured forward, we followed him to where Scott was.

"I'm not sure we can get through this way," Scott said to Ray as we caught up to him. "Hopefully, the others heard your tapping and can figure out a way to get us out of here."

"That's not going to happen," Ray said, shining his light at us.

"Why are you guys here? Did you figure out a way to get back under that piece of steel?"

"Let's just say there was a little bit of a communication error," I said, giving Ray a dirty look. "I'm sure if we truly can't get out by going forward, the six of us can figure out some way to pry that steel plate up."

"I hope so," Scott replied. "It doesn't look real promising. Come on, I'll show you."

Ray turned his flashlight off and we followed Scott another hundred yards into the tunnel. Coming to a stop, he pointed his flashlight towards the ground. Just as we'd feared, the tunnel had been compromised and water had been making its way in.

"This is as far as I came. I'm not sure how deep it gets from here, but it definitely slopes downhill."

"You guys make the call," I said. "We know getting across the bridge would take nothing short of a miracle. Hell, by now it might not even be standing anymore. We could try a boat attempt or we can tread water."

"What do you think?" Ray asked.

"I personally think this is our only option," I replied. "We can go through that train car and find some items that float; that would at least give us a chance to rest if we needed to."

We all came to an agreement and decided to push ahead. First, we went back to the train and located what we needed. We found two lunch boxes and a few seat cushions. Making our way back to the edge of the water, I could tell we were all beginning to have second thoughts. After all, we weren't trained Navy SEALs; we were just normal, everyday people. If someone had asked us to do this just a few months earlier, we would've told him to go fly a kite.

Deciding to make the first move, I entered the water with the others right behind me. The first few hundred yards weren't too bad, just extremely cold. Gradually, however, it got deeper and deeper, until finally coming to the point where we actually had to swim. There was still plenty of room above us, so it wasn't as if we were totally submerged — at least not yet.

Once we began swimming, we could all feel the tunnel closing in on us. Not only that, but the air quality was terrible. Those of us with the nanites weren't affected, but I could tell Robert was having a hard time just trying to stay awake. He passed out a few times, only to have Cornelius slap him.

"Sorry, Rob," he would say. "I'm only doing that to keep you going."

Robert wasn't the only one looking as if he might succumb to the lack of good air. Both Scott and Ray showed severe signs of fatigue.

At one point, it got so bad that we all decided to sing to keep them awake. That was a great way to pass the time and keep from drifting off, but it was really hard on the ears. We sang, laughed, hollered, and just about anything else we could figure out that would help.

Then we came across the bodies. Just one at first, but soon we saw close to twenty or thirty of them. We were all thinking the same thing, but for a while, nobody said a word. Then, finally, Robert shared his thoughts with us.

"This is fucked up," he bluntly said. "I can already touch the ceiling, and we're not even close to the end of this damn thing."

"It's going to be OK, Rob," I said, hoping to calm him down.

"That's bullshit, Steve, and you know it. We're going to drown, just like every one of these poor bastards did."

Cornelius pulled out his flashlight and examined a body.

"Steve's right, Rob. I think we'll be OK."

"I am?" I asked questioningly.

"Yes, these people didn't drown. It appears they died of asphyxiation."

"What the hell are you talking about?" Robert asked, still not convinced.

"When the quake first hit, there were hundreds if not thousands of fires. These tunnels must've been filled with carbon monoxide. There's a good chance there was little to no water in the tunnels at that point. That's why there doesn't appear to be evidence of drowning. The gases would've caused them to pass out like you did earlier. If there had been much water in here at all, they still would've drowned after losing consciousness. However, that's not the case."

"So, will the gases kill us too?" Scott asked, swimming over to him.

"I don't think so," Cornelius continued. "The water probably started entering the tunnel after an aftershock or possibly there's some type of pump system in here. When the power operating them went out, the tubes naturally started filling with water. That in turn created a vacuum, sucking clean air in from one end while expelling it out the other. That's a good indication to me that the other end of this tunnel has a lot less obstruction."

"So, what are you saying?" Robert asked as he turned over to float on his back.

"I'm saying there's a high probability your dumbass will be around to see your son being born."

"That's good enough for me," he said cheerfully. "Now come on, you lazy fucks. Let's get the hell out of here."

With that, Robert pulled out his flashlight and turned it on. Then, resting it on his lunch box, he swam past Ray and took the lead. With a renewed sense of optimism, everyone else gained a sudden burst of energy and took off after him.

We passed a few more bodies over the next few hundred yards. Then we came to a section where the tunnel seemed to have a slight bend in the walls and the ceiling was folded somewhat like an accordion. We couldn't see the actual tear in the structure, but we could feel the pile of silt beneath our feet that came in with the water. Given another week or two, the whole tunnel would've been completely filled.

We stopped momentarily and stood on the soft pile. It wasn't a long break, but after nearly a mile and a half in cold water, it felt good to just stand and stretch. Then Robert's flashlight went out.

"Break is over, bitches," he yelled, diving forward into the darkness.

We had two more working flashlights but opted not to use them at that point. If debris were in our way at the other end, we'd need the light to get through it. For the next ten minutes, we swam on in complete darkness. Then, off in the distance, a ray of light glimmered off the surface of the water.

"Hey, guys, there's light up ahead," Robert shouted to us.

"Damn, Rob, you're getting pretty good at pointing out the obvious," I shot back happily.

Turning towards me, Robert hurled the lunch box he'd been using as a float.

"Screw you, Steve!" he yelled.

He wasn't mad; he was actually elated. We all were. The water depth had been dropping further and further since we passed the bend in the tube. After what seemed like an eternity, we could finally touch the bottom once again. A few more yards and our swim would be over, making it possible to walk the last half mile or so.

Each step of the way, the light in the tunnel increased. In doing so, it revealed to us that this end of the tunnel hadn't collapsed but had done just as Cornelius figured. Fire had consumed a large section of the BART station, filling the tunnel with smoke and gases, and killing the last of the survivors from the train.

Reaching the platform, we all felt a sense of relief. Not only had we managed to safely make it through the tunnel, but we also had done so undetected. Still, we weren't out yet. There was so much damage down there that we questioned whether the stairs leading up to the street would be accessible.

We had our answer before we even reached them. Dozens of shadows on the ground showed us where the bodies of those killed by the fire had once been. The fact that the bodies had been removed told us that there was, in fact, a way out.

We followed a ray of sunlight to what was left of one of the stairwells. Large chunks of concrete blocked most of it, barely leaving enough room to squeeze through. One by one, we helped each other past the narrow opening and slowly made our way through the rubble to the surface.

Back outside, we all just stood and stared for a moment. We couldn't believe the amount of devastation before us. We'd all heard about the huge quake hitting this area, but the news made it seem less destructive. Yet nothing had gone unscathed; the majestic towers that once stood over the city had either collapsed or been damaged so badly that they appeared ready to. Those that had fallen left enormous mountains of steel, concrete, and broken glass in their wake. Jagged pieces of rebar protruded from these mounds, making them look like they could easily tear through flesh and bone.

Suddenly, we heard a loud explosion off in the distance, followed by what sounded like two fast-moving trains colliding. That told us the bridge we'd been fighting to cross was no more. Then, for a brief moment, silence filled the air. We all froze, praying to God to hear something, any sound at all that might tell us our comrades were still alive. After what seemed like an eternity, we heard gunfire.

"They're still alive!" Ray yelled joyfully. "Come on, guys! We have to jam that signal."

Cornelius quickly removed the locating device from the lunch box he'd been using to float with. It was a little wet but still fully operational. Honing in on the signal, he turned back towards the bay.

"It's this way!" he called out, taking the lead.

We all took off after him, staying hidden the best we could. Many times we left the nearly unsurpassable roadways to cut through buildings that were still standing. Occasionally, we found it necessary to alter our course slightly to avoid the destruction of one that had fallen across our path. We were forever vigilant, not only to the gunfire that assured us the fight continued, but also for the rogue drones that seemed to be flying about randomly.

These weren't battle drones, but more of the type you'd find at a hobby store. They had the typical four rotors and even a camera mounted below. At one point, we were nearly trapped as one came around the corner of a building. With no place to hide and only seconds until it was on us, we all dove into the pile of debris we were climbing. We stayed motionless, our heads facing down to hide our eyes from the camera, as the drone slowly hovered over us. Then, after we could no longer hear the hum from its motors, we stood up and continued on.

Scott was nearing the point of exhaustion. Beaten and bloodied from the treacherous conditions, his breaths grew more and more labored.

"I can't go on, you guys," he called out as he lay across the hood of a partially crushed taxi.

Looking ahead, I could see the road becoming clearer. That's when Ray turned around and walked calmly back to Scott. I figured he was going to either give him some words of encouragement or a shoulder to lean on for a while. Man, was I ever wrong.

"Get your ass up, you filthy little maggot," he screamed, getting his face within inches of Scott's. "I didn't come all this way to let some out-of-shape pussy get me and my friends killed."

Scott's eyes shot open as Ray lit in to him again.

"Get you eyes off me, you piece of rat shit, before I beat the holy hell out of you with your own arms. Do you understand me, you lazy fuck?"

His tactics caught everyone else off guard. The sudden barrage of insults and threats forced a wave of adrenaline through Scott that sent him right back into Ray's face.

"You want a piece of me, asshole?" he screamed as he stood up.

"Do you even have the strength to man up and fight, you little pussy?" Ray yelled, pushing him back against the taxi.

Then, using the cab to push off from, Scott shoved Ray with all he had.

"I have enough to kick your ass!" he yelled, trembling from the adrenaline rush.

"Good," Ray responded calmly, with a smile. "Now let's go kick some ass."

Still fuming, Scott caught back up to the rest of us. "I know why he did it, but damn, I'm pissed right now."

He made sure he said it loud enough for us all to hear.

"I'm just glad you're back up here with us, you little pussy," Robert said, ribbing him.

He grunted under his breath and then laughed. "I'm never going to live this down, am I?" he asked, shaking his head.

"Not if I can help it," Robert said, slapping him on the back.

We were on the last pile of rubble we had to climb, and for the first time our target was in sight. It wasn't a building with a cell tower as we'd expected. No, they were controlling the drones from inside a yacht.

There was still about two city blocks between us and the boat, but the terrain was different. We could see that several large pieces of equipment had removed all the debris, leaving the roads clear. Even though the buildings that were left standing were heavily damaged, they'd no longer be obstacles. In fact, they'd prove to be very beneficial in our attack. We could move from building to building, only exposing ourselves long enough to cross the streets. However, getting onto the yacht could prove to be a little more difficult.

We made our way off the pile and into the first building we came to. It was on our right and gave us a view from the higher floors of not only the yacht but also of the battle that still raged on.

Making our way through the building was more difficult than we planned. The quake may have left the outside pretty much intact, but the inside was in shambles. Broken glass and shelving covered nearly every square inch of the floor. The main interior wall had crumbled, dropping a large section of the second level down onto the first. It took some doing, but eventually we located what was left of the stairs and climbed our way up to the fourth floor. It was mainly made up of small offices, along with rooms used for storage.

Pushing open the door to one office, we found ourselves in the perfect spot for reconnaissance. It was a nice large corner office with windows facing both east and south. All the glass had been broken out, which allowed a cool breeze of salt air to pass through. Robert especially enjoyed chasing after the birds that had made this room their home.

From our current vantage point, we watched as the drones relentlessly pounded the last of our troops. They were still holding on the best they could, but the bridge was now a total loss. With over half of it now resting at the bottom of the bay, it was useless to them.

Turning our focus to the yacht, we spotted three men standing guard. As far as we could tell, they were the only ones between our goal and us.

"Doesn't seem like a lot of protection for such a valuable asset," I mentioned as I began to wonder if this really was our target.

"They probably never figured there'd be anyone left to dispute their takeover. I'm sure here in a few minutes they're going to wish they would've thought things out a little better."

We all sat and watched the guards for a few more minutes, trying to see if we might be missing something. The three of them were about fifty feet from the boat, all within an arm's length of one another. They were standing on a large concrete jetty, facing away from the city. The battle across the bay seemed to have their attention, which allowed us a clear shot to reach them.

Ray pointed out what was left of some sort of structure not far from them. We couldn't tell what it had been originally; all that remained was a lone brick wall. Running nearly parallel to the guards, it would allow us a closer point from which to attack.

We made our move out of the building and quickly over to it. Not once did the guards remove their focus from the ongoing battle. With less than twenty yards between them and us, we were in position. I could feel the tension in the group as everyone made one last check of their weapons.

"Cornelius and I will take the lead," I said as I slid my safety off. "I want the rest of you to watch our backs the best you can. Once on the boat, we'll split up into three groups, the same ones we had earlier. This isn't a rescue mission, so if it moves, shoot it. Any questions?"

Each member of the group nodded his head and prepared for whatever happened next. Taking a deep breath, I slowly poked my head around the corner to get one last look.

"Get down!" I said, pulling my head back behind the cover. "There's a helicopter coming this way."

We froze, with our backs against the wall, waiting for the helicopter to pass over. Ben had his head down almost as if he were about to throw up.

"You OK, Ben?" Robert asked.

"Yeah, just saying a quick prayer. I figured we could use all the help we can get."

"Be sure to tell him Scott's here with us," Ray joked. "Maybe that'll have some pull with him."

After a moment, we realized it wasn't flying over; it was landing right there on the jetty. I carefully poked my head around again to see if I could tell what they were up to.

"Someone is getting off the chopper," I quietly informed the others.

"Is it another guard?" Rob asked.

"I can't tell yet. They're getting off on the other side."

"Let me take a look," Cornelius said. "I may be able to see more than you."

We traded spots and Cornelius carefully peered around the wall.

"Son of a bitch!" he exclaimed, turning back towards us. "It's Josh!"

"They have Josh's body?" I asked in confusion.

"No, they don't have his body. He's the one who got off. Josh is alive! From the looks of things, he isn't a prisoner either. I think he's actually with them."

Squeezing past Cornelius, I took a look for myself. Josh was shaking hands with some nerd in a suit. Then, as the chopper took off again, the two of them made their way onto the yacht.

Feeling my blood begin to boil, I ducked back behind the wall and clenched my fists.

"Well, he's definitely with them," I said angrily.

"How can that be?" Robert asked. "He's been with us since the beginning."

"Not the whole time," Cornelius said. "Remember, he was going to look for his family when we left him at the lake."

"I was wondering how he found us," Robert said. "I bet they sent him to see if we survived the drone or not."

"You make the call, Steve," Ray said, pulling out his knife. "Do you want me to slit the fucker's throat or would you like to?"

I raised my gun towards Ben. "You were away from us at the lake too."

"Hey, wait," Ben nervously said. "I was in the cave the whole time. I swear to you the only person I saw after you left was Josh."

"Then why did you tell us he had a broken neck?"

"It looked to me like he did, and I didn't want to get blown up confirming it. Now, please, put the gun down."

Robert reached over with his left hand and lowered my barrel. "Don't shoot him, Steve. I believe he's telling the truth."

"Why do you say that?" I asked, still not convinced.

"He loves Amy and her little girl. Do you honestly think he'd have left them behind to come with us if he were a traitor? Heck no, he would've just snuck off with them."

I holstered my firearm and extended my hand to his.

"I'm sorry, Ben. I should know better than that. Josh has been acting strange ever since he found us at the lake."

Ray held the knife out so I could see it.

"Well, can I kill him?" he asked.

"No, I don't want anyone killing Josh," I said, removing my weapon. "I want you to bring him to me."

Josh may have changed sides, but that didn't slow us down. If anything, it renewed our desire to kill those bastards.

Hearing the helicopter lift off, I stuck my head back out around the wall. The guards were all facing away from us as they watched it head back towards the battle.

"Let's move!" I said, taking off towards them.

We closed the gap between them and us as quickly as possible, while not allowing our footsteps to draw attention. We weren't exactly running, but it was close.

With their knives in hand, Cornelius and Ray were right beside me. Robert, Ben, and Scott followed close behind, their guns drawn. They were not only watching our rear, but they also kept an eye out for movement on the yacht. With about ten feet to go, I holstered my pistol and pulled out my knife.

The three of us reached our target at the same time. Then, with the sound of the rotors from the helicopter still drowning out the noise, we raised our blades to their throats, cutting through their windpipes as well as their arteries. The three men dropped silently to the ground.

Robert and Ben had passed us and were already stepping onto the yacht. Scott was still facing the opposite direction, protecting us from any possible threats. With the area secure, we all joined Robert and Ben.

Using hand signals, Ben assured us the upper deck was secure. A second later, Robert stepped out from the bridge and gave me the thumbs-up, his knife still dripping with blood. We split up into our groups and carefully scoured the rest of the vessel. Other than the captain that Robert had eliminated, the boat was nearly deserted.

We knew there were at least two more people to find — Josh and that piece of shit he was shaking hands with. Robert was just about ready to call the main deck clear when he opened up the bathroom door and found Josh. He was washing his face in the sink and nearly turned white as a ghost as Robert stuck the cold steel against his throat.

"I should kill you right here, you fucking traitor," he said coldly.

Josh closed his eyes and lowered his head. "I just—"

"Don't say a word! Steve wants you alive for some reason. I just know you'll say something to piss me off and cause me to spoil that for him."

I could hear Robert and came over to see what was going on. Just as I reached him, I heard yelling followed by several shots coming from below us.

Staring coldly at our traitorous friend, Robert and I waited in anticipation until we heard Ray call out all clear. A second later, Cornelius called out from the front, "All clear here too."

"We're all clear also," I yelled out, "and we have Josh."

I put the barrel of my gun against his head. "What the hell are you doing, Josh?" I screamed.

"I'm so sorry, Steve," he said, breaking down and beginning to cry. "They found me after I left my house. I was distraught and was walking aimlessly around my old neighborhood. At first, they were going to kill me, until I told them I was with you. They promised all I had to do was get them some pictures and a little information about everyone in the group. If I did that, they'd let me live. I didn't want to help them, but I was scared. You have to believe me. I didn't share anything with them that could hurt you. I only told them you were part of a small group that had lived through the attacks."

I wasn't sure what to do. Josh had been with us since the beginning and was like family to me. It just seemed so heartless to kill the guy.

"How did you live through the crash?" I asked, shaking with anger. "Ben said it looked as if you had a broken neck."

"The other guy was lying on top of me, and I could tell he was dead. When Ben came over to check on me, I tried to look like he did. I guess Ben was so shaken up, he didn't bother to look closer."

"That part bugs me the most. Why the hell did you pretend to be dead instead of coming with us? It seems to me you and your dead friend downstairs were pretty chummy together."

"I figured that would be my best chance of getting them the information they asked for. I couldn't do it with everyone around."

"That's bullshit, Josh, and you know it. Once you were back with us, they were no longer a threat to you."

That's where you're wrong, Steve. They were still in control. Before I was turned loose, they injected me with something. I'm not sure what it was, but they assured me they could kill me at any time. I swear to you, I only gave them enough information to get the antidote."

"How did you contact them to pick you up?" Robert asked as he pressed his knife harder against Josh's throat.

His voice cracking, he quickly answered him. "They gave me the frequency they're using. Here, I have it written on a piece of paper."

Josh handed Robert the paper and then turned to face me.

"What do you want me to do with him, Steve?" Robert asked, still holding the knife to his throat.

Removing my gun from Josh's head, I thought for a moment. "Just hold onto him for now," I said, still trying to wrap my head around his betrayal. "This is one of those decisions we should make as a group."

Suddenly, Scott came running into the room, a frantic look on his face.

"Steve, you and Rob need to see this."

Dragging Josh behind him, Robert followed us down the staircase into a large room filled with computers. There were five bodies lying on the floor near them; one of them was that piece of shit we had seen with Josh.

"It appears to be the main control for every drone on the West Coast," Scott said, motioning to the monitors. "That one on the end has something on it you need to see!"

I made my way over to it and took a look. There on the screen was the picture of Michelle that Josh had taken the night before. In the background was a view from Google Earth of my property.

"What does this mean?" I asked, turning to Josh.

"They're going after Michelle," he said, his voice shaking.

Turning back towards the screen, I read the words at the bottom: "Launch complete."

"What the hell are we going to do?" Robert nervously asked.

Turning around, I pushed Josh up against the wall and looked him right in the eyes. Feeling a sense of rage deep inside me like I'd never felt before, I answered Robert.

"KILL HIM!"

TO BE CONTINUED

www.ingramcontent.com/pod-product-compliance
Lightning Source LLC
Chambersburg PA
CBHW071155250626
47159CB00001B/99